NORA I

LITTLE
BOLTON

THE STORY OF A LANCASHIRE
WORKING CLASS FAMILY AT THE START
OF THE INDUSTRIAL REVOLUTION

SKRIV
IN ENGLISH

To Bill Hall's great grandson

CONTENTS

ACKNOWLEDGMENTS

I would like to thank all those who helped me to gather as much factual information as possible for this book, especially the Bolton Library Archives and Local Studies Service, Manchester Central Library, and the Manchester and Lancashire Family History Society. Special thanks to John Lawson who spent hours amongst the records, feeding me with new information, and helping discover long-forgotten parts of our family.

Thanks to Jenny Puronne who not only had great ideas for the book cover, but is also a fantastic photographer and artist. Thanks too to my model who cooperated wonderfully, even in the crazy summer heat.

To my amazing editor Jennifer Quinlan. For your vast knowledge, for pulling this book together, and for being on hand when I needed help. I really cannot imagine a better historical fiction editor.

To my test group readers who read all or some of my book at some stage. For your great feedback and encouragement: Anna, Annika, Ashia, Kathryn, Lisa, Michelle, Ragnar, and Socrates.

To Annika for expert layout help and for swiftly banishing my indents and page numbering demons.

To my girls, A & I, for inspiring me each day. Always follow your dreams, and always be yourselves.

And finally to R. For your never ending support and encouragement. For keeping me on track with this book and making quite intelligent suggestions! Without your support I'm pretty sure I never would have finished it. *Tack, din apa. Älskar dig!*

PREFACE

I first got the idea of writing this book while sitting on a train from Colombo to Kandy in Sri Lanka. As a keen amateur genealogist, I had been trying to trace the last movements of an ancestor who had lived in Colombo. As the rickety and sweltering train trundled through the countryside, the idea for this book suddenly struck me. I had always loved writing but never felt I had a good enough story to tell before. What could be better than a story about extraordinary people living what they considered to be ordinary lives? We will never know just how tough our ancestors had it, but their hard work, sorrows and joys have lain the foundations for our lives today. Everyone has a great character, a hero, or a villain lurking in their family tree. Hopefully, not all of them will be forgotten as the years roll by.

These are some of the characters, heroes and villains in my family. I am sure I have many more. While most of this story is based on fact – birth, marriage and death records, parish records, census entries, immigration data, newspapers, handed down stories, etc., some is undoubtedly fiction. I hope I have done none of them an injustice.

Nora Lönn
January 2017, Stockholm, Sweden.

THE HALLS

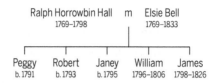

Ralph Horrowbin Hall m Elsie Bell
1769–1798 1769–1833

Peggy	Robert	Janey	William	James
b. 1791	b. 1793	b. 1795	1796–1806	1798–1826

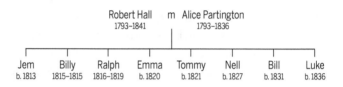

Robert Hall m Alice Partington
1793–1841 1793–1836

Jem	Billy	Ralph	Emma	Tommy	Nell	Bill	Luke
b. 1813	1815–1815	1816–1819	b. 1820	b. 1821	b. 1827	b. 1831	b. 1836

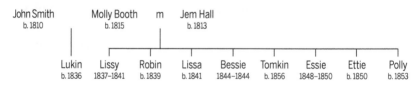

John Smith Molly Booth m Jem Hall
b. 1810 b. 1815 b. 1813

Lukin	Lissy	Robin	Lissa	Bessie	Tomkin	Essie	Ettie	Polly
b. 1836	1837–1841	b. 1839	b. 1841	1844–1844	b. 1856	1848–1850	b. 1850	b. 1853

Jem and Molly's family include only those children born up until the book ends, in 1853.

THE BOOTHS

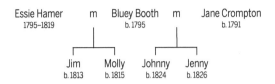

Essie Hamer   m   Bluey Booth   m   Jane Crompton
1795–1819   b. 1795   b. 1791

Jim   Molly   Johnny   Jenny
b. 1813   b. 1815   b. 1824   b. 1826

THE FLEMINGS

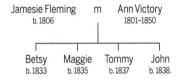

Jamesie Fleming   m   Ann Victory
b. 1806   1801–1850

Betsy   Maggie   Tommy   John
b. 1833   b. 1835   b. 1837   b. 1838.

PART 1

1841

Unable to compete with the price and productivity of the new mills, spinners and weavers became forced to leave their rural homes and move to towns for work. People moved into cellars, hastily built insufficient housing, or shared rooms with several other families as the demand for housing exceeded supply. The first modern census was taken on 6th June 1841.

CHAPTER 1

THE FUNERAL
JANUARY 1841

Wedged in between his father's coffin and his sister, Bill couldn't help but feel the whole thing was just a bad dream. As the horse pulled the cart slowly over the uneven narrow dirt road out of town, rhythmically bumping his back against the driver's seat, he wished he could wake up and everything would be back to normal. He closed his eyes and willed his mind to conjure up familiar scenes – his father sitting by the fire, too sick to go to work. Bill himself going out the door, heading for a day's work at the mill, even though he was only nine. His thirteen-year-old sister Nell fetching water from the pump two streets down, and his four-year-old brother Luke either helping her or getting into trouble, usually being marched back by a neighbour after a scolding or a beating, only to be let go by their father, who seemed to have lost interest. As far as Bill was concerned, their family consisted of just him, Nell, Luke and their father. His older siblings were all grown up and never came around. Jem had his own family and rarely visited, and no one had seen Tommy or Emma in years.

The horse plodded on, and the wheel passed over a large rut, shaking the rickety cart and bumping Bill hard into Nell. Bill looked up at his older sister, her small frame racked with sobs. He wanted to comfort her, to make her feel less sad, but he couldn't tell her it was all going to be all right because he wasn't sure that it would be. And if he didn't concentrate hard, he might start crying too.

His father had been sick for a while, progressively getting worse. Some days he couldn't even stand, let alone go to work, coughing into a rag and then hiding it away quickly so no one would see. But Bill had seen, and he had seen that sometimes there was a lot of blood. One

15

night their father had been so bad, racking coughs shaking his frail frame, unable to catch his breath, that Nell had rushed out the door to get help. She returned half-frozen, teeth chattering and lips blue, with their eldest brother, Jem, in tow. But Jem had sent for the surgeon, even though his father had said not to, that they didn't have the money.

Nothing good ever came from sending for the surgeon. Even Bill knew that. He and Jimmy Taylor from across the court once saw the surgeon visit Mr. Johnson down the street. Two days later, Mr. Johnson's eldest lads had come back with a laying out board. Bill hadn't wanted to see a dead body. They were scary. What if they suddenly sat up? Jimmy Taylor said his grandfather had done that. Sat right up on the laying out board and looked straight at Jimmy's Pa. That story always made Bill shiver.

Bill had been too scared to "pay his respects" when his father had been laid out, but Jem had dragged him there by his collar and made him look. Jem had said Bill would thank him later, but Bill didn't think he would. Robert Hall had looked far worse dead than the last time Bill had seen him alive. His pale, almost rubbery-looking skin was so taught across his face that Bill could see his father's skull quite clearly. His eyes were sunken, and he had hideous dark blue bruises in several places. He had been dressed in a Sunday suit, but the yards of fabric hung from him. He'd been laid out for two days, and then they had put his father in this box. Bill tried hard to wipe that image of his father out of his head, but so far he was losing the fight.

Nell's sobbing grew louder. "How can he be dead?" she wailed. "What are we going to do?" Bill bit his lip hard, but it didn't stop the tears from rolling down his cheeks. Not only was it the thought of sitting next to his father's cold and stiff empty shell, but he was scared for himself and his siblings. What was going to happen to them now? Their Jem hadn't said anything, but as Bill, Nell and Luke were all under age, they would surely end up in the orphanage. Bill had seen the place. A gruesome building where they made pies out of the naughtiest children, or shipped you off to foreign countries where there were monsters and no houses. Bill was most scared of being separated from his brother and sister and never seeing them again. He even preferred to go back to the house they all hated than be locked away in that godforsaken place. At least in their old house, he, Nell and Luke had been together.

Their old house was in the closed yard of Wellington Court, one of the worst slum areas in Bolton. As soon as you reached the gap between the houses on Dean Street, the stench from the street became oppressive. Rotting scraps mixed with human waste and dark, stagnant water that never drained. Rats scurried about, raiding anything that looked remotely edible, often other decomposing rats. The seven grey houses, leaning on each other for support, looked ready to fall down. Their doors were patched up with odd pieces of wood, rotting at the bottom and almost hanging off their rusty hinges. They were long past their prime and ready to take their last breath. Three sides of the courtyard were lined with the backs of other houses, oppressively closing in the small yard so that the air became stale. Ugly, large buildings with bricks and slates missing. Their only windows looked out onto the courtyard, but most inhabitants chose to cover these with whatever cloth they could find in an attempt to try to ignore the view of the poorest going about their business. There were no middens around – one had to go three streets away and usually queue, so dirty water and the contents of chamber pots were often thrown out into the courtyard and never cleared. The stench from the street was clearly present even indoors. There was no escaping it. Bill hated that they'd had to move there, but today he found himself promising that he'd never be so ungrateful again. At least he'd had a home. Angrily wiping away the few tears that had escaped, he hugged Nell tightly, the pair of them clinging to each other as the cart continued slowly over the road's bumps and holes, rocking them from side to side.

It was early in the morning, and the grass, bushes and tips of the trees were still painted with frost. Their clothing was thin and threadbare in places, and despite having a rug over them, the slight icy breeze whipped at them, chilling them to the bone. Their noses and hands were red-raw, and their breath exhaled clouds of steam, their throats choked icy in the late January air. Bill didn't know how far they were travelling, but Jem had said it would be a long journey. They would pass through several towns and run close to the moors before they got to the church where their father was to be buried, where he used to live with their mother and Jem, Emma and Tommy a long time ago. Jem hadn't allowed Luke to come with them. Said he was too young. Bill had argued with him, then pleaded with him, but Jem had been adamant. So they had left Luke at home with a neighbour who had already helped them so much.

After several hours, the cart eventually moved through Prestwich town. Bill saw mostly fields, undulating hills covered in white-tipped grass, a few farm cottages dotted about. As the cart turned left off the main street, he saw a cluster of terraced houses and a few larger buildings up ahead. They continued down the short, narrow street leading up to the church. On the left, small cottages lined the street, and a pub resided farther down on the right, surrounded by more fields and the church grounds. Where the cottages petered out, two large iron gates marked the opening to the church grounds. The driver stopped the cart on the gravelled path in front of the church entrance, and Jem climbed down, lifting out Nell while Bill tried to scramble over the side, his hands stiff and cold. He stood there, his back to the cart, and looked around at his new surroundings.

St. Bartholomew's was an imposing red sandstone building. Two extensions, almost as wide as the main building itself, jutted out from either side, making the church appear fat and healthy. Its height dwarfed everything in the vicinity and made Bill dizzy as he craned his neck to look up at the turrets reaching towards the clouds. Gravestones were scattered to the right of the grounds like crooked teeth, in no particular rows or order. To the left of the church were more orderly, flat gravestones, great slabs of smooth slate spread out over the frost-bitten grass. It was so peaceful. So quiet. Bill walked over to the gravestones, closed his eyes and gulped in the fresh air.

When Bill opened his eyes again, he saw Jem talking to the rector and a handful of people standing outside the church entrance. Scanning their faces, Bill tried to make out his brother Tommy, whom they hadn't seen in such a long time. His eyes came to rest on a familiar blond mop of hair with the same oval face as his own, and he smiled. Tommy hadn't changed at all. Nell, noticing Tommy at the same time, gave a shriek and ran to him, flinging herself on him. Bill set off behind, slightly less enthusiastic.

As Tommy hugged Nell, Bill heard a tut, followed by a haughty voice exclaiming, "Such behaviour!" He turned around and stared at two older, quite large ladies standing there. The owner of the voice displayed deep-rooted frown lines in her pudgy face. Her hair, or what little he could see of it, was almost completely grey and pulled up into a severe style encased in her black silk bonnet.

"Now, Peggy, don't be so cruel," exclaimed the slightly smaller one, blond wisps of hair escaping her bonnet and softly framing her pale face. Her expression was one of concern rather than disapproval. "They're orphans now, poor little lambs."

She walked over to Bill and took his hands in hers, bending over slightly so that she was more at his height.

"Hello, dearie. You probably don't remember me. I'm your Aunt Janey."

Bill snatched his hands away and stared at her while Nell lifted her head from Tommy's chest and immediately stopped snivelling.

"But we don't have any aunts."

A loud harrumphing sound came from the older lady, followed once again by tutting and two short taps of her silver-tipped black cane on the ground. The younger one merely smiled sweetly.

"Of course you do, love, why ever would you think that? You probably just don't remember us. I'm your father's younger sister , and that there is your Aunt Peggy – she's the eldest of us all. And a bit of a crosspatch," she added, winking at Bill. He looked up at Tommy, his mouth trying to form words but failing. Just as well, as he had no idea what he was going to say anyway. Tommy said nothing, so Bill then looked across at Jem, who nodded.

"But, but ... Father never said we had family! Not in all those years!" Nell exclaimed.

Bill didn't know what to think. First they had no family, now here were these expensively dressed fat ladies claiming to be his father's sisters.

"Oh, poor, poor Bobby!" exclaimed Janey. "He did take it all so hard. Maybe he didn't talk about us out loud very much. He was so ashamed, you see. But I'm sure he thought about us often."

Bill wondered who Bobby was and what he was taking so hard when he realised they were talking about his father. He'd never heard him called Bobby before. He was just about to ask one of the hundreds of questions that were milling round in his head when the younger lady interrupted him.

Janey pinched Bill's cheeks, making him squirm.

"My, you're a fine looking lad! A bit on the thin side though. But I guess boys your age tend to be."

"I'm not good looking. Our Luke's the handsome one," replied Bill, moving away, embarrassed but trying to be polite.

"Luke?" Janey's face clouded over.

"Luke's only four; he's the youngest, and Jem wouldn't let him come. Said he was too young and wouldn't understand. He understands Father's dead though," he added, muttering angrily. Janey looked up quizzically at Jem, but at that moment the rector interrupted them and suggested they make their way into church for the service.

As Nell, Peggy and Janey stepped inside the church entrance, Bill hung back and watched his elder brothers turn to the cart and their father's coffin.

"Is our Emma coming?" he heard Jem ask as he lifted his arms over the side of the cart and tried to slide the heavy wooden casket towards the edge. Tommy leaned in to help him.

"No. Did you think she would?" Tommy said.

"Well, it is her father's funeral," Jem snapped. "She ought to pay her respects."

"What, like he showed her respect?" Tommy asked angrily. "She'll probably head back to Bolton now she knows he's dead. I can't say I blame her."

"Oh, that's great, speaking ill of the dead," Jem said. "He was only our father."

"I didn't mean ..." Tommy let out a sigh and gingerly touched the top of the wooden casket. "Did he ... was he in a lot of pain?" He looked up at his elder brother.

"Well, if you had been here, you would have known," Jem snapped.

Tommy didn't reply. Instead, he seemed to be in his own world. He patted the coffin and whispered something that Bill couldn't make out. "Bye, Father," he eventually said loudly. He then looked up at Jem and squared his shoulders. He was already slightly taller than Jem, and when he stood up straight, Bill thought that Tommy looked in command, someone you could trust, which is more than he could say for Jem.

"Look," said Tommy, "it feels wrong to argue when it's Father's funeral. Let's just have a truce between us, just for today." He put his hand on Jem's shoulder.

Jem jerked his shoulder and tore his arm away as if he'd been scalded. Bill looked from one brother to the other. Of course Jem had told them stories over the years about Tommy's scandalous behaviour, about him getting into fights and losing his job, but looking at them today, those stories didn't ring quite true. Jem always seemed to be easily agitated, and Tommy, at least today, seemed mostly calm.

"I heard you went to speak to Aunt Peggy in an attempt to find me," he heard Tommy say, "that couldn't have been easy." Bill was starting to admire his brother. There was no way he could be so patiently kind when faced with Jem's antics. Jem was annoying when he got like this.

Jem grunted in response.

"Look, Jem, we've had our differences, but can't we just put them aside for today? For Father's sake?"

Jem almost exploded with rage.

"You have no idea what it's been like! I've had to manage everything myself. Do you know how it is to watch your father die, to try and support your own family and his? To watch the little 'uns work their fingers to the bone and still go hungry?"

"I'm sorry!" Tommy was almost shouting back. "No one told me it was that bad. I would have tried to help if I could."

"No, you wouldn't," Jem spat back, stopping to face his brother. "You have never done anything to help this family."

"What could I do? I'm still an apprentice. I won't be my own man for another year, so I don't have any money, and I can't just take time off when I feel like it. And your Molly was helping out. And her family. What could I have done to have made it any better?"

"You sided with THEM!" Jem almost screamed. Bill jumped.

"I did NOT!" Tommy yelled, "I tried to smooth things over with

21

them. Do you know how hard that was? I was trying to do the best by our family. I was only fifteen back then, and it wasn't my job."

"Oh, that's right. Nothing is ever your fault." Jem wagged his finger in Tommy's face. "Do you know how hard it was to be left there to deal with it all alone? You and Emma ran away. Left it all up to me."

"I didn't run away," Tommy said quietly. "I was sent away."

Jem stopped mid-gesture, looking intently at his younger brother. After a few seconds, he dropped his hand and turned away. Bill looked from one to the other with his mouth open. He wanted to leave and not listen to this shouting, but at the same time he wanted to know why Jem and Tommy didn't like each other. His feet were rooted to the ground for fear of them noticing him standing there and giving him a telling off.

"I'm here now," Tommy continued. "Let me do whatever I can."

"Well, you and I need to discuss what is going to happen to Nell, Bill and Luke. I can't take care of them all."

"Aunt Peggy said she had some ideas, and perhaps she'll help out. She said we'd discuss it later."

"Her plans won't include Luke."

"Why does she dislike him so much? He's only a baby."

"Have you met him lately?" Jem began to bristle again. "He's a little savage. But I guess you can't expect much when he grew up without a mother, with a father who ignored him and siblings too busy to give him enough attention."

Tommy looked down at his hands. "I didn't know."

"No, and that's because you never came back!" Jem was starting to shout again.

"I couldn't come back!" Bill could see Tommy's face and neck were starting to get red, and his fists were clenched. If he was Jem, he'd be worried about getting punched right now. Maybe the stories about Tommy were true.

Just then, two gravediggers walked up to the cart and nodded to Jem and Tommy.

"Why don't we leave this discussion until after Father's buried?" Tommy said evenly. "We'll see then what can be done. I'm sure Aunt Peggy won't leave you to just deal with everything yourself."

Jem's shoulders dropped, and he looked down at the coffin. He nodded to Tommy and the other two men standing there, then the four of them lifted the coffin onto their shoulders and walked towards the church door.

They carried Robert Hall down the aisle. Peggy, hooking Janey's arm on one side and leaning heavily on her cane on the other, followed them closely behind, leaving Nell and Bill to bring up the rear.

As they paraded behind the wooden coffin, Bill couldn't help but look round the church in awe. This was nothing like the church they went to every Sunday. For a start, the sheer size made him giddy. The arched ceiling contained beautifully carved sunken panels, crisscrossed with ornate bosses. Large chandeliers hung down at intervals, containing hundreds of small candles. The church's inner walls, along with the columns and archways between the pews, were made from the same bare, large slabs of the sandstone seen on the outside. But as they had not been subjected to the same weathering, they were still the original beautiful red-pink colour – like the rare sunsets you sometimes saw if you were lucky enough to get a break before the end of the day and could step outside for a breath of fresh air. The floor was a creamy veined marble inlaid with squares of different-coloured stones.

Bill looked down at his feet as he walked. Each of his footsteps contrasted with the fine polished ornate stones. His shoes were Sunday best, but the badly scuffed and split leather, his foot almost poking out of the front of his left shoe and the broken, knotted laces made him really feel out of place. Perhaps he should take his shoes off so as not to dirty the floor? But then his socks were more darns and holes than wool, so perhaps he should just leave them on and try to tread carefully. For the first time, he was acutely aware of his dress. Jem had made him wash his hands, face and neck and put on his Sunday suit that morning. But he had grown recently, and his arms and legs appeared longer than his sleeves and trousers. They were also terribly creased and a little damp and dirty as a result of the long cart journey. And of course they were patched in several places. He pulled his jacket as tight around him as it would go. At least that would hide the worst of his mended vest and the shirt that had seen better days.

The parade came to an end as they laid his father's coffin in front of the altar. Up close, Bill could now see that the altar rails and pulpit were ornately carved in dark wood. He was still looking around the excesses of the church in awe when Nell yanked him into his seat.

As the rector began the service, several people entered and took places at the back. Bill turned round to stare at them, trying to see if he recognised anyone, until Nell pinched him. He didn't hear much of the service – well, not that he could remember. He was too busy not being able to take his eyes off the architecture. This was all too much. There was his father, lying there in a pauper's box in the most ornate church Bill had ever seen. He couldn't understand why they would be allowed in here, let alone why they would light all those hundreds of candles for just his father. Candles were expensive, at least that many were. He looked at his aunts, but they seemed focused on the rector's words and oblivious to their environment. Nell was staring down at her fingers, and Bill knew her well enough to know she was fighting back tears. But his brothers sitting in front of them also seemed not to notice their surroundings.

The service was over quickly. Jem had said a few words, but Bill had not been listening. They followed the coffin again out to an open grave. Bill wandered over to stare at some of the inscriptions on the neighbouring headstones, but the letters made no sense to him. He had never been to school, and none of his siblings had ever had the chance to learn to read either. Not many people did apart from the rich and a few people who were lucky enough or clever enough to learn at Sunday school. Sometimes Bill wished he knew his letters – it would make him feel smart and important – but you didn't need that kind of knowledge to work in a mill.

The six members of the Hall family stood around the grave, shivering. It had started to rain a little, the cold air turning the droplets to sleet or hail at repetitive intervals. Several of those who had entered the church late had followed them to the graveside but stood a respectful distance away. Bill couldn't help noticing the contrast in not only the clothing of his aunts compared to him and his siblings, but also in the way they stood, talked and moved. Why had his father never mentioned them? Aunt Peggy seemed a bit fierce, but Aunt Janey seemed nice. Did that mean that they might have even more family? He should remember to ask them that after the funeral. He turned his attention to the grave and tried to concentrate on the words being said.

Janey took his hand and whispered, "Your mother's buried there too, you know. They'll be happy to be reunited again." Bill didn't really want to continue holding his aunt's hand. He didn't know her and just wanted to stuff his hands in his pockets, where they wouldn't be as numb from the cold. But he thought it might be a bit rude to pull away from her a second time, so he continued to stand still. He stood still until they started shovelling soil on top of his father's coffin. It all seemed so final. His father was in the ground with his mother, and he would never see him again.

Something – a noise, or a movement, Bill wasn't sure – made him look up. He didn't know why at first, but as he looked around, he saw a man leaning against a tree by one of the graves. At first he thought he might be another gravedigger, but he was not dressed like the two who stood a respectable distance away, caps in hand. For a start, this man had his hat on, a top hat, and did not have a shovel. Bill knew it was rude to stare, Nell was forever pinching him for doing just that, but the man was staring at them. Janey looked up and saw what Bill was looking at, nudged Peggy and pointed. Peggy squinted, taking up her monocle to her eye and away again, but it wasn't until Janey whispered something in her ear that Bill saw her react. She exploded with indignation, making Bill and Nell jump, and went striding off, waving her cane, as fast as her sheer size and ample layers of frills and black silk would allow.

"Get out of here, Ainsworth, you, you ... how dare you!"

Suddenly, the peaceful burial erupted into chaos. Janey started crying. Bill looked up at Jem, who was peering into the distance, his eyes screwed up. As soon as Peggy started yelling, Bill heard his brother gasp and saw his face drain of colour.

"Edward Ainsworth! Of all the rotten inexcusable things to do, turning up here like that!" Jem yelled and started running, winding his way through the gravestones in a bid to reach the man. Ainsworth had begun to run out of the grounds when Jem yelled, but then he slowed down to a walk, turned around and started walking back towards the gate. Bill watched Jem also slow down, coming face-to-face with the thin, tall man with straggly silver-streaked dark hair escaping from his top hat.

"Come," said Tommy, grabbing Bill's shoulders and trying to steer him away. "No one needs to see this. Come, I said!"

Bill squirmed and twisted out of Tommy's grasp. Before Tommy could grab him again, Bill had started running towards the low stone wall that was connected to the side gate, ignoring Tommy's shouts and trying to get a better view of Jem and the old man.

Crouching down between the stone wall and the laurel bush, Bill hoped he couldn't be seen. Jem and Ainsworth were still a little way off, but their raised voices carried through the crisp air.

"What the hell are you doing here? How dare you turn up!" Jem almost spat his words out. "Get out of here!"

Edward Ainsworth leered at Jem, smiling slowly and showing his rotting teeth.

"Public place this, isn't it? I'm as entitled to be here as any man. Are you going to make me leave, you sorry excuse for a man?" He spat on the ground just inches from Jem's boots and leaned back with a self-satisfied smile. Jem swung at his face with his right fist, missing completely as Ainsworth stepped back and grinned.

"Come on, Jem, you can do better than that. Or maybe you can't. Them Halls, they shouldn't send a woman to do a man's work. Although I've heard your sister Emma is a strong lass. Always ready for a fight."

Jem lunged at the old man again, but Ainsworth was quick. He caught Jem's arm and spun him round, placing his other arm under Jem's shoulders and round the back of his head in a lock. Bill gasped and looked around for Tommy, not sure what to do.

Ainsworth whispered menacingly in Jem's ear, but Bill couldn't hear what he was saying. Jem tried to struggle free, but Ainsworth just tightened his grip, and Jem grimaced in pain.

After a few more words, Jem stopped struggling and nodded slowly in response. Ainsworth released him, shoving him to the ground. Edward Ainsworth was taller than Jem but much older, so Bill was surprised how easily he had managed to hold Jem still.

"You really are an embarrassment, Jem, you know that? If you were my son, I'd disown you." Ainsworth started laughing.

Bill felt himself being yanked backwards by his collar and came face-to-face with an angry Tommy.

"You! I said come on. Get back up there before I give you a good hiding," he said, pointing to the church entrance.

Bill started walking with Tommy behind him, occasionally shoving Bill forwards when he slowed down, craning his neck to see what happened next between Jem and Ainsworth. Even when he couldn't see, Bill could recognise Jem's angry tones.

"You stay away from my family now, or I will kill you myself!"

Bill turned around to see Jem pointing a finger at Ainsworth and the old man laughing hysterically, almost doubling over with mirth. Tommy grabbed hold of Bill's shoulders tightly and marched him away, but not before Bill saw just how dejected Jem looked. For the first time, Bill truly felt sorry for his eldest brother.

CHAPTER 2

THE WAKE
JANUARY 1841

As they reached the church doors, Tommy released one hand and grabbed Nell, quickly ushering the two of them towards the inn. As they passed the group of strangers that had been paying their respects, Bill noticed some of them staring with open mouths. Others refused to meet his eye, whispering to each other while covering their mouths with their hands. Bill squirmed a little, trying to turn round and see what was happening, but Tommy still had a tight hold on him and kept pushing him forwards.

"Who was that?" Bill asked. "Tommy, who was that man and why – "

"He's no one," Tommy said and then paused, seeming to change his mind. "His name is Edward Ainsworth," he said curtly, "and you should never have anything to do with him. Do you hear? If you ever see him again, walk away and do not speak to him. Do not listen to anything he has to say."

"Why? What has he done? Why was he fighting with Jem?" Bill's interest was piqued now.

"Never you mind," Tommy said through gritted teeth.

"He's just a bad man, and I don't want to hear any more about it."

Bill stuffed his hands into his pockets and scuffed protestingly at the hail-covered grass with his feet. It just isn't fair, he thought, treating me like a child when I'm old enough to know things. Nobody ever tells me anything, and I'm tired of it.

Janey and Peggy, arms linked, as usual, quickly caught them up. Bill immediately took his hands out of his pockets and stood up straight.

"Well, I don't know about you, but I need a stiff drink after that spectacle," said Peggy, huffing and puffing. "Shall we retire to the inn?"

Peggy's question was more of a politely veiled order, and she wasn't the type of woman you said no to. Tommy held open the large iron-studded wooden door for Peggy and Janey, then pushed Nell and Bill in before entering himself.

Once inside the inn, the odd-looking party immediately made their way towards the open fire, and Peggy ordered six brandies, suggesting they were purely medicinal after the cold weather and shock. Bill's face quickly started burning from the heat of the open fireplace after the wintry air, and he shuffled his feet uncomfortably.

When all the brandies had been distributed, Peggy stood up and raised her glass.

"To Bobby Hall. Bad decisions aside, may he finally rest in peace."

Bill pricked up his ears. What decisions?

"Bobby Hall," muttered Janey, Tommy and Nell, and everyone sipped their drinks. Bill obligingly copied them, trying not to let the vile, strong-smelling liquid touch more than this lip, which it stung.

Janey sobbed loudly and exaggeratedly raised the back of her hand to her forehead.

Peggy gave her a sharp dig in the ribs with her elbow, and Janey yelped. She glared at her sister, then pulled out a white lace-trimmed handkerchief and dabbed her eyes theatrically. Bill smiled and looked over at Nell, who smiled back at him from behind her glass.

"Pull yourself together!" hissed Peggy. "You're making a public spectacle of yourself, and at your own brother's funeral too."

Janey immediately stopped dabbing her eyes and looked at her sister.

"I'm making a public spectacle of myself? I wasn't the one chasing off that dreadful Ainsworth fellow with a stick!"

Peggy harrumphed, put her nose in the air and turned her back on Janey. Janey went back to dabbing her eyes, more discreetly this time.

A few minutes later, Jem stomped through the entrance to the inn. His shirt and jacket were dishevelled, and his hands intermittently slapped away a piece of dirt or a twig. Bill felt pity for his brother but realised he'd better watch what he said until Jem calmed down. He'd seen him in this mood too many times before.

"Come now," Tommy said quietly. "Forget him. Have a brandy."

Jem exploded. "Forget him? Do you remember what he's done to our family? And do you know what he just said to me?"

"Not here, Jem. We can't do anything about it right now."

Jem glared at Tommy for a split second and then rushed at him, grabbing his jacket by both lapels.

"No, no no no, NO!" Peggy rushed forwards and hit Jem about the head and shoulders with her silver cane. "Release your brother!"

Jem let go and covered his head with his arms.

"Remember where you are!" Peggy commanded. "For heaven's sake! Why can you two boys not get along?"

Tommy looked down at the floor.

"This will never do," she said, tutting. "Behaving like commoners. A bar brawl? Really? Who do you think you are?"

"We are commoners," said Jem. "Father saw to that."

"Well, that's as may be," Peggy consented, "but you can still behave civilly. Shame on you!" She turned to her sister. "You deal with the children," she nodded in Bill and Nell's direction, "while I go and have a chat with these two."

Janey nodded, and Peggy ushered Jem and Tommy into a private room, barking out orders for soup and more brandies on her way.

"What bad decisions?" Bill asked, looking up at Janey.

"What's that, dear?"

"Aunt Peggy said Father made bad decisions. What decisions?"

"Oh, I don't know." She smiled sweetly at Bill. "Maybe she didn't think him starting a chandling business was a good idea." She gave a tinkling laugh.

"Why not?"

"Oh, people just have different opinions. You are a curious one, aren't you?" She smiled and ruffled his hair. "Now why don't we sit down and have something to eat. They may be quite a while."

"Why?"

Janey smiled blankly.

"Who is Ainsworth, why is he a bad man and we're to have nothing to do with him, and why was he fighting with Jem?"

Janey's smile faded.

"Well, I, err ... I don't think that is something to be discussed at your father's funeral," she said, flustered. "You might ask Jem about it all later. But not today, love. Lets all take our time to grieve. Maybe when things have calmed down a bit, Jem'll tell you all about it."

"He won't," said Bill. "He never tells us anything."

"Oh, I'm sure that's not true." Janey flashed them another smile. "Anyway," she patted Bill's knee, "it just doesn't do to be worrying about things you don't need to. And today we have other things to worry about. Now," she looked around, "I'm supposed to get you two some food. Where shall I order? Peggy usually takes care of this sort of thing." Janey stood up and wandered over to the serving hatch at the back of the room.

Nell turned to Bill. "What happened? I didn't really see much of the fight. Tommy made me go back and stand in the doorway, and then he went to get you. What did that man say to Jem?"

"He was taunting Jem about being weak, then he said something about our Emma. Jem tried to hit him, but the old man grabbed him and held him fast. Either our Jem's really weak or that Ainsworth fella is really strong. Then he said something to Jem and just let go and threw our Jem to the ground. Tommy grabbed me then, and I don't know what else happened until I heard Jem threatening to kill Ainsworth."

"But who is Ainsworth? Why did he come causing trouble? What did he say to Jem?"

"I don't know, other than what Tommy just told us about Ainsworth being a bad man and we are to have nothing to do with him. I didn't get close enough to hear what Ainsworth said. And they won't tell us anything more, I'm sure. I bet they're sitting there in the other room talking about it all now though." Bill folded his arms and pouted.

Nell laughed and stood up. "Tell Aunt Janey that I've gone to find the privy." She winked at Bill and started to walk away.

"Where are you really going?"

"I'm going to find out who Ainsworth is and what he said to Jem." Bill stared at his sister. "Come back, you'll get into trouble!"

"Just make sure you tell her that I've gone to the privy, and we won't be in any trouble at all."

"We will be if they catch you."

"Pah!" And with that, Nell slipped out of his sight. Bill turned back towards the fire and waited for his aunt to return, dreading having to entertain her on his own.

31

Nell walked down the long, narrow corridor, its walls newly white-washed. Off the corridor were three doors. One stood wide open, and Nell could see its occupants. Definitely not Jem and Tommy! The other two doors were slightly open. Nell approached the first one and tried to peer through the crack in the door, but she couldn't see anyone. She put her ear to the door instead and heard a familiar voice.

"Now then, we need to discuss the small matter of what is to become of Nellie and Billy," said an older woman's voice. Aunt Peggy!

"Yes, and Luke." Nell recognised Jem's nasal, whining tones instantly.

"What you do with that child does not concern me. The other two, however, I will help you with. I have had some ideas. I assume you are their guardian now?" asked Peggy.

"I suppose. It's not like there's anyone else," Jem said.

I suppose? thought Nell. Well, that's nice. Doesn't sound like he even wants us around. And why won't she help Luke? Maybe she she thinks he's still a baby?

"Well then," Peggy continued, "the boy should get an apprenticeship. He needs a trade. He needs to be able to get himself a steady job once he's of age. There is no money for any of you – you know that."

There was silence. Nell wished she could see Jem's and Tommy's faces, but this would have to do.

"Find him a decent trade, Jem. Nothing too expensive, I'm not made of money, but something where he can learn a skilled job," said Peggy.

"But I can't afford to pay for an apprenticeship," said Jem.

"I will pay, as I did yours and Tommy's. Didn't I just say that?"

Nell gasped and raised her hand to her mouth. Her father didn't pay for his own sons' apprenticeships? Why did Aunt Peggy pay instead? Did this mean she had been in their lives a lot? Until today, Nell had never heard of her. But that would mean things her father had said about them not having enough money because it was going to Tommy's apprenticeship were lies. Why would he say that? What else did he lie about? Did Jem know their father was lying?

"That's very generous, Aunt Peggy." Tommy's deep tone brought Nell back to the present.

"Yes, quite. Contact me again when the boy is thirteen and ready for his apprenticeship. What you do with him in the meantime is up to you," Peggy said decidedly.

Jem started to protest. "But we have no room. We only have two small rooms above my father-in-law's shop for me, my wife, three children and another on the way. There just isn't room for three more."

Peggy's voice rose, making Nell jump. "They are your siblings, and he was your father. I have offered to help out of the goodness of my heart, as I did for you and your brother many years ago. I do not need to do that. You are not my children. I will not take you all on and rectify the mistakes your father made, do you hear me? What you do with those children for the next few years is your problem. I will help with the girl now and the older boy when he's thirteen. I think I've been more than kind. Treated everyone equally."

There was a pause for what seemed like several minutes, but Nell knew it couldn't have been that long.

"You may thank me now."

"Thank you Aunt Peggy," Jem and Tommy mumbled obediently. Nell began to wonder why the sour old woman wasn't prepared to help them out more. It wasn't as if she was lacking financially, by the looks of her dress, or the fact that she'd paid for two apprenticeships and was offering to pay for Bill's too.

"Excuse me, miss!" A stout woman carrying three bowls of steaming soup almost bumped into Nell as she tried to pass her. Nell straightened up quickly and stepped out of the way so Jem, Tommy and Peggy wouldn't see her when the door opened. On her way out again, the woman pulled the door to, but the stubborn door refused to stay closed and creaked open slightly. Nell stepped back into position and put her ear up to the opening again. All she could hear was spoons scraping porcelain and slurping. After a clattering of spoons signifying the meal was over, Peggy spoke again.

"As for the girl, how old is she now?"

"Just turned thirteen," answered Jem.

"Hmmm. We'll tell people fifteen. Shame she's not a bit bigger for her age. I'll ask around and see if I can find her a place in service."

Service? Service! They're going to send me away? Away from Bill?

Nell's heart started to beat faster, and she started to feel slightly sick and clammy.

"In service!" she heard Jem exclaim. "Does that mean you're going to send her away?"

"Be grateful," Aunt Peggy snapped. "She'll earn more than in one of those mills, and I'll make sure she's placed with a good family that doesn't treat her unkindly. You've just said you can't take them all in. She – and you – could end up a lot worse off. What's your alternative? Pack them all off to the orphanage?"

Nobody spoke for several minutes.

"I think I'll go and join Janey now," said Peggy. "You two have more to discuss, I assume? Join us when you're ready." Nell pulled away from the door, briefly looked up and down the corridor trying to decide which was the best route of escape, and decided to flee back to Janey and Bill.

Her cheeks flushed, and her mind full of what she'd just heard, she found it hard to concentrate on what Janey was saying.

"She's not feeling too well," she heard Bill say. "Maybe she caught a chill on the way here."

"Oh, Nellie dear," said Janey. "Come closer to the fire. Here, have some soup. I'll order you some more brandy. Drink up mine to be going on with."

Nell did as she was told, coughing as the strong liquid burned her throat. At that moment, Peggy swept into the room and seated herself with what only she could assume was grace and femininity.

Jem and Tommy eventually returned to their small family group. Nell looked up and noticed for the first time how unlike each other they were. Everyone had always said the Halls were like peas in a pod – the same short, stocky build, blond hair (although usually never combed), blue eyes set back in round eye sockets and high cheekbones in an oval face. The other thing people said about the Halls was that they got progressively better looking. Of course that was cruel to Jem, being the eldest, but his eyes and nose were out of proportion, and his chin was rather weak. In contrast, everyone remarked that Luke looked like an angel. His Hall facial features had been thrown together in an extremely pleasing manner. Bill was a fine-looking boy, Nell thought, but Luke was something special. It was just a shame he didn't have the charm or good behaviour to go with it.

"Come," said Jem, nodding at Nell and tapping Bill on his shoulder. He turned to their aunts. "It was nice seeing you again, even though it was under such unfortunate circumstances."

"Oh, do stay a bit longer," said Janey, "we hardly ever see you. We'd all love to have a chat with you, have the family together, wouldn't we, Tommy?"

"Mmm," Tommy said noncommittally.

"It's just that the cart belongs to my brother-in-law, and he needs it back by this afternoon, and we've a long way to go," said Jem. Nell stared at Jem, but he wouldn't look directly back at her. She then looked up at Tommy and caught his eye, but Tommy quickly looked away.

"Then we'd better see you off, lovelies!" said Janey. She got up and threw her arms around Jem, who looked surprised. Nell went to hug Tommy.

"Don't let them send me away," she whispered. Tommy drew back as if he'd been stung.

"What? How ... ?"

Nell just stared at him, then flung her arms round his neck as if she'd never let go.

"I promise I won't let anything bad happen to you," Tommy whispered into her hair. Nell hugged her brother tighter.

Janey released Jem and scooped up Bill instead. "Sweet boy," she muttered into his hair. "I hope we'll see a lot more of you now." Bill smiled politely back and broke free. Janey turned to Peggy, who was standing to one side, refusing to demonstrate any signs of affection.

"Can't we take in the little boy, Peggy? I'm sure he'd be no trouble. I'd love to have a child about the place."

Peggy turned round and looked at her, aghast. "Are you out of your mind? No, we cannot take in a child! And a boy too? Horrible little creatures."

Nell lifted her head from Tommy's neck and stared at them.

"That's my brother you're talking about," Tommy said evenly.

"Well, you know what I mean," Peggy said, looking at him.

Tommy raised his eyebrows.

"You were practically an adult. How would we know what to do with children? They're noisy and dirty."

These "aunts" are just the worst, thought Nell. I'm so glad I never met them before today.

"The girl, then?" said Janey. "She's almost an adult and very quiet and sweet."

Nell was horrified. Say no, say no! she silently urged Peggy. Really, she'd rather be sent away than have to live with them.

"Janey!" Peggy said sharply. "We simply cannot take in those children, and that's the end of it. They are not our responsibility. Bobby made his choice when he left. Even you know he did." She looked pointedly at Tommy over the edge of her glasses.

"But they're family and the closest I'll ever have to having children. You saw to that. Now we're given a gift like this, a second chance. Can you deny me this as well?" Janey stood there and pouted.

Peggy turned to face her sister, but just before she managed to open her mouth, Jem, who had already climbed up into the cart next to the driver, shouted, "We really have to be going now. Bill, Nell, get in the cart."

Nell reluctantly released Tommy and scrambled up into the back of the cart after Bill. Janey fussed, covering Nell and Bill up with the thin blanket, making a big show of tucking it in until Jem insisted they really had to leave or they would be late back. Finally, she was forced to let go as the cart pulled away, and she stood back, waving.

Nell waved at Tommy until she could no longer see him. With a heavy heart, she sank down, pulled the blanket up to her chin and rested her head on Bill's shoulder. Should she tell him their brothers were going to send her away? How long did she have left with Bill and Luke? Would they send her far away? Would she ever see them again? Or just at family funerals, like with Tommy? Maybe she shouldn't tell Bill. Maybe it would be better that he didn't know until the last minute so he wouldn't spend so much time worrying or being upset or trying to stop them. It was hard enough for them all right now without adding to the misery. If she didn't tell him, perhaps they could spend what was left of their time together happy. But Nell didn't know how to be happy right now. Not only had she lost Tommy, she was now going to lose Bill. She closed her eyes, and the tears flowed.

CHAPTER 3

BACK TO BOLTON
JANUARY 1841

As soon as they could no longer see their relatives, Nell felt Jem lean back on his bench seat and heard him let out a long sigh. Nell sat in silence, occasional tears rolling down her face. She huddled up next to Bill, who pulled the rug tighter around their shoulders. It was a bit warmer than it had been early in the morning, but it was still cold. Nell started to think about Tommy. It had been such a long time since she'd last seen him. She had been almost nine when Tommy had left home, aged fifteen, and she missed him terribly. He had always been the one she'd run to if she was hurt or upset, and he was always so friendly and gentle. He was the one who would give her a hug and help wash her cuts and scrapes when she fell down. He would sympathise with her torn dress when her mother or Emma would just shout at her for making more work. And then one day Tommy came to tell her he had to leave. It was the week after Luke had been born and their Ma had died. They were all in shock and tired from trying to look after a baby who constantly screamed and never slept. Emma had just left the day before in a barrage of yelling and screaming, taking only her shawl, and turning to curse their father before slamming the door behind her. Nell remembered hiding behind Tommy's back, watching the awful scene and wishing she could stop them all arguing. And then the next day Tommy was gone. Just like that. It was almost worse than losing her mother. She waited and waited for Tommy to come back, but he never did.

Nell had toiled trying to run the house, looking after the baby, and Bill, who was only five, cooking and cleaning for them all, falling into bed exhausted each night. It was the worst and most exhausting few years of her short life. Their father was mostly absent, coming home late, occasionally giving Nell money to buy them all food. Jem came round and told them stories of Tommy's new life in Manchester, all about the fine people whom Tommy was learning to make clothes for, but also about Tommy getting into fights and nearly losing his apprenticeship. About the real reason Tommy never came home to visit – he now only thought of himself and didn't want to help them. But that just didn't sound like Tommy to Nell. Even so, she had become angry with him for not coming back when she needed him.

But today when she saw him again, it was the old Tommy she remembered. He hadn't changed at all. Well, maybe he was taller and a little heavier, more solid than the thin fifteen-year-old she'd last seen. Perhaps his face had changed and his voice was a little deeper. But the gentle way about him and the lopsided smile was still the same. She'd been so happy to see him, yet she was annoyed at the same time because he had acted like there was nothing wrong. She didn't know whether to hit him or hug him, so she just clung to him, not wanting to let go in case he disappeared again. There had been so many questions she'd wanted to ask him, but there hadn't been time. And who knew when she'd see him again?

As the cart horse plodded slowly and the hedgerows and brambles slipped by, her mind started to wander, and scenes from the day popped up in her head. Why did Tommy not speak up for her when Aunt Peggy talked about sending her into service? She had been surprised that Jem had – after all, he had made it clear that he didn't want her, Bill and Luke living with him. And then there was that funny thing that Aunt Peggy had said when they were leaving: "You were practically an adult." What did she mean by that? Tommy left home to go and live with the aunts? Or had he left home and then some time later went to live with the aunts? Why had Jem not said anything? None of his stories had involved the aunts. In fact, Nell had never heard of them before today. No one ever said Tommy was living with family. Why?

She looked up at Bill, and he smiled at her.

"Are you all right?" he asked.

"I will be." She smiled back. She wanted to ask him so many things about his impressions from today, but she didn't want Jem overhearing them. It was obvious to her now that Jem liked to keep family things secret. Or change facts. They continued in silence until the cart pulled into the outskirts of Bolton town.

The horse and cart trudged up Folds Road. The street was packed with hawkers, carters, men spilling out of the myriad pubs along the main street, women either going about their business or standing outside neighbours' houses chatting. Nowhere in this town is it ever quiet, thought Nell. The made their way past the foundry where Jem worked, up Hulme Street and onto Dean Street. The driver skilfully manoeuvred the tired and reluctant horse through the gap in the houses and into the courtyard. Nell and Bill sat up.

"Why are we back here?" Bill asked Jem. "You said we don't live here anymore."

"Somebody needs to clear out the house," said Jem. "The landlord said he has a new family needing to move in tomorrow." He climbed down and walked to the back of the cart, where he helped lift Nell and Bill down.

"Right, Bill, you go and fetch Luke. Nell, you come with me. I need help loading some things onto the cart, and the house needs to be swept too."

Nell nodded and looked around. She was happy to see the place, but it felt strange now. Like she didn't belong here either. The place was bustling, as usual. A few young girls were helping their mothers with laundry, dunking faded cloth in large wooden tubs and then scrubbing. Lines of already-washed and hung laundry were tied from one house to another across the courtyard. She knew it wasn't worth hanging up laundry outside – it usually rained or they got soot-blackened from chimney smoke, or the stench from the outside rubbish piles followed them inside. Then again, laundry took forever to dry indoors and made the rooms feel even damper than usual. A few of the older women nodded at Nell before she stepped inside the house but didn't say anything. There was nothing to be said.

Bill stood alone in the courtyard for a moment before making his way over to the Taylors' house directly across from theirs. He looked up at his front door – well, it wasn't his front door any longer. He thought about going in for one last look with Nell, but he just couldn't do it. It didn't matter anyway. Tomorrow this house would belong to someone else, and he could never come back. He lingered by the door, then turned and crossed the courtyard.

At his former neighbours' house, he announced himself as he pushed the door open, as they always did with each other. Bill saw Luke sitting in a chair by the fire with Mrs. Taylor, taking apart a wooden car of Jimmy's that Mr. Taylor had presumably made. Bill's heart lurched, and he wanted to just stand there forever and take in the familiar scene.

"Billy, lad, come in!" Nan Taylor stood up and went over to give Bill a hug, nearly squeezing the breath out of him. "You poor lamb. How are you doing? How's Nellie? I see you've come for this one?" She nodded over at Luke. Bill released himself and tried not to appear ungrateful for the hug, but he just wanted his brother, and he didn't really feel like talking.

"I'm doing all right, thanks," he said. "Nell's helping Jem clean out Father's things."

Nan nodded.

"I'm so sorry we left you behind, Luke," Bill said, sitting down on Nan's chair next to his brother. "I was really angry that Jem wouldn't let you come with us to the funeral, and I told him so." Luke looked up, then suddenly buried his head in Bill's coat. It wasn't often that his brother showed any signs of affection, but when he did, it was as though it melted you from the inside, Bill often thought. He wrapped his arms round his little brother and breathed into his hair.

"I'll not leave you again, Luke, promise. I'll look after you. It's just going to be you, me and Nell from now on, and we're going to be fine."

Nan urged Bill to stay awhile with her by the fire and have something to eat. Bill shook his head, knowing that he'd already had one large meal so far that day, and the Taylors didn't often have food to spare. But he took her up on her offer of staying for awhile. The Taylors were comfortable people. You always felt right at home with them. They said the right things and made everything better. And their house was familiar and warm. Just for a few moments, Bill felt everything was going to be fine. He was amongst people who cared about him. He would go back to worrying about everything else shortly. Just now, he was safe and he was sleepy. Leaning his head against the back of the chair, he drifted off into a deep sleep, not even feeling Luke carefully wriggle free from the chair.

Jem opened the door and stepped inside the house. Nell followed him, letting the door slam after them. She stood inside the entrance and looked around the room. A cold stillness descended, magnified by the noise from outside in the courtyard. The closed curtains, a mark of respect to her father's passing, were so worn that slivers of dim light found their way into the room, creating patterns on the floor and walls. The room was far quieter than Nell ever remembered it. Even with her father so sick, there had always been life in here. Now that seemed to have gone, along with his presence. Jem moved towards the bench at the back of the room and lit the two candles standing there.

"Looks like this will be quick," he said. "You gather together the pots and pans and anything else you have in the kitchen and stand them by the front door. I'll go and check upstairs."

Nell noticed his look of disgust as he glanced around the room.

"We'll have to clean this too, somehow . . ." His voice trailed off, and Nell followed his gaze to a large wet, mouldy patch by the stairs. The walls were uncleanable. They always had been. The mould was now thick, with swirls of black, green and white stains. "Just sweep the floor, Nell."

Nell sighed as Jem went up the stairs to the bedroom, taking one of the candles with him. She gathered their pans and kettle from their shelf, placed the cracked and chipped plates and cups inside them and placed their only knife and four spoons on top. The only other belongings they had downstairs were their father's chair, a breadbox, a small tin bath that she washed their clothes in and the curtains and clothesline Bill had helped her set up. Everything else had been sold off over the years to help buy food when their father became sick and could no longer work. Dragging out the tin bath from the corner, she carried it to the door. Once the clothesline was unhooked from the nails and the pots and pans were placed next to the tin bath, there was nothing more to do but sweep. Nell wondered what was taking Jem so long. All they had up there was some straw on the floor, a few blankets and her father's old trunk. He was probably sleeping, leaving all the work to her. That would be just like him.

Nell crept up the stairs so Jem wouldn't hear her and suddenly pretend he was cleaning. Crouching down, she lifted her head just enough to allow herself to peer over the top step and look around the room. As her eyes grew accustomed to the even dimmer light up there, she saw Jem sitting by the old trunk, the lid wide open and papers spread out all around him. By the glow of the candlelight, she made out a faded leather-bound book in Jem's hands. He was tracing across a page with his finger and moving his mouth slightly as if talking. If she didn't know better, she'd say he was reading. But how could he be? None of the Hall children could read. Most people couldn't. In fact, she didn't know a single person who could read. They had never gone to Sunday school. There was never any money for that, Father had said. So why was Jem sitting there pretending to read instead of helping her clean up? This was just ridiculous. He was being lazy, and she was going to tell him so! But before she could stand up, she heard Jem gasp. She watched him quickly turn a page of the book and then back again several times, muttering to himself.

"Noooo!" he groaned loudly.

Nell jumped and ducked down so he wouldn't see her. A few seconds later, she heard a thud followed by a low scuffling. She slowly peered over the top step again. Jem was scooping up all the papers and throwing them into the trunk. There was another book. Thud! Finally, he slammed the lid shut and turned the key in the lock before shoving it in his pocket. Frozen to the spot, Nell watched Jem pace up and down the room, running his hands through his hair and muttering to himself.

She tiptoed back downstairs and started sweeping with hard, brisk strokes. All the time that trunk had stood there, she had never really wondered what was in it, but now she was curious. First of all, could Jem actually read? It seemed very unlikely. He'd never been to school, and he wasn't so smart, so he couldn't have taught himself, or at least that was the impression he usually gave. A lot of the time he seemed to be drunk or quarrelsome. And he was often looking for a new job. Nell had the impression that he'd been let go from a few jobs because he was unreliable. Or at least that's what she'd heard Nan Taylor say once. And he had trained as a blacksmith but was working as a striker now. Why go through a seven-year-long apprenticeship if you were going to work an unskilled job that anyone could do? Unless you were not so clever. Or you were unreliable, and that was the best job you could get. So she was fairly sure he couldn't read. But yet Nell had seen it with her own eyes. Why would he react like that to a book containing just words if he couldn't read? It just didn't make sense. Unless it contained pictures instead. Nell had half a mind to find out for herself because this was all too confusing.

She swept quickly around the fireplace. But what could be in that book that made him react like that? In words or pictures? What was the book? It was obviously something that belonged to Father, but ...

Her thoughts were interrupted by a rhythmic crash of muffled wood on wood as Jem dragged the trunk down the stairs.

"Nell! Tell the driver to come and give me a hand," Jem said, panting.

Nell ran out into the courtyard and came back in with the driver.

"Go and take up the blankets and sweep upstairs," said Jem.

Nell dutifully obeyed, bundling up the blankets and throwing them down the stairs. She swept the straw into a pile by the top of the stairs.

"Come on, then," said Jem. "Don't dawdle."

That was so like him, thought Nell. He should have been born some fancy rich person with lots of servants because that's how he treated people. She left the pile of straw and ran down the stairs.

The pots and pans, trunk and bathtub were already on the cart, and Nell struggled to find a comfortable spot to sit.

"We don't have all day," Jem said, exasperated. "The driver needs to get back, and we need to deal with all this." He gestured at the back of the cart.

"What about Bill and Luke?" asked Nell.

"They can make their own way back. They know where the house is. We don't have any more space on the cart for them."

Nell settled down into her cramped space, holding on to the tin bath so it didn't slide off when they went over a bump. As the cart was pulled along the short journey to Jem's house, she looked at the trunk a little more intently, running her fingers over the soft black leather. It was small for a travel trunk, but much deeper than you would expect it to be. The craftsmanship was good, even though it was now quite old, the leather finely stretched and held into place with brass studs. A large ornate lock and ornate hinges gave it an air of being grander than it was, and three large initials in curly script gave it an air of importance. Nell knew those initials by heart, even without being able to read them. R.H.H. for Ralph Horrowbin Hall, her grandfather, for whom the suitcase had been made. Of course it almost worked for her father's name, Robert Hall. But there were no more R names in his family – except for Jem's own son Robert, or Robin, as he went by. Nell tried to open the catch, but of course nothing happened. She had seen Jem lock it. She sighed.

After only five minutes, the cart came to a stop outside the back of Jem's father-in-law's paint shop. Jem climbed down to open the gates, and the driver clicked his tongue, whipped the reins, and urged the horse to walk into the flagstoned yard. It must have been late in the day by now because there was no one around. The winter sun had gone down, and Nell's stomach was rumbling.

After unloading the cart, Jem thanked the driver, who led the horse away. The streetlamp shed a dim light over the yard as Nell stood there shivering and watching Jem look around the yard.

"What are we doing now?"

Jem didn't appear to hear her. He walked over to a tarpaulin covering a large pile and pulled it back. Underneath lay wooden pallets, rolls of thick paper and broken wooden handles.

"Aha! The kindling pile. That'll do!" he exclaimed. "Nell, help me drag the trunk over here."

"What? Why, Jem? What are you doing with Father's trunk? You can't leave it here. What if it got burned along with everything else?"

Crouched down with one hand lifting the trunk by the handle, Jem looked up at her. "That's the whole point of leaving it here."

"You can't burn Father's trunk!"

"Of course I can," said Jem.

"Why?"

"Don't question me!"

"But it's Father's trunk. If you don't want it, maybe Bill or Luke will. Or Tommy."

"It's just filled with paper that's only fit for kindling," said Jem. "And people need kindling to light fires."

"What's in there?"

"Never you mind."

Nell opened her mouth to protest but then thought better of it. Jem would never confide anything in her. If she wanted to know what was in that trunk, she'd have to be clever about it. She dutifully helped Jem push the trunk over to the pile and cover it with the tarpaulin.

"Now," Jem said, brushing his hands and turning to Nell, "we'll take the rest upstairs and see if Molly needs any of it. Otherwise, we can try and sell."

"The Taylors might be glad of some pots and pans or plates," said Nell.

"Family needs come first, and the Taylors are not family."

"They've been more like family recently than you have," Nell muttered.

"What?" Jem said absently, picking up the tin bath, chair and blankets.

"Nothing."

"Come, then."

Nell sighed and bent down to pick up the pots and pans. She followed her brother out of the gates and waited for him to open the side door to his home above the shop. How was she going to move that trunk before it got chopped up and its contents burned, and where was she going to hide it?

CHAPTER 4

THE MILL
JANUARY 1841

Bill slept fitfully all night. He never slept well the first few nights in a new place. Not that Jem's place was new to him, but he'd never stayed over before. And he was only ever used to sharing his bed with Luke. Now he had both Luke and their nephew Lukin to contend with in the small space under the kitchen table, and they both kicked him in their sleep. He turned onto his back and lay there in the semidarkness, exploring the cracks in the ceiling highlighted from the soft glow of the flame in the streetlamp outside the window. The room seemed even smaller than he had remembered. At the top of the stairs, there was a short bench along one wall with a shelf running above it, this table and some chairs between the bench and the fireplace and a mattress, which was placed against the wall under the sole window during the day. Even with so little furniture, the room looked cluttered.

His thoughts turned to Nell. He was dying to ask her what she'd overheard Jem, Tommy and Aunt Peggy say at the inn, but he and Luke had gotten back late last night, and it hadn't been possible to get Nell on her own. He would be getting up and going to work in the mill again in a few hours. Maybe he could find some time alone with Nell today. But what about later? The rest of the week? From the way Jem's wife, Molly, had arranged where everyone would sleep, it didn't feel like she and Jem were planning on making their stay permanent. There certainly wasn't enough room on this small mattress for the three of them; Jem wasn't going to accept having baby Robin in bed with him forever, and there wasn't enough room in the bedroom to put a curtain across to give Nell and their niece, Lissy, or Jem and Molly any privacy.

But where would they go? The more Bill thought about it, the more he was sure his brother was going to send them to the orphanage. Then he might never get to talk to Nell or Luke again. Their fate was in Jem's hands, and that was so unfair.

He sat up, almost bumping his head on the table, and looked over at his sleeping brother. Luke's fists were clenched next to his round, flushed baby cheeks and mop of bright blond hair. Jem seemed to really dislike Luke. Bill had even noticed Jem staring at Luke all evening with a strange look on his face. Luke could be difficult, but it wasn't his fault. He'd had it hard right from the beginning. He'd been born in the early hours of a wet October morning almost five years ago. Their mother, Alice, was already dead by the time he'd taken his first breath. She was forty-three years old and had been in labour for three days. Bill still remembered the screams that went on and on. In the end, they told him that his mother just wasn't strong enough. Bill remembered the day his father told him his mother was dead. And the next day, or at least he thought it had been the next day, when Emma and Tommy left. He didn't remember much more than that, but he could see that their father never really acknowledged Luke. Maybe it was because he was sick and Luke was so young and could be a bit of a handful sometimes. But Bill had also noticed that Luke tended to stay out of their father's way, going to Bill if he was hurt or needed comforting. Bill lay back down again, moving closer to his little brother and turning his head so he could be comforted by Luke's breath on his cheek, as he'd been used to every night for the past several years.

It felt like Bill had only just drifted off to sleep again when the knocker-upper tapped on the window. He reluctantly sat up and felt around for his shoes. But he was really tired, and Luke and Lukin hadn't stirred, so he lay back down. Just for a few minutes, willing the ache in his body to stop and trying to draw out those last seconds before the day's toil started. The next thing he knew he was being woken by Jem roughly shaking him. He looked around and realised he was the only one lying on the mattress. He rubbed away the sleep from his eyes, yawned and pulled on his jacket.

It seemed like he'd been the last one to rise. Molly and Nell had already emptied the chamber pots and were ready to take Molly's children and Luke round to her parents' house in Barn Square, a few streets away from the paint shop. Nell was apparently going to help Molly's stepmother mind the children today while Molly was at work, then they "would see" what she was going to do more permanently. Nell and Luke waved a quick good-bye to Bill as they and their nephews and niece were ushered down the stairs and out of the door by Molly. As soon as the door closed, Bill, not wanting to spend any more time in Jem's company than absolutely necessary, tied his shoes, pulled on his cap and rushed for the door.

Bill trudged up the hill to Wellington mill. It was farther from Jem's house than he had been used to walking. He kicked his feet on the debris in the road as he went, trying to draw out the walk as much as possible, but hurried when he heard the first bell ringing. It didn't do to be late – you got your pay docked, and he didn't earn that much to start with. Children were poorly paid. But today he was even more tired than usual. He hoped he'd make it through the day without falling asleep – that would result in getting beaten, or worse, getting mangled in one of the machines. That hadn't happened at his mill yet, at least not while Bill had been working there, but you heard stories, and Bill didn't want to be the first.

He got there on time, took off his hat and coat and went to his machine. The job as a scavenger wasn't easy. Bill couldn't wait until he could do something else. Maybe be a piecer like Molly. Then again, none of the jobs looked easy. The small flecks of cotton floating in the air tickled your throat and made you cough, and you didn't often get a break to go and gulp the tepid water from the bucket and ladle in the corner. Besides, there was always the danger of moving machinery, no matter what part of the mill you worked in.

Bill stood next to his machine watching the rollers, waiting to time the rhythmic movement so he could crawl in under the loom again quickly and scoop up the debris, when something caught his eye. Two children from the next loom stood up slowly, unable to remove their eyes from something behind him. He reeled around to see a child on the next loom caught underneath, arms flailing, his leg pinned between two rollers. Bill froze, not knowing what to do. It was so noisy in the room that not many had heard the accident, but he could see the spinner had already shut down his loom and the mighty machine started to shudder to a standstill with hisses and groans. Bill looked up to see an overlooker come running down from the gallery. The next thing Bill felt was a hand grabbing his collar and pulling him backwards. The hands spun him around and started hitting him around the head and neck, forcing Bill to cradle his head in his arms.

"Pay attention to your own loom, or you're out!" mouthed Pat O'Connor, the spinner from Bill's loom, then he released him roughly. Bill smoothed down his shirt and stared at the rollers. His back was hurting and his right ear was ringing, but he didn't dare look back again.

It was three more hours before the lunch bell rang. Three hours of Bill trying to push all thoughts of the boy out of his head and concentrate on his own loom despite his own pain and tiredness. If the machine had to be stopped, or if the debris caused a spark and a fire, it would be his fault, and he'd get more than just a beating from his spinner. Eventually, the clanging of metal on metal that signalled lunch break became audible over the background noise, and Bill was filled with relief. After the machine groaned to a halt, he took a rag and started to wipe grease and fluff off the warm metal while the spinner poured more dark viscose liquid from a large spouted oil can into the thirsty machine. When the spinner was satisfied, he nodded to Bill, and Bill tore away for his thirty-minute lunch break.

Bill stood at the mill gates, waiting to catch sight of Nell bringing him his lunch as she always did. Finally, she appeared around the corner, and he ran up to greet her.

"You're late!"

"I know, sorry. I had to take Molly's lunch to her over at Hope Mill first. It was on the way. But here you are!" She smiled as she handed over the handle of the small tin pot. Bill tore off the muslin cloth and peered inside. Potatoes and a little meat. What a feast! He was used to the thin gruel Nell made him, very much watered down to make it last longer.

"I could get used to this!" He grinned. Nell smiled back.

"Yes, it all feels so easy right now," said Nell. "Maybe they're just trying to make us feel better about Father."

"What do you mean?"

"Well," said Nell, twisting the handle of the remaining tin lunch pot round her fingers, "I've had a very easy morning. Molly's stepmother, Mrs. Booth – well, she said to call her Aunt Jane – made all the dinners. I didn't have to cook or clean or help with anything except play with the children. And my only task so far has been to take the dinners round. This is for Mr. Booth at the paint shop," she added.

"But that's great!" said Bill. "You deserve to have a rest. You've worked hard looking after us all." His face fell.

"What is it?"

"It's just ... I don't feel so welcome at Jem's. It feels so temporary. And I wish I didn't have to work here any more. I'd do anything other than this. A boy got trapped in the next loom over from mine this morning."

"Oh!" Nell exclaimed. "How awful! How bad was it? Is he going to be all right?"

"I don't know," said Bill. "People are saying different things. But you know that kind of injury is never good."

Nell nodded. Then she poked Bill's arm. Bill smiled.

"What did you hear back at the inn, when our Jem and Tommy and Aunt Peggy were talking? I've been wanting to ask you since yesterday, but Jem was around all the time." Bill watched a frown appear on his sister's face, and her shoulders dropped.

"Not much."

"What do you mean 'not much'? They must have said something."

Nell ran her fingers over the handle of the dinner pot. Back and forth, back and forth. Bill almost started to get irritated.

"Well, they said something about getting you an apprenticeship so you can get a good job when you're older."

A smile spread across Bill's face. "So I won't have to work in the mill forever?"

Nell smiled back at him.

"When?"

"When you're thirteen, like everyone else."

Bill's face fell. He wouldn't be thirteen for a long time yet. But still, it was probably better then spending the rest of his life working at the mill.

"What else?"

"Nothing really," said Nell. "They spent a lot of time eating soup and Aunt Peggy telling them what's what. And then she got up to leave, and I had to run back."

"So they didn't say anything about Ainsworth?"

"No."

Bill scrutinised his sister's face and decided she was being truthful.

"Well, go and eat up, then. I have to get on," said Nell.

Bill smiled at her and turned to leave.

"Bill?"

He turned back again. "What?"

"It might all be temporary," she said, and started playing with the dinner pot handle again.

"What do you mean?"

She looked up. "Us. At Jem's. But that wouldn't be a bad thing, would it? Change isn't always bad. Change has been pretty good for us the past few days."

Bill thought about this for a minute. If they didn't live with Jem, where would they go? There was nowhere else, no one else. Unless ...

"Do you think Jem would send us to the orphanage?"

"What? No!"

"Are you sure? I think he could just send us away." He looked closely at Nell and watched her expression change. So he was right. She thought so too.

"No, I mean, I ..." Nell stammered. "No, Bill, he wouldn't send us to the orphanage. Not ever. Don't think that."

"But where would we go, then?"

Nell sighed, hugged her brother and turned to leave.

"Just go and eat up your dinner and let me worry about things like that."

Bill watched her leave, but he saw the smile was quick to fade from Nell's face and knew his sister was also worried.

Nell walked back down Hulme Street towards the paint shop. As she walked along, weaving her way through the throngs of people out on the street, spilling out into the road amongst the horses and handcarts, she started to think about Bill. He seemed to be so worried about the idea of Jem sending them away that she just couldn't bring herself to tell him that Jem was sending her away. She had been right to keep it to herself. He'd be sad enough when he found out, and Nell hoped that would only be the day before she left. But as long as she knew Bill and Luke were being taken care of and with family, she could stand it. She would miss them dreadfully though. Maybe the aunts would be kind and have her placed somewhere very close to home.

As she turned the corner onto Folds Road she thought about the trunk Jem had left in the paint shop's kindling pile last night. Molly's father, along with some of his brothers, cousins and nephews, owned the paint shop and house painting business. Pretty much everyone knew the Booths around here, and pretty much every Booth in Little Bolton worked as a painter. Even though Jem and Molly had lived above the paint shop for a while now, Nell had never been in the shop itself before, and not the yard before last night. Perhaps she could convince Mr. Booth that the trunk shouldn't be broken up and burned.

Nell pushed open the shop door, and a brass bell on a coiled spring began to ring. The smell of paint fumes hit her immediately. As she stepped inside, a tall young man with wavy dark brown hair and blue eyes like Molly's came out of the back room and grinned at her from behind the counter.

"Can I help you, miss?"

Nell held up the lunch pot. "I brought this round for Mr. Booth."

"Ah. You must be Nell."

Nell nodded.

"I'm Jim. Molly's brother. Pa's in the back. Go in." He gestured at the door behind the counter. Nell smiled quickly in thanks and walked into the back room.

The room was large and bright – whitewashed walls contained light wooden shelves and rows and rows of tins of paint. Directly opposite Nell was a door containing a large glass panel and two very large windows looking out onto the yard. The low winter sun had just made it over the back wall and was shining through the window, hitting the tins of paint and reflecting the glare around the room. Nell looked around and saw a man about her father's age sitting in an armchair in front of a row of tins, or rather he would have been her father's age – she kept forgetting her father was no longer around, and when it hit her, the familiar dull pain in her chest came back. The man looked up and smiled.

"Hello," he said, standing up. "You must be Nell."

Nell nodded.

"My, it's been so long since I last saw you. Molly's wedding, I think. I almost didn't recognise you. You've grown so much."

Nell noticed the man's eyes smiled as much as his face, and she began to relax a little. Mr. Booth's dark, wavy hair was only slightly tinged with grey around the temples. His eyes were a piercing blue, which had led to his nickname of Bluey, but the crinkle lines around them softened their effect. He wasn't a tall man, but he was neither too fat nor too skinny, and his demeanour suggested someone who was friendly and good at putting others at ease. Looks and charm, thought Nell. Yet the charm seemed genuine. No wonder Molly was such a nice person. She hoped their children would take after her and not Jem.

"I've brought your lunch from Mrs. Booth," she said, handing him the pot.

"Thank you very much," said Bluey. "I can imagine you're a great help to Jane today, and I'm very sorry for your father's passing. He was a good man."

Nell hung her head so he wouldn't see the tears starting to fill her eyes.

"If there's anything I or Jane can do to help you children, just say so," Bluey said, smiling.

Nell looked up and out of the window. She could see the tarpaulin from there.

"The woodpile. When do you chop it up for kindling?" she asked.

Bluey laughed. "Why the woodpile? Do you need some kindling?"

"No. It's just that we cleared out Father's house yesterday, and Jem left something there to be burned. It was a trunk of Father's, and I wanted to keep it because it's so beautiful and old and it belonged to Grandfather, but Jem said no. It was Father's, and I just don't want to see it burned." She looked across at Bluey. The smile had left his face, and he was looking at her intently.

"Well then, let's go and have a look at it."

Bluey opened the back door, and they stepped out into the yard. They walked over to the tarpaulin, and Bluey grabbed a corner and yanked it up. There, exactly where they'd left it, was the small black trunk.

"That's it!" Nell pointed excitedly. Bluey bent over and then pulled out the trunk, dropping the tarpaulin again. He let out a low whistle.

"My, that's a nice suitcase. Just look at that craftsmanship. Jem wanted to burn this, you say?"

Nell nodded.

Bluey laughed. "Well, for a start, it's leather, and that doesn't make for great kindling. Jem's none too smart about these matters if he thinks this is good to burn in homes or even here. The stench from the leather alone ..."

Nell nodded politely.

"I don't see why he wouldn't want to keep it either," Bluey mused.

"I want to keep it," said Nell. "I'd keep it for my own house when I'm older and married. Or I'd give it to Bill or Luke when they're older to remind them of their father."

"And so you should!" Bluey said, smiling. "Strange that Jem would want to burn it."

"Perhaps he doesn't have room for it," Nell suggested, looking away.

"Hmm. Well, if you like, I could find somewhere to keep it here for you. Just don't tell Jem I went against his wishes."

Nell squealed and threw her arms around Bluey.

"Steady on!" He laughed. Nell withdrew her arms quickly.

"Sorry."

"No problem. It's only a small favour, really."

"Oh no, it's a huge favour to me – really, it is." Nell's eyes shone as she looked at Bluey, then the trunk, then back at Bluey again.

"Leave it with me, and I'll think of a good place to store it where it won't be disturbed," Bluey said.

"Thank you so much!" Nell said. She turned to leave.

"And thank you for bringing my lunch," Bluey called after her.

Nell practically skipped out of the shop. Now the only other obstacle was to find out what was in that trunk that made Jem react like that. For that she would need time – and the key. She thought back to last night when she saw Jem with the trunk's contents. He must be able to read, she thought. But how? How is that even possible? She began to think that there was more to Jem Hall than met the eye.

CHAPTER 5

ANOTHER NEW HOME
FEBRUARY 1841

It was finally Sunday and a day's rest from the throat-scratching stuffiness and constant clanging of machinery at the mill. The mood at Jem's house was still sombre, and as they sat down to dinner after the church service, Bill noticed Molly looked sad. Perhaps she and Jem had a fight again, he thought. Molly and Jem didn't say much over dinner, and the atmosphere dampened Bill's spirit.

As soon as the last plate had been cleared, Jem rose from the table. "Right, then. Bill, Luke, get your things together."

"Why?" A stab of panic shot through Bill.

"Because you're going to live somewhere where there's more room. Just do as I say and don't keep questioning me all the time."

Is this it? Five days at his house and he's getting rid of us? Where will we go? Bill immediately felt cold and clammy and wished he hadn't eaten so much. Luke sat still in his chair and stared intently at Jem.

"Aren't we all staying together?" Bill managed to get the words out.

Jem looked down, unable to meet Bill's eye.

"You know there's not enough room here."

"You're sending them away?" Nell said incredulously. "Why are you sending them away?

"What do you mean them?" asked Jem.

"I thought it was me you wanted gone."

Jem's jaw dropped, and he just stared at Nell. Bill looked from one to the other. What was going on?

Jem finally cleared this throat. "Bill and Luke, get your stuff together," he repeated, not taking his eyes off Nell.

Bill stood up and went to the corner of the room, where he stuffed his and Luke's weekday clothes into a blanket and tried to tie it, but his fingers were all thumbs, and he felt like he was going to be sick.

"Now," Jem said distractedly, looking up at the clock. "Get a move on; we haven't got all day. Molly will walk you round there."

"You can't do this!" Nell turned to Jem. "Is this how you treat your family? You were never there for us when Father was sick, and now you can't stand to have us living with you, your own siblings. Don't you have a sense of duty?"

Jem's eyebrows shot up. "What do you mean, no sense of duty? I helped out as much as I could, but Father didn't want me around. I took you all in until I could find somewhere better for you. What more can I do? What do you want from me?" he yelled.

Molly wiped her hands on a rag that she used to dry the pots and walked over to them.

"Now come on, love," she said, putting her arm around Bill's shoulders. "You'll like it round at my Pa's. And our Jenny and Johnny have never had younger brothers. They'll probably spoil you. And you'll get your own bed." She smiled brightly.

Bill stopped what he was doing and looked up. "Live at Mr. Booth's?" he asked. "So, so you mean you're not sending us to some stranger ... or to the orphanage?"

"Some stranger? Orphanage?" Jem exploded. "Is that what you think of me? You really think I could do that to you? You ungrateful little sod!" He turned to Molly. "Didn't you tell them?"

"I thought you already told them," she said.

"Ugh!" Jem clenched his fists. He looked at them all, then stormed out, stomping down the stairs and slamming the front door behind him.

"I'm sorry," Molly said, hugging Bill. "No wonder you were so surprised. I really thought he'd told you."

Bill glanced at Molly apologetically.

"You know there really isn't room here for everyone," she said.

Bill nodded. "But I didn't think you'd split us up," he said. "Me, Nell and Luke have always been together. They're all I have left."

"I know, sweetheart," said Molly. "But you do know it's not my decision, don't you? Jem's only trying to do the best for all of us, and my Pa's being very generous and helping not only you two out, but also me and Jem."

Bill considered this for a moment. He didn't really know Molly's parents, but they seemed like very nice people. He just couldn't understand why Nell couldn't come with them.

"But what about Nell?" he asked, looking at his sister. Molly sighed.

"I'm sorry. You must know that I didn't want to split you three up. But we really couldn't find any other way." She paused. "And you're only moving a few streets away."

"You'll have your work cut out looking after Luke," Nell said, grinning. "Don't worry about me. I'll be fine. I'll even get a rest from looking after you lot!"

Bill smiled. Luke was a handful. Although he would rather they all stayed together, but that was one more thing that they had no control over.

"Are you all ready?" Molly asked, picking up the bundle of clothes. Bill nodded.

"Nell, can you stay here and look after my three while I walk your brothers over?"

They hugged each other good-bye.

"Maybe I'll see you later today, Sissy," said Bill.

"And if not, maybe tomorrow," said Nell.

Molly left the house carrying the bundled-up blanket, followed by Bill, who was holding on to Luke's hand. They crossed the wide, busy Barn Street, headed for Water Street but turned off immediately into Barn Square. Here, away from the main road, it was a little quieter at least. A few small houses backed up to the Methodist church, giving way to two large houses at the end of the square. This square was quite an improvement on the courtyard Bill and Luke had lived in. It had pavements; two houses even had their own yards.

They were met at the door by Molly's stepmother, Jane. Immediately, the entire family descended on them, giving them a warm welcome. Bill was slightly overwhelmed. These people didn't even know him, yet their warmth exceeded anything he'd ever felt from his own family, save Nell.

"Let's not leave them standing here," Jane commanded, shooing everyone inside. "They'll probably want to have a look around, see where they're sleeping. Come on." She led Bill and Luke upstairs, followed by her son Johnny, while her daughter Jenny, Molly, and Bluey stayed downstairs chatting.

The house had only two rooms, one upstairs and one downstairs, just like their old home, but they were much larger and brighter than the rooms Bill and Luke were used to. The walls and window frames were covered with fresh paint, and it looked like someone had really taken a sense of pride in making the house as inviting as possible. In the upstairs room, Jane and Bluey slept at the back; a large heavy curtain divided their space from the rest of the room. At the front were two double beds. One had a thinner curtain pulled around it. That was Jenny's, explained Jane. The other bed was Johnny's, and he'd be sharing it with Bill and Luke. Bill looked at Johnny to see if he really minded, but he didn't appear to.

"Don't worry," he said, as if reading Bill's mind. "We usually have cousins over to stay, so I'm used to sharing. As long as you don't kick me all night, we'll get along grand."

Bill grinned. "Luke kicks. And he throws his arms round. It's like trying to fight with a windmill."

"No, I don't," Luke grumbled.

Johnny grinned back. "Then he can sleep against the wall, and you can go in next to him."

"Maybe we can put him at the end of the bed."

"Or under the bed."

Bill stopped when he saw his little brother was not enjoying the teasing.

"We'll let you two unpack and hang up your clothes. There are some hooks on the wall here," Jane said, gesturing. "Come down when you're ready." She traipsed down the stairs again, followed by Johnny. Bill put the blanket bundle on the bed, sat down and looked around the room. Molly had been right. There was much more space here than at Jem's house. Luke plumped himself down next to Bill and swung his legs off the end of the bed.

"So is this our home now?" he asked.

"Yes, this is our home now."

"And we're staying here forever, and no one is going to die?"

Bill swallowed hard. "How am I supposed to know that?"

Luke pondered this for a minute or so.

"Are they our family?" asked Luke.

"Not our family, they're Molly's family"

"Isn't Molly our family?"

"She's married to our Jem, so she's only family by marriage. Look, Luke, the Booths didn't have to take us in. They've been really kind. We could have been sent to the orphanage instead. We should be on our best behaviour for them, otherwise we might still end up there." Bill looked across at his brother.

"I want to go and live with the Taylors," Luke pouted. "And I want our Nell. Why didn't our Nell come with us?"

Bill sighed. How was he to explain all this to a four-year-old when he didn't understand it fully himself?

Eventually, Bill and Luke made their way downstairs. Bill really didn't know how to react to these almost-strangers who had shown them so much kindness. He was still unsure of what was going to happen next, how long they would stay here or what they would do if Luke started acting up.

At the back of the downstairs room was the kitchen. It consisted of a large worktable running along the back wall, two shelves above it and a sturdy wooden table placed a short distance from it. Towards the front of the room was a large fireplace with a good fire going and a few swinging iron hooks on which to hold pots and kettles over the coals. Several chairs, some wooden and some stuffed with straw, and small tables made the room look crowded. Between the fireplace and the dining table was a small bench with a candlestick, small boxes, rows of cotton bobbins, a large pair of scissors and a pincushion. Several paintings were placed on the walls, mostly landscapes, some with pigs or horses on them.

Bill thought he had better start off by being polite. "You have a very nice house, Mrs. Booth," he said, looking around. Laughter was the only response.

"Oh, love, come and sit yourself down. No need to be so formal. You can call us Aunt Jane and Uncle Bluey." Everyone laughed, and

Bill's cheeks flushed hotly. This really would take some getting used to. He went and perched on a wooden chair next to Molly, who smiled broadly at him.

"Our Molly said you thought you were being sent to the orphanage." Bluey's statement was greeted by laughter. "You know, Bill, you have lots of people who care about you." His tone became serious. "And you have a home here. You've all had a hard time lately, and we hope things will be better for you here."

Bill gulped. "Th-Thank you, sir," he managed to stammer. This seemed almost too good to be true. Perhaps this was what he'd been wishing for, a family to call his own – except they weren't really his own and could easily change their minds. He looked over at Luke, who sat in a corner, seemingly oblivious to the rest of the group. As long as Bill could keep him out of trouble and not upset the Booths, they might have a chance at a home life here. He was so thankful for these peoples' kindness, but he really wanted his sister here too.

After a little while longer of laughter and joking, Molly said she'd better get back home, for she had things to do. She said her good-byes and that she and Nell would see Bill at the mill tomorrow or when dropping off or picking up her children. Bill reluctantly said good-bye to her. As soon as she left, Johnny suggested he show Bill around the area. Bluey nodded, saying only that it was getting late, so Luke should stay in. Bill wasn't worried about leaving Luke on his own. After all, his little brother had spent the past several days in this house and was more used to them than he was.

A few hours later, Bill was wide awake and lying in bed. He already missed his sister. Everything was new and unfamiliar again. The Booths were nice, but he didn't know them very well yet, so he couldn't judge whether their kindness was genuine. They could be going out of their way to be nice right now and then go back to their everyday normal, whatever that might be. Then again, surely only very kind people took in orphans whom they weren't related to. Bill started to think back to their conversations just after he'd arrived here earlier today. The joviality and kindness between the Booths felt real, as did the friendliness shown him by Johnny. At the time, it made Bill wish for something he had never had and never known. If only his mother hadn't died. If only his father hadn't been so distant. If only he'd had a family life, like the Booths or the Taylors. A large family where everyone sat around and laughed and joked with each other, where you had adults who were there for you when you were sad or had fallen and hurt yourself. Bill had thought the Taylors were unique in their compassion and generosity and that most people probably had a difficult home life. But now he wasn't so sure. All he knew was that he really, really wanted to be a part of a loving family.

But along with a family, he just wanted to be able to close his eyes and be surrounded by familiar noises and smells. Anything, as long as it wasn't all new and different like this. Perhaps he'd pop in on the Taylors soon. That seemed the only familiar place left now. But as soon as he closed his eyes, he saw his old house, his father's dead body, Jem glaring at him and Nell being taken away from him. Everything was changing too fast. And now he had a chance at a normal family life, but at what cost? Be careful what you wish for, people had always told him when he'd complained about his situation in the past. But he hadn't been careful. And now he felt guilty and scared. If only he'd never wished for anything.

CHAPTER 6

LEAVING FOR MANCHESTER
FEBRUARY 1841

Nell entered the house happy. It had been six days since Bill and Luke had moved out, and today Aunt Jane had said after she'd taken the lunches round to Bill, Molly and Bluey, she could go and visit the Taylors if she liked. As it was Saturday and a half working day, Bill had agreed to join her after he'd picked up his pay packet. It had been a wonderful afternoon. She had been so happy see them again, and now she couldn't stop smiling. But as she got to the top of the stairs, the familiar voices she'd heard as she opened the door hushed. Even Robin and Lukin were quiet.

"You're late," Jem said, looking up from his food.

"I'm sorry," she said, taking off her shawl and pulling out a chair. "Bill and I went to visit the Taylors. I didn't mean to be back late." She looked at Jem, who wouldn't return her gaze. "What's wrong? Has something happened?"

"No, no. Everything's fine," said Jem.

Nell looked at Molly, who turned away quickly, busying herself with her food.

"Tell me," she said evenly.

"We've ... we've found a job for you," Jem said, staring at the wall. "Oh."

"Well, your Aunt Peggy has."

"Ah." Well, she knew this was coming. Now she would find out where they were sending her. She closed her eyes, crossed her fingers tightly in her lap and hoped for the best. "Where?"

"Don't you want to know what the job is?" Jem asked, surprised.

"I know what it is, I just need to know where," replied Nell.

"And what's the job?"

"It's in service. What else would it be?"

She opened her eyes and looked at Jem, who had pushed away his plate and was staring at her.

"You're sending me away, just like you sent away Bill and Luke. It's fine. You have no space here for me, I know. Just tell me where I'm being sent and when, and put me out of my misery," she said wearily.

Molly looked at Jem and back at Nell. "Manchester," she blurted out. "The job's in Manchester."

Manchester, thought Nell. That's far away, but it's not too bad. It's close to Tommy. It could have been a lot worse. She relaxed her fingers.

"It's a really good job and very light work, I'm told," Jem added quickly. "Aunt Peggy found a position in a friend's house. An old man who's really nice and generous and has a housekeeper and a cook. His last domestic just left to get married. Aunt Peggy says you're to say you're fifteen. It's not a big house, so not too much work."

Nell wasn't really listening. "When do I go?" she asked.

"Um, well, that's the thing," said Jem. "It's all a bit short notice, so it has to be, err, tomorrow."

"Tomorrow!"

"Yes, I'm sorry," Jem continued, "but as I said, it was all very short notice. Aunt Peggy sent a telegram this morning and – "

"Can I go?"

"What?"

"Can I go? I need to go and see Bill and Luke."

"Yes, yes," said Jem, pushing back his chair and standing up. "You know, Nell, I didn't want – "

"Jem," she said, "it doesn't matter. It's not like I have a choice, is it?"

"No."

Nell grabbed her shawl, ran down the stairs and out of the door. She wrapped her arms round herself as tightly as she could to try and keep out the cold as she made the short walk over to Barn Square. Tomorrow? Even though she knew she'd be sent away fairly soon, she hadn't expected this. Tomorrow? She impatiently wiped away her stray tears. She didn't want Bill seeing her so sad. By the time she reached the Booths' house, she was shivering. She stood on the front step and knocked loudly.

Jane opened the door and grimaced. "They told you, then?" Nell nodded. "Oh, Nell, lass. Come in."

She stood back and let Nell push past her. The Booths, Bill and Luke were eating dinner. Nell let out a sob, and tears streamed down her face. The five faces at the table looked on with concern.

"What's wrong?" Bill asked, but Nell was sobbing too heavily to answer. Jane fetched a blanket and draped it around Nell's shoulders and made soothing noises.

"There, there. It's not the end of the world, love."

"I know," said Nell. "But I'll just . . ."

"What is it?" asked Bill. "Nell, tell me."

Nell looked up and saw her brother's concerned face. "It's fine," she said. "Bill, it's fine. They've found me a job in service, so I'll have to go away for a while, but it's fine. We'll be fine." She wiped away the tears, looked up and tried to smile. "I'm sorry. I didn't mean to come here like this and upset you."

Bill went and sat next to Nell and hugged her hard. "You're not upsetting anyone, only yourself. Well, maybe me a little bit." He smiled. "Where are you being sent?"

"Manchester."

"Manchester?" Bill exclaimed. "But that's miles away!"

Nell laughed and hiccoughed.

"It's not that far," said Bluey. "I'm sure Nell will get time off to visit. And we can find a way to send her letters in the post."

"How?" said Bill. "We can't write."

"I'm sure we can find someone who can," said Bluey. "And Nell can find someone who can read to her. I'm sure it won't be forever."

"If it helps, Jem didn't want you to go so far away, Nell," Jane added. "He was so afraid to tell you. He nearly turned down the job for you, but times are hard right now. And you know our Molly would much rather have you around."

"I know," said Nell. "I'm just being silly."

"Don't worry, Sissy," said Bill. "We'll just make sure we spend a lot of time together before you go. You'll soon be sick of the sight of me and Luke." He grinned.

Nell smiled and dug her nails into her palms. "That's really why I'm upset. I'm to go tomorrow."

"Tomorrow? Why? But that's too soon!"

Nell sighed. That was exactly what she was thinking too. But maybe it was better this way instead of dragging out a long good-bye, trying to squeeze out every second of every day until they were exhausted.

"You'll be fine, love," said Jane. "You're a good worker, and you'll get some time off to visit at least."

Nell smiled gratefully, but she wasn't reassured. She was scared of the unknown, of what the job and the people would be like, of what would be required of her. Of meeting her Aunt Peggy again. But most of all she was scared of never seeing Bill and Luke again. Of forgetting what they looked like or them getting on with their lives and forgetting her. But she also knew none of them had any say in the matter. Money was a necessary evil. They all needed to survive.

"I don't want you to go," Bill whispered.

"Me neither. Promise me you won't forget me. You too," she said to Luke.

"We'll make a plan," Bill said thoughtfully. "We'll find a way to always keep in touch."

"I'm just scared that time will go by and we'll forget each other," she said.

"We never will. I promise," Bill said. "We've always been there for each other, and that will never change." They hugged, and Nell felt a little more comforted by this, but it was hard to let go of that nagging feeling of dread.

Nell wanted to savour every moment she had left with Bill and Luke, but in all reality, it was only an evening and an early morning. She tried willing the seconds and minutes to stop ticking rhythmically by, but time was not cooperating, and each hour felt like it was over quicker than the last. Jane and Bluey had allowed her to stay so she could spend as much time with her younger brothers as possible. They had lain down blankets in front of the fire, and Nell and Bill sat up talking for as long as they could keep their eyes open. They eventually fell asleep, the three of them curled up together as they always had in their old damp, draughty bedroom.

Nell was woken the next morning by Jane, who shook her shoulder lightly.

"Molly and Jem will be round soon to take you to the station," she said. "Molly's got your things together. I'm not sure if you feel like eating breakfast, but better you come join us at the table and try and eat something. A journey on one of them train things is not to be advised on an empty stomach." She shuddered at the thought. Nell nodded and sat up, wiping the sleep out of her eyes. She looked down at her dress. Hopefully, there would be time to change as she didn't fancy being seen in public in such a creased garment. She shook Bill awake and stood up. She had been dreading this day ever since her father's funeral, but she needed to be brave.

Almost the entire Hall clan, with some Booths in tow, made their way up Bradshawgate together and across town to the train station. As soon as they turned the corner into Trinity Street, the large imposing brown brick building loomed up. The station building spanned two levels on the sloping street, an ornate tower with clock competing in height with the church spire behind it. There was a wide covered entrance where carts and cabs could stop or turn round. Carts piled high with cotton bundles, fabric or parcels competed for space with each other and with passengers dragging their luggage. Everyone wanted to stop as close to the entrance as possible, saving themselves an extra few yards of carrying their heavy wares to the waiting trains. Nell and her family walked through the main door into a long and broad hallway. Two sets of stairs led down to the train platforms. The ticket office and waiting rooms to the right of the entrance were dwarfed by the vastness of the cold, tiled walls.

Jem went to the ticket office to buy a third-class ticket, and the rest stood in a tight group so as to not get separated in the crowds. Nell knew this was it, the last time she would see her family all together for a while. She really didn't know when she'd see them all again. She wanted to turn back time a day or two, to desperately hang on to the feeling of being surrounded by family – what little she had left. She looked around at her loved ones – her younger brothers, Molly, her nephews and niece. She wanted to throw herself on them, to kick up such a fuss that they would abandon the idea and take her home again. But she wasn't a child anymore. She needed to act with dignity, and besides, Jem would just put her on the train anyway.

Tears started to fall once again. It felt like she'd cried more in the past few months than in her whole life. Molly hugged her, looking teary-eyed herself. Then she took off her own shawl and wrapped it around Nell's shoulders, tying it on top of the old grey one she was already wearing. Nell's eyes lit up. She knew Molly loved that blue shawl. She looked so pretty in it, and many times Nell had wished that she had one just like it. She hugged her sister-in-law, clinging to her tightly.

"I'm going to miss you, Sissy," Molly whispered in Nell's ear, and Nell struggled to hold back a tear.

Nell hugged each of her nephews in turn, then her niece, and then turned to her brothers. She swallowed hard. This was not going to be easy. Bill was looking down at his hands, trying not to meet her eye. Luke, hands in his pockets, looked up at her, staring intently, as though he was trying to imprint a picture of her on his mind. She knelt down and hugged him, feeling like she never wanted to let go. To her surprise, the little boy who hated being hugged for once didn't resist. It was only when Jem came back with the ticket and urged her to hurry or she'd miss the train that she released her youngest brother.

There was now almost no time to say good-bye to Bill. Nell put her arms around him and buried her head against his neck.

"Your job is to work out how we can keep in touch every week," she said. She felt Bill's cheek muscles move and knew he was smiling.

"And your job is to come home and visit as often as you can," he replied.

"Nell, we have to go NOW!" Jem commanded, almost pulling her away. Nell waved good-bye as her family all wished her luck, then she turned and followed Jem to the train. Occasionally, she turned back to catch a glimpse of them, almost tripping up or bumping into Jem. The noise of the train as it prepared to move off was deafening. Hisses of steam were released, making Nell jump each time, and swirling smoke filled the platform. People hurried past, porters wheeling luggage to the first class carriages. Another train pulled into the station on the next platform, increasing the overall volume. Nell began to be scared of this heavy, clanking, noisy moving machinery. She didn't want to get into such a loud and dangerous machine, but she had to be brave. She was glad Jem was with her as they rushed to the third-class compartments farther down the platform. Jem was staring at the ticket, then at the carriages, trying to work out the correct one. Nell looked at him curiously. Finally, he opened the door to one of the carriages and told her to climb in. The guard blew a whistle, and the hissing and smoke increased, swirling round the wheels and rising up to the carriages. Nell had no time to ask any questions as Jem slammed the door shut and the train began to move. She leaned out of the window and waved as the train pulled out of the station. She tried to look for Bill and Luke, but smoke and people obscured her view. Finally, she sat down on one of the benches in the carriage.

The rhythmic rocking moved her from side to side. The benches were hard and uncomfortable, but Nell had been told this would not be a long journey. Occasionally, the train jolted, sending Nell into a panic, trying to hold on to the bench around her. She hoped she wouldn't have to travel by train very often; she was really not enjoying the ride.

There were five others besides Nell in the carriage – a family with a young boy Luke's age and two men who appeared to be travelling together. The family had some luggage with them. Nell looked down at her inadequate purse. Even though she was leaving to live somewhere else, she had barely any belongings to take with her. She was wearing her Sunday best, which was very worn by now. So worn, in fact, Jem had not allowed her to even consider taking her weekday clothes with her. They were only fit for rags, he said. Seemed like while they would do in Bolton, they would not do in Manchester, and she began to wonder what kind of place it was.

The train jolted again, and Nell panicked for a few seconds. The scenery whizzed by so fast that it made her dizzy and feel a little nauseous, so she stopped looking out the window. Her thoughts went back to her family she was leaving behind, and she began to cry again. As she was scrambling round in her purse for a handkerchief, she felt a tap on her leg. The mother of the little boy had leaned forward and was offering her handkerchief. Nell smiled gratefully and took it.

"Are you travelling far?" asked the woman.

"I'm going to Manchester," Nell sniffed. "I start a new job there. I'm just sad at leaving my family."

"Going into service, are you?" asked the woman. Nell nodded. "First service job?" Nell nodded again.

"It might not be as bad as you think." The woman winked at her conspiratorially. Nell was glad of the kind words, and she and the woman chatted a little until the train juddered to a halt in Stoneclough and the family got off.

Nell panicked again as the train began to pull away. She was sure it would fall apart beneath her, leaving her sitting on the tracks amongst the rubble. Not even the worst and most rickety carts felt as bad as this. Nell could not understand why some people raved about trains. Said they were the future. Not in her future, she hoped.

As the train neared Salford, she began to think about what her new life in Manchester might be like. She was unsure about everything else – the job, the city, being on her own – but she was looking forward to seeing her brother Tommy again. She worried about the job. What if she wasn't up to it? What if they sent her out on an errand and she got lost? Jem had said Manchester was a huge bustling city, so much bigger than Bolton. Lots more factories, places that a respectable girl should stay away from, dangerous areas, poor areas, rich areas. She imagined it was so big that she would never be able to find her way round. What if she was returned home in shame after only a few weeks? She'd run their home since she was eight years old, cooking, washing and cleaning and looking after her father and brothers, but perhaps her loose standards of cleaning would not be accepted here. What if they expected her to know exactly what to do, and she didn't? What if the other domestics didn't like her? What if her master had her beaten? You heard such stories ...

Nell was beginning to get herself worked up. These were all thoughts she'd put to the back of her mind in the hope that Jem would change his mind and she wouldn't have to go. But here she was, and the train was rushing her along at such a speed that she couldn't stop it all and go back home now anyway.

As the train pulled into Salford Station, Nell felt more and more apprehensive. Firstly, Tommy was to meet her here, but how would she ever find him? The platform was already filled with far more people than it was in Bolton. As angry as she still was with Jem, she wished her older brother had come with her.

As she followed the last of the passengers out of the carriage and onto the platform, she was struck by how much busier this station was than Bolton. People were pushing and jostling, porters were everywhere, their trolleys piled high with luggage, coming at her out of the swirling smoke so that she had to quickly move out of the way. Whistles being blown made her jump each time. The clanking and hissing of the trains and the slamming doors sounded even louder here. Nell looked around as she was gently nudged forwards by the moving throng. The station was quite dark. Large pillars held up a roof that already looked like it had seen better days. She couldn't see so far in front of her due to the smoke, which was getting thicker the closer to the engine she walked. She was beginning to get really worried that she would miss Tommy in the crowd. Then she would be here in this unfamiliar city knowing no one and not knowing where to go.

She tried to stand on her toes but simply could not see over the heads of everyone else – her thirteen-year-old frame was much shorter than most of the people. Eventually, she came to the end of the platform. Here, the crowd thinned out, and she saw the ticket office with its long queues and the station clock. Finding an empty spot to stand in, Nell watched all the people go by. Some were in a hurry, some relaxed and jovial, joking with each other and taking their time. Nell was fascinated by the dresses. Some women were dressed somewhat like her, others in much finer clothing. She studied them for a while, wishing she had learned to sew like Jenny Booth had. But she began to worry after several minutes had gone by and she still hadn't seen Tommy.

Perhaps if she changed her location, he would see her, but she didn't know the best place to stand. Where would he look? Just as she started to move closer to the ticket office, she felt a hand on her shoulder and heard her name being called. She spun around to see a familiar face.

"Tommy!" She flung her arms around her brother and hugged him tight.

"You're looking well, Sissy!" He grinned at her. He opened his mouth to say something else, but at the same time, a nearby train let off a loud, long hiss, drowning out his words and making Nell jump and cling to him in fright. Tommy laughed as he took his little sister by the arm and led her outside into the cooling, drizzling rain.

"I think I've gone deaf," Nell said, shaking her head. Tommy smiled.

"Come on, let's get you to Aunt Peggy's. It'll be a lot quieter there, no matter how bad her bark is."

The two of them walked through the bustling Salford streets parallel to the river and headed for the bridge. They chatted a little on the way. Nell knew so little about her brother's life now, and she had so many questions. Tommy had known about their aunts, for a start, so what else did he know? And what had he been up to these past five years? But every time she started to ask him something important, he'd interrupt her by pointing out a landmark or start telling her a funny story. She should probably save all her questions until there was more time. For now, she was just happy to be in her brother's company again.

As they neared the bridge, Tommy stopped at the top of a street.

"See that house there?" Nell followed to where his finger was pointing and nodded. It was a large three-storey house with a grand door up a flight of steps. Or at least it might have been grand once. Next to it, the corner house had an entrance level with the street and a large bay window. It was hard to see inside from where they stood, but there was a faded sign above the window, so Nell guessed it was a shop. The street was short, and Nell could see all the way down to the river. The houses on the other side of the street looked like they had been recently knocked down. Bricks lay strewn on the wasteland, and a large hole had been dug and left.

"I was born in that house," Tommy said triumphantly.

Nell looked at him, incredulous. "In your dreams."

"No, I was. And Father owned the shop too. It was grander around here back then, Aunt Peggy says, but they had to make way for more and more houses. More mills and foundries mean more workers."

Nell looked carefully at her brother. Too many thoughts and questions were going round her head now. This was a side of the family she had never known anything about, and now she was going to be in the middle of it.

"Our family had money once," Tommy said, a far-off look in his eye. "That's why Aunt Peggy and Aunt Janey live so comfortably." He looked down at her. "Remember this, Nell, that we did have money once, so don't ever go thinking you're not as good as anyone else."

Nell looked at Tommy to see if he was joking. He was looking straight ahead and didn't return her look. Nell looked at the building again, and her jaw dropped. They had been rich once?

"What happened?"

Tommy shrugged. "I don't know exactly, but Father lost all his money, and then we moved to Bolton. Come, let's go. It won't do to be late."

They continued on in silence for a while. Nell didn't know what to believe or where to start asking questions.

Then a thought struck her.

"Tommy, can our Jem read?"

"Jem?" he asked thoughtfully. "It wouldn't surprise me."

"Why?"

"Why what?"

"Why wouldn't it surprise you?"

"Well, he did go to one of the best schools in Manchester when he was a lad."

"What?" Nell suddenly stopped walking. Thoughts raced round her head. Jem went to school?

Tommy turned and walked back to her. "Yes, Sissy. As I said, we were well-off once. Jem went to school, and we had a maid."

"So that's why Jem likes to order people around?"

Tommy burst out laughing. "I suppose so." He stopped laughing and offered his arm to Nell, who took it and started walking again.

"Why did you wonder that?" he asked gently.

"Just something I saw. I thought I saw him reading something, but I wasn't sure. Then I wondered how he would have known something if he hadn't read it."

"Well, that was clear," said Tommy, laughing again. Nell smiled.

"I'll maybe tell you about it later, when you tell me all the family history and why we ended up in Wellington Court if Father was well off."

"Well then, we'll have a lot to catch up on," said Tommy.

Nell thought for a minute. "Can you read?"

"Um, a little. Not really."

"Why 'not really'?"

"I never got to go to school like Jem did. The money was mostly gone by then, but Mother did insist I go to Sunday school. So I learned a bit. And I can read certain words that I need to for work like 'inside leg measurement' and 'neck size'."

Nell stepped back to look at him, and Tommy started laughing again. Nell joined in.

"Well, that's good because Bill is going to write to me, and I'll need someone to read his letters."

"Bill is going to write to you about tailoring measurements?" Tommy asked with mock seriousness. Nell slapped his arm gently and laughed.

"Don't be silly." She was so glad to be with Tommy again. He always managed to cheer her up.

As they reached the end of the bridge and were on land again, the contrast could not have been any greater. The small crowded area had given way to more carefully laid out buildings.

"Welcome to Manchester," Tommy said, smiling.

"This is Manchester?" she asked, looking up at the wide roads and mix of ornate buildings and warehouses.

"A part of it, yes." They stood there and looked around. Nell had never seen such wide roads in her life before. And so many large buildings with intricate stonework, some standing as warehouses, some containing shops on the ground floor. No rows and rows of hastily built houses leaning against each other here, although Tommy told her they were not far away and increasing in number even here. Above the buildings, Nell could see the many factory chimneys billowing out black smoke; some looked quite close by. On the roads was a mixture of carters driving their horse and carts piled high with goods, smart horse-drawn cabs, handcarts and hawkers. Ladies and gentlemen in finer clothing walked aside others with very worn clothes, sometimes rags. Children ran around, playing games and dodging the oncoming carts. It was just a huge mishmash of sights and sounds.

They turned immediately right into Parsonage, a wide street off the main road. They walked past a hat manufacturing factory and a cotton warehouse, then the road began to narrow and give way to large houses. Even from the start of the road, Nell could see a large church looming over the roofs. Farther down the street, horses were being led into stables, and the unmistakable smell of them filled the air. The street was a remarkable mix of well-to-do houses and industry, the like of which Nell had never seen before.

"This way," said Tommy, pulling Nell's hand and leading her up the steps of a three-storey terraced house just to their right. Nell's eyes opened wide.

"They live here?"

"Just remember," Tommy whispered after he had rung the doorbell, "don't ever think you're not as good as them."

The housekeeper opened the door and took their outer garments. "They're upstairs in the drawing room. They've been expecting you." She sniffed haughtily.

"Come on, then." Tommy pulled his sister up the stairs. Nell had hardly any time to admire the tiled floor and stairway with its ornate banister. Halfway up the staircase, a stained-glass window shed colourful light onto the floor, illuminating the floor tiles in places. She suddenly found herself on the first floor, and Tommy was knocking on a closed door.

"Come in."

They entered the crowded room. Nell's eyes took in the scene. Fat, greedy sofas in yellows and rust browns looked like their insides would spill out as soon as you sat on them. That was if you could find a place to perch amongst all the cushions. Against each wall were large dark wood cabinets of different sizes, giving a closed-in feel to the room. Delicate occasional tables by the sofas were filled with ornaments and clashed with the heaviness of the rest of the furniture. Portrait paintings adorned almost every space on the busily papered walls. There was more furniture crammed into this room than Nell had ever seen in her life, yet the room did not look lived in or loved. She desperately wanted to go and study all the portraits; they fascinated her, and she fancied maybe even one day she would have her portrait painted. But this was her aunts' home, and politeness had to come first. She was only glad she didn't have to live in this stuffy house.

"Nellie, dear!" Nell was almost knocked off her feet with a large hug from Aunt Janey. She tentatively hugged her aunt back. Aunt Peggy then rose from her seat.

"Nell, dear. Let me take a look at you." Without a look of kindness or warmth, Aunt Peggy held her by the shoulders and looked her up and down.

"I think a bath straightaway is in order," she decided. "We can wait to eat, but I think you've collected quite a bit of soot from your train journey, my dear. Great dirty things. I don't know how anyone can travel on them." She flicked her wrist, as if commanding the whole railway system to stay away from her.

Nell was embarrassed. She suspected her aunt was being tactful. She'd had a quick wash on Thursday, as per mill rules, but it had been awhile since she'd had a bath. Peggy rang the rope bell by the fireplace, and shortly Mrs. Mitchum, the housekeeper, entered the room.

"We shall sit here and chat with Tommy for a while, but the girl needs a bath. Can you prepare one for her?"

"Yes, ma'am."

Nell felt even more embarrassed when the housekeeper looked at her with distaste.

"Now then," Peggy commanded, "take a seat. No, no, no, not you, girl!" she shouted when Nell tried to sit down. "Janey, fetch some newspaper for her to sit on."

Nell looked at Tommy and felt like she could cry. She was not prepared for this. She wanted to be back home, where no one died of a little dirt and folk were far friendlier. Tommy gestured to her to hold her chin up, which she did as she slowly lowered herself onto the spread out newspaper.

"So," said Peggy, "here we are."

Nell smiled weakly as Janey gave her a big smile.

"How is everything with you, Nell? How are your brothers doing? Did you enjoy your journey here? Are you looking forward to your new job?" Janey continued to witter on, seemingly not really requiring an answer to her questions, until her sister interrupted her.

"Janey, go and fetch those dresses you picked out. Nell can choose a couple, and the rest we can give to the needy."

Nell could not have felt any worse as Janey got up to leave the room. She clearly was not good enough here in Manchester, no matter what Tommy said. These were her father's sisters, and they were treating her like a charity case. And she was way out of her depth. The sooner this was over, the better. Hopefully, in her new job they would not care how the domestic looked or what clothes she wore. Tommy looked at her with concern and squeezed her hand.

After her bath, where she was scrubbed raw by Mrs. Mitchum, who deemed her incapable of getting herself sufficiently clean – a humiliating experience – her hair was braided and pinned up (which hurt) and she tried on some of Janey's old dresses. Even though Janey was fairly small, the dresses swamped Nell's tiny frame. Janey stood back, trying to admire her handiwork, but even she could not accept that the dresses fit anything less than terribly.

"Never mind," she said, winking at Nell. "Lucky we have a tailor in training here. Go and fetch Tommy, Mitchum." Mrs. Mitchum nodded and left the room.

Tommy came in and winked at her. He walked around her, looked her up and down and asked Mrs. Mitchum to pass him the pins. After several minutes of expertly pinning darts and hemlines, Nell was allowed to dress again. This time it was in the smallest (ugliest) dress they could find, and the porridge colour looked terrible on her, draining her of what little colour she had. But Nell remembered what Tommy had said, and she swallowed hard, lifted her chin and followed Janey back into the drawing room.

Tommy had been invited to dine with them that evening, and Nell was glad of his company. She really didn't know how to approach or talk to her aunts. If it had been just Janey, she was sure she would have felt easier. As it was, Peggy was quite intimidating. As dinner was served, Nell was surprised to see it was only potatoes and bread.

She had expected to be faced with something fancy and inedible. Delightedly, she set about her food, suddenly finding herself hungry. As she glanced across the table at Tommy, he grinned and pushed his chin in the air, a slight gesture unseen by their aunts. Nell smiled to herself and wondered exactly how much money her aunts really had. Perhaps she could think of herself as good as they were after all.

After dinner, Tommy said his good-byes and promised to get the dresses back to her the next day. Nell clung to him as though she would never let go. Now her only familiar relative was leaving her with these two women that she'd only met once before. Tommy told her he'd see her in only a few hours and released her. As the front door closed, Nell suddenly felt more alone than she'd ever felt in her life.

PART 2

1845–1848

The factory act of 1844 had improved working conditions for women and children by limiting them to ten hours a day. Children aged 8–13 were only allowed to work six and a half hours a day, but many lied about their age. The Chartist movement reached its peak, and demonstrations and marches demanding male suffrage occurred in several Lancashire towns.

CHAPTER 7

APPRENTICED
FEBRUARY 1845

Bill groaned as he was rudely awoken by Luke turning over in bed and kicking him squarely in the face. What the hell was his brother doing, sleeping at the wrong end of the bed again? Luke had been so restless lately that Bill didn't get much sleep at night, and thirteen-year-old boys needed their sleep! Snuggling down under the worn blanket, Bill turned over and rubbed his nose, waiting for the discomfort to subside. The embers from the fire had gone cold, and Bill hoped to be able to get a little more sleep before another Monday morning started. But Luke was still thrashing around. He slept more like a small child these days than an eight-year-old, tossing and turning every two minutes. Finally, Bill sat up, exasperated.

"Can't you just stop moving around and go to sleep? What is wrong with you?"

Luke stopped moving, then eventually sat up, rubbing his eyes. "I was asleep. Why did you have to wake me?"

"You were asleep?" Bill asked incredulously. "Were you having nightmares or something?"

"Someone was chasing me," Luke mumbled. "It wasn't fun. I stole some paint from the shop, and you were supposed to look out, but you weren't there, and then someone saw me and chased me with a knife."

"Are you sure it was a dream? Sounds like something you would do." Bill lay down again, making a point of turning his back on his brother and pulling at the blanket.

"I wouldn't steal from family," Luke said indignantly. Then he paused and thought for a while. "Unless it was like our Jem had a lot of money and lived in a big house, and you and me were starving and they wouldn't buy us any food."

Bill smiled and closed his eyes. Eventually, Luke lay down too. They were just beginning to drift off when they heard a familiar distant ratt-a-tatt-tat. The knocking got closer and louder, and Bill pulled the pillow over his head.

The next thing Bill heard was Aunt Jane laying the fire. "Get up, lazy bones!" she said. "You know your Jem's coming over to take you to the foundry to start your apprenticeship today. And you, trouble," she pointed at Luke, "are starting at the mill today, so be sharp."

Bill and Luke looked at each other, and Bill slowly pulled himself out of bed.

Jane blew on the small flames, making them rise up and lick at the coals until the edges started to glow.

"Now then," said Jane, standing up. "Bill, Jem says you need to be dressed in your Sunday best. You can both have a crust of bread, and then I'm taking Luke up to the mill. No time to be making any breakfast."

They both reluctantly pulled their clothes over their full-length undergarments. Bill had just finished getting changed into his suit when there was a knock at the door followed by Jem's voice announcing himself as he stepped inside. He nodded briefly at Jane.

"All ready to go, then, Bill?"

"Sure."

"Make sure you behave yourself," Luke said, laughing.

Bill pretended to cuff him. "The day you behave will be a miracle," he said, smiling.

Jane rolled her eyes and laughed at them. "Now you just show them how good you are," she said, straightening Bill's tie, planting a kiss on his cheek and shoving a crust of bread into his hand.

Bill waved good-bye to Jane and followed Jem out into the cool, crisp December air. The streetlamps were still lit, the flames casting flickering pools of light onto the road at intervals. The quietness of the roads belied the earliness of the hour. Few people were out yet – making the most of their last precious minutes before dragging themselves to the factory for another long day – and Bill's eyes felt prickly and sore from the lack of sleep.

They walked in silence from Slater Street, where the Booths had moved a year previously, down Duke Street to Bark Street. Here they had to cross over the River Croal to get to Deansgate. Streetlamps were lacking here, and there was no light from the moon. Bill had to make sure to tread carefully so he didn't stumble, but Jem seemed to know exactly where the streets turned and where the bridge was. As they turned the corner from the well-lit Deansgate into Blackhorse Street, Bill saw Union Foundry before him. It was the largest foundry he'd ever seen in his life. There was no end to the red brick buildings with their saw-toothed roofs and high chimneys belching out grey and black smoke.

All around him people hurried, some on bicycles, some on foot, rushing through the gates before the bell sounded. Bill followed Jem through the entrance and across the courtyard. Blocks and tackle and parts of steam engines waiting to be lifted and put together lay by every raised docking platform. Jem stopped to ask someone the way, and they pointed him towards the largest door Bill had ever seen. In they went, up the narrow wooden stairs immediately on their right to a balcony overlooking the main foundry. Several furnaces and smaller kilns punctuated the huge room. Behind the balcony was a set of windowed offices. Jem and Bill took their place in line behind several other potential apprentices, all waiting with a guardian of some sort. The queue was forming quickly behind them. After about ten minutes, the queue reached all the way down the stairs. Luckily, there were only five boys in front of them, and they were quickly dealt with.

"Next!"

Jem stood up and walked into the office; Bill followed.

"Henry Robinson!" said the man behind the desk, offering a hand to Jem. His blue velvet waistcoat matched his eye colour, making a strong contrast against his pale skin and bouffant white hair. He placed a pince-nez on the bridge of his narrow nose, the chain looping down and disappearing under his collar.

"James Hall," replied Jem, shaking the proffered hand.

"And who do we have here?"

"William Hall, sir," said Bill. Henry smiled at him.

"Right then, William Hall. All ready to be a boilermaker apprentice?"

Without expecting any answer, he turned to Jem.

"Here's the indenture, Mr. Hall. If you'd just sign below, here," he said, pointing out the bottom of the paper to Jem, "we'll take on young William. Seven years he'll be with us." Jem nodded and moved towards the paper. He picked up the pencil and, after glancing sideways at Bill, left his mark.

"Good, good," said Henry. "Now, William, say good-bye and go and wait at the end of the corridor with the other apprentices. We'll get you sorted with clothes and lodging. Next!"

Bill stood there with his mouth open, and Jem grabbed his jacket and pushed him out the door. They stood there in the corridor in silence before Jem spoke.

"Right then, I'll say good-bye. Be good, work hard and we'll see you on Saturday."

"What? What lodging? I'm to stay here?"

"Where did you think you'd be staying? Apprentices live in the apprentice house."

"But I didn't even get to say good-bye to Bluey. Or Luke, properly. Or Jane," he added.

"Don't be so soft," Jem said crossly. "They're only a walk across town. You can be there from Saturday night to Monday morning. And be grateful you have a home to go to. It's not like when I was apprenticed – I didn't see my family for seven whole years because Father moved everyone away to here and I was stuck in Salford. Act your age." Bill gasped.

"I didn't even meet you until you were three," Jem muttered.

Bill opened and closed his mouth. He didn't know what to say. He just watched as his brother turned his back, walked down the stairs and out the door.

Bill had been sat in the corridor for what seemed like hours, waiting for the other apprentices to arrive. Finally, Henry Robinson came out of his office and called for their attention.

"As you know, you are all here for the next seven years to be apprenticed as blacksmiths or boilermakers. The first rules are: You turn up for work, punctually, every day unless you are too sick to get out of bed. Any lateness will be docked from your pay. If you have no pay left, you will end up owing us money. You will be fined for swearing, fighting, stealing, not cleaning up after yourselves and any other generally bad behaviour. Take good care not to burn yourself because burns can go bad, and you can end up losing an arm."

Bill watched some of the boys wince at this, then turned his attention back to Henry Robinson.

"You will be living in the apprentice house. The house mistress, Mrs. Lawton, will make sure you have sheets, somewhere to sleep and are fed. You will be provided with new clothes once a year. Anyone running away," he raised his voice, "anyone running away will be found and severely punished. Do not forget, you are the property of Union Foundry for the next seven years."

Bill swallowed hard. Seven years was a long time. Longer than he could even imagine. Bill missed what Mr. Robinson said next, but the other boys were getting up off the floor and following him down the wooden stairs, so Bill followed them too.

Henry Robinson showed them briefly round the foundry. As the noise of the clanking of metal on metal, the crackling of flames and spitting of molten iron made it impossible to hear a conversation, Mr. Robinson just gestured to some of the workers and areas. At one point, Bill thought he was going to faint from the blast of hot air hitting him like a ton of bricks. Seven long years of this all day, every day except Sundays. Suddenly, he felt very young and just wanted Jem to come back and take him home to Bluey. He was relieved when Mr. Robinson led them outside into the cool air, but the heat in his clothes quickly dissipated, and Bill began to feel very cold.

"Over there is the apprentice house." Mr. Robinson pointed at a two-storey building across the courtyard. "Go and get your lunch, and the rest of the day is free before you start tomorrow. I recommend an early bedtime. You will all be here, punctually, at half past five in the morning."

Bill followed the other boys as he groaned inwardly. Half past five? This was going to be worse than working at the mill.

After a lunch of potatoes with a little fried bacon, Bill collected his blankets and stood in line to be assigned a bed. The bedroom was a long, wide room, taking up half of the upper floor of the apprentice house. Large rectangular windows let in light on two sides of the room but added to the whitewashed walls and stone floor to make the room feel even colder. Mrs. Lawton gestured to a bed for each pair of boys standing in line. She pointed at a bed set against the wall for Bill and the tall, gangly boy standing behind him. Bill walked over to the bed and stood there, waiting for the other boy to make the first move. He'd only ever shared a bed before with people he knew – Luke or Johnny Booth. The boy threw a blanket down onto the straw and leapt onto it.

"Bagsy NOT the wall side!" he said, grinning. Bill grinned back.

"How is that fair?" He smiled. "Shouldn't we draw straws or something?"

"If you're too slow, you lose," said the boy, "and you, my friend, are like a snail." He lay on his back trying to get comfortable, but the high wooden-framed bed stuffed deeply with straw was not cooperating to his satisfaction.

"Blimey, where did they get this straw from? It feels like needles. Try it."

Bill placed his blanket on his side of the bed, carefully tucking it in over the edges of the straw while the boy propped himself up on his elbow, watching him carefully.

"You really are like an old woman," he said. "Did you never have a mother to do that for you?"

"No."

The boy sat up. "Me neither. The name's Joe. Joe Walker." He held out his hand, and Bill shook it.

"Bill Hall."

"Do you have a father?"

"No. He died a few years ago."

"Who do you live with, then?"

"My uncle," said Bill. "Well, he's not really an uncle. He's our Molly's father. Molly's married to my brother."

"Right," said Joe. "I was living with my aunt and uncle. They thought this was best for me."

"My brother thought this was best for me."

"Wish we'd had a say in it," Joe said, lying back down.

"Mmm," Bill said, climbing into the bed. He wasn't sure if he was going to get much sleep in this bed, but he may as well try. There was nothing else to do. Lying in the narrow wooden bed next to Joe, he pulled part of the thin, scratchy blanket over him and shivered. The next day would be his first day in the foundry, so he may as well get as much rest as possible and catch up on some sleep. He was not going to enjoy waking up tomorrow.

Luke made his way to the mill, trailing behind Aunt Jane. He had known his time would come; after all, Bill had started much younger, but now you weren't allowed to work officially until you were eight years old. Some people still lied about their age though, so he was lucky that the Booths hadn't made him start earlier. He half wished that Bill was still working there so he could spend more time with him, half wished he could have waited a few more years. This was the worst of both worlds.

He really didn't see why he had to go into that noisy mill with people making him do what he didn't want to when he could just as easily earn the same money catching rats. Luke was good at catching rats. He was fast. And he had a sharp knife for cutting off their tails. Fine, he'd stolen it from Uncle Jim, or rather, was he Brother-in-Law Jim, Molly's brother? Luke didn't really know – or care – who was who to him. They were just all uncles and aunts. But Jim had a sharp knife, and Luke needed one. All hell had broken loose when Jim realised his knife was missing from the back of the shop. But Luke's face remained innocent – he could get away with a lot with those big blue eyes and round baby cheeks – and the fuss eventually died down.

Maybe he could go ratting after work, he thought, patting the knife in his pocket, all snug in its leather cover. He'd be finishing at half past twelve, Aunt Jane had said. New rules for kids under thirteen. Not like in Bill's day. Maybe the factory wasn't as bad as he'd heard it used to be.

Jane led Luke into the mill and up to the offices. They walked past the rows of huge machines, quiet and still, soaking up oil and gurgling greedily as the spinners poured the thick substance into their looms before the start of the day. Jane walked right up to the master's office and knocked on the door.

"Come in."

She pushed Luke inside, and they stood before the middle-aged man poring over a ledger on his desk.

"This is Luke Hall; he's to start today," said Jane.

The man looked up, then took out a pen, dipping it in the ink pot. "Ah yes. Hall. Age and address?"

"Eight years old, 1 Slater Street."

The man started to write in the ledger. Jane was silent.

"Right then, a scavenger. I'll put him on Sam Worthington's loom. Come on, lad, follow me."

"Behave!" Jane hissed as Luke walked past her. Luke shrugged and smiled.

They stopped in front of one of the looms, and Luke was introduced to his spinner, a large, broad-shouldered man with a bushy beard and red hair that stuck out all over his head. His greying sleeves were rolled up, and he had a striped apron on over his shirt and trousers. Luke thought he looked like a lion.

"Right, lad," said Sam. "Watch Jenny here."

Luke turned to look at the other scavenger. She was very thin, but she was taller than him. Her skin was sallow with dark circles around her eyes and under her cheekbones. She moved slowly, like everything was an effort, but what Luke noticed most of all was that her eyes were vacant. It was like looking into a void; the person behind those eyes was no longer there. Luke swallowed.

"You need to climb in under there once the loom is going and pick up any bits of cotton, lint or dirt. I won't be stopping the machine, so you need to time it so you don't get trapped or hit by the rollers. It's important you pick up everything when you see it fall, as we don't want any bits catching on fire from a spark. Kick off your shoes, then, and I'd take off your hat and jacket too."

"What? You want me to crawl in there?" Luke asked incredulously.

Sam's face changed suddenly. The lines around his eyes and mouth disappeared and reappeared on his forehead. He grabbed hold of Luke's shoulder and started to shake him. An overlooker came running down from the balcony and asked what was going on. Sam spat and gestured as he relayed Luke's insolent comment. The overlooker shook Luke and slapped him hard across the face. Then he took out a notebook and a small blunt pencil. Fined for insolence. Insolence? If they thought that was insolence, they were in for a shock. He hadn't even gotten started yet. Just his luck to have to work for idiots. The overlooker walked away, and Sam switched on the loom. Luke sighed. He wasn't going to get beaten to a pulp on his first day, so he'd better look a little willing. It seemed their tolerance for disobedience was very low. So he reluctantly followed Jenny's lead and heard nothing more apart from the clanging and rushing of the machine until the bell rang.

After a few hours, Luke started to get the hang of it. It was backbreaking and tiring work. He had to be fast to avoid getting stuck in the machine. But the worst thing was all the bits of cotton in the air and especially inside the machine. He couldn't help but breathe them in, making his throat scratchy and his nose stuffy. He really wanted a drink of water, but he didn't dare ask for fear of getting another beating. He glanced over at Jenny. The dust didn't seem to affect her at all. His back and legs were aching, and he kept brushing the cotton off his face and eyelashes, coughing and sneezing in between ventures under the machine.

At noon, the bell rang and the machines started to slow down to a stop, but the noise continued ringing in Luke's ears, making him feel slightly deaf.

"Now we need to clean the machines before you go," said Sam. "Jenny will show you what to do."

For the first time in his life, Luke felt defeated. Goodness knows how he'd feel after a few years working here.

How does everyone else manage? he wondered. Bill seems fine, typically serious and too tired to play, but fine. And this Jenny is quiet and ill-looking, but who is to say she isn't normally like that? Luke decided there and then that the stupid mill would not break him. He wasn't going to spend his life working here, drudging, getting ill, feeling miserable. He was going to do something else with his life. He just needed to work out what. He needed a plan. A plan that would allow him to be anywhere but here.

Jane was waiting for him at the mill gates.

"Checking up on me?"

"Just wondered how you got on today."

"I got fined."

"Oh, for the love of Christ. What for?"

"Insolence."

"Of course, what else? Do you understand that if you carry on with your ways, you'll end up working there all day and even owing them money? Best to keep your mouth shut and just get on with it."

They walked on in silence.

"Now we only have a short time for lunch, and then I'm taking you to school."

"School?" Luke stopped. Nobody had mentioned school. "Why do I have to go to school?"

Jane stopped walking and turned round to face him. "You're getting an opportunity your brother never did. Bill would have loved to have gone to school."

"Then he can do my schoolwork, and I'll go and build engines in the foundry."

"It doesn't work like that," Jane sighed.

"Why not?"

"How would the world be if we all just did as we pleased? Sometimes, Luke, I think you're either really smart or really stupid."

"Learning is a waste of time. I could be earning more money."

"Well, you can't," said Jane. "The law says you can't work full-time until you're thirteen, and even then you can't work as many hours as a man. And learning is not a waste." Jane wagged her finger at him. "One day you'll be grateful for your learning."

"No, I won't."

Jane sighed. "Come on."

Luke followed her home and then meekly to school, where he sat, for the first and last time, at the back of the class. For three hours, he mostly stared out of the window, watching the hard rain falling onto the roofs and running down the slates like small rivers. He got his hands rapped four times for being inattentive. Luke realised that this was not going to suit him. He had to think of an alternative. Preferably before tomorrow.

The next morning, Luke gulped down his breakfast and was reaching for his hat and coat before Bluey had even taken his first bite.

"You're keen!" Jane laughed. "Liking it at the mill, are you?"

Luke pulled a face. "No, not really, but it won't do to be late." He made for the door.

"You've plenty of time yet," said Jane.

"Leave him be," said Bluey. "I'm sure Luke knows what he's doing." He smiled as Luke slipped out of the door.

The first few minutes of standing outside in the cool February air, the streets dark and quiet, felt good. Peaceful, almost. Until Luke wondered what he was going to do next. He had thought about it a lot last night before going to sleep, and ratting was about all he knew. He was pretty fast, and he could probably earn a few pennies for the tails, especially with his "new" knife. But that wasn't going to earn him the same wage Bluey expected in his hand on Saturday, and there was no way Luke was going back to that mill.

He was also annoyed at Bluey for not telling him Bill was going to live at the apprentice house. Bluey had said he didn't really know that was going to happen and that it was Jem's choice, but Luke didn't really care whose choice it was. He wanted his brother back, or at least to be able to say good-bye to him. As if it wasn't enough that Nell was in Manchester, they had to send Bill to the other side of town and leave Luke alone. Well, if people insisted on making life difficult for Luke, they should all watch out. He kicked at the wall, then started walking towards the canal.

There were few people around, but Luke began to get the distinct feeling he was being followed. He kept stopping to turn around but he couldn't see anyone, although there were only streetlights on one side of the street, so the other side was in darkness. Maybe it was Bluey making sure he went to the mill. Perhaps he'd seen through Luke straightaway. Damn! he thought. I knew I should have pretended to head in the direction of the mill instead.

He doubled back and headed towards the mill, just to be on the safe side. Once at the factory walls, Luke walked up and down, pretending to wait for the bell. As he walked to the corner for the third time, he suddenly turned it and started running as fast as he could. It only took him a few minutes to reach the canal, then he headed down the towpath to a factory where he'd heard there were big rats.

Sitting down on a large stone to catch his breath and wait for it to get light, Luke almost jumped out of his skin at the sound of another voice.

"Hello. What's a young lad like you doing down here?"

Luke spun around, ready to start running again if need be.

"Come now, I don't bite."

Luke edged forwards to where he thought the voice was coming from and tried to make out the looming shape in the semidarkness. He finally saw an old man dressed in a worn and mended jacket, a bow tie, new-looking trousers and a very strange dark-and-light striped baggy hat with a bobble on top. The overall effect was quite eccentric, and Luke had never seen a hat like it.

"Come, lad. Would you like some breakfast? I've some bread here."

"Thank you, but I've already eaten," Luke said, staring at the man. Once it started to get light, it got light quickly, and he began to see the man more clearly.

The man grinned, tore off a hunk of bread and started to chew. "Suit yourself. So then, what are you doing down here?"

"Ratting," said Luke. "I heard there were quite a few here."

The old man bellowed. "Ratting, is it?" He wiped the crumbs from his mouth. "Well, good for you. See that factory? I own it. So I would be most grateful if you could catch all the rats."

"Yes, sir!" Luke stared at the man. He'd never seen a factory owner close up before, but he would have thought he would arrive to his factory in a carriage and wear expensive clothes, not a silly hat like that.

"Ah, this?" the old man seemed to read Luke's mind. "My good jacket is inside. I didn't want to get dirty down here. It's more of a morning ritual coming down here. A bit of peace and quiet before the days starts. And as for the hat," he took it off, looked at it and put it back on, "my granddaughter made me this. She'd be mortally offended if I didn't wear it." He winked at Luke, and Luke smiled back.

"Now, young man, if you catch those rats, bring me the tails here tomorrow morning, same time, and I'll give you a penny a tail. Can't say fairer than that!"

"A penny?" Nowhere else would he get that much!

"I need the rats gone, and you look like you need a job. What, don't you fancy working in the factory?"

"No. I'd rather be outside," said Luke.

The old man laughed. "Well, that I understand," he said. "Tell you what. I need to get a message to someone across town." He reached into his pocket for an envelope, took it out and turned it over. "If you take it over, I'll give you a shilling now and a shilling when you get back here. I'll see you here tomorrow morning. Plus a penny for each rat's tail, of course."

Luke breathed in sharply. More than two shillings in a day? That was a lot of money. Perhaps he would never have to set foot in a mill again! He grinned.

"Yes, of course I'll do it."

The old man smiled and handed Luke the envelope and a coin.

"Good boy! Now the address is 12 Oxford Street, by the new marketplace. It's for a Mr. Isaac Brown. Make sure nobody else sees it, you hear? Don't hand it over to anyone else except Mr. Brown."

Luke nodded.

"Good. Off you go, then."

Luke scrambled up the banking and headed off towards the town centre. What luck. The address was close to Union Foundry, so he could even go and see what Bill was up to. Really, he couldn't believe his luck!

After delivering the envelope and receiving what he thought was quite an odd response from Mr. Brown – still, he was only paid to deliver it, not think about it all day – he walked over to Union Foundry. As it wasn't yet lunchtime, he just sat down on the wall near the gates and watched some of the engineers lowering heavy parts with winches and pulleys down from docking stations into what looked like steam engines. Other than that, he just watched people passing by. This is the life! he thought.

A familiar voice finally interrupted his concentration. "What are you doing here?"

Luke smiled up at his brother. "I came to see you."

"Shouldn't you be at the mill?"

Luke shrugged and smiled. "Bluey told us last night that you were living here now. I didn't know you would have to move out."

"Me neither. Jem didn't say anything about that. But I'll be back on Saturday after work and stay until Monday morning, so we'll see each other at the weekend."

"It's not the same though."

"No."

"So what's it like, then?"

"I'm sweeping floors and keeping the furnaces going with the bellows."

"Fun, then."

"More fun than being a scavenger."

"What isn't?"

Bill smiled. "So what do you think they'll apprentice you in when it's your turn?"

"Oh, they won't apprentice me," Luke said, smiling. "I'm unapprenticeable."

Bill laughed. "So you'd run away?"

"I'd run far away." Luke laughed.

"Like today."

Luke winked and jumped down from the wall. "See you on Saturday, then."

"Wait, where're you going?"

"I just came to see you, and now I'm leaving. Don't you have some apprenticing to be getting on with?"

And with that, he slipped out the gate and ran across the street. Time to go and catch some rats.

CHAPTER 8

THE SOAPBOX
MAY 1847

There was an ear-ringing clang, which Bill felt right through his bones. Near the furnaces, the heat was searing. Sweat dripped from him, the heat trapped behind the protective layer of thick gloves and apron, which did nothing to help him cool down. He was always afraid his hands would get so sweaty that he'd drop the heavy glowing piece of metal he was holding and hurt himself badly. Bill thought the moulders had the worst job – there were so many accidents working with molten iron, anything from small blister burns (which stung anyway) to really bad accidents. A man needed to be strong and resilient for this type of work, and Bill, after a hard day, muscles aching and wanting some sleep, then had to study a few evenings a week at the Mechanics Institute. His apprenticeship included lessons on interpreting boiler blueprints, calculations (lots of calculations), micro measurements and technical drawings. It wasn't easy trying to concentrate when you were so physically tired, but as Bluey always said, "You put the hard work in now while you're learning, and it will become easier when you start working." Bill did like that he was getting stronger though. His arms didn't ache as much as they used to, and he was a lot steadier when taking something out of the furnace. He also liked that, after two years, he and the other apprentices were finally moving on to learn other skills. Bit by bit they were learning to make different parts of boilers, beginning to be proficient in the different skills needed. It was going to be a long time before he was skilled enough to be able to put a whole boiler together, let alone put it together safely. Now he was beginning to realise why it took so long to be apprenticed. Imagine letting a less-skilled person make a boiler. What if it had a weak point somewhere and it blew up, injuring or even killing people? He wouldn't be able to live with himself if he caused an accident like that.

The studying was beginning to take its toll. Bill was ambitious and wanted to be the best he could be, learn as fast as he could, so he would ask to take home extra work to practise over and over again – blueprints used for teaching, calculations to check his work. His maths skills were improving, but he was tired most of the time, and catching up on his extra exercises meant he spent quite a bit of time on Sundays by himself – something that seemed to annoy Jem.

Jem had made it quite clear he thought Bill's extra studying was unnecessary. That he should be spending time with his family, helping them out where needed instead of thinking of himself. Bill also wanted to learn to read, but when he told Jem, he just laughed in his face. Said he could understand why Bill needed to learn calculations, but trying to educate himself beyond the requirements of his job was a pointless task. They were working class, and they would never be anything better. There was no point having ambition – the masters would just knock him right back down, possibly even punish him for getting above his station, so Bill had better watch himself and leave all that studying nonsense to someone better.

There was little opportunity to learn to read anyway. There was no one around who could tell him what the letters said or correct him, and Bill wasn't about to make a fool of himself by asking one of the other apprentices or waste his teacher's time by asking him even more things after the lesson was over. This right here is the problem, thought Bill, mopping the sweat off his brow and neck with an old handkerchief. How were ordinary working-class men supposed to learn when there was no one who could teach them? Then again, most of them were probably more interested in getting to the pub and forgetting their lives for a few hours. And uneducated men who spent most of their free time drunk were more controllable, which the masters preferred. Why would they want to change the status quo and have their workers become more demanding? Forcing them to provide better working conditions? Better pay? Pah! Most workers could only just organise their weary selves to get to the pub and then home, and Bill didn't see that changing anytime soon.

A lot had happened in the past two years. Joe was no longer apprenticed with him. He'd managed to get out and was working as a farmhand instead. Luke, on the other hand, was becoming a worry. He was only ten and was probably up to no good. Since Bluey had put his foot down and told him that he needed to put a wage on the table like everyone else, Luke had been doing so without telling anyone where it was coming from. All they knew was that he definitely wasn't working in the mill, and most nights he didn't come home until the early hours. Bill hadn't even managed to get it out of him. Luke would just smile, tap his nose and say something like, "You don't want to know." He could be really infuriating sometimes.

Bill knew Bluey was at his wit's end, and he wished he could spend more time with them, or even have Luke come live with him. They had closed down the apprentice house because Union Foundry, like everywhere else, wasn't taking in any more apprentices. This system that had served Bill and his brothers was now coming to an end, and a new system was taking its place. Consequently, he'd been put in lodging in a house on Back Spring Gardens. He shared the upstairs room with his landlady, her son and a couple of other foundry workers. It would be great to have Luke live there too, but who would pay for him? Besides, Bill just didn't have the time to keep an eye on him. Maybe when his apprenticeship was finished and he had his own place and perhaps his own family, Luke could live with him. If he hadn't gotten into real trouble by then. Bill was becoming a little afraid of what his brother might be getting into.

When the bell rang, Bill was happy to down his tools. It was Friday evening, and Joe had decided that they were going to go to the pub and drink ale until they had used up all their money. After all, they needed a break and tomorrow was pay day. Not that Bill ever received more than it cost him for a few meals and a bit of ale. As Bill stepped outside the foundry, the cool air hit him, making him shiver. He moved slowly with the throngs making their way down Blackhorse Street. Instead of turning into Ashburner Street as he usually did, he walked down to Deansgate, making his way to the market on Churchgate. There would be enough time to buy a pie at the market before meeting Joe, and hopefully Jimmy Taylor, whom they hadn't seen in a while.

Bill neared the marketplace, bustling with what seemed like hundreds of people. He queued to buy a pie at one of the stalls, handing over a penny. Taking a bite, he hungrily savoured the taste of fat and salt, a welcome change from potatoes. Bill wandered around the market square, watching people. As always, it was packed. Stall sellers shouting out the price of their wares, competing with one another; hawkers pushing their trays of sweets or pegs or cloths into your face whichever way you turned; piles of rotting vegetables from the stalls and horse manure forcing you to constantly watch your step; men standing on soapboxes and preaching out whatever was closest to their heart.

Bill usually avoided the soapboxes. He had little time for other people's opinions on when the world was going to end or that they were all going to hell if they didn't behave in exactly the way the priests wanted them to. Bluey said that there had always been men there in the marketplace shouting that the world was going to end next month. And the month after, they'd come back and prophesy that it was going to end the following month instead, and hadn't they all had a lucky escape, or that there had been an error in the calculated dates. This had been going on since Bluey was a young man, and anyone could see it had been many years now since Bluey had been young.

As he stopped to take another bite and wipe away the juice trickling down his chin, he saw a lad his own age handing out pamphlets beside a man on a soapbox telling the crowds about something. Bill recognised the lad; his curly bronze-red hair escaping from under his cap and the thousands of dark freckles covering his face were not easily forgotten. While Bill was trying to remember where he'd seen the lad before, he noticed quite a crowd drawing around the soapbox.

"Let me tell you about the demon drink," yelled the man on the soapbox. "The demon drink is a tool for our employers to control us. They want us subversive and uneducated and not causing trouble, so they drug us. Sometimes they even pay us in this drug, making us think they are doing us a favour!" Suddenly, a pamphlet was thrust in front of his nose, and Bill automatically took it.

"Hello," the red-haired lad grinned, "I thought I recognised you. Bit far from home tonight." Bill just stared at the lad, then at the pamphlet, then at the lad again. He just couldn't place him.

"What does it say?" he asked.

"Oh, it's about the temperance movement," the lad said. "If you're interested, it says come to our meeting Sunday at ten o'clock. Temperance Hall."

Bill looked down at the jumble of lines and curves on the paper, but before he could ask anything else, the lad had moved off to distribute more pamphlets to the growing crowd.

"And how can we beat this? We can beat this by turning down the drink. Getting educated. Proving to the government that we are responsible enough to vote. If enough of us are educated and sober, there will be enough of us to know what is going on in the country, to work together to demand better working conditions. Do you want your child to be mangled in machinery because there are no safety guards or the ones they use are inadequate? How would that feel if your child or yourself was injured at work, but your master just said it will be all right, it was nobody's fault – here, have some more to drink so you won't feel like protesting?"

Bill felt rooted to the spot. Everything this man had just said was what Bill had been thinking lately, what he had sometimes discussed with Bluey. If you weren't in the pub all night, you had more time on your hands. And the masters couldn't keep you subdued all the time. Bill's heart beat faster as he looked around at the crowd and saw men and women of all ages listening to the man, some silently nodding. Were there really so many others who felt the same way as Bill about this?

But what about education? How did this man propose to educate adults who had never gone to school? That was the biggest obstacle Bill could see. He wanted to ask, or at least speak to the red-haired lad about it, but as he turned to look around for him, he heard a yell and felt a large arm winding its way round his shoulders.

"There you are! Give us a bite."

"Get off!" Bill said good-naturedly to Joe Walker. "Get your own pie." Bill turned around to see his old friend Jimmy Taylor standing behind Joe.

"Jimmy!"

"Haven't seen you since you moved away. Too good for the likes of Wellington Court these days?" Jimmy grinned.

"Not only has he gone and got himself an apprenticeship," Joe said with mock severity, "he's only studying all hours too."

"Blimey, studying?" Jimmy said in awe. "Do we have to bow down to you now and call you sir?" There was a split second of silence before all three of them burst out laughing.

"Give over," Bill said, shoving him gently.

"What's all this, then?" Joe pointed to the pamphlet in Bill's hand.

"Temperance," said Bill. "Actually, it makes a lot of sense."

"What that is, my friend, is a load of nonsense," said Joe. "Spend your money on improving yourself instead of drink? I'm already great and don't need improving on. As for the drink, EVERYTHING is better after a drink or three." He winked at Jimmy. "Come on now, lad, we have some drinking to do." Joe put his arms around his two friends' shoulders and steered them towards the Man & Scythe pub.

It was dark and rowdy inside. After seeing there was no space in the front room, the three of them tried to make their way through the crowds to the back room in the hope of finding a seat. Joe smiled and nodded at many of the men as he brushed past, sometimes exchanging a bit of friendly banter. There was a sharp whistle, and someone shouted Joe's name and waved.

"It's old Jamesie," said Joe. "We'll go and sit with him; he's a right character!" Bill's stomach felt like it was sinking. This was probably going to turn out to be a long, expensive, drunken evening. He looked down at the pamphlet still in his hands, folded it and stuffed it into his jacket pocket.

"Jamesie Fleming!" Joe said, sitting down next to the bloke with black hair, pale brown eyes and a large grin. Bill couldn't guess if the man was in his twenties or forties, he had such a round, young-looking face. "This is Jimmy Taylor and Bill Hall." Joe pointed at them. "Old friends of mine. Lads, Jamesie Fleming, who works on the farm with us sometimes."

"When I'm sober." Jamesie laughed and winked at Joe.

"And sometimes when you're not," Joe laughed back. There was a scraping of chairs and shuffling up of people on the benches to make space for them.

"This one needs an ale," Joe said, pointing at Bill. "He's getting a bit serious in his old age, needs to relax a bit and blow off some steam."

Bill smiled quickly and looked at the wall behind Jamesie's head. He was beginning to think this was a bad idea already. Seeing his best friends was one thing; being in a crowd, meeting new people and being embarrassed into drinking the foul-tasting liquid when he really didn't want to – for he knew how Joe Walker was once he got going – was quite another. Clutching his wet, warm tankard of flat amber ale, Bill turned to Jimmy.

"I saw your Luke yesterday," said Jimmy.

"You did? What was he up to?"

"Well, that was the strange thing," said Jimmy. "I waved at him, but he completely ignored me. He was with two fellas – one old, one really old. Then I saw him a bit later on again. It was dark. He was standing on the corner near the pawnshop. If I didn't know better, I'd say he was looking out for someone."

"What's your Luke up to?" Joe asked.

"I don't know," Bill said. "He keeps going out late at night and not saying where he's going. He's earning money though."

"Earning how?" Jimmy asked.

"I don't know," Bill said quietly.

"You mean you think he's up to no good? Robbing?"

"I hope not. Do you know who those two men were?"

"No, never seen them before. What do you want me to do if I see him again?"

Bill was quiet for a minute, then started to open his mouth when they suddenly heard a scuffle at the bar and looked around. They could see a fight beginning. Two men stood up across the table from each other, knocked over a few drinks and grabbed each other's lapels. Others, sat beside them, possibly the owners of the drinks, started shoving them in retaliation. Suddenly, the table was pushed over, and one man was held in a headlock while the other pummelled him. The barman rushed to separate them, grabbing at one man and forcing him to release the other. The second man sank to the ground, and the barman sighed as he yanked him up by the back of his jacket. Bill could see the man was struggling to stand up, his feet slipping on the floor as he tried to find his balance. As the man's arms flailed and he spun around, Bill saw it was his older brother. His jaw dropped.

He'd heard Jem often got into drunken fights – that was common knowledge. Joe seemed to frequent the same pubs as Jem and regularly reported back to Bill. But seeing it for himself was a different matter, and Bill found himself unable to react. His mind was racing, thinking about being embarrassed to be seen with a pub brawler in front of his friends, not wanting to have to try and half drag Jem back home to Molly when he was in a fighting mood. As Jem was ejected from the pub, Bill's body remained unwilling to leave his seat, and he was very, very disappointed in his own behaviour. No matter what he thought of Jem and his antics, he was his brother, and he'd just let him down.

"Typical iron moulders!" Jamesie laughed. Joe peeked through the doorway.

"That's no iron moulder, that's his brother," he said, pointing at Bill. "What does he do now? I heard he can't get a job."

"It's not that bad," Bill mumbled. "He's having a hard time at the minute. He's still working in the foundry."

"I heard he got let go again," said Joe. "How many foundries won't employ him now, eh?"

Bill shrugged and turned away.

"Times are hard for everyone right now," Jamesie said kindly, noticing Bill's discomfort. "It's not like I have work every day."

"Yeah, times are hard, hard for our Jem, but he still got me an apprenticeship. He'd do anything for family. He has a good heart and doesn't go round saying unkind things about people." Bill looked pointedly at Joe. "Anyway, is it really the workers' fault that they drink to have a break from their day when their day is so long and hard? And that the masters even pay in ale sometimes when there's no money coming in?"

"There's nothing wrong with being paid in ale," said Joe.

"You don't have kids," said Bill. "You don't have to put food on the table. If your all pay goes on beer, there's only you going hungry. Our Jem has four children to feed."

"But you can still drink and not get into fights," said Jamesie. "Take it from someone who drinks a lot."

"But you don't stay in any one job for long," said Joe.

"Nah, I get bored easily," said Jamesie. "But I choose to leave. Mostly." He looked down into his tankard. "I'm just saying that whatever happens at work, there is no need to get into fights."

"Some people are happy drunks," Jimmy said while Joe grinned and pointed to his chest. "While some people are just mean drunks."

"That's not the point," said Bill. "The point is that by paying us in beer, the masters are cheating us, and they're making sure we're not able to better ourselves."

"Better ourselves?" asked Jimmy. "You and I come from slums. We had nothing. Now I'm a weaver, earning enough not to starve, lodging on a decent street, while you're an apprentice, will one day be a journeyman. I'd say that's bettering ourselves."

"But what if we could have more? What if we could learn to read, take part in politics, become managers because we're skilled at what we do instead of all those who are given manager jobs just because they're middle class and have nice clothes? What if we didn't have to work ourselves to the ground every day, live comfortably without worrying if we'll have enough food for the week? Without worrying about what is going to happen when we get sick? Is no one else tired of working for someone less intelligent than we are?"

Joe shook his head. "Things are not going to get better for us," he said. "And we're lucky. Some people have it far worse than we have it."

"I know," said Bill, "I've been there."

"My eldest lad, Tommy, is only ten right now, but I'll be telling him and my daughter Betsy what I'm about to tell you," said Jamesie. "We cannot change things on our own. Even collectively, they will always have more power than us, and they will always have the right to take away our jobs and livelihood and make it difficult for us to get work if we're known troublemakers. They will believe what they want to believe and will never give us the benefit of the doubt. So if you're thinking about trying to stand up to them, don't. Keep your head down. Do no more than is expected of you, and stay out of all this political trouble. In fact, stay out of all trouble. That is what I have learned."

Bill opened his mouth to ask Jamesie more – had he ever been involved in politics? But Joe got in first.

"Well, that's all a bit heavy," he said. "I think we need a bit more ale." He patted Jamesie's shoulder and disappeared. Jamesie looked at Bill, then quickly looked away.

CHAPTER 9

TEMPERANCE
MAY 1847

Ever since last night at the market square, Bill had been thinking about the temperance movement meeting. He was curious about what they discussed, what they did. But would it get him into trouble, as Jamesie had warned him? Should he stay away? Bill mulled this over as he worked under a large boiler case, setting rivets into the seam. Back and forth, back and forth went the discussion in his head. It was like he had two minds – one was telling him to stay out of anything that could potentially lead to trouble, while the other was telling him that if he didn't take the chance to make his situation better, both for himself and for others, how would he ever look his children, if he was lucky enough to have any, in the eye without feeling guilty?

He was thankful to down tools when the bell rang and walked up to the offices, standing in line with all the other workers for his weekly pay. He still received very little as an apprentice – his lodgings were paid directly to his landlady, Mrs. Marsh, and he received just enough to keep him fed. He thought that since Jem was paying for his apprenticeship, by rights, if he had any money left at the end of the week, it should go to him and not on ale. But how would his life be if he became teetotal and gave the money to his brother, whom he knew was struggling right now? It would certainly improve Jem's life at least. And Molly's. But tea and lemonade weren't cheap either. Water was free, but it wasn't always good, and he didn't want to be constantly sick to his stomach. He would see how much money he could save.

Standing in line, he saw the red-haired lad pass him. So that's where he recognised him from! They smiled at each other, and the lad raised his hand in greeting, but there was no talking in line. Slowly, the line inched forwards until it was Bill's turn to put his cross in the big book and collect his packet. One day he'd sign his name. Then the clerk would be surprised!

Bill stepped out into the late afternoon autumn sun to see the red-haired lad was waiting for him.

"I'd maybe better introduce myself properly," the lad said with a big smile. He held out his hand to Bill. "Tam Green, iron moulder, teetotaller and freckle collector." He grinned. Bill took the outstretched hand and grinned back.

"Bill Hall, apprentice boiler maker, orphan and snail, I'm told."

Tam Green chuckled, his eyes crinkling.

"What did you think about Harry's temperance speech last night at the market?" he asked. "Do you fancy coming to the meeting tomorrow?"

Bill gestured to start walking and waited until they were out of the foundry gates before he said anything. "Will it get me into trouble?"

Tam was silent and thought for a minute. "Nah. But it depends how far you want to go," he said. "The temperance movement itself is harmless. We abstain from liquor, and there are many good reasons to do so. We just want to spread the word, get more people interested – the more that become aware, the more that join us. As long as we're not spreading the word in work hours and we're not going to political meetings – the temperance Chartists can get quite passionate about politics, we're not causing any trouble at all."

"But what about when we're paid in ale?" Bill asked. "What about that and being teetotal?"

"Yes, that," said Tam. "We tend to not make it known who's teetotal, otherwise some masters might want to try and scupper that. They want to keep us under their control, you see, and if our brains are pickled in alcohol, we're less likely to think for ourselves." Bill nodded and immediately thought of Jem. "But some of the temperance groups have started to protest against it. And there's something big happening in Leeds – Band of Hope they're calling themselves – but for now, no there's no trouble with our group. I can't guarantee you won't want to get into the politics that go with it though." Tam winked.

"Are you?"

Tam grinned. "Come to the meeting tomorrow, and you'll see what it's all about. If you don't think it's for you, no harm done, and you've learned something new."

"Oh, all right, then," Bill said.

"I have to go now," said Tam. "I have a reading group I'm late for. But it was really nice to meet you, and I hope we'll see you tomorrow." He smiled and held out his hand.

"Wait, you're learning to read?" Bill asked, shaking Tam's hand. "Where?"

"There's a temperance hotel on Newport Street," Tam said. "I'm the teacher."

"What?" Bill's mouth hung open. "You can read? You teach? Do you . . . do you think you could teach me?"

"Of course! We could maybe do something after the meeting tomorrow, if you have time?"

"Yes!"

"Well then," said Tam, "I'll see you tomorrow." Bill watched Tam walk away, then carried on walking to Bluey's house. What were the chances of meeting Tam today? Then again, how could he not have known there was someone at the foundry who was teaching people to read?

After tea, Bluey went to sit in the living room while Aunt Jane and Jenny cleared. Bill went to join him. Luke quickly muttered something and rushed out the door before anyone could tell him to stop.

"Where's he off to now?" Bluey muttered. "I know he's your brother, Bill, but really, he's becoming such hard work."

"I know," said Bill. "He won't talk to me either. I don't know what to do. Do you think he's up to something bad?"

"I hope not, but it wouldn't surprise me. I would like to know who he's hanging round with though. I wish I could do something before he ends up in real trouble."

Bill was silent for a moment. "Do you think it would be any better if he lived with me?"

"I know you miss him," Bluey said, "but you're just in lodgings. I had hoped that him having a home here, somewhere he'll always know he's safe and can stay for as long as he likes, would help. Besides not knowing where we'd find the money for his lodgings, I think it would make him worse. He's almost wild as it is."

Bill sighed. "So what do we do?"

Bluey shrugged. "I don't know. I've tried everything. He won't talk to me. He won't even talk to you. I've punished him, offered rewards for good behaviour, tried to stop him going out, given him free rein – short of following him one night, I'm out of ideas." They both gazed into the fire, trying to distract their thoughts.

"Bluey, what are temperance Chartists?" Bill asked suddenly.

Bluey laughed. "Where did you here that?"

"Oh, just from someone today."

"You know the Chartists want votes for every man? Well, temperance Chartists want to show that by abstaining from drink working-class men are responsible enough to be given the vote."

"What about women?"

Bluey's eyebrows shot up. "Do you think women should be allowed to vote?"

"Well, if they're working, they're contributing just as much as men."

"But they're not. They don't work more than ten hours a day now, same as children. And what about those that are home looking after the children, bearing children, keeping their families in decently mended clothes and their bellies as full as the husband's wage will stretch?"

"Well, I guess they're working too, in a way, so maybe they should have the vote?"

"And what about a family wage so that more women can stay at home and look after the family instead of having to go out and earn with their husbands in low-paid jobs? Or should all women be working too?"

Bill could see Bluey was getting quite worked up about it all. He wanted to have an opinion about all this, a fair one, but he felt way out of his depth. There were so many things to think about, and he was sure that no one solution would help everyone.

"What do you think about that?" Bill asked carefully.

"Well, you know I agree with the Chartist sentiment," said Bluey, "only in my own home though. It's not always safe to discuss it outside, not in these times; some people can be so radical. But why shouldn't every man of sound mind have the right to vote? We should get a say in how the country is run. We contribute. How would it be if we all down tools and the mill owners had to do all the work themselves? And we're men. We need to provide for our women and children. To make our children's lives better than what we had. Although I do think this country is going backwards in that respect. Things were certainly better before everyone came to the towns to work in the factories."

"Why won't they give everyone the vote?"

"That's a very good question! I think that because there are more working-class men than middle and upper class, they're scared that we'll vote for some working-class politician instead of for some rich bloke who owns twenty mills."

"And why would that be bad?"

Bluey snorted. "It wouldn't be. But the rich people want to stay in power and make themselves even richer. And what would they do if there was no one to work in their mills and factories for pittance so they could get richer and richer and buy fancy clothes and live in fancy houses and go to fancy parties? A working-class leader would fight to change things so our working conditions can get better, probably at the expense of lining the rich men's pockets."

"So they make sure we can't vote. So how can our situation get any better?"

"The way I see it, the working class needs to get educated. Get sober. Start a collective movement. If everyone works together instead of just a brave few, there's nothing we can't do. But that requires education, spreading of information via pamphlets, meetings. I doubt there are enough educated or sober souls right now."

"So temperance is a good start?"

"Well, I'd be happier if a lot more people would drink a bit less. I don't know if you have to abstain completely, but maybe some do. You've seen the damage drink does to families."

"You mean Jem?"

"Yes, Jem is a good example. You've seen how it goes. He starts drinking, drinks more, gets mean with his kids and with Molly, loses his job because he's drunk at work or hungover, time after time. There's no money to put food on the table or pay the rent, so Molly has to go out and get work. He sobers up, promises he'll never do it again, gives his pay packet to Molly as soon as he gets a new job and starts again full of good intentions. But then he's begging for a few pennies for a drink. Getting mean again, refusing to hand over his pay packet, drinking more and on and on it goes. He's not the only one, by far."

"Why do people drink so much? I mean, I've heard them say that it's relaxing, that it takes their mind off their worries and their pains when they've worked their bodies to the bone, and that sounds all right. But why go so far that you're drunk at work and lose your job?"

"Many don't let it get that far, but some just can't control it. It's a drug to them. They need it. It becomes their life, even when they're going through a sober period. Maybe temperance will help them. Although I can't see Jem going to a temperance meeting."

"I've tasted beer, and it's horrible!" said Bill.

Bluey laughed. "You're sixteen, Bill. I'm sure that opinion will change!"

"So temperance is a good thing?"

"Definitely, for some. Do you think Molly's life would be better if Jem was teetotal?"

"Sure." He was quiet for a moment. "And a person wouldn't get into trouble for going to a temperance meeting?"

Bluey turned and looked hard at Bill. "What's all this about?"

"Nothing, I mean, just . . . someone at work suggested I go to a temperance meeting with him. He also teaches people to read and said he can help me."

"I know how much you want to learn," said Bluey, "but it doesn't mean you should let yourself get dragged into something you don't want to get dragged into."

"No, it's fine. I was listening to someone on a soapbox at the market yesterday. He was going on about alcohol and temperance, and this lad from work said maybe I can go to the meeting and just see what it's like. That I don't have to go again if I don't want to."

"Well, I guess you should see it for yourself, then. Just don't start getting into politics. You know if you speak out against those in charge, things are going to end badly. And no matter what your opinion is, or how badly you want to help others, I don't want to see a member of my family go to jail for getting involved in the wrong kind of politics."

"I'll be careful," Bill said thoughtfully.

"You're so young," Bluey said. "It's easy to get wrapped up in things at your age, think your way is the only way. But just think about the consequences of your actions before you do anything. I don't want to have to worry about you too!"

It was quite late when Bill went to bed that night. Even so, Luke didn't return until Bill was already asleep. He tried to slip into bed without Bill noticing, but the mattress sagged so much that as soon as Luke climbed onto it, Bill rolled towards the middle of the bed and woke up.

"Luke!" he hissed. "Where have you been?"

"Nowhere. Go to sleep," Luke said, settling down.

Bill sat up. "Tell me where you've been. Are you always out this late now? You're ten years old. Don't you think Bluey and Aunt Jane worry about you?"

Luke shrugged.

"You're being so disrespectful. Can't you think of them for once? After all they've done for us – put a roof over our heads, welcomed us as one of their own, looked after us when we were sick or hurt."

Luke sat up too. "I'm earning money. I'm doing it for all of us. Bluey said I had to put a wage on the table, so I am."

"And you can't do that during the day like a normal person?"

"I'm earning much more than I ever was at the mill. And it's only for a few hours a night. I'm not hurting anyone."

"What are you up to? What are you doing that requires you to work at night?"

"It's best if you don't know."

"What?"

"I said it's best if you – "

"I heard what you said. Tell me right now what you're up to."

111

Luke sighed and lay down with his back to Bill.

"I'm just trying to make our situation better. If we were rich like Father once was, we'd all be better off. The people I work with, they think so too."

"Who? Did they know Father?"

"Does it really matter? I'm just trying to help us all."

Bill thought about this for a while. "If you get into any trouble, you come to me straightaway, you hear me? Luke?" But Luke was already asleep. His hands curled into fists and tucked in under his chin, he looked much younger than his ten years. Bill pulled the covers over his little brother, turned over and tried to get back to sleep.

After church the next morning, Bill sneaked away and made his way to the Temperance Hall on St. Georges Road. The hall was a large, ornate rectangular building on the corner of Higher Bridge Street. The front door stood open, a small, dark mouth dwarfed by white-framed windows. Bill watched several people flow in through the door and disappear. He looked around for Tam but couldn't see him. For a moment, he considered walking away. He should really be up at Jem and Molly's, waiting to have lunch with them. Jem would probably be annoyed with him, but something compelled him to stay. Swallowing hard, he forced his legs to move and walked in through the open door.

As his eyes quickly adjusted to the light inside, he looked around in awe. The main hall was huge. The ceiling was two whole storeys high. Red velvet draped over several of the windows, which were each longer than about four men stood end to end. The luxurious fabric was held in place by ornate gold rosettes. Matching chandeliers hung from several spots in the ceiling, filled with lit candles. At the front of the hall was a speaker's podium, wooden steps either side, consisting of several carved panels, some depicting crests, others depicting scenes. A large St. George's flag hung from the podium. Apart from two galleries running along the sides of the hall containing matching chairs with ornately carved backs and armrests, the remainder of the hall was filled with high-backed benches.

Bill looked around, trying to see if Tam was there, but quickly gave up, thinking it impossible in this crowd. He turned around to go and find a seat and wait and immediately bumped into a lady wearing a crinoline.

"So terribly sorry!" he apologised.

"No harm done." The lady smiled. "First meeting?"

"Y-Yes," he stammered. He looked down at his jacket and tried to smooth out the fabric. Giving up, he placed his hand over his pocket, trying to hide a hole that he kept forgetting to ask Aunt Jane to mend.

"It's a bit overwhelming at first," the lady said conspiratorially, "but no one bites here." She let out a tinkling laugh, and Bill gave a quick, compulsory smile. He should never have come.

"Come now," she said, placing her hand on Bill's shoulder. "Let me show you where to get a cup of tea. You know we have a huge apparatus for boiling tea. Perhaps the largest in Lancashire! We can make tea for nine hundred. Can you imagine that! We shall never run out of tea here." She laughed again and steered Bill towards the back of the hall and through a door. After waiting in line for his cup – Bill didn't want to disappoint the lady who had shown him kindness, but he really wasn't interested in tea – he made his way back into the hall. A speaker was already up on the podium, so he slipped into a seat on the nearest bench.

Speaker after speaker stood up to say their piece. One talked about the temperance movement in Leeds, about young men dying from drinking alcohol, about young children, some as young as eight or nine, drinking and what that does to their state of minds. One mentioned the Temperance Hotel in Bolton, now on Newport Street, a place to go to get away when you needed to or to meet friends, but to drink ginger beer, lemonade, tea or raspberry vinegar instead. In fact, there was never a need to drink alcohol, he declared to rousing applause. Another talked about the upcoming general election and what it might mean for the Chartists. Bill squirmed in his seat. This was all very well, but he didn't have time to sit here every Sunday and listen to people going on. Not knowing what to do with his cup, Bill sipped at the tepid liquid from time to time.

Then a younger speaker stood up. He began to talk about education. About how education and teetotalism went hand in hand. About how, when a man was no longer drinking every night, he had time to learn to read. Or if you help a man learn to read, get him interested in trying to help change the working-class situation, he would drink less and less. He ended his speech with an announcement about reading groups on Saturdays and gestured towards a familiar looking tuft of red hair. Tam! There he was.

After the speeches were over, Bill made his way to the front of the hall where he'd seen Tam. He was surrounded by several people, his face permanently creased into a grin as he laughed and joked with them. He looked up and waved Bill over.

"Bill!" He grabbed Bill's shoulder and pulled him into the group. "This is Bill, my latest pupil and possibly a temperance follower too, but we shall see." He grinned at Bill.

Several of the men in the group reached out to shake Bill's hand. "Good for you, Bill! Well done! He's a great teacher is Tam. Hope to see more of you!" Bill shook each hand, a little stunned, not knowing what to say back, so he just smiled.

Tam took his leave, whisking Bill away to the back of the hall.

"They all seem so friendly here."

"Yes, they are. They're always happy to have new members, encourage more people, but sometimes it's hard to get away." Tam stopped walking. "So shall we take our first lesson? Do you have time now?"

"Oh yes!" Bill said.

"Lets give it a go, then," said Tam. "We can always find a different time for next week that's better." Tam led the way up the stairs and into one of the smaller rooms. It had two large windows at the far end of the whitewashed wall and several small round tables with two to three chairs around each table. Several of the tables were occupied, and all of their residents turned round to wave hello to them.

"This is the reading and writing room," said Tam. "Here we have books, slates, sand trays, pencils, newspapers. Take a seat."

They pulled out chairs round the nearest table. "Best to start with reading," said Tam. "I always find writing is so much harder and so time consuming."

"Where did you learn to read?" Bill asked.

"Sunday school. My father was a stickler for it. Bit of a forward thinker. Taught me a lot about politics too."

"My father didn't have any money for Sunday school. I didn't think much of it at the time. No one round our way went to Sunday school. Now I wish I'd gone."

"Well, you don't need to wish that any longer." Tam grinned. "The important thing is that you're learning now." Bill smiled back.

"Right then, let's make a start." Tam put a newspaper on the table in front of them. "We can see where you're at. Do you know your letters?"

"No," Bill mumbled and looked down at his hands.

"Not to worry," Tam said kindly. "Everyone needs to start somewhere. I'll be back in a minute."

Bill sat back in his chair and stared at the front page of the newspaper until Tam returned. It just looked like someone had thrown random squiggles of different sizes onto the page. How was this ever going to make any sense to him?

Tam returned with a couple of sheets of paper and a pencil. "This," he said, sitting down in his chair, "is the alphabet. I'm afraid it's no fun to learn, but it must be learned first. Each of these is a letter, and each letter makes a different sound. There are twenty-six of them, and when you put them together and sound out each letter, they will make any and every word you care to read."

Bill smiled. This might not be too difficult after all.

"Let's start with the first one." Tam pointed to the sheet. "The letter A. This one says 'ahh'."

Bill dutifully repeated the sound, and the two of them became engrossed in the lesson. It was only when the other remaining reading group got up to leave that Bill looked at the clock and realised how late it was.

"Jem is going to kill me!" He shot up out of his chair.

"Who?"

"Our Jem. My brother. I was supposed to be at his place for Sunday dinner. They've probably all finished eating by now." Bill wrung his cap in his hands, hesitating to leave the table.

"Thanks so much, Tam. I appreciate you took your time to help me. I'd love to stay longer, but I don't want to take up any more of your time, and I'd better be off anyway."

Tam sat back in his chair. "You're welcome. Look, if this time doesn't suit, I have a reading group at four on Saturdays in the Temperance Hotel on Newport Street. Or we can do this here after the meeting again."

"Or both?" Bill said hopefully.

Tam laughed. "Or both. You're in a bit of a hurry to learn!"

"Yes, I am," Bill said. "Thanks again." He held up his hand and rushed out the door.

"Where have you been?" Jem bellowed, looking up as Bill stumbled in though the front door. Jem stood up and slammed his fist on the table. Molly jumped.

"I was just ... I–I lost track of time. I'm sorry."

"I asked you where you'd been," Jem said menacingly. "What is so important to abandon your family like that? You want me to treat you like an adult, yet you act like this? What do you expect?"

"All right," Molly said, standing up hurriedly. "Come, children, let's go for a walk while Jem and Bill talk." She rounded up the three older children and picked up the baby. "Come on, Robin, don't dawdle."

"But I want to stay and watch," Robin said, folding his arms and looking from Jem to Bill and back again. Molly rolled her eyes, ushered her son to the door, grabbed her shawl and four small jackets and closed the door behind them.

"I asked you where you'd been."

"None of your business." Bill stuck his hands in his pockets and faced Jem across the table. He knew he was in the wrong here, so rudely arriving late for dinner, but he was just so tired of Jem laying down the line and telling him what to do and how to think. Bill was going to educate and better himself, and there was nothing Jem could do to stop it.

"What? How dare you. Tell me where you've been."

"Why? Why should I tell you what I get up to? You only complain about what I do. I'm always doing everything wrong. Yet I'm not the one getting drunk and getting into brawls every night."

"How dare you speak to me like that, you ungrateful little swine! If it wasn't for me, you wouldn't be on your way to getting a trade. You'd be rotting in the mill with everyone else."

Bill hung his head and dug his nails into the fleshy part of his palm. He wondered how long Jem was going to go on about that. It's not like he'd ever helped Bill at any other time in his life, but he did one thing and Bill had to hear about it for the rest of his life.

"You should have been here with your family," Jem repeated. "Molly worked hard to prepare this, and we don't have food to waste. Where were you?"

"I was at a temperance meeting."

"What? At some pointless temperance meeting with complete strangers instead of with your own family? What the . . . what . . ." he spat.

"Yes," Bill said coolly, knowing it would make his brother even angrier, but he was past caring. "It was actually very interesting. Did you know that if you stopped drinking, you'd have more money and time and you could even get educated and stop being so stupid? Oh, maybe you couldn't though."

Jem sprang to the other side of the table and cuffed Bill around the ear.

"Ow!"

"Don't you dare give me that!"

Bill gingerly stood upright and put his hand to the now tender side of his face. "At least I won't be drinking and fighting, and I'll have more money and learn to read."

Jem went for him again, but Bill ducked this time. "Are you drunk now?"

Jem roared and shoved Bill backwards towards the fireplace. Bill fell against the edge of the mantelpiece, hurting his back on the sharp metal corner.

"Are you crazy? You could have burned me!" Bill flew at his brother, easily knocking him off balance. He then dove onto Jem and started hitting him around the head. Jem lifted his arms up to try and protect his face, but Bill kept on going.

"Stop! Stop!" Jem yelled, but Bill didn't stop until he heard his brother sobbing. His arm froze in midair, fist clenched. Slowly, he released Jem and stood up. Jem lay on the floor, his forearms covering his face, his body racked with sobs.

Bill moved to help his brother up but then thought better of it. He let his arm fall down by the side of his body, turned and walked out of the door. It took several minutes for the rage to subside, but eventually the horror of what he'd just done hit Bill. What kind of person was he becoming? He'd sworn he would never be like Jem, never. And look what had he just done. He had to keep a check on his temper from now on. He didn't want to end up like Jem. And if he could do what he just did now so easily, surely alcohol would make him ten times worse. Perhaps temperance wasn't only an ideal for him, perhaps it was a necessity. He would go every week to those meetings, avoid drink and hope he never lost his temper like that again. And of course, he'd have to apologise to his brother.

Luke woke up just after the family had left for church. He pulled on his outer clothes and looked around the kitchen for any leftover food. There were some oatcakes in a tin on the counter, so he took two and stuffed them into his mouth. Sitting on the edge of his bed, he bent over to tie his shoes. He sat up for a moment and then flopped backwards onto the mattress. Luke closed his eyes. He still had some work to finish off today, but he was so tired. He just wanted to crawl back into bed, just wanted the familiar, reassuring shape of his brother to still be there. He had to get a grip and head out, but maybe he could take just a few minutes to lie here where he was safe and everything was fine. He'd count to three and then get up. Yes. That's what he'd do.

On the count of three, he reluctantly tore himself off the bed. At least he wasn't working in the mill. At least he was earning more than he would have there. One day he'd make his fortune, and he and Bill could live well without ever having to worry about having a roof over their heads or having to rely on other people to take them in. He knew Bill would like that. Sighing, he walked out through the front door and over to the viaduct arches out by Canal Wharf.

They were waiting for him when he got there, the old fella and his son.

"Where've you been, lad?" said the old man. "We've got to shift this stuff before people start noticing it. Hurry up."

Luke rolled up his sleeves and helped them load the strips of lead from their coverings under the viaduct onto the cart. His shoulders and back ached, and his hands felt raw. He couldn't believe how heavy the metal was. Still, it was easier this morning than it had been last night, prising the metal off the roof.

After the last strip was safely on the cart, the younger man pulled the tarpaulin over, looked around, then jumped up to take the reins.

"You go inside and my father will sort you out. I have to get moving."

Luke watched him drive away, turned and went into the cellar of an abandoned ruin. A lot of buildings around here were being pulled down.

"Luke, my boy. Come. I have some pay for you. Sit down."

Luke looked around the cellar and perched himself on the edge of the only chair.

"Here you go. Have some food." The old man pushed a piece of bread and a tankard of beer into Luke's hands. Luke wolfed down the bread greedily, then swigged at the tankard.

"Now then, ten shillings for you from the last job." The old man dropped several shiny coins into Luke's hands. "We'll need you for a job next week. Wednesday. We need someone small to climb in through a window and let us in. Meet us here in the cellar about eleven o'clock. They should all be asleep by then, our Jackie says. And you'll get your pay from this job then. Jackie should be able to sell the lead today. All right?"

"Yes, Mr. Ainsworth." Luke nodded.

"Go on, then, off with you. I have things to do." He picked up his grey-and-white striped hat with the black bobble and placed it firmly on his head.

"Yes, Mr. Ainsworth." Luke leapt up and was up the steps and out onto the street before the old man could change his mind.

CHAPTER 10

NELL'S HOMECOMING
FEBRUARY 1848

Nell was coming home! She was finally coming home! Bill was beside himself with happiness. Jem had received a telegraph saying to meet Nell on the train from Manchester on Sunday morning. He didn't know all the details, but Nell's master, old Mr. Slater, had passed away, and she was being released from her domestic position. Bill wanted to go to the station too, but Jem had said no, that he wanted to meet Nell alone and Bill could see her when he went around to their place after church. Of course, Bill thought of defying Jem and just going along to the train statin and waiting, but since the day he had beaten Jem, he'd been trying to be good, to behave and mostly stay out of Jem's way apart from the occasional Sunday dinner they'd come to an agreement on.

Why does time pass by so slowly? Bill thought. And on a day off too. Usually days off go by so quickly. He looked at Bluey and Aunt Jane sitting on the pew next to him, Luke once again nowhere to be seen. He hadn't been to church for a good long while now. Aunt Jane usually said, "The good Lord will see fit to save his soul when the time is right," but Bill didn't think that would happen anytime soon. He worried about what would happen to Luke when he got a little older. They still didn't know where he was going at night or what he did during the day, but they no longer questioned him, and that seemed to make Luke more open to spending time with them. Just not at church or at Jem's house either, it seemed. Bill looked up at the ceiling, his eyes following the stone arches and curving vaults punctuated with stone bosses. Another hymn. Just two more and then the service would be over, and they'd all get to see Nell.

Finally, the rector finished his departing blessing and made his way to the front of the church.

"I just have to go and tell Tam I can't make it today," Bill said to Bluey, snatching up his cap.

"Fine," said Bluey. "Just don't be late to Jem's though. We'll walk over there slowly so you can catch us up." Bill nodded and almost sprinted out of the church, drawing tuts and mumbled comments about his behaviour.

He ran all the way down Higher Bridge Street until he came to the Temperance Hall. The door wasn't yet open, but it was unlocked. He pushed his way in and looked around the hall. There were a few people there already, probably speakers, but no Tam. He looked in the tea room, then upstairs in the reading room. No Tam, but there was someone there whom he recognised.

"Ah, you're early!" said the man, stacking books on the shelf.

"Yes, and I can't stop today. Can you give Tam Green a message for me?"

"Of course."

"Tell him my sister is coming home today. She's coming on the train, and she'll be here soon. So I can't make our reading lesson today."

"Fine. Will we see you next week?"

"Of course!"

"And bring your sister too!" He laughed, and Bill wasn't sure whether he was joking or not.

"Right, I will, then," he said hesitatingly and rushed out the door.

Bill didn't manage to catch up to the Booths, but he did manage to get to the house on Monks Row a mere minute or two after them. Nell was already there, and Bill flung himself on her, hugging her as if he never wanted to stop.

"Steady on," Bluey laughed.

"Are you really back for good?" he asked, finally releasing her. Her blue dress with a hint of crinoline under it and no darning or patches looked far too grand for this part of town. Her hair was tightly braided and pinned on top of her head, her skin smooth and pale. She also felt a little different now, slightly like a stranger, even though Bill was sure he knew everything about her. Bill just couldn't put his finger on what it was.

"Yes," she replied. "Mr. Slater passed away a few days ago, and his sons came to sort everything out. They dismissed the whole household but said they would try and find other work for anyone who wanted it."

"But you're not going to go back and work as a maid again?"

"I don't want to." Nell looked up at Jem. "I want to stay here with my family instead. I'll work in the mill, anything."

"You're twenty now, you should be finding yourself a husband, getting married," Jem said. "I can't imagine anyone would take you on for mill work now, not having had the experience at your age."

"They took me on," Molly said. Jem glared at her.

"I'll ask up at the mill," Molly continued. "In the meantime, you can help out here. I'll be needing it." She patted her expanding stomach, and Nell smiled. With four surviving children – Lukin, Robin, Lissa and Tomkin (Lissy had died from croup, as had a baby they'd had a few years ago), and another on the way, Molly needed all the help she could get, coming home exhausted after ten hours at the mill and then making supper for her family.

"Where are you staying?" Bill asked.

"She'll stay here," Molly said quickly. Jem was silent. "We had room for you before, and we have room for you again. Especially since this house is bigger than the two rooms we used to have above Pa's shop. Besides, both Jem and I are bringing in a wage now, and Lukin's doing a bit of work for Pa. We're a lot better off than we were when you left. Another adult wage wouldn't hurt either," she added.

Nell smiled again.

"And I have so much to tell you!" Bill said, squeezing his sister's hand.

It was another week before Bill got to see his sister again. That Saturday afternoon was one of those rare afternoons where it wasn't raining. Nell suggested she and Bill go for a walk. Bill got his coat, and they stepped outside, linking arms and heading out of town, past the bleach works and towards the long green fields belonging to one of the local farms.

"So tell me what you get up to these days then, little brother. What does Bolton have to offer you? I feel like I don't know anything about most of my family anymore."

"Well, the apprenticeship keeps me busy. And in the evenings I usually need to study," he began.

"Any young ladies in your sights?" she teased.

"No," Bill chuckled. "What would be the point anyway? The foundry owns me until I'm twenty-one."

"What do you do for fun, then, in your free time?"

"Well, on Sundays I go to meetings at the Temperance Hall and – "

"Temperance?"

"Yes, you know, when you're teetotal and – "

"I know what temperance is," Nell said. "So are you telling me you're teetotal?"

"Yes."

"Crikey."

"Crikey, what?"

"My serious little brother! Well, I think abstaining from alcohol is very commendable. I can't believe my own little brother feels the same way, especially since you work in the foundry. It can't be easy."

"No," said Bill. "Believe me, I get grief from Joe and Jimmy about it, but . . ." He paused and inspected a split in his thumbnail. "If I'm completely honest, I've lost my temper a few times, badly. And I think I shocked a few people. Anyway, I don't want to end up like Jem, so I thought I'd better stay away from the drink, as that can only make rage worse."

Nell nodded slowly. "So what are these temperance meetings like?"

"Oh, people are really friendly, really kind. And they drink endless cups of tea! And they talk about what's going on with other temperance groups around the country, or they talk about examples of men or boys whose lives have been destroyed by drink or about those who stopped drinking and got educated and are now teaching others to read. Just anything, really, to make you inspired to keep on avoiding alcohol."

"Educated?" Nell asked.

"Yes, they have a reading room. I've been getting help to learn to read for the past year."

"Really?"

"Yes, and I can read some now. Nothing complicated though, and it takes me a long time just to read a sentence still. But I'm not giving up."

Nell's eyes widened, and she broke into a huge smile. "Good for you! Do you think I could learn too?"

"What? Why would you want to learn?"

"Why shouldn't I?"

"Well, I mean, I've just never heard you say you wanted to read before," he said hurriedly.

"There's a lot of things you've never heard me say before," Nell said. Bill went quiet. Of course they had spent a long time apart – seven years. They were bound to have changed without the other one's knowledge.

"Well, they did tell me to bring my sister next time, so why don't you come along? Although I don't think Jem would like it," he muttered.

"Jem, why not?"

"We've had words." Bill told her about the fight and about Jem not wanting Bill to go to the meetings or the reading lessons at the expense of helping his family out. When he'd finished, Nell just sat there silently.

"Then we'll just not tell him," she said decisively. Bill looked at her in admiration. There she was, the sister he knew so well.

"What will we tell him instead?" he asked. "You live with him. It's not like he won't notice when you're not home."

"Oh, we'll tell him I'm rescuing kittens or stepping out with a well-to-do character or finding myself a husband." She waved her hand dismissively.

Bill smiled. "You know who you remind me of right now?"

"No, who?"

"Luke."

Nell started laughing. "Then maybe Luke will turn out all right after all," she said, linking her arm with Bill's again. The corners of her mouth turned up in a mischievous smile. "Now come on. A brisk walk is good for your constitution!"

The following Saturday, Nell suggested she join Bill for his reading lesson with the group. Bill was a little hesitant at first, saying that the group was maybe at a more advanced stage than was suitable for beginners and that she'd be better off joining him on Sunday when it was only him and Tam. But when Nell said she'd just go anyway and sit and sip tea by herself, Bill sighed.

"All right, all right! But if Tam says no, then that's not my fault!"

They walked in silence to Newport Street, entering the establishment with its fresh-curtained windows and matching white tablecloths.

"Bill!" Tam looked up and waved.

Bill walked over to the table. "This is my sister, Nell. Nell, this is Sammy, Dobin, Blackie and Tam."

"Ah," Tam said, grinning, "the famous sister who arrived back the other week. Very nice to meet you!"

"Nell wants to learn to read too," Bill said. Dobin and Blackie started laughing, but Tam pulled out a chair beside him.

"Of course, Miss Hall. Everyone is welcome here. Take a seat!" Nell smiled and sat down. Blackie stopped laughing and looked across between Tam and Nell, his mouth still open.

"We're working on this pamphlet today," Tam said, waving the black-and-white typed sheet of paper.

"I'm not sitting here learning with no woman," Blackie said, standing up.

"I'm sorry you feel that way, Blackie," Tam said. "But women and children have the right to be educated too, so I'm not going to say no to anyone who wants to join our group. Perhaps you should come by after the temperance meeting tomorrow, and we can find you another group to work with?"

Blackie grunted and left.

"I hope he comes back," Tam said quietly. "You tell him, Dobin, that we'd like him back and that reading is women's work too. There are many upper-class ladies who read and write letters to their friends." Dobin nodded, and Bill glanced at Nell. Was that it? Did his sister have designs on being a lady now that she'd lived in Manchester and had much finer clothes than all of them?

The lesson continued slowly until Sammy and Dobin had to leave.

"Right then," said Tam, grinning at Nell and Bill. "We shall take a well-deserved rest and have some tea. You can tell me how you thought your first lesson went!"

Nell continued to join them on Saturdays and even started to meet them at the Temperance Hall on Sundays. They'd fallen into a routine where they would drink tea and chat with Tam after the Saturday class, and sometimes all three would take a walk together after the Sunday class. Bill was still struggling, but became renewed by Nell's enthusiasm. In fact, if anything he wanted to make sure he was a better reader than her, so he tried even harder. Their reading material and discussions progressed from the Bible and a few pamphlets on temperance to political comments in newspapers and even The Northern Star.

One Sunday Tam produced a new pamphlet and said, "Here you are. Let's work through this. I think you'll like this one, Nell." After the first few sentences, Bill reading the words slowly and Nell managing to make out a few words herself, they suddenly realised what it was about. Women's suffrage.

"Finally, some sensible reading material!" Nell giggled. Bill looked up.

They started to read the next sentences. Suddenly, Nell sat back in her chair.

"Who wrote this?"

"Will and Frances Roberts," said Tam. "They are here a lot, a young married couple. You could meet them if you like."

"Isn't this all a little bit too mild?" Nell asked. "I mean, there's not even a mention of women's rights. They run their families and go out to work, but outside the home they are second-class citizens. I just get so angry when I see women's suffrage swept out of the way by the Chartists, who strongly advocate men's suffrage – like they can't fight for both at the same time."

Bill's jaw dropped. Not only were his sister's views on the subject quite strong, they were a lot better thought out than his own. Where had she learned all this?

"Sounds like you've discussed this subject a few times before," Tam laughed.

"Yes, with my brother in Salford. He met a lady there who was very actively into women's suffrage, so he started to learn about it. They both educated me."

"Tommy?" Bill's eyes were wide.

"How many brothers in Salford do you think we have?"

Tam laughed, and Bill's cheeks flushed red.

"You remember he married Bella a few years ago?" Nell asked. "Well, I know you've never met her, but yes, she campaigns."

"So Tommy and you discussed politics?"

Nell smiled. "You and he are not so different, you know."

A warm feeling spread through Bill. It was both comforting and nice to find out a brother he barely knew was still similar to him. Jem and Luke were just so different. If only he could get to see Tommy again. Perhaps they would have a lot to discuss.

"If we're going to campaign for men's suffrage, why not campaign for women's suffrage at the same time?" Nell continued. "Votes for everyone of full age and sound mind. Women should have equal rights because they are the backbone of the family; they bear and bring up the children – the future generation. That is one of the most important jobs in the world because women – not men – are the key to modelling the young child's mind. If the mother is a strong woman, the family will do well. But there are many women who are treated badly by their husbands because they think they have no say. If Parliament recognised that women do have a say, that would prevent a lot of unnecessarily bad treatment by their husbands."

"Nell definitely has a good point there," Tam said, looking hard at her. "In fact, it's one of the most interesting points I've ever heard anyone make."

"Thank you for not saying it was the most interesting point you've heard a woman make," Nell said.

Tam smiled, but this time it wasn't his usual whole-face grin. "Equal rights should begin at home or in the Temperance Hall."

Nell smiled and looked down at the table. Bill just looked from one to the other, but they both seemed a little preoccupied. He watched Nell look up first, a blush forming on her cheeks.

CHAPTER 11

THE SUITCASE
MARCH 1848

Nell had joined Bill and Tam for another reading lesson in the bright, comfortable room above the Temperance Hall. Tam sat down and pulled out part of a newspaper, apologising for his lack of variety in reading material this week.

"I was late to grab the paper today, so all the interesting parts were taken by the other teachers." He smiled bashfully.

"Maybe that's why I'm struggling," Bill joked. "My brain isn't interested in altercations outside butcher shops."

Nell smiled and patted her brother's arm. It was true he was struggling right now. She had watched him try but noticed he was giving up more easily than he had a few weeks ago when she'd first joined in the lessons with them. She was still finding it very exciting, and the attention from Tam helped, but Bill seemed to have lost his motivation. She hoped it was only temporary. "I think you're doing rather well," said Tam. "You just need something more exciting to read than this and the Bible. I bet if you found something you really wanted to read, your reading would come on no end. A book perhaps? Shall we try and find a story you like? I remember having my head in a book all the time when I was younger. I think that was the only thing that really helped me."

"Oh!" Nell took a sharp breath in, and the others turned to look at her.

"Nell, what's wrong?" Bill asked.

Of course! Nell thought. If ever there was something that could motivate them to read, this was it!

"Nell?"

"I know of some reading material that might be interesting to us both," she said. "And maybe you can help us, Tam."

"What is it?" asked Bill.

"Something I hid from our Jem," Nell said, grinning. Tam started laughing.

"Well that sounds more interesting than this newspaper already!" Bill said, chuckling. "What is it?"

Nell lowered her voice and moved her head closer to Bill and Tam, who looked around the room and moved in closer too. "Remember after Father's funeral, when I had to go and help Jem clear out the house and you went to fetch Luke?"

"Mmm, not really," said Bill.

"Well," Nell said, ignoring him, "Jem went upstairs and was there for ages. I crept up there to see what he was doing, and he had Father's trunk open and was looking at a book."

"So the book might be interesting? Doesn't sound very interesting. It was probably only pictures, haha."

"I haven't finished yet," Nell said. Bill could be very annoying at times. "It was how Jem reacted to the book that made me wonder what was in there."

"How did he react?" Tam asked quietly.

"He yelled. Said, 'Nooooo! Can't be true.' Got all worked up, paced up and down the room, threw the book. Then he said we had to get rid of the trunk, and we left it at the paint shop to be chopped up and burned."

"What? Why?" said Bill. "Why didn't you tell me about this before?"

"I didn't know what was in it. And then I was sent away to Manchester just a few weeks later, so I couldn't very well go and check on it, could I? And then I just, well, forgot about it until now. I did have other things to think about, you know!" She glared at her brother.

Tam sat back in his chair. "But wasn't the trunk burned?"

"No," said Nell. "It's safe at the paint shop. I told Bluey the next day I wanted to keep it because it was Father's, or really, Granddad's, so he took it out of the rubbish pile and hid it for me."

"I didn't realise you were so sneaky!" Bill said. Nell kicked him under the table.

"And you want to find out what he read that made him so upset," said Tam.

"Yes," Nell said, her eyes sparkling. "It also might make for more exciting reading material. Can you help us?"

"Of course." Tam smiled. "Sounds very interesting. Unless you'd rather I didn't hear about possible family secrets?"

Nell waved her hand dismissively. "I think you can be trusted not to gossip!" Tam winked at her.

"But Jem can't read," Bill said. "It's probably all nothing. You know what he's like."

"Jem can read," Nell said evenly.

"Jem?" Bill laughed. "No, he can't."

"I didn't believe it myself, so I asked our Tommy, and he said yes, and that Jem went to school."

"But that can't be right!" Bill exclaimed. "No!" He sat back and folded his arms.

Nell watched her brother's facial expressions turn from shock to disbelief.

"No, he can't."

"Bill ..." she began.

"But that doesn't make any sense," said Bill. "How could Jem have gone to school? I would have heard about that. And how could Father have paid for it? We were always so poor." He scratched the back of his neck over and over again. Nell wanted to grab his hand to make him stop.

"Father wasn't always poor," Nell said quietly. She watched Bill turn to her, his forehead creased as though in pain. She had always known she would have to tell Bill about this at some point, but maybe she shouldn't have started here, in a public place.

"What? How?" Bill almost whispered.

Nell leaned forwards across the table and lowered her voice. "Tommy told me that they'd been rich when they lived in Manchester. He showed me the house he'd been born in. It was huge. Why do you think Aunt Peggy and Aunt Janey are so well off? They all were, Father and all his siblings. But Father lost all his money before you and I were born."

Bill swallowed hard, and Nell could see he was having a hard time taking this in. She herself had been very surprised, but why care about something you can't do anything about?

"How long have you known?"

"I only found out when I went to work in Manchester. I didn't tell you because I didn't see what good it would do. It's not like we could do anything about it. And really, is it going to make you feel any better about your life? No."

Bill leaned forwards and said in a low voice, "So you're saying that Father was rich once, and he paid for our Jem to go to school and get an education? While all this time Jem's been telling me not to better myself. Not to waste my time learning to read, that it wasn't for working-class people like us? The bloody bugger! Just wait until I see him!"

"Bill!" Nell exclaimed.

Bill sat back in his chair and folded his arms again.

"Look, Bill," Tam said, putting his hand on Bill's shoulder, "I'd be really upset too if I found out my brother had been lying to me all this time. Especially about something that shows he has complete double standards. But we don't know what the circumstances are yet."

Bill shook Tam's hand away without unfolding his arms. "The circumstances are obvious!" he said, staring down at the table. "I don't care about what Father did or didn't do. I care that my own brother has been such a complete hypocrite, trying to stop me from getting educated, when all the time he'd already had an education himself. Paid for, even. The best that money could buy, I suspect."

Tam looked across at Nell, then tried again. "Why don't we go and get the suitcase and have a look at what's inside?" he said. "We don't know why your Jem has been lying, and my guess is that we won't find out from him. But there might be something of interest in there. Hey, anything that helps you learn to read faster, right?"

"We might even find out something about that old man who caused a scene at Father's funeral," Nell added.

"Him? I'd forgotten about him," Bill said, lifting his head.

"See, easily done," said Nell. "I forgot about the suitcase!" She wasn't sure, but she might have just seen a flicker of a smile on Bill's face.

"Who?" Tam asked, looking from one to the other.

"Oh, he's not important." Nell waved her hand dismissively.

"Maybe it won't hurt to look, then," Bill said, unfolding his arms. "I'm still really angry with Jem though, so we'd better avoid him for a while."

Nell smiled. "We'll go back to Slater Street and ask Bluey where the suitcase is. And we'll keep you away from our Jem until you calm down."

"That'll be a very long time," Bill muttered.

The three of them left the Temperance Hall, Nell and Tam on either side of Bill, linking his arms, and walked the short distance back to Slater Street to go and find Bluey.

Bill knelt over the suitcase and rifled through the papers, examining the script on each of the flat sheets of thin yellow parchment. Nell sat on the floor by the fire, dipping into the suitcase every now and again. Bluey had the suitcase moved from the paint shop to Slater Street some years ago and kept it hidden under his bed. They had been repainting the shop, he'd said, and he wanted to make sure it wouldn't get ruined, paint dripped on it, or lost. He'd brought it down to the kitchen immediately, and Nell, Bill and Tam set about wading through it.

"This is it!" Nell squealed, pulling out a faded leather-bound book. "This is the one I saw Jem reading. See, it's not pictures, it's words!"

"Give me that!" Bill said, snatching it off her. He flicked through it. Definitely no pictures in sight, just pages and pages of looped handwriting. He handed it to Tam.

"Here's another one," Nell said, pulling out a slightly newer version.

Bill checked the rest of the suitcase. Only these two bound books, the rest were documents and envelopes. He peered over Nell's shoulder as she flicked through it. More looped handwriting but slightly different, slightly easier to decipher. Even so, it would take him forever to read even a page at the rate he was currently at.

"A diary," said Tam. "Most of the entries are from the 1700s." He had a quick look at the newer book Nell passed him. "And this is from the early part of this century. Last entry is 1836."

"Whose are they?" asked Nell.

Tam shuffled a little. "I don't really want to start prying into another man's diary," he said. "It seems like a very private thing."

"But if you help us, or even just Bill, to read the pages, surely that would be all right?"

Tam pulled a face. "I can maybe help a little, but really you should be reading it yourselves without me. It's your family, not mine."

"I understand," said Nell. "Maybe it will motivate Bill a little more to practise his reading, then."

Bill smiled at her. "These are really thick journals. They'd better be more interesting than what the owner had for dinner each day!"

Nell and Tam started laughing.

"Let's see what else is in there," said Tam. "What have you found, Bill?"

Bill picked up the bundle he'd been looking at. He'd made out the words Bolton Boys Grammar School and The Manchester Grammar School.

"Looks like school papers."

"School papers?" echoed Nell. "School papers for Jem?"

Bill glared at her and looked back through the parchments.

"It says 'Robert Hall'," he said slowly. "Robert Hall? So Father went to school too?"

"Tommy said Father was always reading – newspapers, pamphlets, books – so yes, I'd imagine he did go to school."

Bill dropped the papers and stared at his sister. He could feel himself getting annoyed again. Nell was making him feel like a stranger to his own family.

"Really, how much do you know about our family that I don't? Do you have anything else to tell me?"

"I only found out a few things from our Tommy after they sent me to Manchester. It just seemed like a completely different world there. But I can't say I care too much about what our brothers and Father may or may not have done ..." Nell's voice trailed off.

"Anything else?"

"Anything else what?" Nell asked.

"Anything else you'd like to tell me about our family?"

"You now know all I know," she said.

"Look at this!" Tam said, trying to change the subject. "Here's your father's school report! And Jem's."

"Read it to us, please!" Nell said.

"Right. Jem's. James Hall is inattentive, lacks discipline and does not assert himself."

Bill looked up at Nell, and they both burst into laughter.

"He's not changed much," said Bill. "What does Father's say?"

"Bobby Hall talks too much and is overenthusiastic. His energy would be better spent on learning his grammar rules than playing practical jokes."

Nell started to giggle again.

"I never thought of Father as being like that," said Bill. "He was always solemn, quite quiet."

"I don't think we ever really know our fathers," said Tam. "Brothers, maybe, but remember our fathers had a whole life before we came along. Then they had to raise us and discipline us. Show another side of themselves. He could have been quite a different person amongst his friends."

"I never thought about it like that," said Bill. "How did you get so smart?" He playfully punched his friend's arm.

"I read a lot!" Tam said and laughed. "Here, I've been looking through these. They seem to be wills."

"Wills?" Bill said. "Whose wills?"

Tam looked up at the top of each page, searching for names. "It seems that although there are a few versions, they are for two different people – a Ralph Horrowbin Hall is the first."

"Granddad," said Bill. "Was Granddad rich too? I thought only rich people had wills."

"Well, if Father had been well off, there's a good chance his father was too," Nell said.

"Wait, so you're saying that we are from a middle-class family? That we were all middle class, and our Jem and Emma and Tommy lived as middle class? But we ended up poor and in Wellington Court?"

"It looks very much like that," said Nell.

"So really we are middle class, and we should be being treated better?"

"I don't think it works like that," Tam interrupted. "Once you go down a class, you're not going back up again."

"Why?"

"Who is going to accept you? Certainly not the middle class. You don't belong in their social circle anymore, probably caused a huge scandal by losing your money and your home. And the working class are going to think you're trying to be better than you are, think you think you're better than they are, and they'll turn their back on you too."

"But why will the working class accept you if you've gone down to join them?" Nell asked.

"A man down on his luck? Someone scraping a living now, just like us? Same circumstances? What's not to accept? We're all in it together. As long as you don't show you think you're any better than the next man."

But Bill wasn't listening. Those words spoken by Tam had been said to him by Jem, over and over again. That they were working class and would never be anything any better. That any sign of ambition would result in him being knocked right back down for getting above his station. Was this what Jem had meant all along? Had he just been warning Bill, looking out for him? Had Jem once tried to pull himself back up and got knocked back down? Bill realised he was experiencing a newfound understanding for his older brother. There were so many things he didn't know about and Jem not explaining them didn't help. Perhaps he should be more lenient with Jem.

Had fortune smiled a little differently, Bill might have had a much easier life. But was it really better to have had so much and lost it, just to even experience the good life for a while, like Jem and Tommy, and even Emma, or was it better to have only ever known poverty and not have to accept less or miss the good life, like himself, Nell and Luke? Maybe it was better to need to build yourself up than to have everything handed to you and then suddenly taken away. Then a thought struck him. He was no longer jealous of Jem or even angry. He just felt sorry for him. Yes, Jem had had the education that Bill had only dreamed of, the advantages that Bill wished he could have experienced, but he was no better off than Bill was now. In fact, he was worse off. Perhaps it would be easier now for them to get along.

Tam's voice interrupted his train of thought. "Hmmm. Seems that this suitcase is mentioned in the will. Says he bequeathed it to his eldest son, Robert Hall."

"Father!" Nell exclaimed. "So it definitely is Granddad Hall's suitcase!"

"A family heirloom," said Tam. "How great is it to have that documented? So good that you had the foresight to save it."

Bill watched as Tam smiled at his sister and Nell turned away and blushed. He'd never taken his sister to be the blushing type. Perhaps that was something else she'd learned in Manchester.

"What else does it say?" he asked.

Tam jumped and cleared his throat. "Yes, let's see," he said, looking up and down the page. "Yes. Last Will and Testament of Ralph Horrowbin Hall. I, Ralph Horrowbin Hall, leave all my monies and worldly goods to be divided between my children Margaret, Robert, Jane, William and James. In addition, my eldest son, Robert, is to receive the leather suitcase and gold pocket watch. A sum of ten pounds is bequeathed to Edward Ainsworth of Blackburn."

"Edward Ainsworth!" Bill and Nell exclaimed in unison.

"How strange! Why is he in Granddad's will?" asked Bill.

"So he knew Granddad!" said Nell. "I wonder how. Doesn't explain why he was at Father's funeral though. There must be more answers in here somewhere." She started rifling through the suitcase again.

"Who is this Edward Ainsworth?" asked Tam.

"He's a very bad man, and you're to stay away from him!" Bill said in mock severity. Nell almost collapsed laughing.

Nell and Bill pulled themselves together and told him the story of Ainsworth turning up to their father's funeral. Of his fight with Jem. Of Tommy not telling them anything other than he was a bad man and they shouldn't have anything to do with him or listen to him. Of Nell creeping off to eavesdrop on Jem, Tommy and Aunt Peggy, but not finding anything out of real value.

Tam's eyes became wider and wider. "Well, that's quite a story," he said.

"But there must be some family connection to Ainsworth, otherwise why would he be in Granddad's will?" asked Bill.

"He could have worked with your granddad," Tam offered, "or been the son of a good friend. Perhaps your granddad was some sort of guardian to him."

"The aunts seemed to be very upset that he'd turned up," said Bill. "They knew him. Jem and Tommy knew him, but no one would tell us who he was."

"Maybe there's a clue in some of these other papers," said Tam. "There are some more wills here." He picked up the other sheets from his lap.

"Now let's see. It seems the other wills are all by a Robert Hall. One will dates from 1818 and the last seems to be 1830."

"Ohh. Read the 1818 one first," Nell pleaded.

"I, Robert Hall, of sound body and mind, leave my grocery stores to my wife, Alice, to do with as she feels fit. The proceeds from the sale of my stocks and bonds will be used as provision to educate my surviving sons, James and Ralph, until they reach the age of eighteen. At such a time, if there is any remaining monies from the sale of the stocks and bonds, they are to be split equally between them. The gold pocket watch is bequeathed to my son James."

Bill whistled. How much money must he have had in stocks and bonds? Where did it all go? And who was Ralph?

"Who is Ralph?" Tam asked.

"An older brother who died when he was three," Nell said. "That was before Emma and Tommy were even born."

"I never knew that," Bill said.

Nell sighed. "That's because you never listen."

"So your father had grocery stores?" Tam asked. "More than one?"

"He had three," Nell said.

"How rich must he have been?" Bill wondered. "Three grocery stores and enough money in stocks and bonds to educate his sons until the age of eighteen!"

"I wonder what happened?" Tam said.

"Tommy said he didn't know," Nell said. "That he was too young to know anything, and then suddenly they had to move. After that, he said it seemed like they were moving all the time, several different places in a year. Sometimes staying with relatives he'd never met, other times it was just them. Then they ended up moving here to Bolton."

"What does the 1830 will say?" Bill asked.

"Last Will and Testament of Robert Hall. All monies from the sale of the tallow chandling business, materials and stock to go to my wife, Alice. In the event of Alice dying first, monies from the sale to be split equally between my surviving children James, Emma, Thomas and Ellen. The gold pocket watch is bequeathed to my son James. The suitcase and all its contents are bequeathed to my son Thomas to do with them as he feels fit."

"That's it?" Bill asked.

"That's all there is," said Tam.

That must have been the total amount of goods he had left at that stage, Bill thought. No clue there, then.

Bill reached into the suitcase for some more bundles. It took awhile to decipher them, but the rest seemed to be old invoices, letters between his father and mother, letters between his father and Aunt Peggy. Bill opened each bundle, trying to read the script carefully or passing them to Tam. This was going to take ages. It was getting very late, and Nell and Tam were yawning.

He untied the red ribbon on the next envelope. A stack of papers fell out. The papers were old and yellowed, printed on one side. They were all identical. Odd. There was a fancy printed border around each and pictures of a steam engine, mountains and rivers. After a while, he made out the words Darlington and Bryant, Ltd. across the top in curved lettering. Shares 100 pounds each was typed at the bottom, with the date: 1825.

"Look at these!" he exclaimed.

Nell and Tam each grabbed one.

"What are these?" Bill asked. "Could they really be worth a hundred pounds each? There are loads of them. Is this where Father's money went? Are we rich?"

"Look at this one," Tam said, turning his over. "It says, Worthless!! I was lured. Never trust Irishmen or half brothers."

The three of them looked at each other.

"What does that mean?" Nell asked. Bill shrugged and looked at Tam.

"Blowed if I know," Tam said, shaking his head.

"But are these real?" Nell asked.

"I would guess they're either fake or they lost their value completely," said Tam. "'Worthless, I was lured'. That would be my guess, but maybe you should take them to the bank and see if they have any information on them."

"But if they were worthless, then why would he have kept them? I would have burned them all," said Bill.

"So this is how Father lost all his money?" Nell asked, turning the yellowed paper over and over in her hands. "This is how it all went wrong?"

The three of them stared at the shares in silence. How must it have felt to have had all that money and then just lost it all? Bill wondered. And how did it happen? I was lured. Lured. Irishmen? Half brothers?

"Wait," he said, almost jumping up. "He was lured by an Irishman or a half brother? Father had a half brother?"

"We don't know so much about Father's family," said Nell, "but I'm sure there were no half brothers. There were Peggy and Janey and two brothers who died young, Peggy said."

"Tam, where's Granddad's will? What are the names of Father's siblings?"

Tam scrabbled through some of the sheets he'd cast behind him, finally locating it. " . . . And worldly goods to be divided between my children Margaret, Robert, Jane, William and James."

"William or James?" asked Bill.

"Those would be the brothers who died young," said Nell.

Bill sighed. "What else does it say again, Tam?"

"In addition, my eldest son, Robert, is to receive the leather suitcase and gold pocket watch. A sum of ten pounds is bequeathed to Edward Ainsworth of Blackburn."

Nell and Bill looked at each other. That can't be true, can it? Bill thought. They would have known, wouldn't they? Tommy would have told them, surely. Then again, they only met their father's sisters at his funeral.

"What if Edward Ainsworth was Father's half brother?" Nell said. "That would explain why he was in the will. And if that was true, no wonder he'd hold a grudge if Father inherited everything and Ainsworth only received ten pounds. Maybe he was even angry enough to take revenge on Father."

"No!" Bill exclaimed. "Could he really be?"

"Well, that's quite a vivid imagination you have!" Tam said.

"But what if it was true?" said Bill. "It's possible. I'm not sure if it's likely though. But how would we ever find out?"

"Maybe ask your Jem or Tommy?" Tam suggested.

Bill let out a sarcastic laugh.

"Maybe there's something else in here, maybe some more answers. We haven't looked through everything yet."

"No, please, Bill," Nell pleaded. "As much as I want answers, I'm so tired. And I have to walk back to Jem's."

"I'll walk you," Tam said quickly. Nell smiled.

"Best I do it," Bill said, getting up. "Nell being escorted back at this hour by some young man unknown to him is likely to set Jem off."

"I thought you wanted to stay away from Jem?" Nell said.

Bill shrugged. "Maybe I misjudged him."

Nell's eyebrows shot up, but she remained silent.

The three of them left together, Tam to head home and Bill to take Nell home. On his way back to Bluey's, Bill couldn't stop thinking about what they had potentially discovered. How were they going to find out the truth for sure? He could maybe talk to Bluey about it; Bluey always had some good ideas and always offered solutions whenever Bill had a problem. But it was late Sunday night, and Bluey was probably asleep. Now Bill wouldn't see him or the suitcase until next Saturday because of having to go back to his lodgings. How could he wait that long?

140

CHAPTER 12

ANSWERS
MARCH 1848

Bill had been thinking about the suitcase contents almost constantly. What had happened to those shares? Who was the half brother or the Irishman? What did Ainsworth have to do with his family? Could he really have been his father's half brother? The thoughts raced around until Bill became almost too tired to think anymore. By Tuesday, after having burned his fingers twice, and his head aching, Bill couldn't stand it any longer. As soon as the lunch bell rang, he grabbed his jacket and ran out the door. Fingering the couple of shares he'd kept folded up in his pocket, he headed straight for the bank. He just had to know if they were fake. Or if not, what had happened to the company? He was certain that the shares were now worthless, but why? How? He hoped someone at the bank could help answer his questions because he didn't know who else could.

The bank clerk furrowed his brow and peered at Bill through his thick round glasses when he explained his request and handed over the shares. Turning them over in his hands, then holding one and then another up to the light, the clerk clasped his hands and leaned forwards, subjecting Bill to a barrage of questions about how he had come to possess the shares. Bill could feel the back of his neck becoming warm and uncomfortable against his scratchy shirt as he stammered that they belonged to his father, who had passed away. Finally, after staring at Bill for what felt like several minutes, the clerk rang a bell. An older man in a fine suit walked up to the desk and asked how he could be of assistance. The clerk explained about the shares while Bill kept quiet. The older man picked up one of the papers, turned it over and over in his hands and then held it up to the light.

"I would say that this is most likely to be a fake, sir." He handed one of the papers back to Bill. "See? If you hold it up to the light, you should be able to see a watermark."

Bill obliged, holding up his paper and looking at it, but he wasn't quite sure of what he was supposed to be looking at.

"However, I am familiar with the company," said the older man. "Darlington and Bryant, Ltd. do exist. Or at least did."

"So these were fake rather than being real and the company going bankrupt?" Bill asked. "I know they're not worth anything now, and it may seem unimportant, but I would be most grateful for any information. We're trying to solve a mystery."

The older man smiled. "Then I shall go and check our ledgers and try and provide you with as much information on the company as I can. Please take a seat."

Bill sat in the brown leather chair and waited for what seemed like ages. He was anxious to get back to work. His master, Henry Robinson, would surely fine him and probably punish him with some extra work for being late. He looked up at the large clock over the doorway. He'd just have to run back to the foundry as fast as he could. There was no time to eat now, so he hoped he could hold out until dinner at seven. Eventually, he saw the two bankers in the distance discussing something. The elder one was holding a ledger and something else. Occasionally, they would gesture and then look over at him. Bill started to feel uneasy, part excitement, part dread. Finally, they both walked back to the desk, and Bill stood up.

"Good afternoon again, sir," the elder man said. "I have managed to find some information for you. Please sit down."

Bill sat down again as the elder man pulled his chair in and lowered himself onto it, placing the ledger to one side of the desk. The younger clerk remained standing by his side.

"We've checked the name of the company, and I can tell you that Darlington and Bryant was a British-registered company from 1820 until 1845. From what I remember personally about them – I was a young bank clerk in the 1820s," he whispered conspiratorially at Bill, who smiled, "they were an extremely successful transport company building railways and roads in several South American countries. Of course they were only one of many companies doing that at the time, but in the mid-1820s, they were giving people high returns on their money."

"So the shares weren't worthless?" Bill asked.

The elder man looked down at his desk and cleared his throat before looking up directly at Bill.

"Well, ordinarily, no, but the real ones contain a watermark with the company name and crown, it says here. We could write to the head office to ask them to try and find out whether the issue numbers at the bottom here correspond to those registered as shares from that company, but I think they'd just tell you the same as I have."

"Then that shouldn't be necessary," Bill said. "So they were fake." He sighed. He didn't know why, but since he'd stepped into the bank, he'd had a slight hope of them still being worth something.

"Yes, I'm afraid so," replied the elder man. "That was my initial feeling when I saw they were missing the watermark, but of course it's always better to check."

Thoughts began to race around Bill's head again. So someone forged these shares and sold them to Father instead of the real ones. That's where all Father's money went. Although the will did show he had three grocer shops, so surely he must have had some money left? What had happened to them? And who forged the shares? The half brother or Irishman, of course! And who was he? Surely, it couldn't have been Ainsworth because Father would have recognised his half brother. How would they ever find out what happened? A discreet cough brought Bill back to the present. He quickly stood up and thanked them for their time.

"I do hope your family hasn't been too badly affected," the elder man said kindly. Bill gave him a quick smile and assured him not. Then he paused.

"Was there ever any report of someone forging these shares?" he asked.

"Well, I would think it may have gone on a lot with shares from many different companies, and probably many unsuspecting investors were swindled. But as to records of this, I can only think that those who were caught would have a police record, while the others we will never know about."

Bill nodded. "And those investors who were lured, what tended to happen to them?"

"I would say that if they had invested more than they could afford, which many did because it was seen as a very easy way of making a fortune for a time, they probably would have had to sell their every last possession to pay their debts. There were stories of some even putting up their businesses as collateral when they couldn't find ready cash. Others who did not invest as much may have escaped relatively unscathed."

Bill's jaw dropped. He had a very uneasy feeling his father belonged to the former group. He nodded his thanks once again, then walked out in a daze. Someone forged these shares, lured his father out of all his savings and possibly his businesses, and landed them all in poverty. He shook his head as he walked back to the foundry. He no longer cared about running. His punishment was not going to be any more severe if he was a further five minutes late. For a while, the facts were pointing to Ainsworth being the half brother. Perhaps he wanted to destroy Robert's good fortune after being denied by his father and watching Robert be given everything. Bill could understand how that would hurt, but why go so far? Why spend your whole life trying to get even? But the only flaw with that was that surely his father would have recognised his half brother. Bill began to mull this over and over in his head. Father was lured by his half brother. Why did he not recognise him? Was he in disguise? Did father not know he had a half brother? And if Ainsworth wasn't the half brother, then who was he, what was he doing in Granddad's will, and why did he turn up at Father's funeral and threaten Jem? Where was Bill going to find all the answers?

The questions plagued Bill until Saturday afternoon when he finished work. He, Tam and Nell had a standing arrangement to meet at the Temperance Hotel on Newport Street for their Saturday reading lesson, but Bill really wanted to go back, have another look in the suitcase and talk to Bluey.

As he reached the gates of the Union Foundry, instead of turning right to head into town, he turned left to head to Little Bolton and

Bluey's house on Slater Street. Bluey was already home as Bill pushed open the front door and stepped inside. The house, as usual, was filled with noise and laughter. Aunt Jane, Bluey, Johnny Booth's wife and their children from next door, and Jenny Booth and a friend of hers were all sat chatting and joking.

"Bill! We don't usually see you this early. No Tam today?" Bluey smiled.

"I just had to come back to look at the papers we found in the suitcase again," Bill said. "We found some interesting things about Father and Jem that I never knew about. I really need some advice."

"Let's go into the kitchen, where it's a bit quieter," Bluey said, standing up and putting his hand on Bill's shoulder. Jenny and Jane looked up momentarily, then continued their conversation. Bluey let go of Bill's shoulder and led him into the smaller room that doubled as his and Luke's bedroom. The suitcase, with all its contents, stood in the corner.

"What is it?" asked Bluey.

Bill sat down on his bed and pulled out the shares from his pocket.

"These," he said, passing them to Bluey. Bluey sat down next to Bill and took the papers. He turned them over in his hands and passed them back.

"What are they?"

"Shares. Shares that Father owned that are now worthless. There are hundreds of them. A fortune. I went to the bank, and they said these were forgeries. On the back of one of them, Father had written, Worthless!! I was lured. Never trust Irishmen or half brothers." He looked up at Bluey and noticed Bluey was staring straight ahead.

"Bluey? Do you know anything about this?"

"I'm sorry," said Bluey. "Yes, I knew about the shares and that your Father had been swindled."

Bill felt hope for the first time since he'd learned about all this.

"What happened?"

"Where do I start?" Bluey gave a nervous laugh. "Well, you know that your father and I had been friends for a long time. That's how your Jem and our Molly met."

Bill nodded.

"Yes, we went back a long way. I've probably told you some stories about my father and your granddad working together, building some of the first mills here. The pay was pretty good for plasterers and glaziers back then. Your father was only two years older than me, so we played together quite often, either in the paint shop, which my uncle owned at the time, or round at your granddad's house. Ah, we had some good times!" Bluey started to stare out of the window, then shook himself, looked at Bill and returned to his story.

"Well, we were about eleven or twelve or so when your granddad sent your father and his brothers to school, and my father had me apprentice with him. Wasn't much time for playing after that."

"Brothers?"

"Yes, your father had two brothers – and two sisters, I think. I remember Peggy was the eldest, anyway, then your father. She was a bossy madam! Always had an opinion on everything. Then there was a younger sister – she never said a word. Looked as though she'd blow away in the wind."

Bill smiled.

"I never had much to do with the younger boys. They were quite a bit younger than me and your father, but I remember one of them was quite sickly. Anyway, your granddad eventually decided to go back to Manchester – they were from there, and there was a lot of building going on there too. I don't think your grandmother liked Bolton that much. I was about sixteen when your father left. I didn't hear from him again until round about when Nell was born."

"But you know what happened? Why did Father come back?"

"He said he'd lost all his money, investments. He lost his shops, couldn't afford his house anymore. They were all living with your other grandparents, your mother's parents, and your father really needed to get on his feet again."

"So he came here, then? Why?"

"He wrote to me – well, wrote to me at the paint shop, hoping we were all still here. I got the rector to read me the letter and help me reply. He needed to start over again in a new place. So I helped him move back here, found him somewhere to stay. My uncles gave him a bit of space in the shop's backyard for him to start his chandling business until he got on his feet, which he did rather quickly. He had a good head for business, your father, he certainly did."

"Not if he lost all his money," said Bill. "What happened?"

"All your father told me at the time was that someone had stolen all his money and he was still in danger from this man. That's why he needed to move to another town, hopefully where this man couldn't find him."

Bill held his breath and felt his heart beating fast in his ears.

"Your father didn't say much more than that. He was a proud man, so he didn't really talk about it. Maybe he was embarrassed to have been swindled like that, or embarrassed to be seen to be running away. He said he had moved around several times in the year before he came to Bolton, but each time the man found him. He also said something about the man threatening his whole family, otherwise he would have just tried to disappear himself."

Bill took a deep breath. "What's the man's name? Are we in danger?"

"His name is Edward Ainsworth," Bluey said, shaking his head. "I don't know, Bill. I never heard of Ainsworth coming to Bolton or your father ever hearing from him again. I assumed that was the end of it."

Bill gasped. Ainsworth! It was him! So was he Father's half brother? Why would they be in danger from him? What did he want? He'd already taken Father's fortune.

Bluey continued, "I don't know much more apart from your father had had too much to drink one night, not long after your mother died, and told me what Ainsworth had said to him and that he would not stop until every last one of your father's heirs were destroyed. Now I don't know how much of that was the drink talking, but he seemed distraught."

Bill just sat there, rooted to the chair, not knowing what to say. Finally, he croaked, "Did Father have a half brother?"

Bluey shuffled uncomfortably. "Yes, he did. No one knew about it until after your granddad died. It was a bit of a scandal by all accounts. My father got to hear about it, but your father never said anything to me. I suppose they hushed it all up."

"What was his name?" Bill closed his eyes.

"I don't know."

Bill's eyes shot open, and he looked at Bluey.

"Could the half brother be Edward Ainsworth?"

Bluey looked down at Bill and narrowed his eyes. "What makes you think that?"

"The back of the shares. Worthless!! I was lured. Never trust Irishmen or half brothers. He was lured by his half brother, but I can't work out why he wouldn't recognise him. You said he was lured by Edward Ainsworth. And Granddad bequeathed Ainsworth ten pounds in his will . . ." Bill's voice trailed off as he noticed the expression on Bluey's face.

"Oh, Bill!" Bluey put his arm round him. "Your father never met his half brother, that I know about. He never said anything about it to me."

"So it could have been Ainsworth? He turned up at Father's funeral and threatened our Jem."

"He did? Jem never said anything about that." Bill noticed that Bluey looked a little worried.

"Jem never says anything about a lot of things," Bill said. "Did you know he could read?"

"Yes – well, no, not specifically. I can't say I ever thought about it. But Ainsworth turned up to Robert's funeral? Does he know you're all here in Bolton, then?"

"I don't know," Bill said. "I haven't seen him, and it's been seven years now. Maybe he doesn't know where we are." They sat in silence for a while, each occupied with their own thoughts.

"Do you think we're still in danger from this Ainsworth?" Bill asked after a while.

Bluey hugged Bill tighter. "I was hoping not, but I really don't know."

Bill went out for a walk to try to clear his head. He wanted to find somewhere quiet, away from everyone and all the noise, but there were so many buildings and people in that part of town that it was almost impossible. Eventually, he made his way to the parish church and sat down amongst the gravestones. If his parents had been buried here, he could have come to their graves and asked them questions. It wasn't like he'd get any answers, but it would make him feel better. But no, his parents were buried far away on their request, returned to a part of their life that Bill had no access to. Bluey didn't know any more, so the only person left to provide answers was Jem. But Bill was almost certain that Jem wouldn't tell him anything.

He sat there for what felt like hours. Dusk started to fall, and the air and ground became chillier. Bill pulled his jacket closer around him. Really, he may as well go and ask Jem. He had nothing to lose. He got up and made his way round the back of Churchgate, down Water Street and back to Folds Road. Coming to the public house on the corner of Monks Row and Folds Road, he opened the outer door and took a step in.

The Eagle and Vulcan was no different than any of the other shops or houses on the street with its double-fronted windows and yellowed curtains, but the noise and the smell of tobacco and stale ale every time the door opened gave it away as a beer house. Standing on the low step, Bill took a deep breath and pushed open the inner door. The thick cloud of smoke made it hard for him to catch his breath for a second, and the sour smell of alcohol filled his nostrils. After a few seconds, his senses became used to the thick, dim atmosphere, and he looked around for his brother. It was very unlikely Jem would be anywhere else at this time. He finally spotted the familiar blond hair, and clenching his jaw, he strode over to the table. Jem was sitting alone on a bench in the corner, bent forward over his glass, which he clasped in both hands as if he was afraid of it being snatched away. Bill pulled out a stool and sat down opposite him before Jem even looked up.

"Billy boy! What are you doing here? Let me get you a drink." Jem waved over to the hatch at the back of the room, and the landlady gave a curt nod, then rolled her eyes. Jem turned back around to face his brother, exaggerating his body movements and keeping his smile fixed on his face. Bill had never seen his brother smile for as long as this before. The fact that his older brother was beer-induced happy riled Bill. Spending his money on this stuff when it could be going towards better things. Better food for a start. He'd seen Molly drying the used tea leaves on the windowsill, to be used over and over again, even if there was very little flavour left. He was sure they didn't get to eat much meat in that family either.

The landlady came over with several glasses of ale on a tray, slammed one down in front of Bill, sloshing the brew onto the table, and walked away.

"Go on, drink!" Jem gestured to the glass. "It's not just for looking at."

Bill grimaced and pushed the glass away. Jem stopped laughing and glared at him.

"What's wrong with you?"

"Look, Jem, I have two questions for you. They're important. Then I'll leave you alone. You can have my beer."

Jem sat back, leaning against the wall as he grinned and took a swig from his glass.

"Is Ainsworth Father's half brother?"

Jem choked on his ale. "What?" The blood drained completely from his face, and he wiped his mouth with his sleeve.

"Just tell me what you know about Ainsworth, Jem. I'm seventeen now; I'm a man. I know all about Father being rich, you having gone to school, Father having been swindled out of his fortune. I just need to know about Ainsworth and whether we are in danger. Why did he threaten you at Father's funeral?"

"How, how ... ?" Jem stammered.

"Remember that suitcase of Father's you wanted to get rid of?" Bill began. "Well, it still exists. And it contains lots of documents. Some school reports, some wills, Father's shares, which are now worthless."

Jem swallowed hard and slowly lowered his glass. "What?"

"You heard."

Jem sat back in his chair. "Bill, you need to get rid of that suitcase."

"Right. So Edward Ainsworth. Was he Father's half brother or not?"

Jem gulped and looked around.

"Are we in danger from him? Bluey said – " He stopped mid-sentence, distracted by Jem looking around the room again.

"Shhh, shhhh," Jem said, putting his finger to his lips. "You don't talk about that man, ever."

"But I just – "

"It's not safe here."

Bill leaned in and whispered across to Jem. "Is he here in Bolton?"

Jem nodded so lightly that Bill wasn't even sure it was a nod. He sat up and looked around the pub.

"Where is it safe to talk? At your house? When can we talk about this?"

Jem looked right at Bill. "Just go home and get rid of that suitcase," he said.

"So you're not going to tell me anything?"

"Not here," Jem said quietly.

Bill leaned back in and hissed at his brother, "How am I supposed to know if I'm in danger? Who to look out for? If I get hurt, it'll all be your fault!" With that, Bill stormed out of the pub.

Jem was being unhelpful as usual. Bill should have realised that he'd never change. It wasn't as if he even liked Jem anyway. Well, he'd just have to find out more by himself, but how? Bill started to walk up Hulme Street back to Bluey's. He cut through a back street, the lack of light from the gas streetlamps forcing him to squint hard to try and avoid the potholes. Just as he crossed over, nearing the junction with Union Street where the light was stronger, he felt his jacket being grabbed and he was pulled backwards and slammed up against a wall.

Bill gasped and tried to fight back, but his attacker rammed him against the wall again and stuck his forearm under Bill's chin. Bill squirmed until the man pressed hard with his arm, blocking off air to Bill's lungs. Bill stopped moving, and the man released his grip slightly so Bill could breathe.

"Well, well, well!" croaked a voice. "Who do we have here? If it isn't young William Hall."

Bill could smell the man's rotting teeth and feel his warm breath on his cheek. He tried to turn his head away, but the man just pressed his arm into Bill's throat again until Bill stood still.

"Now then, William. You don't mind if I call you by your Sunday name, do you? Let's see if you manage to live until Sunday." He laughed. Bill squeezed his eyes shut.

"I've been hearing you've been asking around about me. Asking people about your father's shares. Mentioning my name."

Bill's eyes shot open. He tried to turn around to see the man's face properly, but every time he struggled, the man pressed harder.

"So we're going to do this," said the man. "You're going to keep quiet, not ask any more questions and never mention my name again, and if you do, I'll leave you alone. For now. You hear? YOU HEAR?"

Bill nodded.

"Because if you don't, you'll get what's coming to you. And let me tell you it won't be pleasant. It WILL involve blood and broken bones. I have my eye on you. You and your brothers."

Bill blinked hard.

"It's such a shame you all have to suffer," the man continued. "But as I told your father, I won't rest until you all feel the pain and loss that I did. All of you." The man leaned in so closely that Bill could almost feel its warmth on his cheek. The stench from his breath was overpowering.

"Ah, the sins of the father. A terrible burden," he whispered into Bill's ear.

Bill squeezed his eyes tightly shut and stood as still as he could. After what felt like several minutes, the man started to release him, stopped, and just as Bill tried to brace himself for worse, released him completely with a laugh.

"There you go," he said, smoothing down Bill's jacket. "Off you run."

Bill tore away as fast as he could. He didn't stop until he got to Slater Street, ran into the house and bolted the door behind him.

"Steady on," Aunt Jane said. "That lock's not been used since the Queen wed. You're scaring it."

"What happened?" Bluey asked.

Bill looked from one to the other, rubbing his neck.

"Nothing. I'm just . . . just tired," he said. "Good night."

He walked into the kitchen and flopped down onto his bed, pulling the blanket up over himself completely. He noticed he was shaking, his teeth chattering, even though the fire in the kitchen was lit. So Edward Ainsworth was in Bolton, and they were all still in danger. What in hell was he going to do?

CHAPTER 13

THE CHARTIST MARCH
APRIL 1848

Nell looked up as Bill entered the reading room. She hadn't seen him since last Sunday when he'd walked her home. He hadn't turned up to the reading lesson yesterday or church this morning or the temperance meeting.

"Where have you been?" she said, noticing his dishevelled appearance. "What's wrong with you?"

"Nothing," he said, pulling out a chair and sitting down at the table. "Where's Tam?"

"He's on his way up. Have you thought any more about the shares and Ainsworth? I can't stop thinking about – "

"Just drop it," Bill said shortly.

Nell was a little taken aback. What had possibly made her brother go from being so excited about this mystery to behaving like this?

"What do you mean, drop it? Why?"

Bill took off his cap and ran his fingers through his hair. Nell noticed the dark rings under his eyes.

"We don't need to discuss it further," he said. "We found some old papers that aren't so important, that's all. We all have better things to worry about."

"But, Bill ..." Nell couldn't believe her ears. Something had happened. Had he had a run-in with Jem again?

"Just leave it, Nell. Please."

Nell was about to open her mouth again when Tam burst through the door, eyes shining.

"Bill, you're here! Where have you been? Did you miss the meeting? Did you hear about the riots in Manchester?" he asked excitedly.

"No! What happened?"

"Well, some lads attacked a workhouse and several mills. Nothing big. But some of the Chartist leaders helped the police put down the riots, and now there's going to be a march here in Bolton."

"March?" Bill said.

"Yes. There's going to be some demonstrations in different towns today, and they're going to take a petition to Parliament again soon."

"Third time."

"It's got to work this time," said Nell. "The government must see that the working class are becoming better organised, more educated about their rights and won't give up."

"They'll never allow it," Bill said. "The government has too much to lose giving us the vote."

"But they don't put down the meetings as harshly as they used to," Nell said. "Do you remember when we were kids? You couldn't even talk about Chartism without getting into trouble."

"Do you even remember hearing about Chartism when we were kids?" Bill stuck out his tongue at Nell, but she ignored him.

"There's definitely progress," Tam agreed. "But is there enough progress? It's not like we three are involved in the politics. I'm sure there are so many working class like us who are still afraid to get involved, and that's what the government is banking on."

"Then maybe it's time we got involved," Nell said. The other two looked at her.

"What if we got arrested? Ended up in gaol? Got beaten up, killed?" Bill said.

"Maybe it's time to get involved by supporting the peaceful meetings," Tam said. "Help educate others. Spread the word quietly. It's not like we're going to go into Manchester and take part in a riot."

"Exactly!" Nell said, and Tam grinned at her.

"When's the march?" Bill asked.

Nell stole a glance at Tam. The pale skin covering his cheekbones was sprinkled with golden freckles, and she longed to touch him to feel how soft his cheeks were. Tam caught her looking and grinned, his eyes crinkling up and the well-worn lines appearing. Nell quickly turned away, embarrassed to have been caught and annoyed with herself to be knocked off guard. Tam was her brother's friend. Now he'd know she liked him, and if he didn't feel the same, it would risk spoiling their friendship. She had loved these past few months of spending so much time with Bill and Tam and didn't want it to change.

"Nell! Will you be joining us?" Nell looked up to see both boys looking at her quizzically.

"Joining you where?"

Bill sighed. "The Temperance Hotel. There's a meeting this afternoon to discuss the Chartists submitting another petition to Parliament next month, and then the march is starting."

"Do come join us!" said Tam. "I could do with some intelligent company at the meeting."

"Haha!" Bill said sarcastically.

"Coming, then?" Tam looked directly at her. "Maybe we should stay away from the march though. It might not be safe."

Nell couldn't read anything in his face other than the question he just asked. She nodded.

"Think yourselves lucky to have me come along as the voice of reason," she said, smiling. Tam burst out laughing as Bill groaned.

The Temperance Hotel was crowded, but Nell, Tam and Bill managed to squeeze in. As a few more bodies entered the room, Nell felt herself being pushed closer towards Tam. She looked up at him, and he smiled. One of the usual speakers at the Temperance Hall was stood on a chair barking out information. The room was getting hot, and Nell had the distinct impression that this "meeting" was less about the Chartists submitting another petition and more about whipping up emotions ready for the march. As more people poured into the room, Nell began to lose sight of Bill. Eventually, the speaker stopped talking, and with a few rousing cheers, people began to leave and march towards the marketplace. Tam grabbed her arm to prevent her from being ushered out with the rest, holding on tight until most of the crowd had left.

"Where's Bill?" Nell asked, looking around.

"I'm not sure. I didn't see him leave. Maybe he joined the march. I'm not sure there won't be trouble. We could avoid it if you prefer?"

"Certainly not!"

"Well, let's go, then." Tam smiled, his eyes crinkling. He offered Nell his arm, and they set off.

"So, Nell. Tell me more about your interest in the cause. We've never really had a chance to discuss it. You seem to know quite a lot about it, or rather women's suffrage," Tam said as they made their way through the crowded town streets.

"It was my brother's wife, Bella," Nell said. "Or rather, before she became his wife. I didn't know much about it before I met her. Our Tommy had been to Chartist meetings, and they'd met there. She's a lovely person, but very outspoken. She has a confidence about her that I could only admire. I wanted to be like her."

"Why?" Tam asked gently.

"Because she is so knowledgeable. She always has good points to argue with. And what she said made sense. I mean, why should we be treated with no respect just because we don't have money to eat meat every day or live in a big fancy house? I've been looking after our family since I was nine years old. That doesn't mean I'm worthless and don't deserve any rights. Quite the opposite, in fact."

Tam smiled. "I love that you're so passionate about suffrage. If only more people were!"

Nell blushed and looked away.

"I mean, I mean ... when I say passionate ..." Tam stammered.

Nell didn't know where to look. Luckily, they were distracted by the noise from the march. It was getting louder and could only be a few streets away now, but it was hard to judge which direction the chants were coming from.

Tam looked around. "Come, this way," he said as he pulled Nell into the next street. They stood there, looking around. "There!" He pointed down the street to the junction with the main road. They were about five yards away. A sea of dull brown and grey coats, some carrying placards, some carrying sticks or torches, passed by. They could clearly hear the chanting.

Nell looked up at Tam and smiled. "Come on, then!" They walked towards the main road.

"Right then, everybody ready?"

Luke nodded reluctantly. He stood by the doorway, as far away from Ainsworth as he could get. It just wasn't fun anymore. He'd tried to stop working for them, just not turn up, but Jackie Ainsworth had come looking for him and threatened to break both his legs. In the beginning, he'd just been helping old Mr. Ainsworth move things, run errands. He'd load up carts, move building supplies, sometimes vegetables that they'd got cheap, do some petty stealing, nothing so serious. But now he was involved in break-ins and scams. He didn't really care about what happened to the victims. After all, they were never harmed, just their possessions or money taken, and they were all quite well-off and thus deserved to part with some money. Rather, he was scared of getting caught, of being sent to gaol, being locked up. He just couldn't imagine how he'd survive being locked in a tiny room all day and all night.

Right now, until he could work out what to do, he had no choice. He just had to make sure he didn't get caught. Today Ainsworth wanted him and a few other children to pick pockets during the march this afternoon. Luke hated pickpocketing. He preferred less hands-on jobs, preferably when the person he was stealing from wasn't present. Plus it was hard work – you had to pick a lot of pockets to get lucky, and there was a big chance of getting caught. Perhaps he could rob a shop or something and pretend he got the money from pickpocketing. But he didn't know how to do that alone without getting caught either.

Edward Ainsworth opened the door, but as Luke moved to go through it, he barred his arm across Luke's chest.

"Not so fast," he said, closing the door after the others had left. "I know you don't want to do this. I can see it in your face."

Luke shrugged.

"You're a difficult one. And do you know what we do with difficult ones?"

"Break both their legs?"

"Ah, you're a comedian too. No, son. I need you to work for me. So if you don't, I'll have our Jackie break your brother's legs instead. He'll never walk again. Bill, is it?"

Luke's heart raced. He knew enough about Ainsworth to know he followed out his threats. "No! You leave my brother alone. He's done nothing!"

Ainsworth grinned and rubbed his hands. "Ah, so you do have feelings. I was beginning to wonder."

Luke gritted his teeth and said nothing.

"And how about your sister? Pretty one, she is. I think our Jackie's a bit keen on her. I'm a bit keen on her myself."

Luke remained silent.

"No?" Ainsworth bent down slightly so he was level with Luke's face. "No?" he said, searching Luke's expression for any signs of feeling. "Just your brother, then?"

Luke flew at Ainsworth, but the old man was too quick and grabbed Luke's arms before he could do any damage.

"Well then," Ainsworth said, letting go of one arm and quickly twisting the other one behind Luke's back. "I'll tell you what we'll do." He put his face so close to Luke's that he could feel the old man's stubble and smell his rotting teeth. Luke squeezed his eyes shut tight. "You bring in enough pennies today and we'll let your Bill keep his legs intact for a little while longer." He released Luke, shoving him to the floor. "Now just remember. It's your choice and your consequence." He opened the door, and Luke scrambled up and ran out. The light blinded him slightly, but he kept going until he got a few streets away. He leaned against a wall while he got his breath back. How much longer was it going to be before his luck ran out?

Luke walked towards the march. He could hear the noise from several streets away and took a detour. Better he didn't start working where all the other kids were – that would be a recipe for disaster. He rounded the corner and waited. The legions of men and women shouting and waving placards and batons were heading quickly towards him. He ran across the road and slipped into the watching crowd. Pushing roughly past a few bystanders, he quickly slipped his hand into a few pockets, plying whatever he found into his own large jacket pockets without even looking. From what he could feel, he wasn't getting lucky. Gold watches were the best to steal but also the hardest to unbutton, and short of yanking them off a fellow and running for all he was worth, Luke wasn't going to succeed with that.

As the rabble made their way down the street, Luke made his way through the crowd. This was ridiculous, he thought. How was he supposed to bring in enough to satisfy Ainsworth today? This was a really stupid idea. Most of the people watching the march were just like the people taking part in the march – working class, who didn't have many pennies in their pockets. Fine, it was the day after pay day, but even so. An audience of richer people would have got the job done a lot faster.

Deciding to take a break, find a quiet corner and see what he'd managed to steal, Luke looked up across the street and saw some of the other kids weaving in and out of the crowds. One was even walking along in the march, and Luke clearly saw him lift the back of a man's jacket. Guaranteed to get the police involved, that is! Luke thought. Right in front of a huge crowd? Was the boy mad? Sure enough, he saw another man grab the boy from behind and cuff his ears. At the same time, a whistle was blown, and two policemen ran to the opposite side of the road from Luke and grabbed two more kids. Luke stood still, back against a wall, and put his hands in his pockets. He wasn't going to attract attention to himself by moving around right now.

As he stood there, eyes on the crowd, he spotted a familiar face. Nell! What was she doing here? It would be really bad luck now if she spotted him. He tried to look away and pull his hat down over his eyes – people could always sense when you were staring at them, Ainsworth had taught him – but something kept dragging his eyes back. She was standing there with Tam. He couldn't see Bill at all. Strange. The three of them were usually together, so that must mean Bill was close by somewhere. But that wasn't what caught his eye. The crowd was quite thick where they were standing, and as people pushed past them, they bumped Nell closer to Tam. They were standing too close now, Luke thought. She was being ridiculous, smiling up at him like that.

A shout went up from the middle of the march, and Luke snapped his head back. There was a scuffle, then someone else waded in with a baton. A crowd formed around the fighters – some trying to stop them, others joining in. The crowd got pushed back and surged right in Nell and Tam's direction. He heard shrieks and saw people being pushed up against the wall. Some were being trampled on underfoot. He looked around and couldn't see Nell or Tam. He had to make a split-second decision – go and try and help those being trampled on in case one of them was his sister? Or disappear and dump off his takings with Ainsworth before the police came and rounded them all up? Basically, it boiled down to saving his sister (if she was even there – she could already be in safety) and possibly getting caught with stolen goods, or saving his brother from a mauling by Ainsworth.

Within seconds, Luke wound his way out of the crowd and started to cross the road. Part of the march had moved on, but all hell was breaking loose in this part of the street. He was about to cross over and make his way back to Ainsworth's cellar to empty his pockets when he spotted an elderly man dressed in a top hat and burgundy velvet jacket in front of him. Luke almost rubbed his hands in glee. Easy pickings! he thought as he slipped silently past the man, withdrawing a fat leather wallet and tucking it up his sleeve.

Luke turned down a side street and heard someone running behind him. Keeping calm, he continued walking, hoping they were not running after him. He was sure he could get away anyway, even if they were coming for him – he was fast! The footsteps got closer. They sounded youthful, feet encased in sturdy boots. Probably a foundry worker. Luke relaxed. He hadn't ripped off any young workers. No point, as many were apprenticed and therefore penniless. Yes, Ainsworth had taught him a lot about people – who were easy marks and who weren't. And when to run.

The footsteps slowed down, and he felt someone shove him from behind. "What the hell do you think you're doing?" came an angry, familiar voice. The surprise of the push made Luke drop the wallet. As he picked it up and spun around in one fast movement, he came face-to-face with Bill.

"I said, what the hell do you think you're doing?" Bill said, his eyes flashing. "I saw you take that old man's wallet. You can come with me and give it right back and apologise."

"No. Go away, Bill," Luke muttered and started to walk away. Bill ran around him and blocked his path.

"What the hell are you doing?"

"Leave me alone! You have no idea what's going on here. I have somewhere to be."

"Somewhere to be? Luke, you don't need to steal. You have a roof over your head; Aunt Jane feeds you. Why are you doing this?"

"Look," Luke took a step towards him and put his face just inches away from Bill's, "if I go back there, they will certainly arrest me and send me to gaol. There are coppers everywhere right now, and you are bringing attention to me. Is that what you want? For me to be arrested?"

Luke saw a muscle in Bill's jaw twitch.

"No. But this isn't right. You can't go around doing this, Luke."

"I have to."

"No you don't."

"You don't understand!" Luke practically shouted. "I have to go. Leave me alone." He tried to walk away, but Bill grabbed his sleeve.

"Let go!" Luke yelled and ripped his arm away violently. There was a harsh splitting sound as the sleeve came away. The two of them momentarily stopped and stared at each other with open mouths.

"Now look what you've done!" Bill said.

A bolt of heat surged up inside Luke, and he grabbed his brother, catching him off balance and ramming him into the wall.

"Leave me alone!" he hissed. He dropped his hands and walked away, but Bill's wide eyes were now etched on his brain. He started to run and didn't stop until he got to Church Wharf. He knew Bill was only trying to help him, but God, he could be annoying with his older, know-it-all, this is right, that is wrong attitude. Deep down, Luke knew his brother was only looking out for him, as he'd always done. He didn't want to see him get into trouble, but it was too late. It was too late for him now, even though he was only eleven years old. And not only that, it was now up to Luke to protect Bill from getting hurt. And Bill didn't have a clue.

Arriving at the cellar of the old building, breathless and worried, Luke almost stumbled down the steps. In the dim light, he emptied his pockets onto the table and threw the wallet towards Ainsworth, who was sat in his chair playing with a pocket watch.

"Ah, Luke. What do we have here?"

Luke stood in stony silence while Ainsworth counted the money.

"Not bad, not bad. But not great either." He looked up.

"The place is teeming with coppers," Luke said, still breathing hard. "No one in their right mind would go back out there. I saw two of the kids grabbed by the police as I left. I'm sure more were captured."

Ainsworth stared at him.

"I mean, we would have to go out somewhere else. Somewhere away from the march." He got ready to duck in case Ainsworth moved to hit him. Instead, Ainsworth smiled.

"Ahhh. Smart. Right then, we'll wait here and see who else comes back. Take a seat, Luke."

Luke sat down uneasily. Either he or Bill was going to be in trouble very shortly.

After what felt like hours, Jackie walked in through the door.

"It's chaos out there!" he said, removing his hat. He looked at Luke. "What are you doing here? Why aren't you out there?"

"Because it's chaos out there."

Jackie lunged at him, and Luke felt a sickening crack across his cheek.

"That's for being so insolent."

His cheek was on fire, but Luke refused to complain.

"Looks like quite a few of them were rounded up," he said to Ainsworth. "Coppers everywhere. I'm sure some just ran off though. Like this one here."

"I came here to leave my pickings," Luke said.

"Not much we can do about the police and those kids," Ainsworth said. "But we do need to decide what to do with this one. Should we let him off, or should we pay his brother a visit?"

"No! You can't do that!" Luke said, springing up out of his chair. "I did what you asked me. It wasn't my fault so many coppers turned up." He wagged his finger at the old man. In a flash, Jackie grabbed him and put him in a headlock. Luke went still.

"Don't you point at my father like that," he hissed.

"Now, now," Ainsworth said, slowly walking around the table. "Perhaps Luke is right. Maybe we could give you a choice now, Luke, seeing as you were good enough to come back. You haven't brought in enough pickings, certainly not enough to cover what the others would have lost ..."

"What? You didn't say I had to ..." Luke struggled, but Jackie tightened his grip. Luke started to feel like he might pass out.

"Yes, I'll be generous enough to give you a choice," said Ainsworth. "Either Jackie here can go and break one of Bill's legs, or he can break a couple of your fingers."

"Noooo!" Luke struggled again.

"Your choice."

He couldn't let them hurt Bill, he just couldn't. None of this was Bill's fault. It wasn't right. He'd got himself into this mess with Ainsworth and his thug son, so he had to take the consequence himself. And then find a way out.

"Bill?"

Luke shook his head.

"Yourself then?"

Luke nodded. Ainsworth smiled a vicious smile. "Right then, Jackie, in your own time."

Jackie released Luke's head and neck, and grabbed his left arm.

"No," Luke pleaded, tears starting to fall.

The sickening crack was accompanied seconds later by a searing pain. Luke doubled over and vomited. Standing up, he banged his other fist repeatedly against the wall as if trying to dull the pain in his hand by inducing it elsewhere. Jackie and the old man laughed.

Luke doubled over again. Suddenly, he was being pulled up by his hair, and Ainsworth placed his stinking face next to Luke's.

"When I tell you to do something, you make sure you do something." Luke nodded. He let go of Luke's hair. "Now get out! And I want you back here next Saturday, you hear."

Luke nodded and stumbled up the cellar steps. As the fresh air hit him, he gasped, tears running down his face. He looked down at his left hand. Two of his fingers stuck out at completely the wrong angle, and he couldn't move them. He'd never known such pain. He vomited again and swore not to look at his hand until someone had fixed it. He'd go to Molly. She was good with things like this.

Luke made his way slowly back up towards the parish church, then down Bank Street and over to Molly and Jem's house. It felt like a long walk with the number of times he had to lean against a wall when he started to feel dizzy and clammy, drawing strange looks from passersby. He hadn't known Ainsworth was this crazy from the beginning. He had believed everything he'd told him, especially those lies about him being a factory owner and only wanting Luke to run errands and catch rats for him. And now he was in so deep that he couldn't get out. What was he going to do?

CHAPTER 14

THE DIARY
APRIL 1848

Bill sat on the bed, shaking his head. If he was going to be honest with himself, he knew Luke was up to no good, but it was still a shock to see him actually stealing. Why? I just don't understand why? Luke was well looked after by the Booths. Why would he feel he needed to go and steal things? And why was it that nothing he or Bluey could say to Luke would make him behave any better? Bill was at a complete loss. If Luke carried on like this, he was going to end up in gaol. But what about all the people he'd stolen from? How must they be feeling? Work your fingers to the bone and then have your pay stolen? How were they going to even eat that week? Did Luke ever think about that?

He looked down at the suitcase sitting next to the bed and gave it a kick. Ainsworth had given him a real scare last week. There was no way he was going to go asking any more questions after that threat. But what if the answers to all his questions were in this suitcase? Ainsworth wouldn't have any idea that Bill was reading those documents.

Bill glanced into the living room and then out the kitchen window into the yard. Only Aunt Jane was home now. He bent down and lifted the lid. Rummaging around, he found one of the leather-bound books and pulled it out. He ran his fingers over the cover. The tan leather was worn and cracked, and it gave off an earthy, musty smell. Opening it up, he saw the pages were yellowed and beginning to come apart where they had been creased. The writing, sometimes smudged, was long and loopy, letters bumping into others above and below them. Bill sighed. His reading ability still wasn't anywhere near great yet, and this handwriting was so hard to read, but he knew if he wanted answers, he had to check everything. Sitting back on his bed, his fingers traced the first entry: March 28, 1793. The day his father was born. This was going to take forever.

It had taken Bill the best part of nine months to get this far through the diary, and the exercise had felt quite laboured and pointless. Christmas was nearly upon him and frustratingly, he'd discovered absolutely nothing of interest. It didn't help that he was too fearful of it getting lost or discovered if he took it back to his lodgings, so he kept it safely in the suitcase, pushing it far under his bed before leaving Bluey's each Monday morning. Consequently, he had much less time to read through it than he would have liked, and felt it was taking him forever. It also didn't help that his granddad's life seemed so utterly, utterly dull. He rarely wrote about his feelings on anything. One child was born after another, and Granddad merely reported aspects of the christenings, that his wife was championing along after each birth, visiting some local politicians, discussing aspects of building with them, particularly windows and window material (Granddad had been a glazier by trade). The only exciting entry Bill had found so far was a mention of working with a Luke Booth, whom Bill guessed was Bluey's father. Several times Bill had to ask Tam to come round and decipher a word or two – fearful of even taking the diary out of the house.

Nine months of reading the diary two evenings a week and all Bill had learned was that their grandfather must have been a really boring person. Nothing seemed to have ever happened in his life, and reading his diary quite often made Bill fall asleep. It would have been fascinating to read about Manchester back in the late eighteenth century, when farmland was starting to be claimed and all the factories and housing starting to be built. It must have been a completely different life back then, he thought. But none of that was really documented here. Bill felt ready to give up. He'd push on just a bit longer, then he'd start on the other diary.

"26 May 1798. He had finally found me," Bill began slowly on a Sunday evening just before Christmas. "I had been wondering when this day would happen. I did not think he would find me in Manchester. I sent him away."

Who is 'he'? Bill wondered. He would have remembered if Granddad had written about someone looking for him.

He looked at the next entry.

"27 May 1798. He was there again when I came home, standing outside my front door in the rain. I told him to leave. He shouted that his mother had died and that he had some questions for me. He pleaded with me. He was only a child. But I couldn't let him in the house, I just couldn't.

"I dreamed a lot that night. Elsie said I'd been so restless. I dreamed about Mary and about our John. And the court case. My father's face when he found out and sent me away. Far away to Manchester. With a bride. I don't know who I felt most sorry for – Mary or Elsie."

Bill reread the passage. Who was Mary? Granddad's brother was called John, but his wife wasn't Mary. Wait – did Granddad want to marry Mary but was sent away to marry Elsie, Bill's grandmother? Why would he be sent away for wanting to be with Mary? Was she a bad person? Or perhaps he had a child with her? Could this be the half brother Bill had been looking for?

Bill looked down at the yellow parchment again and tried reading fast, but he couldn't get it to make sense, so he slowed down again, frustrated.

"It wasn't that I hadn't ever thought about him – Edward, but I'd been so young back then. Granted, I was nineteen, but I'd had little experience of life. And after Mary taking John to court over their bastard child ..."

Edward? Was this him? Granddad's child? But Mary had the child with Grandad's brother. Then there was no half brother. Bill was confused. His finger traced the next line.

"I regret to this day my relationship with Mary Ainsworth. And the child it produced, not long after John's own child. At least he'd had the grace to acknowledge his son. I just could not acknowledge mine or the irreparable damage I'd done to the relationship with my brother, and especially my father."

What? Bill dropped the diary. So Granddad did have a son with a Mary Ainsworth. Edward. Edward Ainsworth. I knew it! But what about all the other stuff? He looked back at the page again, rereading the entry several times.

Bill finally looked up. Granddad had a son with his brother's lover! He started to grin. Naughty Granddad! Seems this Mary Ainsworth had a thing for the Hall men, which resulted in two bastard children. But what about Edward Ainsworth? His father never acknowledged him. He received a small amount in Granddad's will while his half siblings inherited a fortune. And he apparently had a half brother whose father was Granddad's brother. Ainsworth probably grew up seeing his brother receiving attention from his father, only for himself to be rejected after he's found his own father. No wonder Ainsworth held a grudge. But to go to these lengths to extract revenge, the man was clearly mad. It was starting to dawn on Bill that knowing why Ainsworth was out to get them was probably not going to help him.

PART 3

1850–1852

The old-style apprenticeships where a boy was owned by his master for seven years came to an end. Hundreds of thousands of Irish immigrants escaping the potato famine had made their way to Lancashire. For the first time in Lancashire history, more people now lived in towns than in rural areas.

CHAPTER 15

THE FAMILY SECRET
MARCH 1850

Bill had been reading the diaries off and on for the best part of two years now. He'd finished his granddad's diary – not much more information in there unfortunately, and certainly no more mention of Edward Ainsworth. His father's diary, however, had revealed how he felt when he discovered the shares were fake, and about the "Irishman" he'd gone into business with over them. Bill wished he could talk about what he'd found to Tam and Nell, but he really didn't want them getting involved and maybe talking about it somewhere and Ainsworth overhearing. Who knew where he was and how he found out so much about their whereabouts? Besides, Nell and Tam were spending a lot of time together now without him, and Bill was feeling a bit left out.

It seemed that the Irishman had revealed exactly who he was when Robert Hall confronted him about the fake shares. His father had written, "My own brother! My own half brother, whom I knew NOTHING about. Why? How can he be so angry with ME so that he'd destroy my livelihood? I am not my father. While it's terrible that Father did not tell any of us about this man, our brother, I cannot be held accountable for that. It is not my fault this man has felt he has suffered so much because of what my father did. I would have felt sorry for him had he not tried to destroy me. But now, unfortunately, this means war!"

Bill had thought a lot about that. It must have been a complete shock to Father – losing his money and then finding out he'd been swindled by a brother he never knew he had. Bill couldn't even begin to imagine how his father felt. But from the diary entries, it was clear that his father had been determined to get back on his feet somewhere where Ainsworth couldn't find him, and maybe if he hadn't got sick, he might have achieved it.

Bill looked down at the diary. He'd almost finished it. This seemed to be the next to last entry, 3 April 1836, and it was quite short. His father had stopped writing much at that point, only one more entry, a much longer one, in November that year, just after Luke was born.

"Seven years in Bolton. Seven blasted years in this town I've been exiled to for the sake of one man. I thought I'd managed to escape him, to never once again see or hear evil personified. But no. He's been here all along, interfering in my life, working behind the scenes."

Bill took a deep breath. It was almost painful reading this. He had hoped his father had at least been free of Ainsworth. Then again, how had Ainsworth even found out where Bill was?

"Tonight Alice, my Alice, told me quite coldly that this child is not mine."

Bill gasped. Which child? Was he talking about Bill? As a chill crept over him, Bill tried to read the next part as fast as possible.

"And who do we have to blame for that?"

The entry ended there, and Bill almost tore the page turning it over so fast.

"15 November 1836 – The bastard child just lies there and screams. I never asked for this. I never asked for him. I do not want to even look at him, much less name him, for he killed my beloved Alice. And he is the bastard child of the man I despise. The man who destroyed my life, who took everything from me.

"They tell me that I must hold 'my' baby. That he needs a father. Oh, he has a father all right. A father who lies and cheats and takes whatever he wants. I wouldn't put it past him to kill. Like father, like son.

"But how can I tell anyone? How can I tell them why I won't touch the baby? He is Alice's flesh and blood after all, and the last I have of her. But he's also part him. Edward Ainsworth. Even the name invokes such rage inside me. The baby knows. He knows I hate him. That's why he won't stop screaming.

"So now I am pained to listen to that child. He will not sleep. He is amusing himself by torturing me, I'm sure. I'm forced to be a cuckold to prevent people from knowing that I let this happen to Alice and me. And Ainsworth will never know that this is his child. Not as long as I live and breathe.

"And now Emma's gone. She's done everything for us the last four weeks since the baby was born and Alice died. So much that I just had to tell her the truth. She said she'd take the baby away, far away, say it was her own. Keep him safe. But I wouldn't let her ruin her own life like that. We argued. I never meant to beat her. I was grieving. I wasn't myself. And she had to keep pushing, trying different ways to convince me to let her take the baby and keep him safe. I'd just had enough. I've never seen her so scared. Another of my big regrets. I don't think she'll ever come back."

Bill dropped the diary and watched its pages fall open at a different part of his father's life. Luke. Luke! For a second, Bill could barely even think. Not only was Luke not his brother, Luke's father was Edward Ainsworth. Bill's stomach began to spasm so much he was almost sick.

Luke's father destroyed our family. He is the reason Father lost all his money and we ended up in poverty. And Father knew!

Bill stood and paced up and down the kitchen, hands on his head. Luke. Ainsworth was Luke's father! Did Ainsworth know? Did Jem know? He sat back down on his bed, picked up the diary and slung it across the room. It hit the wall with a slap, and several pages came away from the binding.

I should throw it on the fire! he thought. Wait – was that why Jem wanted the whole suitcase and its contents destroyed? Could that be what he read, the reaction that Nell witnessed all those years ago? Finding out that Luke wasn't their brother? Even worse, finding out who Luke's real father was? Maybe Jem was right after all. Maybe it was better if no one knew about this. Then again, Luke had a right to know who his father was. Bill sat and pondered this. If it was he who had a different father, would he really want to know? Would it really make any difference? He'd have grown up thinking he knew who his parents were, that he was fully related to all his siblings. Knowing any different would surely just upset him. It would feel like his whole life had been a lie, that he wasn't who he thought he was. Bill sighed. No, it wouldn't do any good telling Luke, or even Nell and Tam. This was something he needed to keep to himself. Especially when Luke's real father was someone so evil. Bill stood up and went to go and pick up the diary. He pulled out the last two entries, crumpled them up and threw them on the fire. As he watched the flames lick at them and the yellow parchment curl, blacken and diminish, Bill's heart felt heavy with the awful secret he now had to carry.

CHAPTER 16

THE WEDDING
MAY 1850

Bill knew his sister had been planning for and looking forward to this day for a long time. Unlike most people, who took an hour off work during the week and headed to the church in their Sunday best to get married, Nell had booked her wedding on a Sunday. To be honest, Bill thought that was mainly so Tommy could come down from Salford to attend. He knew Nell had become close to Tommy when she lived in Manchester and probably couldn't imagine him not being there, as much as she couldn't imagine Bill not being there. Just think. All the Hall siblings in one place again. Well, all except their older sister Emma. There was a rumour that she was back living in Bolton again, but she'd never been in touch. Bill didn't think he'd even recognise her if he walked past her in the street now – it had been so long since she'd been part of their family.

Bill thought his sister was going a bit over the top for this wedding – getting a new dress made by Jenny Booth just to get married in when she already had so many fine clothes given to her by their aunts not so long ago. Nell had certainly learned some fine habits while she'd been living in Manchester, and she wanted everything just so. He couldn't begrudge his sister her happiness on this day though. She was one of the nicest, smartest women he had ever met. And it was clear that she and his best friend, Tam Green, loved each other. They were a great match. It had taken him a while to accept that. He still longed for the days when it was just the three of them, good friends talking about politics and religion, going to temperance meetings, Tam teaching them both to read and write. How could he not have seen his best friend and his sister falling in love during the past year, right under his nose?

Bill whistled, hands in his pockets, as he made his way over to the parish church with the Booths. He'd stayed over last night after helping Nell with her wedding preparations. The Booths' house on Slater Street still felt like home to him, even though he only stayed Saturday and Sunday evenings now. He had less than two years left on his apprenticeship, although he couldn't imagine them letting him come and live back there permanently once he'd finished. Jenny was married now, and her own family was living there, and Luke was still there – sometimes. Bill would probably just stay in his lodgings until he found himself a wife and a house. Although the thought of moving out from the Booths' permanently made Bill feel sad, so he tried not to think about it.

"It'll be you next then, sonny!" Bluey playfully cuffed at Bill's ear as they walked along, a large group of adults and children amongst them.

Bill ducked out of the way and laughed. "Not a chance!" he said.

Bluey let out a loud laugh. "I'll remind you you said that."

They reached the church and took a seat inside on the bride's side, the last person in their row closing the small door to their dark wooden pew. Bill looked around. A second-storey row of pews up to the left, framed by stone archways and a dark wooden balcony, looked down on them. Level with this row and in front of him was a large stained-glass window. A few rays of light were coming in through the coloured panes and making red and blue patterns on the dark wooden floor. The aisle was narrow, and the pale stone walls with their pointed archways gave a claustrophobic feeling, even though the church was quite large. Looking at the light panes of glass for a tad too long, Bill's eyes became unaccustomed to the gloom around him. The lit candles on their iron stands, bolted to the walls and the pulpit, their flames shielded with frosted glass globes, did very little to light up the church's interior or give a feeling of warmth. Their parish church, the church where Bill himself had been christened and Jem married, was nowhere near as ornate and spectacular as the one which had held his father's funeral and taken Bill's breath away.

The church bells started ringing, and Bill turned around in his seat to see Nell being walked up the aisle by their Jem. He knew she'd asked Jem to give her away out of politeness and etiquette, probably preferring Tommy or himself. Jem should really have been last choice. But it was probably the best thing to do, seeing Jem's proud, beaming face. Bill had to admit that Nell, always thoughtful of others, had probably made the right decision to keep the peace. He just hated the fact that they all had to pander to Jem and make sure they didn't upset him so he wouldn't go off on one of his drinking binges again. Surely, the man could be stronger than that?

Watching Nell walk past him, Bill had to admit that his sister looked lovely today and was glowing with happiness. He turned and grinned at his brother Luke sitting next to him, and then turned back to take in his sister. Jenny had done her proud with that dress. It was a lovely blue colour, not too fussy and fancy – nothing that she couldn't wear on a normal Sunday – with a pleated panel at the chest and a small ribbon. It looked like she had a crinoline underneath to make the skirt stand out a bit. A darker blue shawl draped around her shoulders, and a matching hat made from the same material as the dress perched on top of her blond hair instead of her usual grey bonnet. Nell loved blue, and it suited her, brought out the colour of her eyes.

As they reached the front of the church where Tam was standing, Nell turned round to smile at her fiancé with such a look of love that Bill's heart leapt. How he wished he could find someone who looked at him like that. But on the other hand, he couldn't marry until he'd finished his apprenticeship. How tired he was of having to think about that. It was like his life was on hold until he was twenty-one, so there was no point even thinking about courting for another few years. No wonder they had stopped that form of apprenticeship a few years ago. He just wished he'd been able to be apprenticed under the new system. He picked up the tattered hymn book in front of him and turned the pages, reading while the clergyman, church ushers and parish clerk did their jobs.

Bill looked up when the ceremony was over. He'd been so engrossed in the black printed words on the yellowing tattered paper that he'd missed most of the ceremony. Now Nell and Tam were signing their names. The congregation applauded and called out well wishes as Nell and Tam walked back up the aisle together and out of the church, trying to keep their eyes straight ahead and trying not to break into big smiles –

a feat impossible for Tam, of course, his eyes crinkling up immediately. Bill thought that as much as Tam pretended that the ceremony and fuss was all for his new bride, you couldn't help but see he was extremely happy and proud to be exactly where he was right then.

Outside, Bill managed to get near his sister for a few seconds, kissing her on the cheek and hugging Tam before being dragged away by others who wanted their chance to congratulate the happy couple personally. Outside the church, the flat stone-flagged ground was raised up above some of the nearby house roofs. It was a viewpoint from which you could see quite a bit of the east side of the town – several tall red brick chimneys belching out their thin grey smoke, the bleach works leaving ugly gaping gashes of foul-smelling, discoloured reservoirs, and out in the distance, the farms stretching out with their cattle or sheep grazing – small light dots punctuating the hillside.

Bill wandered over to the far side of the graveyard, where it was a bit quieter. He was happy to have some time alone. Nothing was ever going to be the same again. Nell and Tam had each other now, and Bill felt like an intruder sometimes. First it had been Bill and Nell, then Bill and Tam. He was close to both of them and never imagined they would ever become closer to each other than they were to him. Of course, it was a good thing too. Imagine if Nell had married someone miserable, or if Tam had married someone who took up all his time and they never got to see him anymore. Bill was indeed lucky that his sister had married his best friend, but he was also a little sad because it signified the end of an era. He'd be left to read and think about politics himself while they brought up lots of children.

He heard a shout and stood up. Jem was waving him over. Guests were leaving the church and heading to Nell and Tam's new home on Back Barlow Row. Of course, Nell had managed to organise everything in the short month they'd been engaged, from the church, her new dress and renting a house. They'd received the keys last week, and Bill and Molly had been round there in the evenings, cleaning it out and fixing furniture to make it homely for their first night. Bill joined the small crowd, acknowledging Tommy and shaking hands with Tommy's wife, Bella, for the first time. Tommy even had two children now: six-year-old Janey and two-year-old Nancy. They were strangers to Bill

– even Tommy, whom he'd only seen once, nine years ago now, since he'd left home.

Once inside the house, many of the guests unloaded their baskets of bread and small cuts of meat wrapped in muslin cloth while Nell produced the buns she had baked herself, having saved up for the ingredients for quite a while. The pitchers of lemonade that Bill had helped her make the night before were produced, and the celebrations began. Bill thought it was funny that, while there was no alcohol at all, and several guests complained about that, everyone seemed to be as boisterous and jovial as if they had been drinking. Bluey, Tommy, Tam's father and Jem had all made speeches, Tommy's being by far the best and most entertaining, in which he took out a whole trousseau commissioned by their aunts and sewn by himself. Everyone went to coo over the expertly sewn baby clothing, embroidered pillowcases and a patchwork quilt large enough to fit a double bed.

After the speeches, Bill went to find Tommy. Everything that Nell had said about the two of them being so alike had made an impression, and Bill wanted to judge for himself. Besides, he also wanted to talk to the amazing Bella, as Nell called her, to see if everything Nell had said was true. He found Tommy in the kitchen talking with Tam and one of the neighbours – Mr. Thompson – on politics and the failure of the petition to Parliament. He looked up as Bill entered.

"Ah, Bill! It's been a long time," he said. "You're all grown up now. I hear you're a Chartist too." He winked.

Bill smiled. "Well, I'm not sure if I'd go that far, but yes, it definitely interests me. Why wouldn't it!"

Tommy smiled.

"You took part in the march a few years back," Tam said. "I'd say that makes you a Chartist!"

"You did?" Tommy asked. "I'm impressed! Many people just talk but don't actually do anything to change their situation. Not like you, eh?" He tapped Bill on the chest.

"Well, that's all I did," he said shyly. "Shame it didn't help anything."

"You've also been helping me with pamphlets."

"Yes, Tam's been telling me about that," said Tommy. "I'm certainly impressed, little brother!"

"It's not much," said Bill. "It's not like I'm helping write anything I'm going to risk getting in trouble for."

Tommy smiled and took a sip from his glass.

"So how are you doing? How's the apprenticeship going? Do you like the work?"

Tam and Mr. Thompson started to drift away.

"It's good," Bill said. "Only two years left now and I'll be able to get a decent job. I have to say, I'm so grateful to our Jem."

"Jem? Why?"

"He paid for the whole thing. Otherwise, I'd still be working in the mill."

"What?" Tommy asked, laughing. "No, he didn't. The aunts did. Jem no more paid for yours than he did for mine. Why would you think that?"

"He told me he did," Bill said indignantly.

"Ah well, you can't believe everything he says, especially not after he's had a drink . . . or seven."

"But why would he . . . ?" Bill started to think back. Had Jem really said anything, or had Bill just assumed? Then again, why would he lead Bill to believe that he'd paid for everything? Bill had felt indebted to him. Well, no more! He turned round and saw Jem standing by the door and glared at him.

"I hear you read," Tommy said. "What do you think about this?" He pulled a paper out of his pocket and showed Bill. "I know the Chartists have all but disappeared now after their last failure, but Parliament is coming under pressure now to do something about representing the working class. It's not like the landowners can control us all on rural farms anymore. There are too many of us in the towns and cities, and if it wasn't for us, there would be very little manufacturing."

"Gladstone certainly does seem to talk sense," Bill said, looking down at the paper.

"That's what I think. The Peelites would stand us far better than the Conservatives."

"But how would they get in if we're not allowed to vote?" Bill wondered.

The two engaged in an intense conversation on the matter. They didn't even notice Luke walk up and stand next to them until he pulled at Bill's arm.

"I'm going," he hissed.

"What? Wait," said Bill. "Are you going home? Shall I come with you?"

"You don't have to. I'm just tired. I just want to go home and sleep."

"All right. I'll be home in a bit, then."

Luke grunted and looked up at Tommy. "So you're the brother I've never met."

Tommy's face turned red. "It's not because I didn't want to," he said. "I really wanted to see you grow up, but circumstances . . ."

"Doesn't matter," Luke said, turning away.

"See you later, then." Bill put his arm around his little brother's shoulders, but Luke just ducked and pulled away.

"What's wrong with you?"

"Nothing."

"You're even more grumpy than usual."

Luke walked away. Bill sighed.

Who knows what he's thinking? Bill thought. He wished he knew. Luke was either in trouble, or he was fine. Problem was Luke acted the same no matter what was going on inside his head.

"Is he all right?" Tommy asked.

"He's just being Luke. I don't know if he's really all right, and I don't know what to do about it."

Tommy nodded. At that moment, Nell joined them and asked Bill to go and find the remaining bottles of lemonade because they were running out. After that, he got caught up talking to the Taylors. He didn't get another chance to talk with Tommy.

It was fairly late when he arrived home with Bluey and Aunt Jane. Luke was lying in bed but obviously not sleeping.

"Have you just been lying here?"

"Couldn't sleep."

Bill took off his shoes and outer clothing and crawled into bed next to his brother.

"You know what I found out from Tommy? Jem didn't pay for my apprenticeship after all! He made me believe he did, and made me feel indebted to him, when all the time it was our aunts that paid. Why would Jem do that? Why would he be so sneaky? Did he think I wouldn't find out?"

Luke sat up in bed. "Who the hell cares who paid for it?" he practically yelled. "Really? Is that the biggest problem you have right now? Who paid for your apprenticeship? It was paid for, and nobody asked you to do a damned thing in return. No one is paying for me to learn anything."

Bill went quiet. Was that what the problem was? Luke felt like no one was doing anything for him? He didn't know quite what to say. He was already feeling guilty about what he'd read in the diary. Perhaps the aunts had known about Luke's real father and that was why they wouldn't help him? It was so unjust. Luke had been ignored by Father ever since he was a baby. How was Bill going to be able to put things right?

CHAPTER 17

HEAD OVER HEELS
AUGUST 1850

"You!" Bill, who had one hand on Joe Walker's front door and was about to push it open, swung round to make sure the owner of the voice wasn't addressing him.

"I say, you there!"

Bill's hand dropped as the owner of the voice took a step closer.

"Are you deaf?"

Bill stared. A slightly built girl – well, maybe not a girl, Bill thought, she's probably around my age – stood just a few paces from him. Her arms were crossed and her brows furrowed. Bill looked around.

"You mean me?"

"Of course I mean you! Who else would I mean?"

Bill looked closer at her. He almost towered over her, and he wasn't so tall himself. Her grey dress was patched and quite dirty along the hem. Her knitted black shawl had holes in it, but it was her face that he noticed most. Black hair with the palest creamy-white skin he had ever seen. And not a single blemish, not even a streak of coal dust or oil. The contrast was mesmerising. He racked his brain. Did he know her from somewhere? He didn't know many girls. Even Joe's sister or Jenny Booth's friends he wasn't so familiar with. He didn't usually know what to say to them.

The girl took another step forwards and prodded Bill in the chest.

"You tell your brother to stay away from my sister!"

"What? Which brother? Who's your sister?" Surely, she must be talking about Luke. But Luke was only thirteen. His other brothers were married. It didn't make any sense.

She dropped her hand and glared at him. Those eyes! He would have certainly remembered someone with such pale brown eyes with golden flecks in them. Eyes that seemed to emit sparks.

"Sammy. Your brother Sammy!" she almost shouted. "How many brothers do you have that go round harassing young girls? My sister is only fifteen, for heaven's sake."

It suddenly dawned on Bill who she meant, and started to smile. This made the girl's brows furrow and her eyes spark even more.

"Is this funny to you?"

"I'm sorry," said Bill. "I think you may have got the wrong man. My name's Bill."

"Bill Walker?"

"No, Bill Hall. You mean Sammy Walker?" He started smiling again. "I'm not his brother, Joe. Joe lodges here, but I'm just calling on him."

"Oh." The girl's frown disappeared, and she momentarily looked down at her feet before taking a deep breath and folding her arms again.

"Then if you wouldn't mind giving Joe that message, just so I don't repeat myself."

Bill nodded.

"Right so." She turned to leave, then turned back to Bill, opened her mouth, closed it again and then strode off. Bill grinned, looked back at Joe's front door, then back down the street.

"Wait!" He started running to catch up with the girl. She could certainly walk fast!

"Wait, miss," he said as he reached her just past the corner of the street. The girl stopped and turned around.

"You again?"

"Well, I, er ..." he began.

She looked up at him, eyebrows raised, hands on hips. "Did you want something?"

"Mmm, yes. I, er, need to tell Joe which sister his brother needs to stay away from. I mean, in case there are more than one. Not more than one of your sisters, that is." Bill winced. He really needed to practise talking to girls. He wasn't like Joe or Jimmy Taylor. They never seemed to have a problem. "Just be yourself," Joe would say. But he couldn't.

The girl let her arms drop. "Maggie," she said. "My sister's name is Maggie. Maggie Fleming."

"And you are?"

"Betsy."

"Then I'll do what I can, Betsy." She nodded, and Bill got the impression that she expected nothing less.. She started to walk away, more slowly this time. Bill caught her up again.

"May I walk you home?" he asked. "After all, you came all this way." He gave a quick smile and could feel himself sweating. He hoped his face wasn't red.

"Thanks, but I live just there." She pointed over at a house on the next street, and Bill marked that her voice was a little softer.

"Then I'll leave you to it." Bill gave a short bow, smiled and turned away. Idiot! he told himself. She probably thinks you're really stupid now. You don't bow to people. Who bows to people in the street? But as he turned and looked behind him, he saw Betsy was still sanding there, watching him walk away.

"Where have you been?" Joe asked as he answered the door. "I thought I saw you there, and then suddenly you weren't."

"I was talking to someone who gave me a message for you."

"Me? Who? What message?"

"She said to warn your Sammy off her sister. Apparently, he's been harassing some girl."

"Oh no. Not again. We'll go over and have a word with him on the way to Jimmy's. He might be at home with Uncle Robert. Then again, he might be anywhere. You know what younger brothers are like." Bill rolled his eyes and followed his friend.

It had been two weeks since he'd seen Betsy. He was walking up Newport Street on his way to see Tam at the Temperance Hotel, as he usually did on a Saturday afternoon after work, when he spotted her. She was waiting outside a door farther down the street, so he decided to walk up to her and say hello.

She saw him before he even got close, grinned and waved. As Bill waved back, he watched her look up at a window, wrap her shawl tighter around her and walk over to him.

"Hello, Bill Hall." She smiled.

"Hello, Betsy Fleming."

She burst out laughing and shuffled from one foot to the other. "What are you doing here, then?"

"I'm meeting my brother-in-law," said Bill. "We usually meet most Saturdays, and well, Sundays too. He has this reading class, and I've been learning to read, so ..."

"You read?" she said. "Blimey. What else do you do?"

Bill heard a shout from one of the windows above where Betsy had been waiting. They both turned around and looked up.

"Is that for you?" he asked.

"Come," said Betsy, taking his arm and starting to run. Bill followed her automatically, weaving their way through the crowded market street and not stopping until they rounded the corner. Breathless and giggling, they stood and waited until they got their breath back.

"What was all that about?" Bill asked.

"Oh," Betsy waved her arm dismissively, "I was supposed to buy some medicine for me Mam. She's sick. But I've decided against it now."

Bill stopped and looked at her. "Medicine? But there was nowhere there to buy medicine."

"Potcheen," said Betsy. "She says it's medicinal, but I think that's why she's sick. She doesn't need more of it, in my opinion, but we do all need food instead."

Bill swallowed. "That must be hard on you if she's drinking so much she's making herself sick."

Betsy stared at him, almost without blinking, Bill noted. She was starting to make him uncomfortable.

"Yes, well, doesn't everybody drink?" Her tone had become hard again.

"Not me," Bill said quietly. "And I know a lot of others that don't. But I also know some that do drink, a lot, and I see what it does to their families. Sometimes things get better, but then they get worse again."

"You don't drink?" she said slowly. "So you read, and you don't drink?"

Bill smiled and looked down at his feet. "I just want a better life for myself than I had growing up," he said. "And I think not drinking and getting educated are the only things that are going to help me."

Betsy sucked in her cheeks, then let out a sigh. "Personally, after seeing me Mam like she is, not that me Pa is exactly teetotal, I've sworn to never touch the stuff. But it just seems like everyone else does. People are going to think I'm strange if I say no to an ale."

Bill smiled. "You should come to a temperance meeting with us, then."

"Well, I don't know if I'd go that far . . ."

Bill looked at her and tilted his head to one side. "You could meet our Nell, my sister. And Tam, her husband. They don't drink. And they're really nice. They won't think you're strange."

Betsy considered this for a moment, and Bill watched her twist her mouth one way and then the other.

"It might be nice," she conceded.

Bill smiled.

"It's our older brother who drinks," he said. "Just now, he seems to be doing fine, but he's lost his job so many times, and he's unreliable. I know it's not the same as what you're going through with your mother though, because we don't have to live with Jem. We can ignore him sometimes."

Betsy looked down at her hands, twisting her fingers backwards and forwards. "Makes me feel like I'm the parent most of the time. Mam needs looking after all the time now. And Pa is completely unreliable. Not that he drinks all the time, but he disappears, or he doesn't work for a few days. If I didn't steal money from Mam's purse to buy us bread, we'd all starve."

Bill just wanted to put his arms around Betsy and tell her it was all going to be all right. But firstly, she might hit him, and secondly, he didn't know if it would be for her. He wanted to make it all better, make her situation better, more stable, but he'd also wanted to do that for Nell and Luke several years ago, and he still remembered that same helpless feeling. That he couldn't get his siblings out of their dire situation, and that he so hated their lives being left up to Jem. He had only been nine years old back then, but now at nineteen, he wasn't in any better a place to help anyone. It would be another eighteen months before he would be his own man, free from his apprenticeship and free to start working and earning a wage. Money. That's what helped all situations. And education – that was the only way of being able to earn a decent wage.

He sighed and looked at Betsy. He didn't know what it was about her, but he just wanted to save her. And this was only the second time he'd ever met her. She looked up at him with those pale brown eyes with the golden flecks, and his stomach lurched.

"Why don't you come with me to meet our Tam?" he asked. "I usually walk back with him after the lesson, and we buy some pies on the way, take them home to Nell and spend a few hours there. Maybe you can take an afternoon off from being the parent, take your mind off your troubles for a few hours. I'm sure you deserve it."

Betsy looked at him. Then she looked back towards Newport Street and sighed. "That sounds like a wonderful idea. But I don't know if I should leave my sister and brother all day without any food. I'm holding the only money we have until Pa turns up at some point today with his wage. But when that will be, I don't know. He could be all happy or he could be sitting in a public house right now with his friends."

"Then we'll go and buy some bread, take it back and run!" Bill said. Betsy laughed.

"Well, Mam would kill me anyway for not bring her the potcheen, so it's not like I'm going to be in any more trouble than I already am."

"Maybe your sister could look after your brothers just for one afternoon," he said. "Didn't you say she's fifteen? How old are your brothers?"

"Maggie?" Betsy said. "Oh, but she's a bit soft in the head. She's very sweet but completely useless. It's like she's seven years old sometimes. My brothers are nine and ten."

"Well then," Bill said, "your brothers can look after themselves. I was orphaned at nine and before then, me, Nell and our Luke, who was just a baby, basically had to look after ourselves. It didn't hurt us."

He grinned.

"Oh, I'm so sorry." Betsy's hand flew to her mouth. "That must have been really hard."

"It didn't seem so much harder than before we were orphaned," Bill said. "Mother died when I was about five, and Father had been sick for a long time. The hardest was when we were separated. Nell was sent to Manchester to work, but a really kind relative – well, not really a relative, but of sorts – took me and our Luke in."

"I can't imagine being away from our Maggie, even for a day," said Betsy. "That must have been terrible." Her eyes looked so sad that Bill felt an overwhelming feeling of wanting to kiss her. Pull yourself together, he told himself crossly. He looked up and stared over at the market.

"It was hard, but now Nell is back and married to my best friend." He smiled. "So it all worked out well in the end."

Betsy continued to look sad. "That's what I keep telling myself, that it will all be fine in the end."

"Well, at least Sammy Walker isn't harassing your Maggie anymore. That's always something," Bill said.

Betsy burst out laughing. "So true. Oh, that boy was such a pain. Thank you for helping there."

"I can't take all the credit," Bill said, smiling. "Joe was pretty hard on him. I just stood there and looked stern."

Betsy laughed again.

"Come on, then. Let's go and buy some bread to deliver, then you can take a break for a few hours. You never know, tomorrow might be better."

Betsy nodded, and they walked through the throngs of shoppers, handcarts and hawkers towards the market stalls.

"Bill!" Tam looked up from the cream-clothed table in the Temperance Hotel. "We've just finished the lesson. You're a bit late today."

"Sorry," Bill said, nodding at the man sat across from Tam and pulling out a chair for Betsy. "I was just helping Betsy run some errands."

"Pleased to meet you, Betsy," Tam said, putting out his hand. "I'm Tam."

The man across the table stood up and grabbed his hat. "I'll be seeing you, then," he said. "Got to go."

"Thanks, Dickie," Tam said, standing up to shake his hand. "You made great progress today. Same time next week?"

The man nodded and walked out the door.

"Now there's a man of few words," said Tam.

"Not like Bill," Betsy said, grinning.

"Oh really?" Tam smiled. "Chatty today, is he?" He looked across at Bill, who'd found himself a chair, and winked. Bill blushed.

"Yes," Betsy said, missing the wink. "He's been kind too."

"Yes, Bill is kind," Tam said, smiling and squeezing Bill's shoulder. "My life would certainly be less happy without Bill in it."

"Oh, give over," Bill said, blushing. Tam laughed.

"Once you get to know Tam, you'll realise he thinks everything is one big joke," Bill said, leaning towards Betsy.

"Better that than crying every day," said Tam.

"Quite," Betsy said as she turned round to scrutinise him.

Tam collected his papers together and shuffled them. "Right. We're done here, so I'm off to buy some tasty treats to take home to my beloved. Will you two be joining us?" He looked across from one to the other. Betsy blushed.

"Yes, if that's all right?" Bill said, looking directly at Betsy.

"That would be nice." Betsy smiled.

"Right then." Tam stood up. "Betsy, I'm not sure where you're from, but how familiar are you with Little Bolton?"

Betsy laughed. "Not at all. I'm from the opposite side of town."

"Well then, time for an adventure!" Tam offered Betsy his arm, and she took it, smiling at Bill.

Back at Nell and Tam's house, it seemed like they'd all been friends for years. Betsy giggled at Tam's comments and gossiped with Nell. Most of all, they seemed to appreciate her razor-sharp wit, as did he. Sometimes her daring, quick comments almost took his breath away.

He'd never met anyone like her.

Of course, the conversation inevitably turned political. Nell started talking about women's suffrage, showing Bill a leaflet that Bella had sent to them.

"Well, I don't know about any of that, and I can't read like you all can," said Betsy, "but I do hate it when people tell me I can't do something just because I'm a woman. As if that had anything to do with it. Nonsense. As women, we have to do everything."

"I completely agree," Tam said. "We say women are the fairer sex, but they have to go out and work, keep a home, be strong enough to carry babies, then birth them. And I know from my own upbringing, whatever my mother said went."

Nell started laughing. "Oh, if only you did as I tell you!"

Tam smiled.

"But seriously, Betsy," Nell continued, "I agree with you completely. Things are hard enough without having to be told we can't do something. But what I don't understand is when we're fighting for men's suffrage, why can we not fight for women at the same time? Do we have to wait for all men to get the vote before all women can vote too? That just doesn't make sense to me."

"Now that you put it like that," said Betsy, "I hadn't really thought about it before."

They carried on discussing until Bill realised what time it was. How could several hours pass so quickly? And they hadn't even eaten.

"It's past ten o'clock," he said. "Maybe Betsy and I should be getting home."

Betsy jumped and turned round to look at the clock, her hand flying to her mouth.

"How is it so late? I should have been home hours ago! They'll be wondering where I am."

"I'll walk you," Bill said. She smiled at him.

"It has been a pleasure, Betsy," Nell said, hugging her. "We hope to see you again very soon."

"That would be lovely," Betsy replied, hugging Nell back and then Tam.

They stepped out into the balmy air. It wasn't often the evenings were slightly warm. It just made the evening feel even more special.

"You all seemed to get along well," Bill said as they made their way through town.

"Your sister is so lovely," Betsy said. "And I'd never heard people say half those things before. It really made me think. Are all teetotallers like that?"

Bill laughed. "I don't know. Probably not. I'm sure some are very dull."

Betsy laughed. "Then I would very much like to spend time with the not-dull ones again!"

They carried on walking in silence until they came to the end of Betsy's street.

"This is me. Hopefully, Mam will be asleep now," she said, nervously looking up at the row of houses.

"Well, people who drink a lot often have really bad memories, so maybe you can tell her you already brought her the potcheen, and she drank it," Bill said, smiling.

"Bill Hall!" she exclaimed, lightly pushing him in the chest. "For someone who seems to be really nice all the time, you can certainly be a bit sneaky!"

Bill flinched at the prodding and grinned. "Oh, I'm not nice all the time."

"I think you are," Betsy said quietly. Bill's heart leapt, and they walked on in silence.

"Well, this is me." She stopped at the end of the row of houses.

"I could walk you to your door," said Bill.

"Ah, best not. Just in case Pa is about. I don't want him to see me coming home this late accompanied by a boy. Even if I am already seventeen," she added.

Bill nodded. "Well, good night, then, Betsy. It was lovely spending the afternoon with you."

Betsy smiled, her whole face seeming to light up, even in the dim glow of the streetlamp.

"It was lovely." She looked down at her feet.

"If you need to get away again, we'll all be at the Temperance Hall from about ten o'clock tomorrow – Nell too. So come along if you fancy a cup of tea. They serve lots of tea. They have a very big tea urn."

Betsy burst out laughing. "I'll remember that," she said. "If I fancy a cup of tea."

"Well, bye, then."

"Bye."

Bill watched her walk away and disappear down some steps a few houses away. No wonder she didn't want him to see where she lived. A cellar? Poor Betsy. Still, it couldn't be much worse than their house on Wellington Court had been.

Bill turned and began the long walk home to Bluey's. His body had never felt so light, and he couldn't stop smiling.

"So then! Tell us all about her." He felt a punch in the arm and turned round to see Tam's freckled face grinning at him. Nell pushed past someone in the crowded hall, stepped towards Bill and handed him a cup of tea.

"Who is she? When did you meet her?" she asked, eyes sparkling.

"Stop it," Bill said. "We're not courting or anything. She's just someone I was helping out."

"Ah," Tam said as Nell grabbed his shoulder and pulled him out of the way of a few people who wanted to pass. "Just helping out. You mean like I was just helping Nell out with reading right up until we married?"

Nell smirked as Bill felt his cheeks getting hot.

"I mean, I've just met her, and I don't know if she likes me," he said.

"Well, we think she's nice," Nell said, sipping at her cup. "Very opinionated, but nice. So we approve."

Bill felt a tap on his shoulder. He turned round to face a pair of golden-brown eyes.

"Betsy!" He felt his stomach flip.

"Betsy!" Tam said. "We were just talking about you. How are you, my dear?"

"I'm well, thank you," Betsy said, smiling. "Happy to know I'm approved."

Nell almost choked on her tea.

"So where's this famous tea I've been hearing about?"

"Tam and I will get you a cup," said Nell. "Come, Tam. Tam!"

As his sister and Tam disappeared into the crowd, Bill turned to Betsy.

"So great you could come. How did it go yesterday when you got home?"

"Mam was asleep. She was this morning when I left too. I told Pa as we were leaving for church this morning that I needed a break from being a nurse to Mam and a mother and father to everyone else."

"Ooo. What did he say to that?"

"He looked guilty. Said not to worry, he'd sort it all out today. Said I could have the day to myself. Even let me keep some of my wages."

Bill gave her a hug and quickly pulled away. "That's great! Good for you!"

"Yes, well, Pa can be great sometimes, when he's around, but he's usually completely unreliable. He never takes anything seriously."

Nell had made her way back and pushed a cup into Betsy's hands. "There you go."

"Thanks," Betsy said as she sipped the dark liquid. Bill realised they were all staring at her.

"Well, it's better than we have at home, that's certain," was her verdict, and they all laughed.

"Then you should come here again, just for the tea," said Tam. "I hear there's plenty to go round." He winked at her.

"So, Betsy," Nell said, "what are your plans for today?"

"Well, I was planning to go for a walk with Bill. Maybe down by the canal."

"You were?" Bill said hopefully. "I mean, yes. Sounds like a great idea. I mean . . ."

"You mean you want to abandon our plans and go with Betsy?" Tam said in mock seriousness. "Well, I don't blame you. Your sister can be a bit bossy sometimes."

"Oy!" Nell elbowed Tam in the ribs. "What my impolite husband means is that we were planning to go for a picnic, but you two are more than welcome to take the picnic basket and go yourselves. I'm feeling a bit tired anyway."

"Oh no, no," said Betsy. "That's far too generous."

"No, it's not," said Nell. "Tam, give them the basket. We'll make plans for next weekend instead."

"Well, if you're sure," said Bill.

"Quite sure!" She grinned at him. "Just drop it off later before you go home."

"Will do." Bill smiled and offered his arm to Betsy.

It didn't take them long to walk down to Church Wharf, where the canal started. They stepped down onto the towpath and started to walk alongside the water. Being led along the path in front of them was a cart horse slowly pulling an open barge stacked with sacks of coal. As they neared its pale, feathered fetlocks and its swishing tail, they climbed up the banking to go around it, Bill helping Betsy so she wouldn't trip over her impractically long skirt. They quickly passed the plodding horse and climbed back onto the towpath, giving a curt wave to the boatman, who waved back. There were a few other people walking along the path, but it was so quiet and peaceful compared to almost every other place Bill knew in town.

"I love being close to the water," Betsy said absently. "It calms me." She looked up at Bill and smiled. They'd linked arms to climb the banking, and neither had yet let go.

"I know what you mean," he said. "It's so peaceful here too. Away from all the noise."

"Heaven," Betsy agreed. "I come here whenever I can, which isn't so often. But it's days like these when it's warm, a little sunny and quiet – away from daily life – that make me feel like I can carry on, you know? No matter how bad things get, you can always find something to make you feel better for a while."

"I know what you mean," Bill said. "The place that makes me happy is the graveyard behind the parish church. It's – what?"

Betsy's peals of laughter interrupted him.

"What?" he said, smiling. "It's peaceful there."

"Depressingly peaceful," Betsy giggled. "Don't you think it's sad with all those dead bodies?"

"They're not bothering anyone," Bill said, playfully pulling Betsy's arm. "Maybe I like depressingly peaceful."

Betsy burst into another fit of giggles. Bill watched her. Her eyes were almost yellow now, when the sunlight hit them. But it was her smile that made all the difference to her face. It was like happiness radiated out of her when she smiled, and it was infectious. How could he not be happy with Betsy around?

They found a quiet place to sit and spread a rug out on the ground. Nell had packed bread, cold cuts of ham, some tomatoes and a bottle of lemonade. Bill opened the bottle, poured a glass and handed it to Betsy. Then they both delved into the basket and made their own sandwiches. Their spot overlooked the water and towpath, and the midday sun shone down on them. Bill leaned back onto his elbows and sighed. It had been a long time since he'd been this happy.

Betsy moved closer to him. "Just so you know," she said. "I do like you."

Bill's mouth dropped open, and he shot upright.

"You were saying earlier," she clarified. "You didn't know if I liked you. Well, now you know."

"Oh."

They sat in silence, watching the water. What was he supposed to say now? Of course he liked her too. But what should he say? Maybe if he didn't say anything, she'd do all the talking.

After a few minutes, Betsy turned to him. "Well?"

Bill swallowed. "Well what?"

Betsy sighed. "You're hard work. I didn't expect to have to ask the first boy to kiss me to kiss me."

Bill's heart almost stopped.

"Well, are you going to kiss me or not?"

"Oh, er ..." Bill took off his cap and twisted it in his hands. Betsy rolled her eyes.

Bill placed his hand on her back and leaned in to kiss her. Betsy's lips met his, and he felt like the ground had dropped from under him. His stomach was doing somersaults.

CHAPTER 18

LIES

NOVEMBER 1850

As Bill rounded the corner, heading deep into the woods, away from the mills and foundries, he saw her standing under their usual tree. There she was, punctual as ever. Her dark hair catching the autumn light, shining like a raven's wing, a halo of badly behaved strands frizzing out in a way that fascinated him and annoyed her. Her way of standing was so familiar to him. He still felt his heart leap every time he saw her.

"Hello there." His eyes twinkled at her, and he received that familiar lopsided smile in return. They hugged for what seemed like ages, neither wanting to let go. Their time together was always so limited and so precious.

"So how are you?" he asked gently.

"Come," Betsy said, taking his hand. "Let's go for a walk. I've something I need to tell you."

Bill had an uneasy feeling in the pit of his stomach and felt like his world was about to change abruptly. He could feel her hand trembling.

"What's wrong?" he asked. They stopped walking.

"Well," she said, "there's only one way to say this, so best get it over with." She took a deep breath as Bill's stomach plunged deeper. He closed his eyes. He wasn't ready for this.

"I'm expecting."

Bill opened his eyes. For a moment, his heart seemed to stop beating. Then a huge smile spread across his face. So she wasn't going to end it with him?

"A baby? We're going to have a baby?" He threw his arms around her. He just couldn't stop smiling. They were going to be a family! His own family!

He released her, still smiling.

"Well, I'm glad you think it's all fun because, quite frankly, I'm feeling terrible," she scowled.

Bill laughed. "You poor thing," he said, hugging her again. "Have you been sick? If I could make you feel better, I would."

Betsy's frown melted, and she began to smile too.

"I was so worried how you'd react," she said. "I was dreading telling you."

"Why?" he asked. "You have no idea how happy I am right now! We have to make plans now. Find a house, decide on a church. I can ... oh."

"Oh, what? Was that a marriage proposal? Because I have dreamed of better ones." Betsy was grinning.

"Bets," Bill said, taking her hand. "I would go down on one knee right here and now and ask you to marry me, if you could," he swallowed hard, "if you could wait a couple of years. I mean, well, more like a year and a half."

Betsy snatched her hand away. "What do you mean wait two years?" Her eyes were flashing angrily.

"I'm still only an apprentice. I'm not allowed to marry until I'm finished. Not to mention I don't get any pay – only pennies each week for food. And I can't quit because then I'll have to pay back all the costs: rent, training, clothing, food for the past five and a half years. I don't see how I can do that." He looked up at her, his eyes starting to prick. What was he going to do?

Betsy walked away and went to sit on a fallen tree trunk. Bill followed her.

"So what are we going to do?" she asked. "What am I going to tell my father?"

"I don't know," Bill said, his head in his hands. He looked up, staring ahead at a clearing in the trees.

"I know how hard it was for my sister-in-law, Molly, when she had a baby and the father refused to marry her. I promised myself I would never be that man."

"Well, now you are," Betsy said sharply.

Bill winced.

"Bets, I promise you, I would marry you tomorrow if I could. I just can't. It's beyond my control."

"So you're saying that you want me – us – to wait for two years for you? And in the meantime, what am I supposed to do?"

"One and a half years," Bill muttered. Betsy was right. How could he expect her to wait for him? Better she find another man, like Molly did, someone who could look after her and the baby. His baby. A stabbing pain shot through his chest. The thought of not being a family with Betsy and this child hurt him more than he could ever have imagined. And up until a few minutes ago, he'd been completely oblivious to all this.

"Oh well, pardon me!" Betsy said.

Bill sighed. He needed more time to think about this, work out what he was going to do, what he could do.

"Can I try and think about it?" he said. "I mean, I have no idea right now what I can possibly do to make it better, but I want to try."

Betsy looked at him, and just for a second, Bill thought he saw her shoulders relax. But then she stiffened again.

"Meet me here same time next week," she said. "Tell me then what you've come up with. I can't hold on, hoping for something that's not going to happen, Bill. I have to think of myself."

"I know, I know," he said, leaning over to hug her. He rested his head on hers and breathed in the scent of her hair. He didn't want to let go in case this was the last time he ever got to do this. Eventually, Betsy moved out of his grasp. Bill sat up.

"I have to go." She stood up. Bill nodded. He watched her disappear amongst the trees as he sat there completely alone. What was he going to do now? He could talk to Bluey, but Bluey was going to be really upset with him, especially after the same thing had happened to Molly. But he had no one else to turn to, and he had no idea how he could solve this on his own.

A week later, Bill was making his way back to their spot in the forest. His heart was a lot lighter than it had been, and he couldn't wait to tell Betsy. Bluey, after giving Bill a piece of his mind, and Aunt

Jane saying how disappointed she was in him, decided they would help. A Booth cousin who lived over on Kay Street said they would take in Betsy and the baby – they had room. If Betsy got started working in the mill after the baby was born, Aunt Jane would, as she did with Molly's children, look after the baby during the day. Bill would help out, giving as much of his measly allowance as he could to Bluey and Jane, and in return Jenny would sew up a set of baby clothes for them. And Bill had to promise to marry as soon as he was released from his apprenticeship. The first Sunday after his release, the banns would be read. Bill gladly agreed. It wouldn't be easy on any of them for the next year and a half, but now Bluey had made the impossible possible. Right at that moment, Bill felt that with love and a supportive family, he could achieve anything.

He sat on the fallen tree trunk and waited, a huge smile on his face. It had started drizzling, but Bill didn't even feel it. After a while, the smile on his face started to fade. Betsy was usually punctual. Had something happened? Perhaps she'd told her father, and he'd become really angry. Or perhaps she was sick and couldn't come? After about ten more minutes, he got up and walked towards his lodgings. Betsy lived in the next street. He'd often walked her home but left her at the corner because she didn't want anyone gossiping. Still, Bill had always stayed to watch her enter her front door safely, so he knew where she lived – in a cellar dwelling under the seventh house from the corner.

He walked down the worn grey stone steps to the cellar and knocked on the door, trying to avoid standing in the deep, rubbish-strewn puddle. This place reminded him of Wellington Court, the house he'd grown up in. The smell was similar – the rotting rubbish from the streets being washed down to their front door with every heavy rainfall. The front door itself was thoroughly rotten at the bottom, and from what Bill could see, there was only one very small window to the whole room, high up at street level.

The door was yanked open, and Bill stepped backwards.

"Bill! What are you doing here?" Jamesie Fleming looked up the steps behind Bill and back again. "Joe not with you?"

Bill tried to gather his wits. Jamesie was Betsy's father? Oh Lord, he was going to be in real trouble when Jamesie found out.

"N-no, sir," Bill stammered. "I'm-I'm here to give Betsy a message."
Jamesie cocked his head to one side. "Betsy?"

"From my sister, I mean. She knows my sister." That wasn't a complete lie, he thought.

"Ah," Jamesie said and punched Bill on the arm. "Come in, so." He opened the door wider, and Bill stepped through. He gave his eyes a little time to adjust to the poor light. Looking around the room, the first thing that struck him was that there was no fireplace. There was also no sign of the kitchen nor a bench where you could prepare food, just a long table with two small candles, their burning fat adding to the vile stench. The walls were all bare brick. Some of the bricks stuck out a little or were missing, leaving gaping holes. The floor was made up of dirt and goodness knows what else. In one corner, it was so damp that Bill could hear the drip, drip, drip of water trickling down the wall. Two double beds were the only other furniture in the room, and Bill could make out Betsy and her sister sitting there in the gloom. Apart from the opened door, the only source of light coming into the room was through the small, dirty, cracked window Bill had seen at street level. This was even worse than Wellington Court. Poor Betsy. No wonder she didn't want me to follow her home.

"It's just a temporary thing while we look for a better place," said Jamesie. "You know how it is, you can't find a place to live in this crowded town these days for love nor money." He gave a short chuckle and quickly looked down at his feet. Bill nodded.

"Bets, someone here to see you!" Jamesie shouted. Betsy, who hadn't stirred when Bill walked in, reluctantly stood up.

"What do you want?" she asked, a scowl on her face.

Bill was a little taken aback. "I, er, I have a message for you from our Nell," he said.

"I don't get any privacy in this place!" Betsy said as she tugged her shawl off its hook and angrily slung it around her shoulders. "Come on, then, let's go." She barged past Bill and up the steps.

Bill nodded at Jamesie, who smiled briefly back, then followed Betsy up the steps. Betsy was stomping down the street, and Bill had to almost run to keep up with her.

"Wait, what's wrong?" he said.

Betsy ignored him. He saw her mouth was set firm, and she was staring straight ahead. He knew he was in trouble.

"Bets? What have I done?"

"Done?" Betsy spun round and practically spat at him. "Done? You know bloody well what you've done!"

Two middle-aged women stepped out into the road to pass around them and smirked. Betsy looked around and pulled Bill into the next street and then a back street. She released him and stood glaring at him, arms braced across her chest.

"I'm sorry," Bill said. "But I have a solution. That's what I came to tell you, but you didn't turn up. Everything's going to be fine."

"Oh?" Betsy raised her eyebrows, the scowl still there. Bill was beginning to feel uncomfortable. "So you're going to marry me, then?"

"You know I can't just yet, but we have a solution until I can."

Betsy pulled her shawl tighter around her body. "He said you'd say that!" she fumed.

"Who said what?" Bill asked. "You haven't even heard what I'm proposing."

Betsy stepped forward and prodded Bill in the chest. "Don't think I don't know what's going on," she said. "I know full well why you won't marry me. Do you think I'm stupid? I know you've been seeing someone else all along. And what? You're going to keep us both? Marry neither of us? Or her?"

Bill stepped backwards. Where was all this coming from? Why would she even get this idea? He started to think back. Was there any woman who he'd been talking to that she might have gotten the wrong idea about? Maybe someone from the Temperance Hall? Maybe one of Jenny Booth's friends? There wasn't a woman in his reading group. He racked his brains but couldn't come up with anything. He usually never knew what to say around women. Betsy was the exception.

"Ah. So it is true!" Betsy yelled.

"No!" he said. "I was just trying to think –"

"Oh yes, think of an excuse?"

"No! Where is all this coming from?"

Betsy moved closer to him again. "You were seen. A neighbour saw you and told me. Warned me."

"Well, that neighbour is wrong!" he said. "It's not true."

"He said you'd say that. In fact, you're behaving exactly how he said you would, so I think you're guilty."

"Let me talk to this neighbour," Bill said. "He's wrong. He's mistaken."

Betsy folded her arms and looked up at the chimneys and roofs. Bill could see that tears were starting to form in her eyes.

"Bets," he said gently. "It's not true. I would never see someone else. You're all I want." He smiled and made to hug her.

Betsy shook his arm away.

"Don't," she said. "Don't lie to me. The neighbour told me everything. Said his wife had seen you with this girl many times over on the other side of town. He said he didn't want to see me make the same mistake as his daughter did, waiting for a man who wasn't ever going to marry her." The tears rolled down her cheeks. She gasped and looked at Bill again.

"I don't want to hear your solution," she said. "I don't want to see you ever again."

"But ..." Bill felt his heart sink into his shoes. He knew it was so hard to get Betsy to change her mind once she'd made it up. How was he going to prove to her that he hadn't been seeing someone else? That the neighbour was mistaken? He didn't even know which neighbour it was.

"I'll let you know when the baby is born," she said. "I'll send word to Nell. But I won't do more than that. You don't deserve more than that."

"But it's not true!" Bill yelled in frustration. Betsy turned her back and walked towards the road.

As she walked away from him, Bill stood there helplessly, his eyes filling up, making the walls and cobbles around him blurry. He loved Betsy. They hadn't been together more than a few months, but he'd really fallen for her. He admired her sharp tongue and razor wit, her huge, infectious smile. The way the corners of her mouth twitched when she was amused and trying not to laugh. She always made him smile, the tough little girl that she was. He also loved her wavy black hair that she twisted up and pinned on top of her head, the way it frizzed out in the damp as she tried everything to tame it. And now she was carrying his baby. But everything had gone wrong when he'd said they had to wait so long to marry. And now she was going to meet someone else eventually – someone who could take care of her, like their Jem did for Molly. And his child was going to be brought up by another man. The thought of that was like a knife through his heart.

He walked away, kicking at the leaves littering the ground, his heart breaking. He'd ruined the life of the woman he loved and also the life of his first child. He'd often condemned Jem for his heartless behaviour, but at least Jem had taken on Molly and her child, and that made Jem a much better man than he. He had been wrong all along. It was he, Bill, who was the bad one, not Jem. Now he had to deal with that realisation on top of losing Betsy and his baby.

CHAPTER 19

A DAUGHTER

JUNE 1851

"Come," Nell said, discreetly taking Bill's arm as they came out of church.

"Where?" he asked.

"Just come, will you?" Nell started walking slowly, her protruding belly causing her to waddle, her hand resting on the small of her back for support. "I've told Tam to say I'm not feeling well and you've walked me home. He'll join us shortly."

"What's going on?" Bill asked.

Nell smiled. "You'll see." Bill was a little surprised but happy to be spending time as just the three of them again. It rarely was these days, and as Nell was due to have her first baby in a month or so, they'd have even less time after that to get together. Bill followed his sister as she turned the corner, walked up to her front door, pushed it open and stepped inside.

Standing behind Nell, Bill didn't see her at first, sitting by the fireplace, a tiny being wrapped in a shawl in her arms. But when she looked up and met his eyes, he almost couldn't breathe.

"Well, go on, then." Nell smiled. "Say hello to your daughter."

"Daughter ..." Bill whispered, finally removing his cap. "My daughter?" He looked from Nell to Betsy and back again, a huge smile lighting up his face. Betsy pulled down a part of the shawl, and Bill saw her shock of black hair, red-pink skin and his own oval face.

"Betsy!" he breathed. "She's beautiful." He put out his hand to cradle his daughter's head. A jolt of pride shot through him.

"Of course she is!" Betsy said sharply. They both sat there, heads almost touching, looking at the tiny little baby, grunting and trying to move her hands in her sleep. "She's two weeks old now."

"Thank you so, so much for bringing her to see me. You have no idea how much it means to me."

Betsy looked straight at him. "Of course I do. Your sister told me over and over and over again. I was sick of hearing about it!"

Bill grinned and thought he saw the corners of Betsy's mouth flicker upwards.

"You know there was never anyone else," he said. "Never."

"I don't want to talk about that right now," she said.

"But I need you to believe me. I can't stand to know you think so badly of me. I don't want my daughter thinking I'm that sort of person either."

"Bill," Betsy said softly, "I said I don't want to discuss it right now. Turns out the neighbour might have been wrong."

"See, I told you!" he almost shouted, "I promise you, Betsy, I never, ever, EVER –"

"Shush. Just concentrate on your daughter, will you?"

Bill looked down, put his finger in her tiny hand and felt his stomach lurch as she grasped it. This was his little girl. His! He smoothed down the baby's gown with his other hand.

"Are these the clothes Jenny Booth made?"

"Yes," Betsy said. "Thanks for those. They're beautifully made."

"I just wanted her to have something nice, something new," Bill said. "And Jenny's really good with a needle. She practically made all my clothes."

"They are nice," Betsy said.

The sound of the front door scraping as it opened made Bill jump. Tam peered around the front door at them before closing it.

"Congratulations, you two!" he said, walking over to Bill and shaking him by the hand. "Let me have a look, then. Ah, the latest Hall baby."

"She'll be a Fleming," Betsy said sharply and stiffened her shoulders. She pulled the shawl a little closer around that baby's head and turned, moving her out of Bill's and Tam's reach.

"Of course," Tam said. "Sorry, of course she'll be a Fleming. Just look at that hair. She's beautiful, like her mother. Does she have your lovely brown eyes too?" Betsy seemed to relax a little.

"Yes, her eyes are brown," she said. "And I'm naming her Anne."

Bill sat down beside her. "Anne," he said. "After your mother."

"You remembered."

"I remember everything about you," he said softly. Betsy's shoulders dropped, and she looked away.

"Would it be possible to name her after my mother too?" he asked. "Alice?"

"You remembered." He smiled and Betsy laughed.

"She'll be known as Anne," she said. Bill gave a rueful smile and nodded. He really had no right to ask this of her. Besides the fact that he was never going to get the chance to bring her up, he knew Betsy's mother had passed away a few months ago. He just sat and looked in wonder at his precious little daughter.

"Alice Anne, then," Betsy said suddenly. Bill's heart leapt. He beamed at Betsy, then turned to his daughter.

"Hello, Alice."

"Alice Anne."

"Hello, Alice Anne."

Bill and Betsy sat and chatted for an hour or so, their conversation punctuated with comments from Nell and Tam. It just felt all so familiar to Bill, yet also new. He needed to talk to Betsy about what had happened last time they spoke, but he also wanted to just stay in this bubble with her for as long as he could. Alice Anne woke, and Betsy began to feed her. Bill was amazed at his daughter's tiny hands and tiny feet covered by long layers of dress. Betsy had been telling them that her father was a different person now. He'd been working almost every day, and they'd moved out of the cellar room a few months ago to a house on Howell Croft. Bill was so happy to hear they were doing well and then immediately felt so guilty that it wasn't him providing for his daughter.

"I really need to get going," Betsy said, finally standing up. "They'll be wondering where I am on a Sunday. I said I was going to visit a friend, show off the baby."

"Will I see you again?" Bill asked, standing close to her, his hand on Alice Anne's back.

"Bill ..." she began. "How can we? After everything?"

"You're always welcome to visit me," Nell said quickly. "I'm due soon too, so maybe Alice Anne would like to come round and have company. I know I'd like it."

"We'll see," said Betsy. "Thanks for the tea. Bye, Bill," she said softly, closing the front door without looking back.

Bill watched the front door close and slumped down into his chair. "I'm never going to see them again, am I?" he asked his sister desperately. "My daughter. My Alice." Tears began to form as he angrily rubbed his eyes. Tam handed him a cup of tea.

"Drink this while it's hot," he said, patting Bill on the shoulder.

"The stupid thing is," Bill said, blinking back more tears, "I thought I was never going to see her. And now that I have, I don't know how I can live without seeing her grow up."

Tam glanced at Nell.

"This is going to be so hard," said Tam. "But there is nothing you can do right now. Nell's been talking to Betsy a lot. Betsy told her about the argument you two had, about the reason why she decided to end it. But over the last few months she's come round to realise that what her neighbour said wasn't true. Now I think she feels really bad about things and she's just going to need a bit of time. It can't be easy for you or for her."

"But who was this person who told her those lies?" Bill demanded. "He's ruined everything for us. Because of him and his meddling, I may not get to see my daughter grow up."

"A neighbour is all she said," Nell said. "She did go back to talk to him after I'd spoken to her – I told her a few truths about your fear of talking to women, let alone the very idea of courting two at the same time – and she said she could no longer find him. No one had heard of him."

"Odd."

"Yes. But she said he was very convincing. Actually told her exactly how you would act when confronted about it, seemingly showing your guilt."

"What? But that sounds ..."

"I know," said Nell. "Really odd. Like someone wanted to break you two up, make your life miserable. I don't know who would do that or why, but I think she's feeling really guilty about it all now. She just needs some time to come around."

But Bill wasn't listening. Someone who wanted to break you two up, make your life miserable. Could it have been Ainsworth? But Bill had promised to leave well enough alone. To stop prying into his family's history or trying to find out what really happened. There was no way Ainsworth could have known that Bill had read the diaries. They had never even been out of Bluey's house.

"Ainsworth?" Bill said.

"Ainsworth, what?" Nell asked.

"Ainsworth might have done this. He told me he'd leave me alone if I stopped trying to find things out about him, about the shares. Otherwise, I'd get what's coming to me."

Nell's hand shot up to her mouth.

"You spoke to Ainsworth? When did you see Ainsworth?" Tam asked. "You never said anything."

"Bill! Why didn't you tell us?" Nell said. "When was this?"

"Why do you think I didn't want to talk about the suitcase contents or Ainsworth anymore?" Bill said. "It was after I'd been to the bank to ask about the shares, then talked to Jem and Bluey about it all. Ainsworth grabbed me when I was walking home that night and threatened me."

"You went to the bank?" Tam asked.

"Oh, Bill!" Nell said and walked over to hug him.

"I have to say he scared me," Bill confessed. "That's why I didn't want to look into it all anymore. He said he'd leave me alone 'for now'. Maybe 'now' has arrived."

"But why?" Nell asked. "Why would he do that?"

Bill shrugged. "Who knows? I got the impression he's crazy. He said to me, 'I won't rest until you all feel the pain and loss that I did'. I remember that clearly."

"So he thinks all you Halls need to feel the same pain and loss that he did?" Tam said carefully. "Does that mean he is your father's half brother and that he was never acknowledged for that?"

"I think so," Bill said. "Bluey confirmed that Father did have a half brother, but he didn't know his name and said as far as he knew, Father had never met him. But Granddad's diary revealed that he had a son named Edward with a Mary Ainsworth. Father's diary mentioned it too, said he couldn't believe what his own brother had done to him and that he wasn't responsible for his father's actions. Oh, and Jem wouldn't answer any of my questions. He seemed scared."

"You read Father's diary?" Nell asked. "And Grandfather's? Why didn't you say anything? What else have you been holding from us?"

"Ainsworth scared me," Bill said. "I didn't want to take them out of the house in case Ainsworth found me and I was carrying them. Or if they got lost."

"We could have come to Bluey's," said Nell.

"Well, Tam did ..." Bill began. "He helped decipher a few words. Granddad's handwriting was useless."

Nell turned round and glared at Tam. "Oh, you did, did you? You both kept me in the dark?"

"It wasn't like that," said Tam.

Nell huffed and turned to face Bill again. "And what else?"

Bill swallowed. Should he tell them now about Luke? He needed to tell someone. Would they think of him differently? Would either of them let it slip one day? He couldn't risk that.

"Nothing."

"Nothing? You look like you're hiding something," Nell said.

"I'm not!" Bill's voice went up a notch.

"Hmm."

"So you said Jem was scared?" Tam asked. Bill was grateful for the change of subject. It was never easy lying to Nell.

"I can only imagine Ainsworth has said or done something to Jem too."

"So you really think it could have been Ainsworth who told Betsy all this nonsense?" Tam asked.

"I think there's a good chance," Bill said. "I need to speak to Betsy and hear from her what this 'neighbour' looks like. It was dark, but I saw his face for a brief second, and I'll never forget it. That face has haunted me."

"I think you need to give Betsy some time," Nell said. "I do think she'll come around eventually, but she needs to do it in her own way. I can try to get her to describe the neighbour to me, tell me a little more about it, but in the end, it's up to her."

"It'll probably be too late by then. She'll have found someone else to marry," Bill sulked.

"Look, Bill," Tam said, "I'd say that would probably be the case with most other women, but do you really think Betsy would? I mean, really, is there anybody else who would like to marry such a prickly tiger with more than a few opinions?"

Bill started laughing. "Maybe you're right."

"Of course I'm right. I'm always right." Tam winked.

"Bit like Betsy in that way," Bill said, chuckling. Nell snorted.

"I'm sure things will work out," said Tam. "There's nothing you can do right now, so what's the point in worrying about something you can't control?"

"You're right. Again," Bill said, standing up. "Thanks for the tea, but I think I need to be on my own for a bit now." He handed the cup back to Tam and went to hug his sister. She swept the hair back from his forehead and kissed his cheek.

"You take care now, favourite brother."

"I will, favourite sister. And you take care of both of you," he said, pointing to Nell's belly. "Oh, and I know I don't have much to give, but can you give this to Betsy next time you see her?" He pulled a small coin out of his pocket. "I'll try and give her something every week for the baby. It's not much, I know, but I can't do nothing."

"But you're still paying whatever you have left over to Bluey for the baby clothes you had Jenny make," Nell said. "How are you going to afford to eat?"

"I'll pay him a little less, and perhaps you'll feed me." He smiled. Nell playfully shoved him out the door.

As he made his way back to Slater Street, he started to think about Ainsworth. There was no way he could have known that Bill had continued to look into family secrets, so he must have just decided to go after him anyway. How was Bill going to stop him next time? He had thought that knowing why Ainsworth was doing all this would help him, but now he realised it wasn't going to make any difference. Ainsworth was not going to rest until he got what he wanted.

CHAPTER 20

THE REUNION
NOVEMBER 1851

It had been just over four months since Bill had seen Betsy and Alice Anne. He was pretty sure Nell had seen them a few times, but when he asked her, she just said, "Oh, Bill! If Betsy wants to see you, she will see you." His heart ached. He tried focussing on his studies and improving his reading to take his mind off it. He still went to temperance meetings with Tam, but Nell now stayed at home with their new baby they had named Alcy. It wasn't easy for Bill to see his little niece when he couldn't see his own daughter and had no idea what she was like or what she was doing.

On Sunday evening, Bill had gone round to visit Nell before heading back to his lodgings. He'd stopped staying at Bluey's on Sunday nights a while ago, giving himself a much-needed extra hour of sleep on Monday mornings. Saying his good-byes to Nell and Tam and stepping outside, he was hit by an icy blast of air. It was freezing cold. He held his jacket close as soft snowflakes started to fall. It was a long walk home to the other side of town through the back streets. Once again he wondered, as he did every night on his way home from work, whether he should take a trip down to Howell Croft just to see if Betsy was there. But just like every time he got the urge to do this, he resisted. There was no point in making a nuisance of himself if it was clear that she wanted nothing more to do with him. As he hurried home, he saw a small figure holding a large bundle walking in front of him. As he passed, he saw the bundle carefully wrapped up in a bunch of rags was a baby. He lifted his cap and smiled as he passed the pair and got such a jolt when he saw a familiar face looking back at him, her brown eyes meeting his.

"Bill!" Betsy exclaimed. She pulled the bundle of rags wrapped around Alice Anne closer to her. "What are you doing here?"

"I'm on my way home from seeing Nell and Tam," he said. "I usually walk this way. How are you? How is Alice Anne? What are you both doing out here so late? It's so cold. Are you both well?"

"Yes. We're just coming back from visiting a friend. I didn't realise how late it was. How have you been, Bill?" She looked up at him, and Bill melted.

"I've been missing you both ... a lot," he said. "I just hoped you were both all right, and I wonder every day what Alice Anne is doing."

"Oh, Bill! We talked about this."

"Yes, I know. I know. It just doesn't make it easier. Have you been getting the money I've given to Nell?"

"Yes, thank you."

"I know it's not much, but it's all that I can spare right now. I finish my apprenticeship in a few months, and then I'll be able to give you both more."

"It's not about the money," Betsy said, looking down at Alice Anne, who was grizzling. "I never asked you for money." She looked up at Bill again. "We're doing well." She smiled. "You know Mam died earlier this year – well, Pa has been holding down a job ever since. He's really making an effort. Said he doesn't want his granddaughter growing up in a cellar, so I think he's trying to make sure we never have to move back to one. I'm looking after the house; it's a nice house too. Our Maggie's still working in the mill, and my younger brothers have just started. Although I don't think they like it very much." She laughed and Bill smiled. Just then, a gust of wind blew down the street, making Betsy stumble a little.

"You shouldn't stand here in the cold," Bill said, "you'll both catch your death. Do you mind if I walk you back?"

Betsy nodded. "As long as you only walk me to the end of our street. I still haven't told Pa you're her father, and I don't want him getting ideas."

Bill stopped. "You haven't? Why?"

"What good will it do? He'd just be angry with you, be thinking all kind of things about you that aren't true. He might even come and find you and give you a bit of a beating."

They walked along in silence for a little while, Bill with so many thoughts flying round his head and at the same time finding it hard to take his eyes off his daughter.

"Have you seen our Nell's new baby?" he asked, trying to think of some way of filling the silence.

"Yes. I visited just after little Alcy was born. She is a very beautiful baby. Then again, you Halls aren't so bad looking." The corner of her mouth twitched into a lopsided smile, one that was very familiar to Bill, and he felt like he'd been transported back just over a year to when they first met.

"Alice Anne is beautiful too," he said.

"That's because she's part Hall." Betsy smiled coyly.

"No, it's because she looks like her mother," Bill said.

Betsy fell silent.

All too so soon they were at the corner of Howell Croft and Great Moor Street. Bill hesitated and then touched Alice Anne on her cheek. She looked up at him and gurgled. Bill cooed at her, then looked directly at Betsy.

"Just let me know if you need anything. If your Tommy really hates it at the mill, maybe I could talk to my master about an apprenticeship or something at the foundry. How old is he now?"

"He's fourteen," Betsy said. "You would really do that for us?"

"Of course. Anything."

Betsy smiled. "I have to go in now. I don't want our Alice Anne to get cold. But maybe I'll look in on Nell next Sunday."

Bill grinned from ear to ear. He said good-bye and walked home feeling happier than he had in a very long time.

Sunday could not come fast enough. Bill practically ran up the street to Nell's house after church and burst through the door without knocking.

"Is she – ?" He stopped as he saw Betsy sitting by the fire. He went over to Alice Anne, who was crawling on the floor and playing with an empty bobbin. Bill walked over to her, sat down and started rolling the bobbin back and forth to her, making her giggle.

"You can certainly move fast when you want to!" Tam Green came in through the door, panting.

"Poor love," Nell said, kissing his cheek as he took off his hat. "Are you getting a bit too old to be walking up that hill?" Bill and Betsy started laughing.

"The insults!" Tam said in mock severity, "and in my home too! How are you doing, Betsy, love? You're the only one who hasn't insulted me yet."

"I can change all that if it makes you happy." Betsy winked at Bill. Tam sighed and threw up his hands while Bill and Nell giggled.

Bill felt so happy and so at ease. It was like going back in time to when they were all friends and he and Betsy were courting. Back when anything was possible. And here they all were again, and there didn't seem to be any hard feelings between him and Betsy. But he really needed to know if it was Ainsworth who ruined everything.

"Bets," he began, "I've been meaning to ask you about that neighbour who told you lies about me."

"Oh, Bill, do we have to bring this up again? It was all going so well here."

"I know you don't want to be reminded of that time again," said Bill. "And I'm sorry, but I think I know who he was – or is. And I think I know why he did it. I just need you to describe him to me to be sure."

Betsy opened her eyes wide and looked up at him. "Well, he was tall. A lot taller than most people I know. Old, not really old, of course, but I'd say a bit older than Pa."

"Do you remember anything about his hair and teeth?" asked Bill.

"His hair was grey and straggly. Came down almost to his shoulders. His teeth were rotten, and his breath was really bad. His eyes were blue – like yours. That kind of blue."

Bill took a sharp breath. "When did you first meet him? Do you remember?"

Betsy stared out into the distance. "I'm not sure," she said. "It was like he'd always been around. I bumped into him one time, literally, and he helped me carry some potatoes home. After that, I'd see him around quite often. He'd wave to me."

"Do you remember seeing him before you bumped into him?"

215

Betsy was silent for a few minutes, then she turned to Bill. "I'm not sure. I can't remember seeing him before then, but I got the feeling that he'd lived around there for ages."

"And when you went to find him to speak to him, there was no trace of him?" Nell asked.

"No. That was the strange thing. I asked around about him, but none of the neighbours recognised him." She looked at Bill again. "What is it? Do you know who he is?"

"That's definitely him," Bill said to Nell.

"Who?" Betsy asked.

Bill sighed. "This man, Edward Ainsworth, turned up to Father's funeral and threatened our Jem. No one would tell us who he was at the time, but Nell found an old suitcase of Father's, and we found out from the wills and things in there that he had something to do with our family. We suspect he could have been Father's half brother, but he was never acknowledged by our family, so he started seeking revenge. We thought he'd got his revenge, but he attacked me one night, said I had to leave well enough alone, stop asking questions about him, and that he would make sure all us Halls suffered the pain that he had. That he would destroy us all. I think he's been watching us, saw I was happy and decided to destroy my life."

Betsy gasped. "Oh, Bill! And I fell for it. I can't believe I took his word instead of yours. I'm so sorry." Tears started to fall from her eyes.

Bill rushed to her side and put his arms around her. "It's not your fault, do you hear? It's not. You did nothing wrong. That man is evil, and apparently he's very convincing."

Betsy clung to him. "He was so convincing," she said. "He told me exactly how you'd act, exactly what you'd say, and you did. How did he know?"

"I don't know," Bill said. "It scares me to know he knows me so well. Makes me wonder what he's done to Jem. Jem was so scared when I mentioned Ainsworth's name that he wouldn't even talk. I worry about him going after Luke too, but Luke's still only a kid, only fourteen. Ainsworth left me alone until I was an adult. Maybe when Luke's a bit older, we need to tell him about Ainsworth."

"I'm so sorry," Betsy sobbed.

Bill held her tight. "It'll all be fine, Betsy," he said, stroking her hair. "We'll all be fine. Don't worry."

After lunch, when both babies were taking a nap. Bill, Betsy, Nell and Tam sat around the table. Tam had just put some more coal on the fire, and it crackled and hissed, the sharp smell of soot temporarily filling the air. It was just as cold as it had been the previous week, so the fire was a warm welcome. A light dusting of snow lay on the ground, mixed with frost. For the first time in a long time, Bill was looking forward to Christmas and wondering what he should make for Alice Anne.

"So then," Tam clasped his hands carefully and leaned over his elbows propped on the table, "does it need to be said, or are you two going to skirt around the issue all day?"

Nell smiled.

"What?" Bill asked, confused. Betsy sat still, her eyes wide.

"Does it need to be said that it is obvious that you are still in love with the lovely Miss Fleming here?"

Bill spluttered, then looked around at Betsy. He could feel the heat rising in his cheeks. Betsy said nothing.

"Well, as you're both as bad as each other, I think it also needs to be said that it's equally obvious that the lovely Miss Fleming is still in love with you too."

Bill stopped protesting and looked at Betsy, who had now turned quite red too.

"What my dear husband is trying to say, in a not very subtle way, is that you two need to talk. Say whatever you like, but you two need to be together," Nell said, leaving the table.

"Subtle?" Tam said. "These two wouldn't get subtle. These two needed to be hit with a brick." Nell pulled at his shirt and steered him towards the door, throwing his jacket at him.

"We'll step out for a bit of fresh air," she said, wrapping two shawls around her shoulders. "Now sort it out quick because it's freezing out there, and there won't be much time before one of the babies wakes up." With that, she placed Tam's hat on his head and pushed him out the door.

Bill sat there, mouth open. Then he turned to Betsy.

"So then," she said. "Do you still want me?"

"Still?" Bill asked incredulously. "I've never stopped wanting you."

"Right then. Now I know."

Bill waited for a few seconds before leaning in and saying, "Does that mean . . . ?"

Betsy looked him up and down, twisting her mouth first one way, then the other in a very familiar expression. "You'll do," she decided.

Bill burst out laughing. "You're not big on compliments, are you?"

Betsy smiled. "It's you who needs to be big on compliments. Let's get that right from the start." Bill threw his arms around her, feeling like he never wanted to let go. Betsy let out a long sigh and hugged him even tighter.

CHAPTER 21

THE PROPOSAL
MARCH 1852

Bill had never thought he'd feel this happy again. He and Betsy had been courting for the past three months. They got so little time together, just the two of them, only on occasional Sundays when Nell said she'd take Alice Anne for an hour or so. But Bill also enjoyed the three of them spending time together – himself, Betsy and Alice Anne. He felt so proud, carrying his little daughter as the three of them took a walk through the forest or over the hills out by one of the surrounding farms, where nobody knew them and nobody would know they were not married. They also had great fun with Nell and Tam and their little daughter, Alcy. Bill had been so wrapped up in Betsy and Alice Anne that he'd had no time for reading or temperance meetings. And now his studying was over because in mid-March, his apprenticeship would finally end.

He'd made it through seven years, and now he was finally going to be his own man, find a good, decently paid job as a journeyman boilermaker and most importantly, propose to Betsy. He'd been planning to propose the day he finished his apprenticeship. They'd get married as soon as the banns were read, and he'd be able to find a place for them all as soon as he got his first real pay packet. Of course, he'd have to save up to buy a ring, and Betsy deserved one, deserved for everyone to know she was now a respectable married woman, but that might have to wait a little while.

Bill still had a smile on his face as he turned into Nell and Tam's street. Just one more week and then he was going to propose. One more week and then the three of them could start planning their lives as a family!

As Bill opened the front door and called, "Only me!" as usual, he saw that Betsy was already there. His grin grew wider as he took off his coat and went to hug her.

After she pulled away, he noticed she was unusually quiet. She'd only given him a quick smile and had pulled away first.

"Are you all right?" he asked gently. Alice Anne was demanding his attention, crawling over to him and trying to pull herself up while becoming tangled in the layers of her baby gown, designed to keep her legs and feet warm. He picked up his daughter and gave her a dozen kisses on her cheek. Alice Anne giggled and wrapped her arms around his neck.

Betsy gave Bill a tired smile and shrugged. Alice Anne grabbed Bill's face and tried to bite his chin.

"Give her here," Betsy said, reaching out her arms. "She's teething. And she's a handful."

Bill obediently handed her over.

"You're looking a bit pale," Nell said to Betsy. "Do you need anything?"

Betsy looked her in the eye. "I don't know," she answered.

Bill started to feel a dull ache in the pit of his stomach. He remembered full well what had happened last time Betsy was all quiet like this.

"Actually, Nell, would you mind if I talked to Bill in private?"

Bill started to feel cold.

Nell nodded. "I'm about to go and take a nap upstairs with Alcy. Tam, could you come up and help me?"

"Help you and Alcy nap?" Tam asked, confused. "I don't think – oh." He noticed his wife's frown and head gestures towards Betsy.

As soon as Nell was out of earshot, Betsy turned to Bill.

"So ..." she began.

Bill swallowed hard.

"Looks like you're going to be a father again."

"What?" Bill's face broke into the biggest smile.

Betsy looked at him and smiled back. Bill hugged her and Alice Anne hard.

"Do you want me to be sick all over you?" She batted him away.

Bill smiled even more.

"You really know how to make a person sweat!" Bill said, releasing a long breath. "I was all worried you were going to say something I didn't want to hear."

"Well, you behave yourself and I'll never have to."

Bill smiled and took a few deep breaths. He took hold of Alice Anne's hand.

"I had planned to do this next week, but it looks like today might be a better time to do it." He released his daughter's hand and knelt down on one knee beside Betsy.

"Betsy, my love, you and Alice Anne make me so happy. I want to be your husband, to let everyone know how proud of you I am, to spend the rest of my life with you. Will you marry me? We could get married next month as soon as the banns are read," he added quickly.

Betsy looked away, and Bill began to feel slightly nauseous.

"Betsy, say something."

"I'll say something when I've finished crying, you stupid man!" She wiped her tears away angrily.

Bill pulled her towards him and held her tightly. Betsy just sobbed and sobbed. After several minutes, the sobbing subsided, and she finally sat up again, turning away from Bill and wiping her eyes and nose with her sleeve.

"That's not me crying," she said. "It's the baby."

Bill laughed. "So now that the baby's finished crying, will you marry me, Betsy?"

She smiled at him. "Yes."

He wrapped his arms around her and never wanted to let go.

"Aha!" came a shout from the stairs as Tam's crinkled, freckled face peered around the door. "Are we celebrating anything?"

Nell appeared after him. "I told him to leave you both be, but does he ever listen to me?" She rolled her eyes, and Betsy smiled.

Bill stood up, keeping hold of Betsy's hand. "Betsy and I are getting married!" he said, looking down at Betsy.

"Finally!" Tam shouted and flung himself at Bill, almost knocking him over. He released him from his bear hug and grabbed him by the shoulders. "I'm so happy for you. After everything you've both been through, you're now getting married."

Bill swallowed hard. It wouldn't do for anyone to see him getting emotional. He couldn't exactly blame his tears on the new baby.

He watched Nell hug and congratulate Betsy, and then she turned to him.

"I'm so happy for you, little brother," she said, hugging him. "Now you're going to get the family you've always dreamed of. Your own family." She released him, and Bill quickly wiped his eyes with the back of his sleeve.

"Yes, and we'll have Luke come live with us and move in next door to you," he joked.

Nell smiled. "That would be perfect."

"Come, come!" Tam said, handing out glasses and opening a large bottle of raspberry vinegar. "We have something to celebrate!"

After much joking and pouring the sweet, dark liquid into everyone's glass, Tam stood up and raised his glass.

"To Bill and Betsy. Finally! May their lives together be plain sailing from now on."

"To Bill and Betsy!" Nell echoed as they downed their drinks.

"And to me and Nell," Tam added, raising his glass again. "Without whom, these two would still be tiptoeing around each other and being miserable."

Betsy rolled her eyes and laughed, then looked up at Bill, and he felt a jolt to his heart. Never had he been more in love with her than at this moment. Two children and a wife, and now his own man. Not a bad life at all! And here they were with his sister and best friend too. Life certainly had improved no end since those dark, desolate childhood days. He was going to make sure his children had a far better childhood than he had.

Bill felt such happiness surging up inside. "Shall we tell them?" he whispered to Betsy.

She pulled her face. "May as well. As long as they don't mention it to anyone else."

Bill turned to Nell and Tam and caught hold of Betsy's hand again.

"There's more," he began. "We're having another baby." He smiled at Betsy.

Nell shrieked and threw herself on Bill. "Congratulations! Oh, Betsy," she said, turning to her and giving her a quick hug.

"Congratulations again," Tam said with his drink in one hand. He put his arm around Bill's shoulders and squeezed hard. "Hence the proposal?"

"I was planning to propose next week." Bill grinned. "I thought under the circumstances, today might be more appropriate."

Tam's eyes crinkled up. "It's so great to see you so happy," he said. "But now more than ever you need to watch out for Ainsworth. He's probably going to be really angry when he finds out his malicious meddling didn't work and you're still happy, not to mention back together, getting married and increasing your family. What can be done to stop him?"

Bill sighed. "Other than looking out for him, I don't know. I don't think he'll stop until he dies."

He saw Nell and Tam exchange looks and wondered how he was going to make sure they all stayed safe.

The next day, after church service, Bill, Betsy, Nell and Tam headed to Jem and Molly's house for dinner. Bill knew how reluctant Betsy was to go with them and meet Jem and Molly for the first time. She had gone home the night before and announced to her father that she was getting married. Apparently, Jamesie Fleming had hit the roof when he heard she was marring Bill. Said Bill was a disgrace for not coming to him first and asking his permission and that he'd give Bill Hall a piece of his mind next time he saw him. Betsy told Bill that she had decided there and then not to tell her father anything else, especially not about the pregnancy. "Maybe people will just think the baby came a bit early," she'd said to him. Bill could understand her reluctance. After all, she'd already been through this once before, alone. He couldn't imagine Jamesie would be as understanding a second time, even if they were getting married.

Bill was relieved when Betsy halfheartedly agreed to join them. He had already told Nell and Tam and Bluey and Aunt Jane, so if Jem found out from someone else first, he would probably blow his top and then sulk for a long time.

"You'll be fine," Bill said. "You'll have to meet them some time.

Better that we tell them now before the first banns get read out next week, or our Jem'll be livid!"

"You've said your Jem can be difficult," Betsy said. "I'm really not in the mood for 'difficult' right now. I'm tired, and arguing with Pa last night hasn't made me feel any better."

"Don't you worry about our Jem," said Bill. "And since when did you care what anyone else thought?"

Betsy was silent for a moment. "Maybe . . . I just can't explain it. I feel a bit vulnerable right now. Like I'm not myself."

"Come here," Bill said, giving her a hug. "Look, the rest of my family is really nice. You know Nell and Tam like you. They've always been on your side. Bluey said last night that he is going to help us find us a house. Molly is as nice as Bluey, so who cares what Jem really thinks? But we have to tell them ourselves before one of them finds out from someone else."

"I suppose."

"Well then," Bill smiled as he picked up Alice Anne and held out his hand, "let's get going."

The room was full of life as Bill and Betsy stepped through the door. Molly was on her knees, two-handedly moving the pan over the newly stoked fire to boil the potatoes and shouting at the four older children to stay away from the heat as they ran around. Nell was sitting with the babies – Alcy and Molly and Jem's Ettie, who was nearly two – and chatting to Molly. Tam was sitting on a stool by the window reading a book, and Jem was seemingly in his own little world, sitting at the table staring down at the faults in the wood. No one seemed to notice at first as Bill stepped in holding the baby, followed by Betsy so closely that she was almost bumping into him. Bill smiled at her and grabbed her hand. As Betsy shut the door, Bill looked around, smiled at them all, and grasped Betsy's hand tighter. The sound of the door closing made Jem look up from the table. Molly turned around, wiped her hands on her apron and smiled back.

"Jem, Molly, everyone," Bill began, "this is Betsy." He turned and smiled at her and she smiled back. "She's going to be my wife."

"Oh! Bill!" Molly stood up and rushed forward, giving him a hug. "We had no idea you were even courting! Did we, Jem?" Still smiling, she turned to face Betsy and threw her arms around her. "Welcome to the family Betsy. I'm looking forward to getting to know you." She then started cooing over Alice Anne, and Bill happily released her into Molly's arms.

Jem held out his hand to Bill and looked at Betsy with narrowed eyes. "Betsy who?"

Bill shook Jem's hand absently. He didn't expect Jem to start hugging everyone, but his tone set Bill on edge. He looked over at Betsy.

"Fleming," replied Betsy. "You must be Jem. Nice to meet you."

"Are you Irish?" he asked. "You look Irish. And with a name like Fleming ..."

Betsy glanced at Bill. "Well, me Mam and Pa are. I mean, were ... I was born here."

"I thought you looked Irish. And that's your baby, I see?"

"Yes. Alice Anne's her name."

"No father?"

"I don't see what that has to do with anything," Betsy said quickly.

"People have children before they marry," said Bill. "Molly had a child before you married. I don't see why it should be so different for us."

"Bill," Jem said, turning to face him, "I don't want you marrying this woman." Molly's mouth dropped.

"What?" Bill was taken aback. "But you don't even know her. How can you say that?"

"I know all I need to know."

Bill looked at Betsy, then at the others in despair.

The children, sensing something serious was happening, went quiet.

"How can you even say that? You've only asked her her name."

Betsy turned to Bill. "I'll go," she whispered.

"No," Bill said, holding her hand tighter. "It's fine. Jem, I don't see what the problem is. We're both of age. I'm now free to marry. It's not like you can stop us."

Jem walked over to Bill and stood in front of him.

"I'll tell you what the problem is, shall I? Shall I? She's Irish. I won't have her marrying into my family."

Nell gasped. Bill and Molly just stood with their mouths open, not knowing what to say or do. Betsy kept quiet, but Bill could see her face was getting red. Suddenly, Nell stood up, handing Alcy over to Tam.

"Oh, for Heavens sake! What is this really all about, Jem?" she asked, hands on hips. "You don't even know her. I do, and I can say she is a good person. Bill couldn't have chosen better."

Bill looked from Nell to Jem and back again. He felt like he was a kid again, his older sister having to stick up for him.

Suddenly, Bill snapped out of his shock. "How dare you! How dare you! She's a lovely person. She's worth a hundred of you any day!" Betsy squeezed his hand.

Jem snorted.

"Lets all just calm down," said Tam. "I'm sure if you get to know her, Jem, you'll love her like we all do."

"I know all I need to know about her," said Jem. He put his mouth close to Bill's ear. "You stay away from the Irish. They just take – our jobs, our money. They steal. They ruin families."

"What?" Bill turned around to face his brother. "Why are you saying all this? Does this have anything to do with what happened to Father? That had nothing to do with Betsy."

Jem glared at Bill and took a step closer. "I told you I'm not going to talk about that."

"You mean you're not going to talk about Ainsworth? Let me tell you he's already come after me, threatened me. He's even gone after Betsy. Are you going to tell me that's Betsy's fault too? She's innocent, but because she's associated with me, she's now been dragged into this, and you won't even tell me what you know."

Bill watch the colour drain from his brother's face and saw him quickly glance in the direction of the window. Was he so scared of Ainsworth hearing anything he said? What had Ainsworth done to him?

"I don't think we're going to change his mind," Nell said. "Let's just go. Betsy's in no fit state to be upset."

"Oh really?" Jem laughed viciously. "She's trapped you, has she, little brother?"

"No one has trapped me," said Bill angrily. "I'm marrying her because I love her." Bill and Jem stood a short distance apart, glaring at each other.

"Let's go, Bill," Nell said, tugging at his sleeve and nodding to Tam. Betsy took Alice Anne from Molly and followed Tam to the door.

"Oh, stay," Molly said. "Let's have something to eat, talk about this."

"No offence to you, Molly, but I won't eat with someone who insults my wife-to-be." Bill turned to Betsy. "I'm sorry I dragged you here only to be insulted. Please ignore my stupid brother."

He hugged his sister-in-law. "Molly, lovely to see you as always. Jem," he turned to face his brother, "you're not welcome at the wedding. And if you can't be civil to Betsy, you will not be welcome at our house either." He walked towards the door, the last one to leave. Nell had held it open, but on reaching it, Bill stopped and turned around.

"You never disappoint, Jem," he hissed. "Apart from when you do." Jem, his face and neck bright red and a vein in his temple standing out prominently, picked up the closest thing to hand – a milk jug – and threw it. Bill quickly pulled the door shut and heard the jug bounce off the other side and shatter into tiny pieces, the precious white liquid seeping under the door and spreading out over the sandstone doorstep.

Bill's heart was beating fast and he was shaking as they started to walk home in silence. He was really angry now. How dare his brother speak like that about his fiancé? Tam tried to break the silence with a few jovial remarks, but clearly none of them were in the mood.

"Well, looks like your guest list is getting shorter and shorter," Tam said. Nell pulled at his arm and tried to shush him, but Betsy just started laughing.

"As long as the important people are there, it doesn't matter to me," she said. "So that's the famous Jem. Now I understand."

"He's just stupid," Bill said. "And nobody listens to him anyway. I'm sorry he said those things to you."

"Well, it's not like I haven't had stick for being Irish before," Betsy said. "Maggie and I used to get it all the time as kids. But I was born here. I've never even been to Ireland."

"He's probably still stuck on what happened to Father, but that doesn't excuse his behaviour."

"Why is he like that?" Betsy asked.

"I imagine there are a million reasons," Bill said. "I probably only know three of them. But did you see his face when I mentioned Ainsworth?"

"He went white," Tam said.

"He looked at the window too," Bill said, "as if he was scared Ainsworth was listening in. I wonder what he did to Jem? Jem won't say anything."

"Then there's not much we can do to try and help him if he won't talk to us," said Tam. "And in any case, I don't think your brother has a good word to say about anybody, generally."

"True," Bill said. "We've missed dinner now, so let's go and get some potatoes and eat them at your place. I'm starving!"

CHAPTER 22

ANOTHER WEDDING
APRIL 1852

It certainly wasn't the lavish affair that Nell and Tam's wedding had been. Just an hour off on a Tuesday morning at Christ Church down the road from the foundry so that Bill could go back to work easily. Tam couldn't even get time off work, his master citing that it wasn't a 'close' relative getting married. Time off for a sibling, fine, but not your wife's brother, apparently. So Bill had asked Joe Walker to be best man. Joe had no problem skipping off work for a few hours. Said the farmer probably wouldn't even notice, and it wasn't like he'd seen Jamesie Fleming in a while. Bill had wanted far more for Betsy, but they didn't really have the luxury of time right now. The banns had been read, and no one had officially objected. Bill had half expected Ainsworth to appear, just to cause problems, but so far no one had received a 'visit' from him.

As Bill stood there at the altar with Joe, he looked around at his guests. Luke, Nell, Alcy and Alice Anne were sat in the front row with Bluey and Aunt Jane behind them. Jem, of course, wasn't invited. Molly couldn't get time off work without Jem noticing her wage was lower than usual, and Tommy couldn't make it down from Manchester on a workday. Still, that was better than Betsy's side of the church. None of her siblings were there yet. Her mother had passed away before Alice Anne was born, and Jamesie should be waiting at the back of the church to walk Betsy down the aisle.

The church doors opened with a crash, and Betsy stood there with her friend and bridesmaid, Polly. As the guests looked round, Betsy just stood there and shrugged. "My father couldn't make it, apparently," she said. Even from that distance, Bill could see she was close to tears.

There was movement from the pews as Bluey started to stand up, but Nell got there first. As Aunt Jane moved forwards to sit with Alcy and Alice Anne, Nell gestured to Luke, and the two of them walked up the aisle and stood either side of Betsy.

"You need someone to give you away?" Nell asked, offering her arm. Betsy burst into tears, smiling, and took it. She turned round to take Luke's proffered arm on the other side, and the three of them walked slowly forwards with Polly behind them. Bill noticed the rector's shocked face, then turned to beam at his siblings. As they came up to where Bill stood, they drew back to leave Betsy there, hiccoughing and smiling at him. Bill gently cupped her face in his hands, then wiped away her tears. Out of the corner of his eye, he saw Luke and Nell sit back down, Bluey leaning forward and patting Luke on the back.

As the rector went through the ceremony, probably for the two hundredth time, it seemed that the church was far too large for such a small gathering. Bill almost felt embarrassed at wasting the rector's time with so few attendees. In fact, the couple getting married before them had quite a lot of guests, the groom giving Bill a broad smile as he walked past, but the rector didn't seem to mind at all. Better to be wed in the eyes of the Lord than live in sin, he'd said. And as long as God was watching, who else really minded? Bill minded. He had always wanted his own family, a wife, lots of children. He'd wanted to be surrounded by people he loved, who loved him. But most of them were not present, and he'd brought it on himself, quarrelling with his brother. Why couldn't he just let it be sometimes? He and Jem would never agree on anything, but at least they should be civil. And Jem should be here; Bill should never had banned him, but Jem should never have said those things about Betsy.

He looked at his bride, standing there in a borrowed dress of Nell's. She was smiling, and Bill could see the joy in her eyes, but there were also tears, and he could see that she was paler than usual. The dark rings dulled her soft light brown tiger eyes that glistened whenever she was angry or mischievous. He'd missed her sense of humour over the past few weeks. She'd become quiet and withdrawn and had been quite sick. Bill was almost worried that she didn't really want to marry him, but she'd said she did. It was probably also his fault that her father wasn't here. If they had been more careful, if Bill had been more careful, they could have had a wedding like Nell's. There would have been no rushing, no family arguments. Maybe her father felt the same way.

The short ceremony was soon over. Bill hugged Betsy as they waited to sign the register. Betsy twisted her thin gold ring around on her finger – Bluey had loaned him the money for one - while Bill picked up the pen.

Making slow, careful swirls on the paper, he signed his name. Pausing for a minute to look at the letters, he realised this was one of his big achievements in life. He had done this, learned how to write, even though he had been denied an education as a child. With perseverance – and it had been very hard at times – he had managed to sign his name on his wedding day, a mark which would still exist long after he was gone. A mark all his children would see. He had made the effort to learn to read and write, and now he had his very own family. At the age of twenty-one, he had already fulfilled all his childhood dreams. Life was going to be so great from now on. He stepped back and handed the pen over to Betsy.

"It's going to be all right now," he whispered to Betsy, "you'll see. We're going to have a great life together."

Betsy smiled quickly at him, took the pen and carefully drew a cross next to where the rector was holding his finger on the page.

Bill wanted to stay with his new bride, to go and celebrate at the Temperance Hotel or even have some food back at Bluey's. But he had to get back to work. As he was now working as a boilermaker and even had some new apprentices to show how to file (oh, how he remembered that part of his life!), his master, Mr. Robinson, was very reluctant to give him more than an hour off work. He hugged Betsy, then released her, noticing she was almost crying.

"What's wrong?" he asked, dread spreading through his chest.

"Oh, nothing," she said. "I just ... I just wish I felt different. I wish I felt married."

Bill pulled her to him again. "I know it wasn't much today," he whispered into her hair, "but we'll have a celebration on Saturday. It'll be fun. Maybe you'll feel more married after that."

Betsy sobbed, and Bill hugged her more tightly.

"None of my family came," she wailed. Bill winced. "Makes it feel like my wedding didn't matter to them."

"I'm sure it did," he said. "You know it's not so easy to get time off work."

"I feel so alone," she said. "I thought this would be such a happy day, but instead I feel let down and alone."

"Hey!" Bill took her face in his hands and made her look at him. "You are not alone. You will always have me. And you'll always have Nell and Tam, Luke and Bluey and Aunt Jane. And I'm pretty sure you'll always have your sister and brothers too. Jamesie will get over it at some point. And we will have the best life – a nice house, lots of happy, beautiful children. Our lives are starting to get so much better, Bets. We're just beginning."

Betsy nodded and wiped her eyes, and Bill released her.

"You're right," she said. "I'm just being silly. We have it better than most, with your job. I'll be fine." She picked up Alice Anne, who started to squirm.

"And we'll soon have another one of these!" Bill grabbed Alice Anne's hands and blew a raspberry on her cheek, which made her laugh.

Betsy rolled her eyes. "Not soon enough!" she said.

"You plan our party with Nell, and I'll be home as soon as I can be," Bill said. He planted dozens of kisses all over Alice Anne's cheek, which made her squeal. Betsy smiled.

"I have to go." He gave Betsy a quick kiss. "I'll see you later." Betsy nodded and walked towards the group waiting for her. Bill watched Nell put her arm around Betsy and Betsy lean her head against Nell's as they started to walk. Bill watched until they were out of sight, then turned to head back to the foundry. He was married now. Married! He carried his head a little higher as he walked back to work.

PART 4

1853

The number of cotton mills in Manchester reached its peak in 1853 before declining. It was then surpassed by Bolton as the largest centre of cotton spinning. The importance of sanitation in crowded towns began to be recognised after a number of cholera outbreaks. Stricter building rules were now enforced which prevented new 'back to back' houses from being built. The Temperance movement continued to grow, as did interest in education.

CHAPTER 23

ACCUSATIONS
MARCH 1853

It was Tuesday evening, and Bill sat by the fire reading a book. Betsy was upstairs with the baby – their son, Jamie, born in October – and Luke was sitting across from Bill in the other faded armchair they had managed to acquire from a cousin of Bluey's. As he looked over at his little brother, who was now living with them, Bill thought that at some point his luck just had to run out. Here he was, a journeyman with a good job, in charge of several apprentices, a house – fine, the furniture was a bit mismatched and some of it old, but it was comfortable, two children and a wife who was smart and funny. He was even helping Tam out a lot now. They were still printing pamphlets, mostly on temperance and education, and they held several reading classes. Although Betsy complained sometimes about him not being around so often, he knew she was proud of him. Teaching others to read! Bill never thought he'd be good enough to be doing that. And best of all, he'd been able to have Luke come live with them, finally. Of course Bill had turned a blind eye to Luke's activities, as long as he didn't get into any trouble or brought problems home, he'd told him. But everything seemed to be working out fine.

Bill looked down at his book again and turned the page.

"Bill?"

He looked up.

"Can I ask you something?" Luke said.

"Sure."

Luke squirmed in his chair and then sat forwards. He glanced towards the back room, then looked at Bill.

"I've got myself into a bit of a problem, and I don't know how to get out of it."

Bill raised his eyebrows but said nothing. Luke didn't really talk much with him anymore, not since the pickpocketing incident.

"I've been working for this gang. Well, for a man mostly, but he has others working for him. I've been trying to leave, but he keeps threatening me – well, you. Says he'll break both your legs if I leave. But I need to." He started picking at a fingernail.

"Me?" Bill said, his heart beating faster. "How does he know me?"

"I don't know," said Luke. "He mentioned Nell as well, just once though. Maybe he's seen me come home, seen you. I don't know. But anyway, what should I do? What can we do?"

"We?" Bill echoed. "Don't drag me into your shady dealings. I can't believe this!"

"Oh, you were fine about it all when it didn't affect you," Luke said sharply.

Bill's mouth dropped open. Of course Luke was right. And now he was in trouble because Luke was in trouble.

"What do you want to do?"

"Maybe we could move away," said Luke. "All of us. He probably wouldn't come looking for us."

Bill put down his book. "You want me to move my family to somewhere where nobody knows us? Away from Bluey and Nell? No."

Luke dug his nails into the palm of his hand.

"I don't see what else we can do. I need to leave, and I don't want him hurting you."

"Well, thanks for that!" said Bill. "Who is this person anyway? Why are you working for him?"

"I started out just running errands for him when I was about eight," said Luke. "It seemed harmless at first. Then it was being a lookout or climbing in houses through slightly open windows and then letting them in through the front door. Helping move lead they'd taken from roofs, that kind of thing. They paid me really well, so I didn't have to go and work in the mill. It wasn't like they ever targeted people who would have suffered from losing some money. And no one got hurt."

Bill swallowed.

Luke continued. "When I got too big for all that, they moved me on to stealing. Not really stealing at first, more like conning people."

"Luke!"

"You knew what I was doing though, didn't you? You're not stupid." He looked up, and Bill saw there was no trace of any emotion in his brother's face.

"I knew you were probably up to no good. But what could I do short of tying you up? You never listened to anyone."

Luke shrugged and gave a wry smile.

"Why do you need my help now? What do you think I can do?"

Luke looked down at his hands again.

"I want to get out. Away from them. I can survive on my own now, and well, old man Ainsworth is crazy. If I don't do what he says, he threatens to break both your legs. He's making me do things I don't want to. He was the one who did this as a reminder that he owned me when I told him I no longer wanted to steal for him." Luke held up his left hand, and Bill looked down at the two crooked fingers. He remembered the incident well. A cold shiver went down his spine.

"Ainsworth?" he whispered.

"Yes. Edward Ainsworth and his son Jackie," Luke continued. "The old man is completely crazy, but Jackie is not much more than an unintelligent thug – wait, what? Do you know him?"

The room had started to swim before Bill's eyes. So Luke had been working for Ainsworth for eight years now? Ainsworth had had his grip on him for that long? He must have known who Luke was from the beginning. Maybe even targeted him. Did he know Luke was his son?

Bill started to speak, but only a squeak came out. He cleared his throat and tried again.

"An Edward Ainsworth stole all Father's money, and that's why we ended up in poverty. He also vowed to destroy all of us. He attacked and threatened me, and I'm sure he's done the same to Jem." How much was he prepared to tell Luke about Ainsworth? Should he tell him everything? Bill hadn't banked on telling him anything at all, but here they both were now, and Luke needed his help. How in the world was he supposed to help him?

"What!" Luke exploded, taking Bill by surprise. "Could it be the same person? If it is, I'll kill him! I'll kill him!" Luke banged hard on the table with his fist.

"White straggly hair, bad teeth, very tall and thin?" Bill asked.

"The bastard!" Luke stood up and kicked a chair.

"Careful," said Bill.

"I will wring his neck with my own bare hands!" Luke spat. "How dare he? Did he know who I was? How dare he steal from Father and then go after you and Jem. All these years and he's been lying to me and ordering me around. I bet he wanted me to get caught, go to gaol."

What more do I tell him? Bill wondered. If he's this upset, knowing Ainsworth is his father might just push him over the edge. Do I even tell him Ainsworth is Father's half brother?

"Bill? Bill!" Luke grabbed Bill roughly, the touch jerking him back to the present. "How long have you known?"

"Ainsworth turned up at Father's funeral. We were just told to stay away from him, that he was a very bad man. We didn't know anything more until a few years ago when we found some documents."

"We?"

"Me and Nell." Bill swallowed. "And Tam."

"Why did no one tell me this?" Luke said, pacing up and down. He stopped to face Bill and grabbed the lapels of his jacket. In one swift movement, he'd pulled Bill up out of his chair and had pinned him against the wall. For the first time in his life, Bill was scared of what his little brother was capable of. He had no idea that Luke was this strong, for a start.

"Bloody Tam knows, but no one thinks to tell me? Am I not important enough?"

"Y-you were just a baby," Bill stammered, staring into his brother's eyes. "Only four. Nell and I weren't so old either, but we thought we could protect you if he ever turned up. Jem refused to tell me anything about him."

Luke stared back unblinkingly.

"Come on, Luke. I didn't know much more myself. It was only around the time Ainsworth threatened me that I started to try and find things out for myself. You're my brother. I was trying to protect you."

"He's already threatened you?"

Bill nodded. "Just before I caught you pickpocketing. About a week before. It was when I was walking home one night. Told me to stop asking around about him or I'd get what was coming for me."

Luke continued to stare at Bill, then suddenly released his grip. "I can't believe it! He started threatening me the very next week that he'd hurt you if I didn't cooperate. He'd already hurt you by then." Luke swiped at the back of a chair, and it fell to the floor with a clatter. Still not satisfied, he turned around and kicked at the front door. There was a crack and the door split. Seconds later, a wail went up from upstairs. They both turned and looked at the ceiling. The crying carried on.

"Sorry," Luke said.

Bill sighed and grimaced. "You'll have Betsy down here in a moment. Pick up that chair and sit down."

Luke collapsed onto the nearest chair.

"He also tried to split up me and Betsy," Bill continued. "He kept telling her untrue things about me, and also how I'd react when she confronted me. In the end, she started to believe him. I almost lost her and Alice Anne because of him. And Jem seems to be terrified of even hearing his name."

Luke stared at him, mouth open. Then he put his hands on his head and groaned.

"You should have told me," he said, his head in his hands. "You should have told me as soon as you found out anything. You don't know what you've done."

Bill's heart was pounding. He had thought he'd done the right thing. Luke stood up, pushing the chair backwards. He took a step towards the broken door and grabbed his jacket and cap.

"Where are you going?"

"I'm going to go and kill him!"

"No, Luke, come back! Ainsworth is crazy."

But the door slammed shut, and Luke was already gone.

"Hall, a word!" Bill jumped. He'd been concentrating hard on laying out boiler parts, showing two apprentices how to interpret the blueprints before they finally started welding the pieces together. He didn't know his master had been watching him; if he had, he would have taken better care. Bill handed the blueprint to one of the apprentices, a thin, gangly lad with a shock of black hair that never seemed to lie straight at the back, and followed his master to the office.

"Now, Bill," said Henry Robinson, closing the door and walking to the other side of his desk. "I've just had word from another foundry that there's been a few workers instigating political unrest, and we need to put a stop to that straightaway. I don't expect this of you because you are one of my best workers, but it would be best for you if you told me what you knew."

Bill swallowed hard and nodded.

"Do you know anything about the passing of pamphlets on suffrage, teaching of workers to read and discussions on striking for better pay and conditions?" Bill swallowed again and looked straight at his master.

"No, sir."

The old man looked closely at Bill. His milky-blue eyes held Bill's gaze for what seemed like several minutes. Bill was forced to keep his eyes steady, thinking Henry Robinson would see right through him if he looked away now. He started to sweat more than he did when he was close to the furnaces. Henry finally lifted his head, crossed his arms and widened his stance.

"For your sake, you need to tell me what you know. We've been very good to you here. You're one of my best workers and one of the most intelligent ones, but if I find out you know something about this and don't say anything now, there is nothing I can do to help you, do you understand?"

"Yes, sir." Bill's heart was racing. He could feel rivulets of sweat running down his back.

"Now, Bill, I know you can read, and I know what kind of man you are. If you know anything, tell me who the instigators are, whether there's anyone at this foundry involved, then you might be able to keep your job." Bill didn't take his eyes off his master and refused to blink. He had a split-second choice here.

"It's true I have helped a few friends learn to read – read the Bible and that – but I don't know of any talk of striking. Nothing in this foundry." No matter what kind of uneasy friendship had grown over the years between Bill and his master, he knew they would never be equals.

And he knew he could not lose his job or give up his brother-in-law. "Then I believe you." Henry Robinson sighed. "That's all. You can go." Bill walked back to the apprentices, who were arguing over the placement of a boiler part. He could feel Henry's eyes burning on his back. He knew Bill knew something. He wasn't stupid. Bill was feeling torn. His master had helped him so many times, shown him kindness, given him more responsibility than many other journeymen at the foundry had been given, and in turn Bill had let him down. He felt pulled between his master and the other workers, whom he knew felt it was unjust that Bill got all the praise, that Bill got fewer tellings-off and fewer fines than anyone else. That Bill was old Henry's favourite. But Henry Robinson was still a master, and as loyal as Bill felt towards him, Henry would never be able to understand what it was like to be working class. But what had just happened? Who had found out about him and Tam teaching the workers, passing pamphlets? He hoped Tam was all right, that they wouldn't find out names. But Bill couldn't shake the feeling that names were known, he'd just personally betrayed his master and that he'd be out of a job in a few hours.

The bell rang for the end of the day, and Bill looked up. No one tapping on his shoulder, no master, no one coming to speak to him. He left the foundry quickly and rushed home. He closed the front door, barred it, then closed the curtains.

"What's wrong with you?" Betsy asked from her chair by the fireplace, feeding Jamie. Alice Anne was sat at the table, scribbling on a piece of newspaper.

"Why aren't these two in bed?" he asked sharply.

"I'm not tired," Alice Anne said, looking up.

"Bedtime!" Bill raised his voice. Betsy glared at him.

"And how am I supposed to get that one to bed while I'm feeding this one?"

Bill ignored her and paced around the kitchen until she finished.

"What is wrong with you?" She looked concerned now.

"I'll tell you once these two are out of the way," he said irritably.

Betsy gave him a strange look as she carried Jamie up the stairs.

"Come on, Alice Anne, you too."

Betsy came back downstairs and wasted no time. "Bill Hall, you just sit down and tell me what's going on."

"They know," he said, wringing his hands.

"Who? Know what?" Bill looked her straight in the eye.

"They know someone has been passing pamphlets, talking about striking for better pay and conditions, and they asked me today if I knew who it was."

"What? Why would they think it's you? Why would they ask you?" Bill hung his head.

"Oh, tell me you haven't!"

Bill remained silent.

"You stupid man!" Betsy shouted. "Not only are you never around because you're always off teaching others, but you've been organising strikes too?"

"I haven't!" he exclaimed. "I may have passed some pamphlets, and I may have discussed them if questions came up, but I haven't been organising strikes or anything. This was all purely theoretical discussion."

"And who wrote these pamphlets?"

"I may have helped Tam write them," he said quietly.

"Oh Lord!" Betsy exclaimed. "Why, Bill? Why did you have to get involved?" She paced up and down the room. "Do you have no regard for your own family? You're supposed to be looking after us, not getting yourself into trouble, probably losing your job. We'll all end up in the poorhouse."

"I didn't think," Bill said, sitting down into his armchair, sinking his head into his calloused hands. "We'd been doing this for so long, Tam and I – the reading, talking politics – that maybe we got careless. I don't know. I just never thought we were writing anything that risky."

"Ugh!" Betsy screamed in frustration.

They sat in silence until she had calmed down enough to speak again.

"So have you lost your job or not?"

"Not yet."

"What do you mean 'not yet'?"

"Mr. Robinson asked me what I knew about it, and I said nothing. He said he believed me."

Betsy stared hard at her husband's face. "So he believes you? They don't have any names? They don't know it's you?"

"Not yet."

"But do they have the authors' names?"

"I don't know."

"Who printed them?"

"Tam. But he usually only did it because his handwriting was the best. Then he'd make copies on the machine at the Temperance Hall. That was his job, even back when I'd first met him."

He was met with a stony silence.

"Betsy, it's not what you think. I'm pretty sure the pamphlets we printed were harmless."

She turned her head slowly to face him. "Pretty sure or sure?"

"Well, I'd have to look at them again. Tam . . ."

Betsy groaned and tossed her head back.

Tam! The gravity of his brother-in-law's situation suddenly hit him. He was surely going to be in more trouble than Bill over this. He'd been working at a different foundry since he and Nell had married and moved to Little Bolton, so Bill couldn't be sure how reasonable Tam's master would be.

"Tam!" he shouted. "Should I go and see if he's all right? If they questioned him as well?"

Betsy thought for a moment. "No," she said. "What if they know it's him and he's being watched? You don't want to give them any reason to suspect you too, if they don't already. No, we'd better wait a few days, carry on as normal. See them after church on Sunday."

Bill was seriously worried. He didn't want to show his face outside or even go to work the next day. This situation could only get worse as the masters gathered more information. He didn't think it could have become so bad. He'd discussed the text with Tam, seen the finished pamphlet, distributed a few in the pubs around Little Bolton. They had never once broken the rules and distributed anything at the foundries. The pamphlets were mostly on temperance and education – the pros of each. This was just a tiny step further. A small comment on a family wage. Linking education with better working conditions. Suffrage. And they'd discussed the contents a little with the men they'd been teaching to read. There had been some good discussions, some jokes. Of course, some discussions had become angry slates against the masters for their cruelty, but no one had been talking of striking, of inciting unrest. Tam had been sure to make sure the pamphlets were written very mildly. Still, Bill had a terrible sense of dread that grew every minute.

Nell thought she heard the front door being pushed open, slowly. Then she heard boots scraping on the wooden floor downstairs. Glancing around the bedroom, all she could find to use as a defensive weapon was the broom she'd been using. Grabbing it, she crept out onto the landing and made her way to the top of the stairs, trying to avoid the creakiest floorboards she knew so well.

She peered down from the top of the stairs but couldn't see anyone. Broom in hand, she crept down, step by step, until she reached the bottom. Breathing hard, she braced the broom handle in front of her body and waited. The footsteps were now clearly in the kitchen, just a few yards from the staircase. As quietly as she could, she peered around the wall of the staircase, then let out a yell.

"Tam! Oh, thank God it's you," she cried. "Don't scare me like that! I couldn't think who it could be, walking in and not calling out. I've just put Alcy down for her nap."

She leaned the broom against the wall, went to go and hug him, then stopped.

"What are you doing home in the middle of the morning?" She was afraid she already knew the answer.

"Oh, Tam, did you get fired? What did you do?"

"Come and sit," he said. Nell went to sit down next to him as he told her what happened.

"I have no idea why they're accusing me of this," said Tam. "We haven't broken any rules. Bent them a little, maybe. Perhaps the comment on a family wage might not have gone down too well with some people, but those pamphlets were harmless, Nell. And we never,

ever, discussed anything at work with anyone. Neither I nor Bill at his foundry."

"Bill!" she exclaimed. "Has he been sacked too?"

"I don't know."

"We have to get word to him, find out what happened."

"Best we leave it right now," said Tam. "If someone doesn't have his name and is watching to see who I contact, it's best for him that we stay away." Nell went quiet and put her head on Tam's chest.

"Oh, Tam!" she sobbed. "What will we do now? Rumours fly so fast in this town. By the time word gets round, you'll be branded a troublemaker and won't be able to get another job. What will we do?"

"Well, I could either become a hawker or a farm labourer or something, or we move far enough away to where word hasn't got and find a job in a foundry." Nell sobbed even harder. Tam just held her, trying to soothe her until her sobs subsided.

"Why? Why must it be like this?" she asked through her tears, thumping his chest. "Why can't the masters just give us all decent working conditions, a family wage and some sort of say? Then we wouldn't have to fight for more rights."

"Every generation has to fight for something," Tam said, catching hold of Nell's wrists and holding them tight. "I just want to do my best to make a better future for my children so their voices and their votes get to be heard. Their struggle won't be this one, but they will have their own to overcome."

Nell laid her head on his chest. "Do you think we'll ever achieve that – the vote – in our lifetime?"

"We better!" Tam laughed. "Otherwise, I will have wasted a lot of time and effort."

Nell laughed. And that was the reason she loved him, his humour and his sense of justice. It seemed to run in her family too, with Bill and Tommy – she sat up suddenly.

"Our Tommy," she said.

"Your Tommy, what?"

"He once said to me, back when I was living in Manchester, that if I ever needed help, to call on him and he'd do what he could. I can't see us needing more help than we do now. Although maybe it's not a good time, after what happened with Bella and all."

"I know," Tam said softly. "Poor Tommy. Must have been a shock when Bella died so suddenly last summer. Who knew she had a weak heart?"

"I wish I could have done more for him," Nell said. "Bella was an amazing woman, such strength. I haven't heard much from him since he sent word that Bella had died. He said he didn't want me to visit, and he only answers my letters briefly now. Last time he answered was several months ago."

Tam sighed. "Poor man must have been heartbroken. He probably wasn't in his right mind, but there's not much you can do if he said he didn't want any help. Is he still living in the same place?"

"I think so." She thought about it for a moment. "I think we have to try him. I feel bad about burdening him now, but where else can we go?"

"I'll collect my pay tomorrow," Tam said, "then we can take the train." He was silent for a moment. "Would that be far enough away?"

"Salford?" Nell sat up again. "We have to try. Otherwise, where else would we go? Blackburn? Preston? Rochdale?"

Tam hugged her. "You know, Nell," he said softly, "few men are lucky enough to have such an understanding woman."

Nell smiled. "As long as we're together, Tam, I think I can deal with just about anything."

CHAPTER 24

LEAVING BOLTON AGAIN
MARCH 1853

Nell hurried to the train station to meet Tam, having just left Alcy with Betsy. Was it really six years ago since she was last on a train? She still remembered that day so clearly – so happy she was at being able to come home. And now she was going to have to leave again.

She had agreed to meet Tam at the ticket office. Where was he? She hoped it had gone as well as could be expected at the foundry. Maybe she should have gone to pick up his pay instead. She was sure they wouldn't have been too happy to see him back there, standing in line, even if it was for the last time. But then she saw him, that wild, curly mop of untameable hair sticking out of his cap, now tinged with straighter grey strands, and that round face with its now fading freckles. His face, usually always framed with a smile, looked pale and worried. She waved, and he smiled and walked towards her.

"How did it go?" she asked.

"We don't need to talk about that," he said, sounding distracted. "I bought us tickets, but there's not a lot left. I don't think we can afford to stay over anywhere tonight."

"What, why?"

"Besides losing my job, I was heavily fined," he said.

"But that's not right," Nell protested loudly. Several people turned around and stared.

"Here's not the time or place," Tam said softly, taking his wife's elbow and guiding her forwards through the crowd towards the steps leading to the platforms.

"But, but they can't do that," she spluttered. "Sack you and take your money?"

"And making a scene at the train station isn't going to make it any better," Tam said quietly. "What do you want them to do? Know where we're heading so they can stop us getting a job somewhere else?"

Nell was quiet. Of course he was right, but she was so angry.

"Why don't you go and sit in the ladies' waiting room? It's a bit cold out," he said.

"I want to stay with you," she said defensively.

Tam smiled. "In that case, I'd be glad of the delightful company." Nell grinned and took his arm. No matter how hard things got sometimes, Tam Green could always make her smile.

So they stood and waited, taking in the passing steam trains, the dirt, smoke and noise, wondering what fate had in store for them next.

Once aboard the train, Nell experienced a vague feeling of the same sadness she'd felt before, in the exact same surroundings. She'd always left Manchester happy, happy to be visiting her family, but the journey back had always been hard. She remembered she'd cried every single time at the thought of not being able to see her brothers again for another few months.

But the journey seemed to go faster than she'd remembered, and the train was soon pulling slowly into the station, accompanied by swirling steam, pistons hissing and creaking. Salford Central was busier than Bolton station, and just as familiar to Nell. Wasting no time, Nell looked around, then purposely strode to the exit.

"You're in your element here, aren't you?" Tam smiled down at her.

"What do you mean?"

"You know this place so well; it must bring back a lot of memories."

"Yes," she said, "a lot of memories of missing my family."

Tam's face fell.

"I didn't mean ..." she started.

"No, you're right," said Tam, "I'm taking you away from your family. As if you haven't already spent so much time away from them. This is all my fault."

Nell swung round to face him. "Don't you ever say or think that. I'm your wife, and unlike most wives, I want to be with my husband."

Tam smiled and she continued. "I love that you're so passionate about your causes, that you want to make the world a better place, but the way the world is right now, we have to pay for that. We have to pay so our children will have it better. My father didn't think of anyone but himself, and look what happened to us all. No, I'd rather have you and your attitude and the consequences that go with that a thousand times over than deal with someone like my father."

Tam scooped her up and held her tight for a long time. Nell eventually wriggled free.

"Tam, we don't have time for this," she said. "Now we need to get to Bury Street and see if our Tommy is still staying at the same house. It's going to be dark soon, and I don't want to have to be wandering round town at night."

They crossed the busy road hemmed in on both sides by two-storey terraced houses. The red brick wound around the rows of windows and doors until it was abruptly stopped by a road. Nell walked up to a door right in the middle of the row and knocked loudly. An upper-floor sash window was raised with a crash, and a young blond head poked out. Nell and Tam stepped back so they could see more clearly.

"What do you want?" said the young woman, staring out at them.

"Oh, er," Nell was taken aback. It didn't look like Tommy was living here after all. Her heart sank. "I'm sorry to bother you. I'm looking for Tommy Hall; he used to live here. His wife's name was Bella. She passed away about six months ago. Do you know them?"

The young lady looked disgusted and slammed the window shut. Tam and Nell looked at each other.

"What now?" Nell started thinking. They could go to the tailor where he used to work and see if anyone was around who knew where Tommy was living. Although most people would have gone home by now. Perhaps they should try some beer houses in the area? It was so hard not being able to stay in touch by letter because Tommy couldn't write and he was too proud to ask anyone for help. But she'd never made an effort either, and the years slipped by so fast. She was just trying to decide which option would give them the best chance when the front door was flung open.

"Why do you want me Pa?" asked a young girl about ten years old, her thin brown hair tied up in pigtails. Nell and Tom turned around.

"Your Pa? Jane? Is that you? My, you've grown so much!" Nell started to smile. "Do you remember me? You came to my wedding. I'm Nell. Your Auntie Nell. This is your Uncle Tam." Jane looked up quizzically, then stared at Nell's face.

"Nope. Don't really remember you."

"That's fine," Nell said, smiling. "It was three years ago after all. Where is your Pa? Maybe I can talk to him?"

"In the pub, probably."

"Who's looking after you?"

"We have a new mother. She's called May." She jerked her head towards the upstairs window. "She's not as nice as our Mam, and she doesn't like hearing about it," she whispered conspiratorially.

"Oh," Nell said, kicking herself. Now she really wished she'd kept better in touch. But Tommy could have at least sent word about this new woman. And only six months after losing Bella? Maybe that's exactly why he didn't.

"I'm so sorry about your Mam."

"Jane! Get inside now!" A voice from inside made Jane roll her eyes, but she obeyed and stepped back into the room.

As the door was pushed to, Nell called out, "May? I'm sorry. I'm Tommy's sister. We haven't been in touch for a while. I didn't know you'd married."

The door opened again slightly, and the young woman peered around the door. She certainly looked very young, thought Nell, noticing that May had a firm grip on the door, her knuckles white and her jaw clenched.

Nell held out her hand. "Nell Green. Was Hall. Very pleased to meet you." May opened the door a little wider and took Nell's hand, her eyes wide.

"This is Tam, my husband." Tam leaned forward, and May shook his hand too. She quickly placed both hands back on the door and held it tightly.

"We're looking for Tommy. Do you know where he is right now?" Nell asked gently.

"Maybe try the Bee Hive," May muttered, looking them both up and down, taking in the cut of Nell's dress and the mended patches on Tam's coat.

"Thank you so much!" Nell said, ignoring the obvious insult. "Where's that again? I haven't lived around here in a long time, and I've forgotten a lot."

"Jane'll show you." May turned around and barked a few instructions at her stepdaughter, who returned to the doorstep with her younger sister.

"Nancy!" Nell exclaimed. "Oh, you were just a baby when I last saw you!"

"She doesn't remember you either," said Jane. "Come on, then."

Nell and Tam walked through the Salford streets with the two small girls leading the way. The factories and foundries were closed, just a few shops still open, but the life and noise had transferred to the many public houses around. After about ten minutes, they came to a wide main street with large buildings on both sides.

"That's it, there." Jane pointed to a large sandstone building. It stood alone, with double bay windows and a painted wooden sign of a hive and three bees hanging over the door.

"He's usually in there. If he's not still in the shop. He works quite late sometimes. May says he'd rather sew suits than be with her, but Pa says he can't turn work down. The shop's a few doors down."

"Thanks," said Nell.

"We'll be off, then." Jane spun around and skipped down the street, followed by her younger sister.

"Shop or pub first?" Tam asked, turning to Nell.

"Lets try the pub first while we're here," she said. "The shop might be shut, and I don't fancy having to start banging on the door while not knowing if anyone's actually there."

The walked into the smoky hallway and looked around the room. It wasn't so easy looking for someone you'd not seen in years. Most of the men were dressed in different shades of the same jacket, hat and haircut, and as a consequence, most of them looked like just slight aged variations of the same face. The air was thick, and the noise level fairly high.

Suddenly, Nell thought she'd spotted him, dragging Tam over to the back of the room.

251

"Nell!" Tommy stood up and came forwards to hug his sister. He looked confused. Nell couldn't get over how much he looked like Bill – just an older version. The two brothers had hardly seen each other over the years, but they looked and dressed so similarly that if you ever did see them together, they'd look like a pair of bookends.

"What – what are you doing here?" he asked, releasing her with a big smile on his face. "Tam, nice to see you again!" He shook Tam's hand.

"I need your help," Nell said. "Do you remember you once said to me that if ever I needed help ..."

"I would help you," he finished. "Yes, and the offer still stands. What's wrong?"

Nell looked at Tam and back at Tommy. "Can we go somewhere else and talk?"

"Of course." They left the pub and started walking towards the canal. Tam turned around to look behind them several times.

"Who are we looking for?" Tommy asked.

"No one," Tam said. "I'm just being paranoid."

"What's going on, then? Tell me."

The three of them walked along the towpath as Nell and Tam relayed their story to Tommy, sparing him the long version.

"Well," Tommy said, "that's quite a pickle. Foundries are not my area, but I daresay I know a couple of chaps who should know of any moulder jobs going round here."

Nell's shoulders started to relax a little. Perhaps things would work out, and at least she had some family here, and the streets were mostly familiar.

"Anything else?" he added.

"Nothing that can't wait."

"Right then!" Tommy said. "It's getting late. Let's head back to my place."

Nell smiled. Once the urgent things were out of the way, they would have plenty of time to talk. About May, for a start!

The house was just as Nell had remembered it when Bella lived there. May seemed an unwilling host, but she dutifully doled out the food and then disappeared up the stairs immediately afterwards. Jane and

Nancy were already in bed.

"She's very pretty!" Nell said.

Tommy smiled.

"And very young."

Tommy rolled his eyes.

"I guess you've been told that before." Nell smiled. "How did you meet her?"

"This is going to sound bad," he said, "but she came into the shop the day after we buried Bella. That was the first time I met her. She was very concerned about me when she heard. Brought me food every day after that. Said it was a tragedy and I was to keep my strength up for my two girls. She was very kind to me. And . . . and I really needed someone to look after my daughters."

"Oh," said Nell. "She knew what she wanted, then."

Tommy was short this time. "What else could I have done? She's been good to me," he said. "My girls are well looked after, even though she's only eight years older than our Jane."

"I wasn't criticising."

"No? Everyone else round here seems to. That's why I didn't tell my family."

"But you could have told me," Nell said. "You know you can talk to me about anything. It must have been an awful time for you all when Bella died so suddenly. Even I miss her."

Tommy looked at the floor. "I felt guilty. I was lost, and she was there. I knew full well how it looked. Lots of people commented. I just didn't want to admit to you that I didn't grieve Bella properly. I know how much you thought of her."

Nell stood up, walked round the table and hugged Tommy hard. What must he have been through? Everyone had their own reasons for doing what they did, and you couldn't really judge them unless you'd been in their shoes. Tommy hugged her back briefly and then broke free.

"I'll put a bed up for you in here," he said. "It's getting late. I'm sorry I only have blankets, but I'm sure we can make it somewhat comfy."

"It's nice and warm in here," said Tam, "we'll be fine!"

"Just leave them with me," Nell said. "You go up, we'll sort ourselves out."

Tommy pulled a bundle of blankets out of the cupboard under the stairs and passed them to Nell. "Good night, Sissy. It's so nice to see you again. I'm just sorry about the circumstances."

She hugged him hard. Then, as he made his way up the stairs, she turned to Tam.

"Let's make up the bed, then."

The next morning, Nell and Tam were woken early by May coming in to light the fire and make breakfast. Nell smirked as May's jaw dropped when Tam offered to take over cooking the gruel.

"He's progressive," Nell said, looking warmly at her husband. "Big on women's suffrage."

"Right," May said, a little unsure.

"We've not had a chance to get to know each other," said Nell. "You seem to be very good for my brother."

May looked at Nell cautiously. After a few minutes she replied, "Well, he doesn't talk about his family much. He did say he saw a lot of you when you lived here though."

Nell smiled. "Yes, we – " She stopped abruptly. How was she not going to mention Bella? Almost all the time she'd been in Manchester, Bella had been part of the family.

Tam interrupted, "Yes, this is only the second time I've met Tommy, so really, we're both new to the in-laws." He winked. May gave a quick smile that didn't reach her eyes.

"So why are you coming back to Salford?" she asked.

"Well, er ..." Nell turned to Tam. This was one thing they hadn't discussed. Could she swear Tommy to secrecy, ask him to keep it from his new wife? What kind of relationship did they have?

"It's a bit embarrassing, really," said Tam. "I'm looking for work. There aren't many jobs going where we are right now, and well, this is a much bigger town, and Nell used to live here, so we thought ..."

Only a slight lie, Nell thought. But when did her husband get so good at lying?

May nodded and continued to prepare breakfast.

After breakfast, May insisted they all get ready for church. She sent the girls upstairs to get changed into their Sunday best while Nell helped her remove the breakfast plates and start washing up, using the water from the bucket she'd already got from the pump on the corner.

"I'll stay here," Tommy said.

"What, why?" May glared at him.

"I need to talk to Nell and Tam. There never seems to be enough time, so it's better if we take this hour, and then we can see Nell off at the train station."

"But I don't understand why you need to talk to them instead of coming with us to church," May protested. "You talked last night. And they'll be moving here soon enough. It's not like you're never going to see them again."

"I haven't seen our Nell in quite a while," Tommy said. "And I've only ever met Tam once before. I have a lot to ask them still." He looked pointedly at Nell.

Nell looked away. She didn't want to listen to someone else's argument. She also hated herself for mentally comparing May with Bella.

"But you know I don't like taking your girls out on my own," May whined. "Jane never listens to me, and I can't stop Nancy disappearing off somewhere. They show me no respect – in church, of all places. And what will people think?"

"I'll have a word with them," Tommy said, getting up from the table. He went over to put his arms round his wife's shoulders. "And I'll make you a new bonnet, trimmed with that new ribbon we got in yesterday. For your trouble." May smiled up at him, then looked at Nell defensively. As Tommy went up the stairs, Nell glanced at Tam, then looked away. At that moment, Nell hoped her husband could read her mind. There was no way she would want May knowing their business. Nell was even beginning to wonder whether it was smart telling Tommy everything.

CHAPTER 25

A CONFESSION
MARCH 1853

Bill had spent the whole of Saturday dreading another tap on the shoulder. He sweated much more than usual, even though he spent the day mostly away from the furnaces. His usually nimble fingers would not work, and he dropped his tools and rivets several times. He was even asked twice whether he was all right. So much for acting normally! Luckily, it was only a half day, and he had Sunday off.

He was relieved to arrive home just before four o'clock, saying a quick hello to Jamie and Alice Anne, who were playing with his niece, Alcy.

"Has our Nell been round? Where is she?" he asked Betsy, hanging up his jacket.

"Salford," Betsy said, looking up from her mending.

"Salford? Why?"

"She and Tam have gone to visit your Tommy. Alcy is staying with us tonight, aren't you, love?" she said, smiling at their niece. Alcy beamed back and carried on playing with her cousins. Betsy glared at Bill, instructing him to shut up, and Bill knew there would be no more information until the children were asleep. Another three hours! Three hours that seemed to pass incredibly slowly. Finally, Betsy took the children up to bed.

"Well?" Bill asked as Betsy came back downstairs.

Betsy pulled a face. "They let Tam go. He's gone to Salford to try and find work. Nell's gone with him. She'll be back tomorrow though. Bill, he'd never get another job here, not with such a reputation as a troublemaker."

Bill sank down into his chair. "But it's not true. It's not fair!"

"You know how it is with politics, and you two took a risk. You could be next. Then we'd have to move as well. Did you think about that? Is what you're doing more important than your own family?"

"Of course not! And we weren't doing anything wrong." Bill started to wonder how Tam's master could have got word of this. How his own master had heard, but not known who was behind it.

"But how did they get his name? Why don't they have mine?"

"I don't know," said Betsy. "Perhaps it was one of the fellas you were teaching to read. Or someone who overheard you."

"But if they knew Tam, they'd know me. Why only Tam? Unless ..."

"Unless what?"

"Unless they have my name too."

"Then why weren't you fired?"

"I don't know," Bill said quietly. "Someone we were helping wouldn't knife us in the back like that. And why target Tam? Everyone likes him."

"Well, he obviously upset someone."

"But we didn't do anything wrong," Bill reiterated, standing up and flinging his arms in the air. "Yes, they could have seen the pamphlets, but all that inciting violence and striking, there's no evidence of that. That's all made up."

"Then you'll be able to prove it."

"You can't prove you didn't do something," he said acerbically. "And they don't need proof that we did something in order to lose our jobs. They don't care about that. They'll go off rumours if they want to." He swung around. "There's no justice."

"So what are you going to do about it?" Betsy asked, folding her arms and tilting her head to one side. "Are you going to hide out here and think it all over until they fire you too? Or are you going to do something about it?"

"What can I do?"

"Well, you can get a job at another foundry, stop the reading groups for a while."

"But Henry Robinson has been good to me."

"Yes, and you have lied to him. Do you think he'll keep you on once he finds out you lied?"

"No," Bill muttered. "Oh, I wish I could find out who did this. I'd ask him why and then wring his bloody neck!"

Bill knew it was inevitable. Henry Robinson was going to find out it was him, if he hadn't already over the weekend. He'd been so good to Bill, better than any other master would have been. He would have to tell Henry Robinson the truth. And one thing was certain – once he did, he wouldn't be able to work there anymore. Betsy was right. Either he found another job now and then told his master the truth, or he waited it out and risked being fired, branded a troublemaker and end up in the same position as Tam.

He'd done nothing but think about his situation all weekend. He'd talked to Nell when she'd come back for Alcy, and for the first time in many years had stayed away from the temperance meeting and the reading groups. He felt angry, sad and let down. Not least, it felt like he was losing his sister all over again. And his best friend. He was in a bad situation, and he had to do something to get out of it before it was too late. So when the bell rang out from the Spring Gardens Mill across the street, Bill put on his cap and coat and walked down to Soho Iron Works to ask for a job there.

It was already nine o'clock by the time Bill made his way back to Union Foundry. Without even stopping to take off his coat, he made his way to Henry Robinson's office. As he ascended the creaky wooden stairs, he thought about the very first time he had come here with Jem, nine years ago. How much things had changed. He had been just a boy then, unable to read, unable to make decisions for himself, not knowing what life had in store for him. That was before he'd seen the suitcase. Before he'd got angry at Jem. Before he'd learned to read and found things out for himself. And now here he was again. Where had reading got him? Nell and Tam having to move away. That was the payoff for them helping others to read. And Luke had been missing since he'd gone out to confront Ainsworth. Granted, Luke went missing quite regularly, but Bill couldn't help but worry this time. Each creaking footstep on the worn wooden steps brought him reluctantly closer to his fate.

He knocked on Henry Robinson's door. The old man looked up from his desk, surprised to see Bill, but waved him in anyway. Looking directly at him, Henry's forehead started to furrow, his wild eyebrows – the only hair not snowy white – moved closer together. "Hall, is there something wrong?"

"Yes, sir, I'm afraid there is."

"Sit down, man."

"I'd prefer to stand, sir. I'll be out of your way in a moment."

Henry Robinson listened patiently while Bill explained. Only after Bill had offered his resignation did the old man speak.

"I appreciate your honesty. I just wish you had told me when I first asked you." The old man's demeanour was icy.

"Sorry, sir," Bill mumbled. "I was scared, and I didn't know what had been said, didn't know what rumours had been put about. I need to support my family, and you just can't defend yourself from rumours."

Henry Robinson brushed at a minute fleck of cotton on his sleeve. "Let's leave it at that, Hall. You have been one of my best workers and one of my most trustworthy up until now. I thank you for telling me the truth, even if it is a little late. But you understand that I cannot keep you on after this."

Bill hung his head. "I understand completely, sir."

"Then we'll leave it at that," said Henry. "As far as I'm concerned, you left here under your own steam. I won't be repeating what you said here today. And if anyone asks, I'll say you're a damned good worker and I'm sorry to lose you."

Bill nodded gratefully. "Thank you, sir. And I'm so sorry to have let you down."

"Best of luck, Hall." Henry smiled, holding out his hand. Bill shook it and turned to leave. Hesitating, he turned back again.

"There is just one thing. Who was it that said we were inciting unrest, encouraging people to strike? Who gave you the pamphlet?"

"It was an old gentleman. Said he knew you from the temperance movement and had overheard you and your brother-in-law talking and didn't like where it was going. Said they didn't want troublemakers associated with them."

"So he told you my name?" Bill asked in surprise.

"He said Bill Hall and his brother-in-law."

Bill's eyes opened wide. "So why didn't you fire me on the spot?"

"I didn't know if there was any truth in it. Thing is, the old man didn't seem to be very trustworthy. I don't know many teetotallers who smell of ale early of a morning." He winked.

Bill thanked him once more, turned and fled. Could it have been? Could it really have been Ainsworth? Was he keeping his promise of destroying Robert Hall's remaining family one by one? Did this mean that he had Luke? Bill suddenly felt a cold shiver. He needed to find his little brother before it was too late.

CHAPTER 26

THE CONFRONTATION
MARCH 1853

Luke arrived at the hut in Church Wharf and flung open the door.

"Ainsworth! Ainsworth, where are you?"

"Don't be speaking to my father like that," Jackie said, standing up and walking towards Luke. "Show some respect!" He cuffed Luke around the ear.

Luke took a step back. "Shall I tell you something about your father? Shall I?" he said, pointing his finger at Jackie. His cheeks felt on fire, and he was shaking with rage. "Your father destroyed mine. Stole all his money, lied, cheated. And then he set out to destroy my siblings when they have done NOTHING."

"Why should I care?" Jackie sneered. Luke lunged at him, forcing him against the wall on the opposite side of the room.

"Now, now, children. No need for that!" came a voice out of the darkness. Luke hadn't even noticed Ainsworth sitting in his chair in the corner with two other men they regularly worked with. He let go of Jackie and walked towards Ainsworth.

"How dare you!" he spat. "You've been threatening to hurt Bill unless I do what you want when all along you've been trying to destroy him anyway. You leave him alone, you decrepit old bastard."

"My, my," Ainsworth sneered. He held up his hand, and Luke looked behind him. Jackie was standing close, about to attack him.

"Little Luke has found his voice. Now what are we going to do about that?" He stood up and put his face so close to Luke, he could feel his breath. Luke wrinkled his nose, disgusted.

"You leave my family alone!" he yelled. "I'm warning you. You mess with Bill once more and I will kill you."

Ainsworth broke into a smile. Luke saw nothing in front of him apart from a red fog. He growled and launched himself at Ainsworth, pushing him back into his chair and pummelling him with all the strength he had.

"That's for my father, who should have done this to you himself, you bastard!"

Luke felt his arms being grabbed, but he angrily and rapidly tugged them free and continued to pummel the old man. Finally, three men pulled him off Ainsworth and held him up so his feet couldn't touch the ground. Luke kicked and screamed and twisted with rage.

"Put him down in the cellar for now, and come and help me," Ainsworth panted. One of the men immediately went to Ainsworth's aid. Luke went still and eyed the doorway. Jackie and the other man dragged Luke outside, then around the corner of the hut. The second Jackie let go of him to open the hatch to the cellar, Luke elbowed the other man hard in the stomach. The man gasped and dropped to his knees. Before Jackie even had time to react, Luke tore off.

He pumped his arms and legs as fast as they would go, as though his life depended on it. For his life did depend on it. The only thing he could think of right now was getting away; trees and ferns blurred as he rushed by them, raindrops splashed into his eyes as he tore his way through the foliage. His legs felt weak, heavier with every step, the bottom of his trousers and his shoes soaked. He felt sick, ice in his throat and lungs about to burst, but the hot blood coursing through his veins kept him going as he willed his legs to move faster and faster. Up over the banking and into the woods.

The shouting had subsided. All Luke could hear now was his breath and the pounding of his heart and his feet. He slowed slightly, turning round to judge how close his chasers were and immediately tripped over a tree root. Pain shot through his ankle. He gasped with the shock, grabbing his foot. But there was no time to rest now, even if he couldn't see them. Thinking quickly, he looked around and spied an old hollowed-out tree trunk. Climbing into the hole, he lowered himself down onto a heap of composted leaves and twigs. His feet reached the squelching mass at the bottom, and he crouched down. He willed his breathing and his heart to slow down – they would surely hear the thudding beat and his rattling breath.

But no one appeared. Perhaps they were waiting for him back on the towpath. He'd have to go back that way to get home. Or perhaps they'd walked around, trying to cut him off farther into the woods. Luke now had no idea which direction was safest. He just knew he couldn't go home now. Not to Bill, who had always looked out for him no matter what trouble he got himself into. But Bill had kept things from him too. If only he'd been open and told him everything. Trying to protect him? How was this protecting him? Leaving him to the likes of old Mr. Ainsworth and his vicious son, Jackie? If only one of his brothers had warned him about the Ainsworths, this could all have been avoided. But now there was no way out. All the risks he'd taken in the past ... and what for? And now people were out to kill him.

If he got out of here, he would have to go far away where Ainsworth couldn't find him, start afresh. He was glad at times like these that he had no wife and family relying on him. He liked to feel free. But at this moment, stuck in a tree, legs cramping and unable to walk, Luke Hall was anything but free. He did not know how he was going to get away without risking being caught. He needed a plan. He needed his big brother. Again. Luke sat there considering his options, but by all probability, his only option now was certain death. Why had he ever got involved with Ainsworth?

CHAPTER 27

THE JOURNEY TO SALFORD
MARCH 1853

Luke had been lucky. He'd managed to get out of the woods after nightfall. The only thing he could think of – as Ainsworth's men would surely find him if he stepped foot in Bolton again – was to try to find Tommy in Salford. So he had set off, racking his brain to try to remember any little information about his brother that would make him easier to find. It had taken him just over two weeks to reach the outskirts of Salford, heading in a roundabout way and staying on the moors or in the forest as much as possible to try and cover his tracks. He had occasionally approached a town to steal food or dry, clean clothing from clotheslines when he'd got wet and cold. But whenever he did come into contact with people, he tried to keep to the shadows and make himself invisible. He'd lived off rainwater and whatever scraps he could find or steal to eat. But sleeping rough in the cold, wet April weather had taken its toll. His ankle was really swollen, and what had begun as a bit of a cold had now turned into a racking cough, but he just had to keep going. At first, he'd used the train tracks and the River Irwell as a guide, keeping a lookout for the steam trains and barges from afar, but after a while he felt safer staying completely out of sight. He didn't want Ainsworth's men getting any information on his whereabouts. And if he could just get to Tommy, then Tommy could get word to Bill to look out for Ainsworth. Unless it was already too late.

The sun was going down, and people were rushing to get home from their jobs. Luke sat on the banks of the Irwell and watched them for a while, trying to decide what to do next. He really wanted to just collapse and lie down somewhere, anywhere, but he wasn't safe yet. He had never even been to Salford before, let alone his brother's house, and had no idea where he lived. All Luke had to go on was that Tommy had mentioned St. Stephen's Church when he was over for Nell's wedding and that Luke knew he was a tailor. It wasn't much, but it wouldn't do him any good to start asking just any old person around here, just in case Ainsworth had his men out looking for him. It seemed like a tall task to find his brother, but he couldn't give up now. Tommy was his last hope, the only one of them not living in Bolton; otherwise, he wouldn't have turned to him.

Luke looked up and saw the top of a steeple. He could be sure a rector wouldn't be in Ainsworth's pocket. Old Mr. Ainsworth had something against men of the cloth. Said they were only fit for distractions so they could rob people while they were at church. Or indeed, rob churches. He gritted his teeth and pushed himself to walk towards it. It took him ages to get there; his ankle was still painful on every step and he was weak from hunger. He didn't want to bring attention to himself by stealing some food here, as he was hardly in a fit state to outrun anyone. Entering the gates, he limped through the grounds and pushed open the church doors.

"Can I help you with something?"

Luke looked up and saw the rector standing by the altar, holding a stack of prayer books. "Please," Luke said, limping over to him, "please help."

The rector rushed over and helped Luke place one arm over his shoulder, supporting him by the waist.

"Steady," he said as he lowered Luke down onto a pew. "What's happened?" He gazed at Luke's clothes – freshly stolen off a clothesline only the day before, partly covered in mud, the lack of a coat and hat in this weather and his shoes. "What happened?"

"I was on my way here from Rochdale," Luke began. "Two fellas stole my coat and money and beat me. I tried to fend them off, but one of them stamped on my foot – almost broke it. I've walked for the past day, not having any money for a coach for the last bit of the way. I'm on my way to meet my cousin, we have some business to attend to together, but I just need to rest for a while."

"Of course, yes!" said the rector. "You poor thing. Come on, I'll help you over to the vicarage. My wife will give you some food, and we'll take a look at your leg."

"I don't mean to ask for charity, I have money. My cousin can pay you back until I arrange something. But you are very kind. Thank you."

The rector beamed. "No trouble at all. Come on, let's get you inside where it's warm."

"Thank you so much," said Luke. "You're very kind. John Cooper is the name."

"Nice to meet your acquaintance," said the rector. "Richard Mills."

They shook hands. Some people are so gullible, Luke thought as he let the rector help him up again. You have to believe your own lies if you want anyone else to believe them, that's what he had been taught.

It took all of Luke's willpower not to fall asleep in the warm cottage. He'd been offered a bath and clean clothes belonging to the rector, and now he just wanted to wolf down the meat pie he'd been given. Instead, he took his fork properly and ate one mouthful at a time, hunger clawing at his stomach and mocking him. He even dabbed at the corners of his mouth with his napkin, smiling at his hosts and thanking them profusely.

"What's the name of this church?" he asked. "So I can send a token of my thanks when I get back home."

"Oh, no need," the rector said, batting the air away with his hand, "we're just happy to help."

"Then maybe I can donate to the church," Luke said. "And thank you for the loan of clean, dry clothes too. It is very much appreciated. I feel like a new man." He gave a quick, charming smile.

"You're very welcome," the rector said. "This is Christ Church."

"Well, thank you," Luke said. "I apologise for my abruptness, but I need to leave. My cousin will be wondering where I am. Now if you would just point me in the direction of St. Stephen's, I will be able to find my way from there."

"I'll do better than that," said the rector. "I'll take you there!"

Luke's smile fixed to his face as he tried not to let his emotions show. "That is very kind of you, but you've already been far to kind to a complete stranger. And I'm sure you have plenty of work to be going on with."

"It really is nothing," the rector said jovially. "Do not neglect to show hospitality to strangers, for by this some have entertained angels without knowing it. Hebrews, chapter 13, verse 2."

"May the Lord now show you kindness and faithfulness, and I too will show you the same favour because you have done this. Samuel, chapter 2, verse 6," Luke countered, glad that Ainsworth had made him learn several Bible verses to cover almost all eventualities when he was in character. Cons took a lot of background work.

"My dear fellow," said the rector, "how refreshing to meet a knowledgeable Christian. Please let me ring for a carriage. It's not far, but you won't make it on that foot. I'll tell the driver to take you to St. Stephen's. And I hope you recover quickly from this ordeal."

"You are so very kind," Luke said, shaking the vicar's hand with his right, placing his left on top. "I will write and send that donation."

"Yes," said the rector. "We would love to know how you got on and be relieved when you reach home safely. Do take care. It was very nice to meet you, Mr. Cooper."

"John, please." Luke gave his hand one last shake and followed him out to the carriage. Settling back into it, he started to think about what to do next. One hurdle over, he was on his way to St. Stephen's. Now he just had to find Tommy. He was so tempted to nod off in the cart, but he needed to keep his wits about him, especially if he was to be convincing.

Climbing down from the cart, Luke thanked the driver and hobbled towards the church. It was a squat, rectangular church, very different from the spire and columns of Christ Church. Even the bell tower was low and squat. The whole impression was of a hen laying an egg, Luke thought. He needed to keep up his pretence of being John Cooper meeting his cousin, in case the rector spoke to someone at this church before he found Tommy. However, he was well dressed and presentable now, so that should help. A chameleon – that's what old Mr. Ainsworth had called him. Never had anyone been able to more easily take on another character than Luke had, he'd said. And that had helped them greatly with their scams, with their selling of goods that Luke had never asked about the origin of. Luke had even managed to get himself out of trouble a few times by turning on the charm and spinning a convincing story. Always believe your own lies, he thought, and he had become those characters. For it was usually better to be someone else than to be himself.

Bracing his shoulders and taking a deep breath, Luke walked inside the church. There was no one there. Cursing his luck, Luke limped outside and looked around to see if he could find the rectory. It wasn't so far away, but a short distance on his painful foot now felt like a mile. He really shouldn't have rested. He reached the rectory and knocked on the door.

"Hello, there," he said to the rector who answered, shaking his hand. "John Cooper. I'm over here from Rochdale to meet my cousin, but I got waylaid, so I missed him. And I'll be darned if I've lost his address." He patted down his pockets theatrically. "All I know is he lives in this parish, and I wondered if you know of him? Tommy Hall. He's a tailor."

"Why, yes!" said the rector. "Tommy Tailor, we call him, if he's the one I'm thinking of. Now let me think. I know his sister, Nell, lives on Uxbridge Street, just moved here. Are you thinking of moving here too? Haha." He seemed amused at his own joke.

Luke's eyebrows shot up before he could help himself. "Ah yes, Nell. I haven't seen her since her wedding. Such a nice man, her husband, Tam."

"Yes, quite. They all seem like a nice family," said the rector. "We've only seen them a few times, but my wife always remarks on how lovely Nell's dresses are. Helps if your brother's a master tailor though!" He winked conspiratorially. Luke forced a chuckle.

"Yes, I think Tommy Tailor lives up on Bury Street. I'm not sure though, but he does work at the tailor's on Blackfriars Street by the Bee Hive. Well, I say works, but he practically runs the place after old Mr. Beasley got sick."

Luke patiently listened to the rector go on about several of his parishioners. He was just so tired now. His head was spinning, and he felt like he might fall into a dead sleep at any moment.

"So that's Bury Street, you say?" he interrupted.

"Yes, up the main road here, and it's the second set of crossroads. Turn right and just follow the road. I can't tell you exactly where on that road – best you ask when you get there. Otherwise, you'll find the tailor's on Blackfriars if you just ask for it, the one by the Bee Hive."

Luke thanked him and started to make his way there. His tiredness and pain made his journey very slow, but he was so close. He couldn't give up now. He turned at the crossroads and looked down the street. A busy main road with lots of shops. How the hell am I going to find him here? He looked around, pretending to stop and look in a shop window. Change of plan. Uxbridge Street. At least I know Nell and Tam are here, but when did they move? And why? Luke limped along and crossed the road over to where a few small children were playing with a hoop.

"Where's Uxbridge Street?" he asked them.

"Over there, mister," said a boy of about seven, pointing with his finger.

"Next street or the one after?"

"The one after."

"Thanks."

Luke continued walking slowly, keeping his head down. He tried to hide his limp, but the pain shot through his swollen ankle every time he placed his weight on it. Don't look around or you'll give yourself away, he thought. Just act normally. But he was dying to check if he was being followed.

He turned into what he thought was Uxbridge Street. Now what number? Was there anywhere he could sit and see if he could spot Nell or Tam coming or going? He'd just walk up the street and scout it out. He pulled his cap farther over his eyes and carried on. About two-thirds up the street, he looked up and saw three men loitering at the end of the street, hands in pockets, chatting and occasionally looking around. Luke could feel them staring directly at him. He pretended to drop something, looked around on the ground, picked up the invisible object and looked up in the opposite direction. No one there. Best he go back down to the main road. He turned around as two of the men started walking down the street. Where was the third? Luke quickened his pace, cursing. Suddenly, he saw a man walking towards him on the other side of the street. There he was. Or was it someone else? Luke was slipping. He really should be more observant right now. The two men behind him were gaining on him fast. As he passed the third man, a door was suddenly flung open onto the street, and he was yanked inside by his collar. Too weak to fight anymore, Luke gave up and collapsed.

CHAPTER 28

SCARLET FEVER
APRIL 1853

The knocker-upper was ratt-a-tatt-tatting on the bedroom window. Bill groaned and reached for the candle and matches. Bleary-eyed, he looked over at Betsy. Her eyes were closed tight, and Jamie was in the bed again – he'd probably had a rough night, but Bill was a heavy sleeper and never usually heard much. He groaned again, drew back the covers and stood up. Suddenly, he heard Betsy scream.

"Bill!"

"What is it?" Bill rushed back to the bed.

"Look at him!" she'd drawn away the blanket, and Bill saw the bright red cheeks and a rough red rash all over his son's chest.

"Scarlatina?"

"I think so." Little Jamie turned his head, then opened his eyes and began to cry.

"Shh, shh," Betsy tried to soothe him, looking helplessly at Bill. "I'm so scared. He's so little. This came on really fast."

"He's strong," Bill said, "you know he's strong." But he knew scarlatina could take even the strongest children. He suddenly felt cold, but he had to be strong for Betsy. She could get really worried when Jamie or Alice Anne got sick.

"Strong didn't help Emmy Benson's children," Betsy said, "and so many died from the last epidemic."

"It will be all right," Bill promised, "you'll see. Our Jamie will be fine. I survived it as a kid. Our Luke was only two, and he survived it." Bill still remembered his brother, not far off Jamie's age, and how sick he'd been. Nobody thought he'd make it. But Luke was a survivor. Bill still hoped that was true. He'd been missing now for two weeks. It wasn't unusual for him to go missing for two to three weeks, granted, but if it wasn't for the fact that he'd gone out to confront Ainsworth, Bill wouldn't be so worried. But what could he do? Where should he start looking? Luke could be anywhere right now.

"What if he isn't all right?" Betsy interrupted his thoughts. "How can I live without my little boy?" Bill hugged her hard. He couldn't even bear thinking about it – losing his son or his brother.

When Bill got home from work that evening, Jamie's fever was raging, and Betsy was beside herself.

"Alice Anne has been whiney and clingy. I just can't deal with her today. And I've tried putting cold wet cloths on Jamie's head and body, but it doesn't help. I don't know what else to do!" Betsy's eyes welled up.

"I'll take him," said Bill. "You get some sleep for now." He looked down at his infant son. He was no longer crying and no longer looking Bill in the eye when he talked to him. He could understand why Betsy was so worried – Jamie was scaring him. He felt completely useless. Not being able to make your own son feel better was a horrible feeling. He could see why Betsy was panicking now. This was a horrible illness, and small children could be perfectly fine one day and be gone the next. He was sure his little son, who looked just like him with his soft blond hair and blue eyes, was a fighter. But even the best fighters cannot continue sometimes.

Bill pulled out the tin bathtub, dragged it close to the fire and lay Jamie next to it. There was a pail of cold water standing on the counter ready for the morning, and Bill tipped it into the tub. Carefully undressing Jamie from his layers of baby clothing, he lowered him into the tub, supporting him in the crook of his arm. They sat there for what felt like hours, Bill's arm becoming stiff and cold, but he didn't move. His discomfort was nothing to what his little son was going through – cheeks very flushed and tiny body ravaged by the scarlet rash. When little Jamie started to cry for the first time in several hours, Bill took him up, wrapped him in a shirt, and took him upstairs. He climbed into bed, placing Jamie between him and Betsy. The three of them lay there, and Bill finally fell into a restless sleep.

The next morning, Bill woke to the sound of the knocker-upper. Betsy's arm was curled around Jamie. Bill got up and silently pulled on his clothes. He went over to check on Jamie again and saw two bright blue eyes looking back at him.

"Hello, you! Are you feeling better?" he whispered, not wanting to wake Betsy. Jamie smiled, and Bill carefully lifted him from the bed.

"Let's see if you want some food, then," he said. "It's been quite a while since you last ate." He grabbed Betsy's shawl from the bedpost, wrapped it around Jamie and silently trod down the wooden stairs.

By the time Betsy had woken, Jamie had taken in some lemonade and was nibbling on a crust of bread. Betsy walked through the door and put her hand to her heart.

"Hello, you!" she said, picking up Jamie from Bill's arms and cuddling him. Jamie briefly tolerated the kisses on his chubby cheeks before struggling to get down. Betsy sat down on a chair and balanced him on her knee.

"Told you he'd be fine," Bill said, grinning.

"You don't know how relieved I am! How's he been?"

"Well, he's not really hungry, and he slept for a long time. He's still not himself, he seems to be quite weak, only wants to sit on my knee and lean against me. I think he'll probably need another nap now, but his fever is gone."

Betsy kissed the top of their son's head. "Where's Alice Anne?"

"Isn't she with you? I thought she was sleeping."

"She never sleeps this long." Betsy handed Jamie back to Bill and stood up.

A few minutes later she came back downstairs. "She has it now. She's asleep. I need to get a cold cloth for her."

Bill's smile faded. "I'm sure she'll be fine too," he said. "She's older than Jamie, so she should be fine." Betsy nodded and handed their son over to him. "Get yourself some food first," he said. "It's going to be another long day. I'll go and take a wet cloth to her. Oh, we need more water too."

Betsy sighed.

Alice Anne was getting worse. She wouldn't take any broth or even the water Betsy had tried spooning into her mouth. When she was awake, she was crying, saying her tummy hurt. The rash was stronger, more vivid, and the fever was causing her to see things, crying and babbling because she didn't want Florrie from next door sitting on her bed and throwing things at her. No matter how many times Bill explained that no one was sitting on her bed, Alice Anne still cried. She no longer saw or heard anyone.

It was a Sunday, and Bill had been home with them all day. He had tried the cold water bath he had used with Jamie, but Alice Anne was restless and fought him. Eventually, Betsy took Alice Anne out and dried her off. Bill carried her upstairs and sat with her, stroking her hair.

"My sweet, sweet girl," he said. "You feel better now."

Alice Anne drifted off to a restless sleep, tossing and turning and occasionally crying out. Bill sat in a chair by her bedside, placing a cold, damp cloth on her forehead. He'd felt this useless when Jamie was so sick. There was nothing that could be done. No medicine that could be given. They just had to wait it out and hope their child was strong enough.

His thoughts turned to Luke again. He felt like he should be doing more, looking for him, but where would he even start? Bill had no idea where Ainsworth lived or hung out. Was it too dangerous to start asking around in public houses and wait for Ainsworth to appear? That would risk a beating, and he'd be no closer to knowing where Luke was. If he even was with Ainsworth. He could have decided to leave. Go far away and then send word later. But then surely Ainsworth would have come after Bill by now? A shiver went up his spine.

Alice Anne cried out and started clawing at her blanket. Bill immediately stood up, placed the cloth on her forehead and tried to soothe her by stroking her hair and talking to her. Eventually, she calmed down, and Bill lay down on the bed next to her. Wherever Luke was, he wished he was here right now because Bill had a terrible feeling he was going to lose one of them.

CHAPTER 29

THE LOSS
APRIL 1853

Bill felt a tap on his shoulder and turned round. His master, Richard Cole, gestured for him to follow, so Bill put down his hammer and pliers, took his apron off and sprang after him. His heart was beating fast. He knew something was wrong.

As they reached the main doors where it was a little quieter and cooler, he caught sight of Sammy Andrews from down the street, and his heart sank.

"What is it, son?" he asked.

"Ma told me to say you've to come home at once. They had to get the doctor round."

Bill looked up at Mr. Cole, who just closed his eyes and nodded. Without even waiting to grab his coat and hat, Bill tore out the door.

He ran home as fast as he could, little Sammy Andrews trailing in his wake. There were a couple of neighbours standing outside his house as he pushed past them.

"They're upstairs," one of them said, and Bill took the stairs two at a time and burst in to the bedroom.

"Betsy, what's wrong?" He stopped as he saw the doctor put down his stethoscope and stand up from the bed. His neighbour, and Sammy's mother, Mrs. Andrews, was standing with her arm around Betsy's shoulders. Betsy was standing with both hands pressed to her mouth.

"I'm sorry," the doctor said. "There's nothing I can do for her now. I don't think she has long left."

"Nooo!" Betsy screamed, falling to her knees. Mrs. Andrews held on to her hard and looked helplessly at Bill.

"But – but she can't," Bill stuttered. "She's going to be fine. Jamie was. She can't just ..." His voice faltered as he gestured to the bed.

"I'm sorry," the doctor said. "Sometimes this comes on too quickly and takes all their strength." He packed his stethoscope into his brown leather bag and snapped it shut. Bill didn't even notice him leave.

"I'll take Jamie round to ours," said Mrs. Andrews. "He can stay over. My lot love to play with him. It's no bother. You can fetch him in the morning."

Bill nodded.

"And I'm so sorry!" Mrs. Andrews picked up Jamie, cooing at him as she walked out the door. Bill went over to the bed and picked up Alice Anne, cradling her in his arms. Betsy walked over to them and ran her hands over Alice Anne's face and hair.

"My sweet girl, my sweet, sweet girl. You just hang on. Don't listen to that doctor. You're strong. You can beat this. Don't leave us." Tears fell down Bill's cheeks as he hugged his daughter even closer.

They stayed like this for several hours, the three of them, as the sun started to go down. Alice Anne sighed, and Bill felt the breath run out of her. He put his ear to her nose and mouth and then his hand on her chest. Betsy looked at him quizzically. He just shook his head and pulled Alice Anne tight against him, feeling her soft cheek against his, the tears flowing fast, wetting her hair. Betsy howled a sound unlike any Bill had ever heard, and the pair of them clung to their little daughter, not wanting to let go for the last time.

Molly was the first to arrive. Bill was sitting up in bed, still holding Alice Anne, while Betsy had fallen asleep, her face stained with tears.

"Come now," Molly said gently. "She's gone now. You need to let go so we can lay her out. Wash her and get her all prettied up. Your Alice Anne has gone. This is only her body left now, and we need to tend to it for her. Come on, give her to me." Bill looked up at Molly and down at Alice Anne again. He hugged her one last time and kissed her forehead. Then he handed her over to Molly.

"I'll take her downstairs," she said. "We'll let Betsy sleep a bit longer. You can find me her Sunday clothes." Bill just stared, then got up to follow after her. Downstairs, some of the neighbours had come round with the laying out board and propped it up on a pair of stools. Another had brought cloths and a bucket of water to start washing her. There was so much food in the kitchen. People coming and going, seeing if there was anything more they could do for Bill and Betsy. Time passed abstractly, and Bill felt like he was in a bubble. He just wanted them all to leave. He wanted to yell out and tell them all to go away, to stop their noise and their bustling. Alice Anne was barely cold, and he wanted more time with her, alone.

Bill came back to earth and looked up at Molly. "Did you hear what I said?" she asked softly. Bill shook his head.

"We need to sort out Alice Anne's funeral."

Bill looked over at his small daughter laid out on the borrowed board. Her tiny hands had been placed together on her chest, and her soft dark hair billowed out onto the wooden plank. Her face was waxy, her lips devoid of colour. Betsy sat beside her, her eyes and nose red and swollen, but tears would no longer fall. They hadn't left her side.

"How do you live with it?" Bill asked, his throat raw.

"You just have to keep on breathing," Molly said. "Focus on Jamie. It will get a little easier, but a part of your heart will always be missing."

Bill turned away and stared at the corner of the mantelpiece as he tried to fight back more silent tears. His little girl. She had been his joy. His beautiful little girl. It was because of her that he and Betsy had got back together, and for that he was forever in her gratitude. And to be taken from them so cruelly like that. Why? She had never done anything bad. Why did she have to suffer?

"We don't know why He chooses who He chooses," Molly said. "God just called her back. But she'll have her cousins to play with. And her grandparents to look after her. She won't be alone." Molly touched him lightly on the shoulder.

"I'll go and talk to the rector," she said, standing up. "I'll ask him to come round, and you can talk with him. I'll go and get a . . . I mean, I'll go and organise a few other things too so you don't have to think about it." She swallowed hard. "Bill. This is a pain you never forget. And you will never stop thinking if you had done just one thing differently, she'd still be here. But you can't. There was nothing that could have been done for her, do you hear me? Don't you ever blame yourself. I have been doing that for years, ever since my Lissy died, and it is torture. Please don't do that to yourself – for Jamie, and for Betsy."

Bill nodded, but he wasn't really listening.

CHAPTER 30

EMIGRATION
APRIL 1853

When Luke came round, he was lying on a soft bed with a blanket over him. Someone was dabbing at his face with a warm cloth and spooning broth into his mouth. He struggled to open his eyes and sit up, but he was barred by a large arm, holding him down.

"Now you lie still, young fella. You don't look in the best of shape. Nearly gave your sister a heart attack passing out like that! Let her tend to you, and you can tell us all about it later." Luke struggled against the arm, coughed, then gave up and relaxed. Didn't he recognise the voice? He opened his eyes slightly.

"Luke, thank God you're all right," he heard his sister say. "We've been so worried. Bill's been so worried. He sent us a message that you went missing. What happened"

"You scared the life out of me, dragging me inside like that," Luke complained.

"Sorry about that," said Tam. "Nell saw you pass by the window. I thought she was seeing things. Then as we opened the door, we saw two fellas right behind you. We thought those fellas were after you, you know, knowing your history, and that you were probably trying to find us."

"They might have been. Have they gone? Please don't tell anyone I'm here. I'm in serious trouble."

Tam looked at Nell. "I haven't seen anyone hanging around since. Look, eat what you can. Rest, get your strength back and then we can work out what to do."

"I need to get out of here," said Luke. "I need help to get away. I have a lot of money stuffed inside my mattress at Bill's, but I can't get at it. They'll kill me."

"Who will?"

"Ainsworth and his men."

Tam patted Luke's shoulder. "Rest. You need to get well first." Luke took in some more bread and broth, then flopped down and fell asleep again.

It was light when he woke again. He looked around the room, taking in the peeling grey walls and the two large mattresses – the sole furniture. The low-ceilinged room ran the depth of the house, windows at the front and an opening for the narrow stairs. Luke pulled the blanket tighter around him. He was grateful for its cover, but he was still shivering underneath. Hearing noises and Nell's voice downstairs, he decided to get up and join them.

Draping the brown woollen blanket around him, he realised his ankle was still very sore, but his cough was a little better. He limped downstairs and put his head round the door to Nell's living room.

"You stay in the back room. We don't want anyone seeing you through the front window," Tam said as Nell ushered Luke into the back. Luke looked around at the minimalist rooms. Two chairs and a chest of drawers filled the front room while a table and three chairs were placed in the back.

"I like what you've done with the place," Luke said, looking around.

"Shut up," Nell said. "We've only been here a few weeks."

"Why didn't you bring your furniture with you? Why did you move here?"

Nell was clearly irritated with him. "It was too far and expensive to move everything. Besides, we needed to move quickly. Tam got into trouble."

"Tam?" Luke exclaimed, eyes wide open. Suddenly, a large grin spread across his face and he started to laugh. "But Tam – he's, well he's a goody two-shoes. Tam never does anything wrong. Tam would rescue all the orphans and puppies and teach them all to read and vote for equality for plants and flowers if he could. What could he have done that was so bad?" He carried on chuckling.

"Look, if you're going to be like that, you can just get out. We're doing you a favour here."

The laughter quickly subsided. "Sorry, Nell. I didn't mean to be rude. It's just that I was surprised. Tam doesn't seem like someone who would get into trouble – take it from someone who does."

Nell tutted as she busied herself with taking down the drying laundry handing from a rope strung between two walls. "Bill was involved too."

"Bill?" Luke's voice sounded a little cracked. "What did he do? Is he all right? Where is he now?"

Tam poked his head around the door.

"I said I'd go and get Tommy when you woke. You need to come and bar the door while I'm out, just in case."

Nell nodded and followed him out. She slid the heavy chest of drawers in front of the door behind him.

"Bill, where's Bill? Is he all right?" Luke repeated.

"He's fine. He got off lightly. Someone let it be known that he and Tam were passing political pamphlets, inciting unrest and encouraging workers to strike for better pay and conditions."

Luke's eyebrows shot up. "They were?"

"Of course they weren't!" Nell said crossly. "Do they look like a pair of troublemakers to you?"

Luke shook his head.

Nell calmed down a little. "Well, then. Tam bore the brunt of it. He was the one who usually printed the pamphlets – that was pretty well known. The rest was rumour. Last I heard, Bill's master accepted that he'd done nothing wrong. But Bill was afraid of losing his job anyway. I don't know what happened since. We moved here. Tommy helped us straightaway."

"How long ago was this?"

"A few weeks. Just after you went missing. Where did you go?"

Luke looked down at his blanket and twisted the ends together. "I may as well tell you all when Tommy gets here," he said.

"Well, sit down and have some tea. We saved you some potatoes. You need to keep your strength up now. How's that cough?"

"I'm feeling a bit better. Nell, I ..."

Suddenly, there was a knock at the door. They both froze, rooted to the spot, staring at each other.

"I'll go," Nell said hesitantly. "It might only be Tam. I'll yell if it's not, and you get upstairs as fast as you can."

Luke hobbled up the stairs anyway but heard no noise except the sound of wood scraping on wood.

"He's in the back," he heard Nell say, followed by a voice that was both slightly familiar yet a little foreign.

"Luke? Luke! Where are you?" Luke peered down from the top of the stairs and caught sight of a familiar blond crop of hair. Goodness, how he looked like Bill! He half walked, half slid down the stairs and flung himself into his brother's arms.

"Steady on!" Tommy said, smiling, but clinging on to Luke just as hard. "You idiot!" he said softly. "What have you got yourself into?"

Luke jumped back as if he'd been stung. "I got myself into this?" he yelled. "I was only nine years old when Ainsworth targeted me. You should have told me. You all should have told me. Protecting me? Don't give me that! All this could have been avoided if you'd just told me. But no, now I'm on the run, can't even go home because if they catch me, they'll kill me. They've already broken my fingers as a warning when I was a kid and said I wanted out!" He held up the crooked fingers on his left hand and saw his brother wince.

"I'm sorry," said Tommy. "I should have said something. But you were so small, so young. And we all had other things on our minds. As time went by and nothing happened, I just thought it had all been forgotten or Ainsworth had died or something. I did think Jem would have told you if there'd been a problem."

"Jem? Jem? Why would you leave something so important to him?"

Tommy hung his head and apologised again. "Look, there are many things I would have done differently had I known, in hindsight. We all would have. Now sit down and tell me what happened."

Luke sat down and filled them all in. On how Ainsworth had approached him, asked him just to run errands at first, paid him generously, shared his idea of how Luke could avoid working in the mill and still survive, got him hooked. Then he turned nasty when the jobs moved on from petty pilfering and Luke had wanted to quit.

Finally, he'd confronted Ainsworth about what he'd done to their father, and that had resulted in Luke running for his life.

"I can't believe you survived two weeks living rough and walked all the way to Salford," Nell said, eyes wide open.

"It's amazing how much strength you find when you think your life is in danger," Luke said.

Nell fell silent.

"I hear a John Cooper, a cousin of mine, has been asking after me?" Tommy said.

"Yeah, that was me," Luke said nonchalantly.

"So we don't have to worry about him." Tommy winked. "But let's try and work out what to do next. I haven't seen anyone hanging around here. Tam?"

"No, nothing today at all. Neither here or on the way to your house."

"Then perhaps we were mistaken," Tommy said.

"Or perhaps they know where I am and they're just waiting, biding their time," said Luke. Tam and Tommy exchanged glances. "Either way, we need to act fast."

"There's a ship leaving from Liverpool on Tuesday," said Tam. "I thought about you when I read that last night in the newspaper."

"Tam!" Nell exclaimed. "We're not sending him away."

"These men are not playing. Either I go far away from here, or . . ." Luke broke off. "I don't have much choice, do I?" He looked up at Tommy. What had he done? He was never going to be able to see any of them again.

Nell started sobbing and rushed to hug him. He clung to her.

"I'll go and get the paper," Tam said. He came back, flicking through the sheets until he came to the information. "Port Adelaide, Australia."

"Australia it is, then," Luke said. Nell continued sobbing, and Tam put his arm around her. Tommy gave Luke the saddest smile, and Luke's heart sank even farther.

"There's only one problem. All my money is stashed at Bill's. How am I going to get that by the day after tomorrow?"

He looked around at his family. How was he going to get to see Bill too? To say good-bye? That thought hit him hard.

"I'll help you," Tommy said quietly. They all turned to look at him. "I have enough saved for a boat ticket and a little extra to tide you over."

"How?"

"Never you mind. You just have to worry about getting on that ship without being seen."

Luke looked intently at his brother's face. Usually, he could read people so well, but not this one. Was he hiding something? How did a tailor have enough money stashed away like that to help someone flee the country?

Tommy stood up. "I need to go and sort out the money. I'll bring it over later, or maybe you can come and fetch it, Tam? You," he nodded at the three of them, "need to worry about getting there and getting him on that ship. And you," he pointed at Luke, "need to stay safe and rest. He walked over and hugged Luke once again, holding him tight for what seemed like several minutes. When he released his brother, Luke thought he saw Tommy's eyes glisten over. "If I don't see you again, Luke, take care of yourself. I mean that."

Luke nodded and watched his brother's back disappear out of the room.

The train rattled along the tracks, jolting Luke against the hard wooden bench and backrest. He and Nell had sat in silence for most of the journey in case anyone overheard him. As an extra measure, Tam had helped him blacken his hair with shoe polish, and Tommy had brought him a suitcase filled with clothing. "If you got on a ship bound for Australia without any luggage, folk would talk," he'd said. A pair of thin wire glasses that Tommy had procured from somewhere (Luke was surprised that he was beginning to really respect his older brother) completed the disguise. "The best thing is not to look like you're trying too hard to disguise yourself," Tommy had said, and Luke had looked at him in wonder. Ainsworth had taught him that, but who had taught Tommy?

Watching the fields and trees fly by, Nell finally turned to Luke.

"It's a shame that you couldn't say good-bye to Bill," she said, tears in her eyes. Luke just hung his head. That was the one regret he had in all of this. Of course he was angry at Bill, Tommy too, for not warning him years ago. But to never see Bill again? Bill had always stood by him, no matter what. He'd always been there. He'd accepted Luke as he was and had never tried to change him or control what he did. Luke felt that Bill had been the only person who'd ever understood him. And while he didn't really mind starting over somewhere far away, somewhere where he knew no one, he knew he'd miss his brother. Nell turned back to the window and stayed silent for the rest of the journey.

The train pulled into Lime Street station in a flurry of hissing and smoke. Whistles were blown and carriage doors flung open. Nell stood up and nodded at Luke, who promptly opened their own door for her. Climbing down the iron steps to the platform, Nell almost disappeared into a cloud of smoke. Luke quickly followed after her, trying not to get distracted. The platform was filled with hundreds of people of all different levels of class. Porters wheeling trunks, ladies in nice dresses, moustachioed men in top hats, urchins running in and out of the crowd, families in patched clothes carrying suitcases and looking lost. Catching up to her, Luke quickly linked Nell's arm with his. She didn't even look at him as they headed for the front of the station.

Outside, the street was no less busy. Across from the station, there was a lot of construction going on. Carts, carriages and handcarts filled the street while people milled around talking, laughing, hawking. Three men spilled out from the ale house into their path and Luke steered Nell around them.

"We need to take a carriage," said Nell. "I have no idea where the dock is, and it's probably best not to ask too many people."

"You're right," Luke said and looked around. He went to stand by the road to hail a passing carriage. Climbing in, Luke easily slipped into another character, getting an odd look from Nell.

"Ah, we'd be heading off to America today," Luke said happily to the driver in a now lilting accent.

"Good luck," said the driver. "I hear there's a lot of Irish heading to America right now. Things must be bad there."

"Ah, 'tis, 'tis," Luke said gravely. "But me Da said to take me chance, so me and our Mary are heading out for a new start." He winked at Nell, and Nell smiled back dutifully. By the time the carriage had reached the docks, Luke had spun a fair yarn to the driver. He found it easy to slip into character, and just as easy to make up facts like having a cousin out there already and a niece and nephew who had died during the famine. The driver lapped it up. Luke was sure he'd heard the same story a thousand times over. Luckily Nell had gone quiet so apart from him having to dig her in the ribs at one point when she looked like she was going to open her mouth, she'd been no trouble. But now they were out of the carriage and had watched it drive away, Nell was glaring at him, arms folded. He ignored her.

"The driver said most ships leave from here, Waterloo Dock. So we just need to make sure it's right and go get a ticket." he said, still in a perfect Irish accent.

"Luke ..."

"I'm Tom Bailey, a labourer from Meath," he hissed. "And you're Mary Bailey. And I don't want to hear anything else right now. If you can't play along, just keep your mouth shut." He pulled Nell roughly by the elbow out of the way of a group of passengers, who turned around and stared at them.

Luke steered her through the throngs of people. Everyone seemed to be selling some kind of food and drink; there were stands of touts selling tickets – fake or otherwise, Luke couldn't tell. Boardinghouse keepers shouting out rates for rooms for the night were standing in people's paths along with all the other sellers. Runners – young boys – were running messages back and forth between the ships and people on the docksides or places in town, crashing into people walking too slowly or piles of luggage left randomly on the docks. Luke knew it was hopeless having Nell with him and tried to persuade her to head home. But she was adamant she was staying until she saw him on the ship and watched it leave. Sighing, Luke dragged Nell farther along the docks, finally finding a stack of crates where she could sit and rest for a while. He was in two minds whether to leave his sister here or not. For one thing, it wasn't completely safe with all the con men and thieves around, and Nell wasn't exactly street smart. But he didn't want her around in case he was spotted and needed to run.

"Stay here until I get back, and don't talk to anyone, you hear?" Nell nodded. "Not anyone. Not even if they look like a gentleman. Not even other ladies." He stood up straight and relaxed his shoulders. "I'll leave my suitcase here so I don't have to carry it around. If the ship sails before I get back, go straight home." He could see the hurt and worry in his sister's eyes but he just turned and left.

It seemed like hours to Nell, sitting there, politely but firmly declining every offer of food, drink, lodging, tickets and company. And now it was getting really cold. She looked at the ships in the dock. Two great clipper ships were tied up, with one waiting out in the estuary. Nell had never seen a ship so big, especially not up close. It had a very long wooden hull, painted a different colour below the waterline. Nell could see the ship had been loaded with more cargo and people during the time she'd sat there because it had sunk down deeper into the water. The three main masts had endless ropes and riggings attached to them, Nell wondered how they didn't mix them all up or get them tangled. What must it be like keeping track of all those ropes and which sails they worked? And making the decision to put some of the sails up or down? She suddenly had much more respect for the captain's job, especially on such a long journey. How would they all survive, and what was to stop the whole ship tipping over in the wind and high waves? She'd changed her mind. She didn't want Luke to go. It wasn't safe.

They had started letting down the main sails, the white fabric billowing in the wind before the ropes were tightened. Suddenly, a shout went up, and dock workers started to remove the gangplank and untie the ropes of one of the ships. Nell stood up, looking around frantically. What had happened to Luke?

She felt a pulling at her shawl and turned around to see her now black-haired brother bending over and panting hard.

"I had to wait ages in line for the bloody medical inspection," he panted. "And all they did was ask me if I was feeling fine, show them my tongue and that was it!" He tried again to catch his breath, wincing. "But now I have everything."

"But the ship's leaving now!"

"I'll run to the dock-gate, some were saying you can get on there. There were several people behind me in the queue, so I won't be the only one. Give me the suitcase." Nell handed over the case and hugged her brother tightly. Luke broke free after a few seconds.

"And tell Bill ... tell him I love him."

Tears fell down Nell's cheeks, but Luke was already gone.

CHAPTER 31

LIFE IN LIVERPOOL
APRIL 1853

There was a knock at the door, and Bill got up to answer it. The postman standing there thrust a letter into Bill's hands. Bill stared silently at it for several minutes, and when he looked up, the postman had disappeared, and all he saw was several neighbours staring at him, talking behind their hands to each other. He slammed the door shut and returned to his chair.

He turned the cream envelope with its red penny stamp over in his hands. That was definitely Tam's handwriting, and for a moment he felt a flash of a feeling other than sorrow and despair. Then the thought hit him. They didn't know about Alice Anne yet. They couldn't. It had only been a day. Or was it two? He would have to write back and tell them the terrible news.

He slid the envelope open with his finger and pulled out the two small sheets of paper. Slowly, he began to read. His heart quickened, and he glanced at the end of the letter, then reread it again. It can't be true. It can't be!

Bill sank back into his chair. His favourite armchair, the slightly more faded and worn of the two, with the upholstery hanging off the back, the one where the springs had been worn into a comfortable dent, and the old leather seat creaked satisfyingly. But today his favourite armchair offered no solace. He closed his eyes as through he could shut out the rest of the world. For a while. For preferably longer than a while. Minutes ticked by; the deafening sound of the mantelpiece clock in the lonely room echoed his own heartbeat and pulled him back into reality. He eventually sighed, realising he'd been holding his breath, his chest now heavy, tight and weighed down with dread that would not shift.

"Why? Why?" Bill cried regretfully into his calloused hands. His dusty blond hair, which had once been a brighter golden colour, now as muted as the dull foggy landscape outside, fell forwards through the tips of his square, nail-bitten fingers. His bristly chin, two days of not having seen a razor – he had other things on his mind – scratched at his palms, but he did not feel it. Over nine years of daily foundry work had rendered his hands insensitive and his skin tough and weathered. He slumped back in his chair, utterly defeated. He'd now lost two of the people most dear to him. Alice Anne and Luke. At least Luke was safe, but Australia? Bill would never see him again as long as he lived.

Closing his eyes, he tried to escape the raw, searing pain that was burning inside. He liked to think he was a tough man, fair, kind. A man who knew right from wrong, who never raised a hand to his wife, no matter how much she seemed to need it. A man who helped others, who didn't drink and was respectable. But perhaps, deep down, he wasn't really the man he liked to think he was. He had shown no respect or kindness to his brother Jem. His actions had banished his sister and his best friend to another town. And now he had destroyed his younger brother's life. A younger brother whom none of them would ever see again. And as for his daughter ... this was his punishment. He looked up at the ceiling, as if looking for confirmation from a higher power, the light in his dark blue eyes – his best feature, Betsy had once said – faded. Gone, along with his strength and enthusiasm.

Luke ran as fast as he could to the dock-gate, his suitcase banging against his leg, along with what seemed like hundreds of men, women and children. It was chaos. People were standing crowd deep already, waiting to fling themselves onto the rigging and try and climb onto the ship to safety. Many of the crew seemed to be helping catch suitcases and trunks flung at them.

Luke hung back slightly and assessed the situation. That's what Ainsworth had told him to always do. Work out what you're dealing with first so there are no surprises. Surprises mean you're going to have to think on your feet, and that's what can get you caught. There was a lot of pushing and shoving at the front of the crowd. Many people were being pushed into the water – luckily, there were several rowing boats down there pulling people and luggage out. The ship was close to this side of the dock, waiting for the ship in front to leave, which was in turn waiting for another ship to come in through the narrow opening. Luke would have to either leave his suitcase here or fling it towards the ship, hoping for the best. Then he'd have to push through the crowd and take a running jump. But there was no space for that. The only space to run up would leave him almost around the back of the ship and thus a much longer jump.

Luke looked up and assessed the ships. The incoming ship had now passed them, and the two waiting ships would be moving off soon. If he went around the crowd, there was still space at the end of the dock-gate where no one was currently standing. His suitcase would have to stay here. He knelt down and opened it, stuffing his money and ticket into his jacket pocket. Then he placed his suitcase behind some coils of rope and walked towards the end of the dock-gate.

As the ships started to move, Luke looked to his left at the many people climbing the rigging and several more in the water. He got ready to time his run up. Just waiting for the right moment . . . but as the ship moved, so did the crowd. The ship was moving too slowly, and the crowd was easily keeping up. They started to approach Luke. Now he was going to have to think on his feet. The crowd would soon be in front of him, blocking any chance of him getting through. He walked forwards and stood as close as he could to the edge. The crowd started surging. There was little space left to his right. If they moved one more time, he'd be pushed off the dock-gate and out into the sea. He looked up at the ship. Not an ideal position, but it was now or never! He got ready to jump just as the crowd surged again.

He felt himself falling, landing with a splash, the cold water enveloping his entire body. The inside of his nose and ears became ice cold, and everything slowed down. He wasn't sure which way was up, but he just struggled and fought, kicking his legs with such force to try and reach the surface again. Suddenly, he could breathe. He took a gasp of air and flailed his arms before the water came up over his head again. The second time he came up, he opened his eyes. He was close to one of the wooden supports from the dock-gate. He kicked and thrashed, trying to get closer to it. His hand just reached the dark wood when he sank down again. At least he had a guide now. He came up again and grabbed onto the support, wrapping both arms around it. His body felt so heavy, and he was exhausted. Perhaps the two weeks sleeping rough and the long walk had taken more of a toll on him than he'd thought. Just as he wondered what to do next, along with where he was going o find the strength to do it, he heard a shout.

"Want a hand, mate?"

Luke turned around as best he could and saw a man sitting in a rowing boat, arms stretched wide, holding on to each oar and expertly keeping his boat away from the ship. Luke nodded and gasped, and the man pushed the boat towards him.

"Here!"

Luke saw the oar being thrust alongside him, let go of the support and clung to the oar. The man stood up, legs wide apart, and pulled on the oar. As Luke got close enough to grab on to the boat, the man dropped the oar and quickly grabbed Luke's lapels.

"Now on three," said the man. "I'm going to need you to push yourself up."

Luke nodded.

"One, two, three!" Luke felt himself being pulled upwards and managed to scramble so that his waist was over the side of the boat. Like lightning, the man grabbed Luke's trousers and hauled his legs so hard Luke somersaulted into the boat. The boat wobbled dangerously as the man fell backwards. He immediately grabbed the oars and moved the boat out of the way, under the dock-gate. Luke just lay there, too exhausted to speak.

After a few minutes, they arrived at a set of ladders. Those few minutes had given Luke's muscles a chance to recover, and he sat up. His teeth were chattering and his hands shaking.

"Th-Thank you!" he mumbled.

"Here you are, safe and sound. Them's the ladders back up." The man nodded towards them. "That'll be five pounds, thanks."

"Five pounds?" Luke exclaimed.

"I don't do this for the good of my health," the man said abruptly. "It's dangerous work. I have to make a living too. Besides, what's five pounds in exchange for your life?"

His hands shaking, Luke reached inside his jacket pocket. Fingers too numb, he pulled out everything.

"Not quite five pounds here, but close enough. I'll take it."

"But that's all I have!" Luke said.

"You have your life," the man said, stuffing the wet notes into his pocket. "Go on, then, I'm sure there are others needing saving."

Luke pulled himself slowly up the shaky rope and wood ladders. Each step took superhuman effort, but he wasn't about to give up until he reached the top. Finally, he felt someone grab his arms and pull him the last few steps.

"Up with you, then!" said a cheerful voice. Luke peered at him but was too weary to reply. He just collapsed onto the dockside and breathed hard.

"We see hundreds of your sort every day down here," continued the voice. "Some don't make it, but you were lucky. Best to go and get dry as fast as you can and have some sweet tea for the shock."

Luke nodded and closed his eyes.

"Up with you, then!" said the voice.

Oh, go away, Luke thought crossly. Just let me lie here. I don't care anymore.

"Argh!"

He was yanked up to standing.

"No good will come of you lying there all frozen like that," said the voice. "I've fallen in a few times loading freight – an occupational hazard – and I can tell you I know what I'm talking about. Often, it's not the cold water that finishes people off, it's the cold air." He released Luke.

Luke realised he couldn't talk because his teeth were chattering so much. He nodded.

"Do you have any dry clothes?"

Luke nodded.

"Well, go and get changed, and then you should go to the nearest inn and sit by the fire. Hot sweet tea, that's my advice." Luke nodded again and held up his arm in thanks.

He walked over to where he'd left his suitcase. It was still there. Standing behind some wooden pallets, he tore open the case and stripped off his wet clothes. One change of clothes later and he was on his way to find an inn.

As the warmth started to seep into his bones, both from the fire and from the hot tea and brandy, Luke started to assess his situation. Firstly, he needed to leave the inn without being noticed since he didn't have any money. Secondly, he needed a place to sleep, preferably a warm place. Thirdly, he needed to find enough money to be able to pay for a new ticket. In the meantime, he needed to stay hidden.

Luke stood up and made his way out to the backyard, where the gentlemen tended to relieve themselves. Not exactly a midden, the initial sour stench inflamed his nostrils. Breathing through his mouth, he looked around. Watching an old man carefully, Luke timed his exit. Bumping into the old man in the corridor, Luke apologised. He watched the old man sit down, then turned around and slipped the old man's wallet out from inside his sleeve. Pulling out a note, he passed it to the landlady and waited for his change.

Once out the inn door, Luke rounded the corner and ran. Not entirely sure where he was going, he found himself running back towards the docks. He'd seen plenty of places to hide or shelter down there, so that might be a good start. He headed to the dock-gate and decided to scout around.

"Hello! Feeling better?"

Luke swung around. He recognised the voice but couldn't place the giant of a man with the light brown cloth cap standing in front of him.

"You look like you're feeling better. Been there myself. This air can make you really sick if you stay wet. Did the tea help?"

Luke looked the man up and down. His clothes were a little on the short side, his face ruddy and weather-beaten. The large grin spreading across his wide, flat face put Luke at ease. A pretty transparent man, he thought. Not intelligent enough to be scheming. Perhaps he could be of help.

Luke stepped forwards and shook the man's hand. "Thank you so much for your help earlier," he said. "I might not have made it if it wasn't for you. You were right!"

The man looked a little surprised but shook Luke's proffered hand anyway. The grin spread across his face again.

"Glad to help," he said. "We see so many poor souls end up in the water. Desperate not to miss their ships. The lads with their boats help fish them out usually, but some don't make it. It's worse when it's children." His face fell.

"I can imagine," Luke said. He gestured towards the ship. "My family is on that ship, heading for Australia. I have no one left here and certainly no money for another ticket. I'm going to have to find a way to earn enough money so I can join them. I'm not sure they even know I'm still alive." He looked down at his hands.

"Well ..." the man began. Luke looked up and saw his brow was furrowed. He took off his cap and scratched his head. "There's likely some work here on the docks – loading and unloading. It doesn't pay so well, but there's a few places nearby where you can sleep, until it gets really cold, of course. Maybe I could show you."

Luke nodded and followed the man. He hated pickpocketing, but maybe that plus some dock work would tide him over until he either earned enough for another ticket or worked out what to do next. Either way, it was going to take him a while, and he wasn't sure how far-reaching Ainsworth and his mob were.

CHAPTER 32

REVENGE
SEPTEMBER 1853

The past few months had been hard, but the pain was lessening. Bill could now think about his daughter and remember her ways of doing things without wanting to cry all the time. The good thing was that Maggie and Jamesie Fleming had been round a lot since Alice Anne's funeral. It had been really nice to see Jamesie making a huge effort to help Betsy, to try and make up for the time they'd been apart. When he wasn't working – which was still quite often – he'd call round and look after Jamie or run errands. Betsy had even brought it up that they should maybe ask her father and Maggie to move in – she'd have more help and they'd have at least Maggie's wage and whatever Jamesie would bring in. Bill said he'd think about it.

No one had heard anything from Luke. Tam had written to say that it took three months for a ship to reach Australia, then three months for one to come back with post. So even if Luke had found someone to help him write as soon as he'd arrived there, they wouldn't hear yet for another few months. Bill tried not to worry, but the worst thing was that Nell hadn't actually seen him get on the ship. At least he was safe from Ainsworth's men now. That's if he'd survived the journey.

Bill looked up and watched Betsy rocking Jamie. Her belly was starting to get quite large. Only a few months left now. Soon they would have two children again. Not that it would ever make up for losing Alice Anne. No one could ever replace her – a piece of his heart would always be missing now. But a new baby was a happy event. Perhaps it would help lessen the sorrow a little. Then again, it wouldn't bring back Nell and Tam or Luke. The Hall siblings were now spread far and wide – Bolton, Salford, Australia, and who knew where Emma was. If fact, the only people who were still around for Bill and helped out when things were bad were not blood related to him at all. Of all his relatives left in Bolton, there were only Jem and Ainsworth. One didn't care about him, and the other probably wanted to see him dead, or at least suffering.

Bill had really tried to work hard and better himself, to provide a decent life for his family and improve his children's situation. Most of all he'd tried to keep Nell and Luke close by because he'd been unable to do that when they had been children. And what had happened? He'd failed at that too. Luke had been banished to Australia. Nell had been banished to Salford. Had it all really been worth it? Had Jem been right? Would he have been better off if he'd never tried so hard? If he'd never learned any of the family secrets? If he'd never learned to read and definitely never tried to teach anyone else? At least Nell would still be around. Would things have been any different for Luke? They would certainly have never known about Ainsworth. Perhaps Luke would have stayed around too and continued working for him until he died. Or gone to gaol. Maybe Jem's idea of keeping quiet about all that was best.

Bill rubbed his forehead. But should he have told Luke everything? Despite everything, shouldn't Luke have the right to know? It was just so awful that he knew about something that affected Luke while Luke was oblivious. It was up to him to reveal something that could bring Luke's world crashing down or continue to keep it secret. Bill wondered if Jem felt the same. If he had pondered this dilemma as much as Bill had? But it was too late now. Bill was never going to get the chance to tell Luke, even if he decided to. Luke would die never knowing who his real father was. Considering what an evil man Ainsworth was, that may be a good thing. But what if Luke had children and they ended up crazy like Ainsworth? That kind of thing could run in families – you never knew. Bill sighed and looked over at Betsy again. Maybe he should just stop thinking about all this. It wasn't going to bring Luke back.

It had been five months since Luke had started working at the docks. He liked that his muscles were now well defined, and he was obviously so much stronger than when he started. He also found, to his surprise, that he quite enjoyed the simple life of working all day – not having to think for himself, not risking being caught for doing anything illegal and receiving a wage, albeit a poor one, on a Saturday afternoon. It had been summer for most of those months, and while it had rained a lot, it hadn't been too bad sleeping in the makeshift hut that he and some other workers had shared. There had been several men in his situation. Men who had missed their ship and were trying to work to save up money for another ticket. The dock work was also strenuous and dangerous, and the turnover of workers was quite high. It was certainly a young man's occupation, Luke thought. Very few men over thirty were still working. Five whole months it had taken him to save up, and that was without paying for accommodation or drinking. But now he had the money, and he had also had the time to try and work out what he was going to do.

He had to admit he had spent those five months looking over his shoulder. He'd changed his name and his story, but still, Ainsworth was good, and if he wanted to track Luke down, he probably could. He spent a lot of time thinking about his family too. How Ainsworth had destroyed his father so that there was nothing left of him while Luke was growing up. No mother and a father that couldn't give him any attention. He was lucky he had even thrived at all. But that was completely thanks to Bill and Nell. If it hadn't been for them caring for him, who knows what would have happened. And Nell – she'd helped him when he needed it the most, her and Tommy. He'd never known Tommy, never even remembered meeting him, but from his brief time in Salford with him, he realised he wanted to get to know his older brother. There was something about Tommy that made Luke feel safe. And as for Bill, who had always been there for him, Luke had left him in a rage. Poor Bill. The last time they may ever see each other and Luke had been angry at him. They were his family, and while he'd always taken them for granted before, he was beginning to realise how important they were to him. He had practically ignored them for a long time, yet they still all helped him when he needed it. So should he leave them all behind and be completely alone? Or should he stay?

The problem with staying was that Ainsworth was likely going to kill him. If Luke left, Ainsworth might also harm Bill like he harmed their father. Perhaps he'd even harm Tommy and Nell. No. Someone had to stop Ainsworth, not to mention get revenge for what he'd done to their family. Luke knew what he had to do.

The thought of putting an end to Ainsworth had obsessed him for weeks now. He realised there really was no other choice. Luke was strong, and Ainsworth was an old man – crafty, but old – so it shouldn't be too hard. The only problem was he would have to take out Jackie Ainsworth too. And make sure he wasn't seen. Luke played over different scenarios in his head while he helped move the crates and luggage onto the ships. He was only going to get one chance at this, so it had better work.

He collected his wage on Saturday afternoon along with everyone else and headed for the train station. Throughout the long journey back, his mind was only on one thing. He patted his trusty knife in his pocket and smiled. Plan and assess the situation – that way you don't have to think on your feet. How many times had Ainsworth said that to him? Now he was going to turn everything Ainsworth had taught Luke against him.

Alighting from Bolton station, Luke carefully checked around and made his way down to Church Wharf. He knew from experience that it was hard to spy on the old hut that Ainsworth had commandeered – that was the main reason Ainsworth had chosen it. But there was another place where Luke could hide out for a while. The old shed, with its partly fallen-in roof and rotting floorboards was across the canal and in a position where Luke could see who came in or out of the area where Ainsworth's hut was. Of course, he could miss anyone who went around the back of the hut, but to get down there, you would have to climb down from the viaduct and slide down the banking. He didn't think an old man like Ainsworth would be doing that on a regular basis.

Luke pushed the door to the shed open and walked inside. He hoped he wouldn't have to stay here tonight; it was in far worse shape than he remembered - half the roof had now fallen in. He took off his jacket and started unbuttoning his shirt, revealing another underneath. Folding it, he laid it on a piece of wood and kicked off his shoes. He unbuttoned his trousers to reveal another pair under and folded them along with the shirt. He looked around the shed for somewhere to hide them and settled on the far corner, placing some bits of broken roofing in front of them. He rooted around for a larger piece of wood, finding a suitable few pieces nailed together. Satisfied, he placed the wood by the door, and then he settled down in front of a hole in the wall to watch.

Dusk was starting to fall, and Luke had to keep blinking to focus. He was starting to get hungry when he saw two familiar shapes in the distance. Ainsworth and Jackie, heading towards the hut. By his calculations, some "helpers" would join them soon, and shortly after, Jackie would leave with them. That would be his opportunity to get Ainsworth on his own. Luke continued to peer through the dim light, but it was starting to get too dark to see. He would have to get closer. Picking up the large piece of wood, he made his way down the banking and slipped into the water. Immediately, the panic of his previous dip at the docks came back to him as he felt the chilly water wash over him. Pull yourself together, he told himself crossly, you have a job to do. Clinging to the wooden make-shift raft, he quietly pushed himself along the breadth of the canal. Reaching the other bank, he hauled himself up onto the tow path and pulled up the raft. Flattening it against the low path wall, he climbed up the banking and hid behind a bush at the bottom of the viaduct.

The sound of voices carried over the crisp air. Luke held his breath and stayed as still as he could. Luckily, there was no moon tonight. The voices died down, and Luke breathed again. He was beginning to get stiff, and his teeth had begun chattering from the cold. But he knew in a short while they'd all come out again. He rubbed his arms hard with his hands and willed himself to warm up.

Sure enough, not fifteen minutes later, the voices returned. One he recognised as Jackie's. Luke clenched his jaw hard and squeezed his eyes shut. He waited until he could no longer hear them, then he waited some more. Finally, he stood up and started to walk towards the hut.

His left leg had gone to sleep, so he started to stamp it on the ground. He needed to be able to run at any given moment, so this was not good. But after a few minutes, the blood began to painfully return and Luke carried on.

He saw a light on in the hut before he even got close. Luke grabbed his knife and took it out of its sheath. Walking silently towards the building, he peered through a crack in the door. Ainsworth was sat there in a chair at the far end of the room. He would see Luke long before Luke could get to him. He took a step back and wiped his forehead with his sleeve. What to do now?

Suddenly, he was grabbed from behind, his arms pinned back. In one swift movement, he twisted the angle of the knife and flung himself backwards, knocking the pair of them off balance. As he fell onto his assailant, his arms were released, and he sprang up. He took a few steps back and looked down at the ground. Looking up at him with a surprised expression was Jackie Ainsworth. Why the hell had he come back right now? They both looked down at the growing pool of blood seeping through his shirt. At that moment, Ainsworth came to the door. Luke was frozen to the spot. Ainsworth took one look at Jackie and one at Luke and pulled a knife out of his pocket.

"What the ... ? Now you're dead, you little bastard!" he roared and lunged at Luke. Luke jumped out of the way. Ainsworth came at him again, and Luke dodged him again. No doubt the old man was getting slow, but he was still dangerous.

Ainsworth had started snarling, spittle forming round his mouth like a rabid dog. Luke clenched his knife, and he felt a flash of cold followed by heat in his chest. He lunged at Ainsworth, who grabbed his arm. In the same movement, Ainsworth smashed Luke's elbow down across his knee. Luke cried out and opened his fist, dropping his knife. Ainsworth grinned and spun Luke around, placing his knife against Luke's throat. Luke grabbed at the shaft of the knife with both hands.

"Thought you could kill me, eh?" he leered.

Luke swallowed hard, the silver metal hurting his neck and making him want to cough. It took him a split second to raise his foot and kick Ainsworth in the shin with all his might. As Ainsworth gasped and released his grip slightly, Luke spun around and thumped the old man under the chin as hard as he could. Ainsworth's head flew backwards, dazing him for a few seconds. Luke turned around and tried to scrabble in the dirt for his knife, but he couldn't find it. He picked up a rock.

"Oh, haha!" Ainsworth mocked. "Looks like you're in trouble now!" He lunged at Luke again as Luke brought the rock crashing down onto Ainsworth's hand. He yelped. Luke brought up his hand again and hit Ainsworth's head as hard as he could. The old man stumbled, dazed. Again the rock came down, and again. Ainsworth fell. Luke hit him several more times, his face now covered in so much blood it was hard to see his eyes. Luke dropped the rock and wrestled the knife out of his hand.

"This is for what you have done to me and my family," he yelled, plunging the knife into Ainsworth's stomach. The old man flinched and coughed. Luke took out the knife and plunged it in again. And again. Finally, Ainsworth stopped moving.

Breathing hard, Luke sat back and looked around, all his senses on high alert. He looked over at Jackie, who gazed back, eyes wide, like a hunted animal.

"Best I put you out of your misery," Luke said. He took the knife and slit Jackie's throat. Without even waiting for the life to run out of him, Luke ran. He ran faster than he'd ever run before, straight to the canal, almost bumping into a couple who were taking a late evening stroll. The couple gasped as Luke grabbed his raft and slid into the water. Kicking hard, Luke made it to the other side and scrambled up the banking to the shed. Tearing off his clothes, he pulled out the dry, clean ones, and put them on quickly. His hands were shaking so hard he couldn't fasten the buttons, so he just left them, pulled on his jacket and ran.

CHAPTER 33

THE TRUTH FINALLY REVEALED
SEPTEMBER–DECEMBER 1853

Bill gazed into the fire, the diary open in his hands. How had it come
to this? He started to think about Luke. In one way, it was lucky that
he'd never see him again, that Luke would never get to know about
this. Then again, he could write to him and tell him, once Luke left
word about how he could be contacted, of course. But to read that in
a letter? Bill couldn't do that to his brother. The flames started to die
down, and the embers glowed red and crackled, warming Bill through
his clothes and lulling him to sleep.

The next thing he knew, the front door was slamming shut with a
crash, making Bill jump awake. He looked at the familiar figure standing
in front of him and squeezed his eyes shut before opening them again.
Where was he? Was he dreaming? "Luke?"

"Mmm."

Luke sat down in the chair across from Bill and put out his hands
to warm them in the heat of the flames. His body movements were
jerky, and he shifted around in his chair as though he was sitting on hot
coals. Bill took in the sight – it was definitely his brother, but now his
hair was black. He was wearing clothes that Bill had never seen before
and had a felt bowler hat.

"What? What are you doing here? Didn't you go to Australia? What
happened?"

Luke continued to gaze into the fire.

"I missed the boat."

"Missed the boat? Missed the boat! Then where the hell have you
been these past five months? We've all been worried sick, waiting for
word from you!"

Luke sighed and leaned back in his chair, fixing Bill with his gaze. There was something about the look in Luke's eyes that unnerved Bill. He thought he knew his brother, but this didn't seem like the old Luke. Something had happened.

"The ship pulled away early. Lots of us were caught out because the queue to the medical inspection had been so long. We ran to the dock-gates where the ships have to wait, and we tried to climb on."

He leaned towards Bill. "Do you know how hard it is to climb onto one of those things? With luggage?" He almost spat out the words. "It was hard. There were whole families trying to climb up the rigging. So many cases fell into the water. There were men with rowing boats fishing luggage and people out for a price."

"What happened to you?"

"I wasn't strong enough. Those two weeks on the run had weakened me. I fell into the water and was fished out. I lost everything."

"Then why didn't you come back?"

"I said I lost everything. I had no money. And I couldn't come back here; Ainsworth would have killed me. And it was doubtful that Salford was safe either."

Bill was silent for a moment, watching Luke shuffle back in his seat.

"Then why are you here now? Won't Ainsworth find you?"

"Ainsworth is no longer a threat."

"Why? How do you know? You just said – "

Luke turned his head slowly towards Bill, his eyes stone cold. Bill was suddenly afraid.

"You don't want to know the answer to that, believe me."

Bill swallowed hard.

"Are you saying what I think you're saying?"

Luke remained silent, looking at Bill without blinking.

"Luke, you're scaring me. Tell me what happened."

"I made sure that he and his son will never again come after you or Nell or anyone in our family. I also made sure they paid for what Ainsworth did to Father. You could call it self-defence. It was either them or me."

Bill felt bile rise in his throat. He stood up and clasped his hands over his head and started to pace up and down the room.

"You know," he said, stopping and clearing his throat, "you know if the police find you, you'll hang for this?"

"They won't find me."

"What if they do? What if someone saw you?"

Luke said nothing for a long time. Then he sighed.

"Then I need to leave. Again. Ironic, really."

Bill released his hands from his head.

"You know I will do what I can to help you, but I cannot hide you here. I have to think of the kids and Betsy."

"Fine," Luke said. "I only came back for my money anyway. I kept all my earnings under my mattress. That's if they're still there?" He looked at Bill and raised his eyebrows.

"I haven't touched it. I didn't even know you'd stashed anything here."

Luke walked into the kitchen and crouched down beside the bed that Bill hadn't had the heart to move, even though no one had used it in the last five months and, according to Betsy, was just taking up space. He lifted up the edge of the straw mattress and felt underneath it. Eventually, he pulled out a fat paper bag.

Bill wandered into the kitchen, saw Luke crouched down, counting the money, and reeled in shock.

"All that was in your mattress?"

Luke looked up. "Where else would I keep it?"

Bill leaned against the door frame, watching his brother carefully stash the bundles of notes into his many pockets.

"Luke, I've been thinking. We need to get you out of here tonight. We'll get the train to Liverpool and find whatever ship is going out first in the next few days."

"You don't have to come with me."

"I want to," Bill said. "I'd like to talk to you. I need more time with you than just half an hour. I need time for this to sink in. And I want to make sure, for my own sanity, that you get on that boat this time."

Luke shrugged and stood up. Bill smiled at the familiar gesture.

"I just need to go up and tell Betsy I'm leaving."

"Fine." Luke smiled, something Bill hadn't seen in quite a long time.

After only a couple of minutes, Bill came running back down the stairs and grabbed his coat and hat. "Come on, then, we haven't got time to lose."

"What did Betsy say?"

Bill was quiet for a moment. "Do you really want to know?"

"No."

The walk to the train station was short, just down onto Crook Street and then turning the corner onto Trinity Street, the large station clock tower looming above the entrance. The dark streets were quiet, only an occasional horse and cart passing by or a worker deciding reluctantly to return to his home, his belly full of ale. The street in front of the station was busier – travellers leaving or arriving, some with luggage, many without.

Bill bought the tickets and joined Luke on the platform. It was only thirty minutes for the next train to Liverpool, but it seemed like an eternity. Bill kept looking around nervously until Luke told him to give over; he'd only bring attention to them, and if he was going to behave like that all the way to Liverpool, then Luke would rather he not come.

It was 1:30 a.m. when the train pulled into Liverpool Lime Street. Bill woke with a start at the screeching brakes and hissing steam. He was a little dazed, but Luke told him to get a move on and strode off in the direction of the docks. Said he'd been working there the past few months and knew of a place they could hang out until the morning without being seen. Bill dutifully followed, his head constantly turning to watch the crowds of people, horses and carts; public houses around the station spilling their inhabitants out onto the roads where men in different stages of inebriation joked or fought with each other. Ladies in various states of undress laughed with the men or each other. Bill watched one grab a glass of ale from one of the men, drink it down without stopping and let out a loud laugh. People stepped over rubbish tipped in the street or tripping over uneven cobbles. Bill though Bolton was crowded and busy, but he'd never seen anything like this. At least in Bolton, the streets were usually quieter by now. At one point, not watching where he was going, Bill tripped and almost fell into Luke.

Luke swung round, fists ready, but it was the look in his eyes that concerned Bill.

"Just watch where you're going, and stop acting like a bloody tourist," he hissed. Bill's cheeks turned red, but he meekly followed his brother. After a while, the streets became quieter, and Bill felt more at ease. The walk to the docks was quite long, but once they seemed to get out of town and past some wasteland, Bill began to question Luke's sense of direction.

"We can stay here until morning," Luke said, stopping and pointing to a makeshift shelter on the edge of a piece of land strewn with iron girders and mounds of bricks and fencing.

"What is this?" Bill asked hesitantly.

"It's where they store some building materials. Don't worry about it. They know me here. They won't bother us as long as we don't steal from them. They have a sort of pact with the dock workers who haven't managed to find a place to live yet."

"How long did you live here?"

"Five months."

"Five months?"

Luke shrugged. "It's not that bad. It's not like it's winter." He pulled back a tarpaulin and revealed a "room" built with empty wooden crates. The inhabitant grunted and pulled his blanket and sack of belongings closer to him.

"And don't wake the others," Luke said.

Others?

Bill had wanted to spend the evening talking to his brother, but Luke seemed to be set on sleeping. Besides, they couldn't discuss what they needed to discuss with others hearing. Bill lay down on a piece of tarpaulin next to his brother and pulled his coat around him. How had Luke slept here every night? At least it seemed dry here. He closed his eyes and tried to sleep.

He woke to Luke kicking his foot. "Come on, then," Luke said. "I've got the ticket. Let's go."

"What? How? What ticket?" Bill rubbed his eyes and struggled to sit up. Luke smirked.

"You were sleeping, so I went to get my ticket. Even had my medical inspection before the queues got long. Ship leaves for Australia today. There's one leaving for Canada tomorrow, but I thought today would be better."

"How could I have slept for so long?" Bill wondered, standing up and brushing down his coat and trousers. He picked up his cap, and they crawled out of the shelter.

They walked towards the dock, which Bill could now see clearly in the morning light. There were two clipper ships moored up, both with incredibly long masts and more rigging and ropes than Bill had ever seen. Sailors were beginning to unfurl the main sails on one ship, and the vast white sheets rippled in the wind until the men caught the ropes and tightened them.

"Wonder which is my ship?" Luke said, staring up at them.

"What's the name of your ship?" asked Bill.

"The Lancaster, they said."

"Then it's that one." Bill pointed to the ship with the billowing sails.

"How do you know?"

"It says Lancaster on the side."

Luke laughed. "Well, looks like your reading came in useful for once. Then again, I could have just asked someone."

They walked towards the ship.

"Well, thanks to my reading, we found out what Ainsworth did," Bill retorted. "And it wasn't like Jem was going to tell us."

"Fine lot of good that did us though. If Jem and Tommy hadn't kept all that from us in the first place, things might have turned out differently. At least for me."

Bill swallowed. Should he tell his brother? This really was the only chance he was going to get now.

"There's something else I found out," he said. "It was in Father's diary."

"Do I really want to know?" Luke asked. "It's not like it's going to change anything now."

They walked on in silence until they reached the gangplank. Despite the early hour, people were milling around, luggage, crates and cases were being hoisted up onto the ship, the ship's crew was shouting and winding in ropes. Some passengers were even beginning to climb the gangplank at the permission of the captain.

"I'd better go up, then," Luke said with a wry smile. "You can never get on the ship too early, I have learned. Don't want to miss this one."

"Luke, this thing I read. I think you really need to know. I'm not ever going to see you again."

"Fine, what is it?"

"Ainsworth was Father's half brother. He was never acknowledged by Granddad so that's probably why he decided to take revenge on Father, and the rest of us. Father having been the son and heir that Ainsworth should have been and all that."

Luke's eyes widened a little, then he shrugged. "Am I supposed to care?" He turned to leave.

"There's more ... " said Bill quickly.

Luke sighed and turned back. "What?"

"Well, Father wrote, well he wrote that, when you were born, that is, and earlier even. That you. You ... "

"What? I what? Spit it out." Bill couldn't tell whether Luke was impatient or slightly worried.

Bill took a deep breath. "That he wasn't your father. Now that doesn't change anything for me," he added hurriedly. "You're still my favourite little brother."

Luke just looked at him. The longer he stared into Bill's eyes with that unflinching gaze, the more Bill became uncomfortable.

After a while, Luke fixed his gaze on some point on the other side of the dock.

"Then who was my father?" he said quietly.

"Do you really want to know?"

"Of course I really want to know!" Luke spun round to face his brother.

"What difference will it make?"

Luke grabbed the collar of Bill's jacket. "What difference does it make? Who the hell are you to come and tell me that Father was not my father and then say what difference does it make?"

Luke suddenly released Bill, and Bill took a step back.

"Just tell me who he was."

"I don't know how true this is, but Father wrote . . . he wrote that it was Edward Ainsworth."

There was no reaction from Luke other than the colour draining from his face. He looked straight at Bill and nodded. Then he turned and slowly walked up the gangplank. Bill watched him until he could no longer see his brother's back.

Bill stayed where he stood until the ship set sail. He didn't dare move, desperate to catch sight of Luke again, but there was so sign of him. After the ship moved off, he turned and went to look for a cab to take him to the train station, his heart heavy.

Bill paced up and down the living room. It had been four months now since Luke had stepped on board the ship, and it felt strange to think of him being on the other side of the world. Christmas was just around the corner and it would be their first one without him. It was just so hard to get used to the fact that he would never see him again.

Another scream came from upstairs and Bill winced. Betsy had been in labour now for about ten hours and Bill hoped it wouldn't go on for much longer, for her sake. Another scream was followed by a deafening silence and Bill started praying. Please don't let me lose any more people in my life! Please! What felt like several minutes later, Bill heard a brief, weak, newborn wail. His heart leapt and a huge smile spread across his face.

He ran to the bottom of the stairs and waited impatiently. The midwife eventually came down, wiping her arms on a towel.

"Congratulations," she beamed at him, "it's a little boy!"

Another son! Secretly, he had been hoping for a girl, not that anyone could replace Alice Anne, but he really would have liked having both a daughter and a son again. But there would be plenty time for more daughters. He was just grateful to have another child and for Betsy to be all right. He looked over at the midwife.

"Well, go on upstairs, then. Have a look at your boy. I'll just put the kettle on."

Bill didn't need telling twice, taking the stairs two at a time. He opened the bedroom door and walked into the room. There, in Betsy's arms, tightly swaddled in a cream blanket, was a very pink face and the most hair he'd ever seen on a baby. It was silky and black, just like Alice

Anne's and Betsy's. He sat down on the bed and hugged Betsy, then pulled back the blanket a little.

"A boy!" Betsy said, smiling.

"I know," Bill said with a grin. "How great are you!" He leaned over to kiss her on the forehead. They both sat there for a while, admiring the perfectly formed little hands and face.

"What shall we call him?" Bill whispered.

"I was thinking Thomas, after my brother," Betsy said, adding, "and yours, of course."

"How about Luke?"

Betsy turned to face him. "I am NOT naming my son after a murderer!"

"Fine, fine!" Bill said, holding up his hands. "Although to be fair, it was like self-defence, for all of us Halls."

Betsy glared at him.

"Fine," he said.

She turned to look at the baby again. "Thomas it'll be." Bill smiled. He knew he had no choice whatsoever. "Thomas, then. Both our brothers are good sorts. He's bound to grow up a good person being named after them." He touched his son's hand again.

"Hello, Thomas. Baby Thomas. Tomby. Toby . . ." He looked up as Betsy did. "What? He can't go by Tommy, like everyone else."

Betsy cocked her head to one side while she considered it. "Maybe you're right."

Bill smiled. "Well then," he said, standing up, "I'd better go and fetch Jamie from your Maggie so he can come and meet his little brother."

"In a while," Betsy said. "We still have time. Let's just enjoy this little one for a little while longer. Just us."

Bill sat down on the bed and put his arm around Betsy. The winter sun was streaming into the room, flecks of dust dancing in its light. Baby Toby lay there sleeping in Betsy's arms, and Bill realised he hadn't felt this happy in what seemed like a long time. Life was full of ups and downs, and no doubt there would be more downs to come, but just for now, Bill was going to bask in his happiness.

ABOUT THE AUTHOR

Nora has been writing since the age of seven, producing reams of unpublished stories. A not so short foray into the world of academia resulted in her first published work. Many scientific articles and an Assistant professorship later, she eventually realised her love for writing was greater than her love for the medical sciences. Changing careers, she produced a number of short stories before progressing to a novel. Little Bolton is her first published work of fiction. Nora lives in Stockholm, Sweden, with her family and two cats.

Made in United States
Troutdale, OR
11/28/2023